THE PUCKING WRONG SERIES

THE ~~PUCKING~~ WRONG ROOKIE

THE PUCKING WRONG BOOK #5

DALLAS KNIGHTS

C.R. JANE

Copyright © 2025 by C.R. Jane
Cover design by Cassie Chapman/Opulent Designs
Photography by Wander Aguiar
Editing by Stephanie H./Hannotek, Ink

ISBN: 978-1-0394-8649-2

Published in 2025 by Podium Publishing
www.podiumentertainment.com

Podium

To my red flag renegades who know it was always about more than the red flags with these men.

Dear Red Flag Renegades,

Logan York wasn't supposed to take over my heart the way he did. He wasn't supposed to make me feel things I couldn't shake. He wasn't supposed to burrow so deep into my mind that I found myself thinking about him long after I'd stopped writing. But that's the thing about Logan: he doesn't take no for an answer. He is relentless, obsessive, a little unhinged, but at his core, he is someone who loves so fiercely that it consumes him. And maybe that's why, for all his sharp edges and red flags, he belongs to Sloane the way she belongs to him.

But this book—this world—isn't just about Logan and Sloane. It's about the people who stand beside them. It's about the circle of trust. It's about teammates who aren't just teammates but brothers. It's about women who hold each other up, who call each other out, and who love each other as fiercely as they love their men. It's about a found family that laughs together, fights together, and would burn the world down if one of their own needed them to.

That's what makes this series so special to me. It's not just about love in the traditional sense; it's about belonging. It's about finding the people who see every broken, jagged part of you and decide to stay anyway. It's about knowing you're never really alone, even when you feel like you are.

To my readers—you are part of this world just as much as Logan, Sloane, Lincoln, Ari, Camden, and the rest of the chaos crew. You've laughed at their antics, swooned over their love stories, screamed at me when they did something questionable (I hear you, I really do). Through it all, you've reminded me why I do this: because stories connect us and characters can feel like home. So thank you for reading, for feeling, and for letting me share this world with you.

And to Logan and Sloane, who are proof that sometimes the wrong kind of love is exactly the right kind.

TEAM ROSTER

PLANERS

LINCOLN DANIELS	Captain, #13, Center
ARI LANCASTER	Captain, #24, Defenseman
WALKER DAVIS	Captain, #1, Goalie
CAS PETERS	#42, Defenseman
KY JONES	#18, Left Wing
ED FREDERICKS	#22, Defenseman
CAMDEN JAMES	#63, Defenseman
SAM HARKNESS	#2, Goalie
NICK ANGELO	#12, Defenseman
ALEXEI IVANOV	#10, Center
MATTY CLIFTON	#5, Defenseman
CAM LARSSON	#25, Left Wing
KEL MARSTEN	#26, Defenseman
DEX MARSDEN	#8, Center
ALEXANDER PORTIERE	#11, Right Wing
LOGAN YORK	#42, Center
COLT JOHNS	#30, Wing
DANIEL STUBBS	#60, Wing
ALEX TURNER	#53, Center
PORTERS MAST	#6, Defenseman
LOGAN EDWARDS	#9, Defenseman
CLARK DOBBINS	#16, Wing
KYLE NETHERLAND	#20, Defenseman

COACHES

TIM PORTER	Head Coach
COLLIER WATTS	Assistant Coach
VANCE CONNOLLY	Assistant Coach
CHARLEY HAMMOND	Assistant Coach

PLAYLIST

CASUAL	CHAPPELL ROAN
WHAT'S LEFT OF YOU	CHORD OVERSTREET
I DON'T WANT TO LOSE YOU	LUCA FOGALE
KISS THE GIRL	BRENT MORGAN
LABYRINTH	TAYLOR SWIFT
I'M NOT THAT GIRL	CYNTHIA ERIVO
FEELS LIKE	GRACIE ABRAMS
BLACKBIRD	THE BEATLES
INFINITY	JAYMES YOUNG
PAINT IT, BLACK	CIARA
ON PURPOSE	NI/CO
LIGHT ON	MAGGIE ROGERS
JUST FOR NOW	IMOGEN HEAP
YOU REMIND ME	ANDY SHAUF
WHERE I STOOD	MISSY HIGGINS
CLEAN (TAYLOR'S VERSION)	TAYLOR SWIFT
MASTERMIND	TAYLOR SWIFT

LISTEN TO THE FULL PLAYLIST HERE

TRIGGER WARNING

Dear readers,

Please be aware that this is a dark romance and as such can and will contain possible triggering content. Elements of this story are purely fantasy and should not be taken as acceptable behavior in real life.

Our love interest is possessive, obsessive, and the perfect shade of red for all you red flag renegades out there. There is absolutely no shade of pink involved when it comes to what Logan York will do to get his girl.

Themes include ice hockey, stalking by the MMC, manipulation, reference to prior sex work, description of a sex auction, reference to parent's death due to cancer and addiction, dark obsessive themes, sexual scenes, death of an animal off page, reference and brief flashback to forced prior abortion, infertility, blackmail, death, and abuse (psychological and physical)—NOT FROM THE LOVE INTEREST. There are no harems, cheating, or sharing involved. Logan York only has eyes for her.

Prepare to enter the world of the Dallas Knights . . . you've been warned.

THE PUCKING WRONG ROOKIE

HALF THE GAME IS MENTAL; THE OTHER HALF IS BEING MENTAL.

—Jim McKenny

Hockey Boyfriends Anonymous ✔
@hockeyboyfriends_anonymous

···

🔥 HOCKEY DRAMA ALERT 🔥 Bunnies, Dallas Knights rookie sensation and hottie, Logan York, just set the Stanley Cup Finals on fire—and not just with his game. After a devastating loss in Game 1, York KISSED Tyler Miller's girl in front of the entire arena. Fans are losing it, teammates are stunned, and Miller? Let's just say the look on his face could melt the ice. Was it mind games or true love? Either way, this rivalry just got personal. 🏒🏒 #NHLFinals #LoganYork #YorkVsMiller #HockeyDrama

8:30 PM · Jun 8, 2025

53.4K Retweets   **22.2K** Quote Tweets   **110.7K** Likes

PROLOGUE
SLOANE

Sixteen Years Old

The bedroom door opened, and I didn't bother to glance up. I was tired. Tired of moving from house to house. Tired of keeping my things in a plastic sack because no one had bothered to buy me a suitcase after my duffel bag had been stolen at my first foster home. Tired of being treated like I was a burden.

I was tired of lingering stares and unwanted touches and never getting enough to eat because my foster parents didn't want to spend their government funds on food for us when they could spend it on themselves.

I was tired.

So very tired.

At this point, I couldn't remember a time when I hadn't been.

A throat cleared, and I reluctantly dragged my attention from the hole in my last pair of black leggings to the door where my social worker, Katherine, was standing with a beaming smile on her face.

That was different.

With all the moves since she'd dropped me at that first disastrous foster home, her ability to fake a grin had faded. Until all I'd been met with was exasperated sighs and disappointing glares.

Until now, evidently.

"I have brilliant news for you," she gushed, clapping her hands together in a show of excitement that had me raising an eyebrow because I hadn't known *brilliant* was in her vocabulary. "Come with me!"

I reluctantly slid off the bed, picking up my things off the floor. The contents of this grocery sack were all I had in the world. I couldn't risk leaving it for even a moment.

Following her out the door and down the hall, I listened to the worn sound of the Beckers' wooden floor creaking beneath my feet.

This house sucked. But then again . . . all my foster homes had sucked.

And so had the tiny apartment I'd lived in with my mother before that.

I wasn't going to think about that place, though.

I wasn't going to think about where and how she'd died, in an apartment that had smelled like throw-up and medication.

Don't think about that.

We made it into the living room, and I glanced around, surprised that there wasn't any sign of the Beckers in here. There was usually one of them around. They were like cockroaches, one springing up every time you thought they were gone. It wasn't until Katherine nodded her head at the sagging, faded couch that I realized someone else was in the room with us at all.

Everett.

I fell back a step in shock, my eyes widening as I stared in disbelief at the sight of my mother's brother—my uncle, I guess. I'd only met him a few times, but every meeting had been memorable. Everett had money, a lot more money than my mom and me, and he'd always treated me to ice cream and fancy toys when he'd come around. I'd lived for those visits, treasuring everything he'd bought me like a dragon hoarding its gold.

I didn't think I'd ever see him again. And yet here he was.

Everett was lounging on the couch like he owned the place, even though it was obvious that he didn't belong there. Tall, broad shoulders filled a fancy-looking suit, and his black hair was combed back in a way that screamed rich guy. His skin had that kind of golden tan that people got when they spent their time on golf courses, not working under the sun.

I fidgeted nervously as he stared, wishing I was wearing something nicer. I could only imagine what he saw. A scroungy sixteen-year-old still growing into her features. I looked like the orphan that I was, with the paper supply–logoed sweatshirt that someone had dropped off to Goodwill and my holey, worn leggings. I belonged in this run-down house.

Everett did not.

"Sloane?" His voice was deep and smooth, with a faint trace of a drawl.

For some reason, a beam of hope suddenly made an appearance in my chest, like the first rays of light as the sun peeked out from the horizon. His voice didn't sound like he was disgusted by the sight of me or that he was annoyed that he was here . . . I mean you couldn't tell that much from some-one saying your name, but still . . .

I blinked, still staring at him like he was some kind of mirage. With everything that had happened, I'd sort of . . . forgotten about him. Katherine had never asked if I had any relatives, so I guess I'd just assumed anyone related to me was dead or didn't want me.

After all, why would someone like *him* want someone like *me*?

"Sloane," he repeated, rising from the couch, his light brown eyes study-ing me. "I'm so sorry I didn't come sooner. I've been out of the country for the past year, and I didn't hear of your mother's passing until I returned."

I remained silent as I took him in, my hands trembling at my sides. Ever-ett walked toward me, slowly, like he thought I was a flight risk that would bolt for the hills with any sudden movement.

"I'm so sorry about your mother, Sloane. I can't even imagine what that was like, caring for her while she had cancer. And with you being all alone. If I'd known . . ."

"What are you doing here?" I finally asked, cutting his excuses off. The words came out hoarse, like I'd been silent for years and was just now speaking for the first time.

"Sloane," Katherine chided, sounding shocked for whatever reason.

Everett held up a hand, shaking his head. "I deserve whatever she wants to give me. I left her there, knowing her mother was . . . wasn't alright."

"It was the pills that actually killed her. Not the cancer. Did they tell you that?" I murmured.

He stared at me with pity, and I hated that. I didn't want pity. I wanted . . . I didn't know what I wanted, actually.

But I didn't want that.

"Your uncle's come to get you, Sloane," Katherine said, still sounding miffed. "He's agreed to become your guardian. All the paperwork has been done."

I blinked at the news, the spark in my chest growing. Even confused that he'd been nowhere to be found these past years, I had good memories with him, little glimmers of happiness in the murky gray of my childhood.

Honestly, though, even if he'd been a grumpy man who'd yelled at me for laughing too loudly or running down the halls . . . he'd be better than what I'd experienced this past year.

And then there was the fact that his eyes were the same as my mom's. Staring into them felt a little like . . . staring into hers.

"You are?" I whispered after a moment, afraid that any second now I was going to wake up under my threadbare sheet, and this was all going to be a dream. I studied him closer, willing this to be happening, noticing how truly nice his suit was and the fact that the gold watch on his wrist had diamonds all around its face. Everett had always had money, but it seemed like he might have gotten even richer since the last time I'd seen him.

"Would that be okay?" he asked, glancing around. His mouth pursed in displeasure as he glared at the water marks on the walls that were probably hiding layers of mold, and the stains on the carpet from the Beckers' dog that they never cleaned up after.

"Yes," I said immediately. "I mean—I mean if you're sure," I added, trying to tamp down the hope building in my chest.

His face gentled, and a small smile peeked on his handsome face. "Of course, I'm sure. As soon as I heard what had happened, I came straight to get you. I wouldn't have it any other way."

The grin that appeared on my face was the first one I'd had in well . . . years. It felt strange, as if it was a stretch for my features to make that movement anymore.

Everett's smile grew, and he nodded, like he was pleased with the turn of events. "Why don't you go get your stuff, and we'll get out of here."

I bit down on my lip, staring at my bag as embarrassment flushed through me. "This is all I have," I said softly, holding up the sack as I tried not to allow my shame to leak out all over my face.

His smile died, and a low growl came from his chest as he turned on Katherine. "Is this how the state treats its wards?" he snapped. "Where's all the money that's supposed to be going to her?"

Katherine straightened, pulling on her ill-fitting suit. "Our families are heavily vetted. We leave it to their discretion to buy what the children in their care need—"

"Does that bag seem like all she *needs*? And look at her shoes. Is that—" He glared aghast at my shoe like it had personally offended him. "Is that *duct tape* holding your shoe together, Sloane?"

I crossed my foot behind my other leg like I could hide it, a blush creeping across my cheeks even though it wasn't my fault.

"The court's order has gone through?" Everett snapped, his eyes heavy with disdain as he looked at Katherine.

She seemed alarmed by how the visit was suddenly going, a tic in her cheek and her eyes wide as she anxiously pulled on her suit coat again. Katherine slowly nodded.

"Sloane, go wait by the door," Everett ordered through gritted teeth, and I hustled down the hall and around the corner to the front door as he began to tear Katherine a new one.

The spark in my chest had grown into a forest fire, spreading across my veins and leaving me tingling.

I had to get out the door first, and even then, I didn't know how long it would take for me to believe that I was getting out of this hellhole.

But this . . . this was a start.

A few minutes later Everett appeared, his features completely calm like nothing had happened. I heard the faint sound of sniffling, but I didn't have it in me to feel that bad for Katherine. Each family she'd placed me with had grown progressively worse, and I'd begun to suspect two houses ago that she was intentionally doing it.

"Shall we go?" he asked pleasantly, no sign of the vicious barbs I'd heard him leveling at my social worker.

"Yep," I told him, and he grinned, gesturing for me to walk through the door first.

I made a note to myself as he ushered me through the front door, though . . . my uncle had a temper.

There was a light rain drizzling down, which seemed like a good omen. There had been sun for the first time in two months on the day of my mother's funeral. It had felt fake . . . wrong . . . like all the mourners there, who had never actually *known* or *cared* about my mother, or for me. Rain today felt right.

A gray-haired man in a fitted suit with a severe-looking face and cold eyes appeared on the sidewalk in front of us, and I jumped, glancing at my uncle uneasily. The man undid a large umbrella and hurried toward us.

I stared at him wide-eyed as he lifted the umbrella over my and my uncle's heads. How rich was Everett? I'd thought he was well-off when he drove a Camry and could afford to take my mom and me out to dinner.

This was on a whole other level.

The man stayed by our side for the whole walk to the shiny black vehicle parked at the curb, opening the back door so we could get in.

Sliding into the passenger seat of my uncle's car felt like stepping into another world—one I had no business being in. The soft leather of the seat hugged me as I settled into it, no doubt costing more than everything I'd ever owned. The air inside smelled like something sharp and expensive, like leather and faint cologne, nothing at all like the old mix of sweat and desperation . . . and cats I was used to.

I ran my fingers along the armrest, feeling the smooth stitching beneath my fingertips.

"You like it?" His voice broke through my thoughts, low and smooth, and I realized I was still staring, my fingers tracing the trim like a kid who'd never been inside a car before.

"It's . . . nice," I said, my voice quiet, almost unsure. *Nice* didn't seem like the right word, but I couldn't think of the *right* words to say.

Everett chuckled, the sound warm. "Someday you'll be used to all of this. It's just the beginning, Sloane."

I wasn't sure what he meant by that, and I didn't ask. Instead, I let my gaze wander, taking in the details—the perfect stitching on the seats, the way the buttons and dials seemed to glisten under the soft lighting. It was the kind of car driven by people who didn't have to check price tags or worry about overdue bills.

A silence filled the cab.

"Who was the man with the umbrella?" I finally asked quietly, fiddling with the hole in my leggings.

"That's Darwin. He's my driver and one of my assistants, I suppose," Everett mused, reclining back in his chair.

There was a partition up between the backseat and the front, and I could only faintly hear the sound of the engine as Darwin started the car and we pulled away from the curb.

"What kind of car is this?" I asked awkwardly, glancing around.

"A Bentley Flying Spur," he responded calmly as he pulled out his phone and began typing something into it.

I nodded like I knew what he was talking about.

"Business must be doing well," I continued lamely, immediately wishing that I hadn't opened my mouth. He was going to tell Darwin to turn the car around or just kick me out right here.

I glanced back, seeing the Beckers' house fading from view.

"It is," he answered, putting down his phone and turning his attention to me as I turned back around. "Now, tell me about yourself. What are your hobbies? What are your favorite things?"

I blinked, not expecting such a heavy question right out of the gate.

"Water?" he asked when I hadn't gotten an answer out after several awkward seconds. I nodded, and he opened up the seat between us, pulling a bottle out of a chilled compartment.

"Thank you," I said, immediately undoing the cap and taking a swallow. I'd been hiding out in my room as much as possible since I'd gotten to the

Beckers', and that meant I hadn't been drinking . . . or eating very much lately. Not that there had been much food to begin with.

Mmm. Rich-people water tasted good.

"I don't know what I like anymore," I finally said after I'd finished half the bottle, and he was still eyeing me expectantly.

It was the truth. The last few years had been horrible and lonely, and I was scared to get my hopes up that this would be any better.

"We're going to change that," he said with a smile. "Hungry?" Everett had pulled out a bag of chips from some other compartment, and I stared longingly at it, trying not to drool.

"Yes," I whispered, unable to keep the eagerness out of my voice as I took the chips and carefully opened them like they were gold.

My uncle pretended not to notice how I gobbled them up like a deranged monster.

"Where do you live?" I asked after I finished and had leaned my head tiredly against the glass.

"Dallas," he muttered as he typed something on his phone. My mouth dropped and I sat up, gaping at him. I'd never been out of Washington.

"We'll get you all set up with school and new clothes and whatever else you need. It's going to be great," he continued distractedly, still staring at his phone and seemingly completely unaware of the fact that I was melting into my seat in shock.

I'd recovered somewhat by the time he finally put his phone down. After all, what was the alternative to moving to Dallas, keep living in shitty foster homes until I aged out and ended up on the streets?

I'd take my chances in Texas.

He patted my knee before reaching down and grabbing a fancy-looking black box. "Chocolates? They're the best money can buy."

The gold lettering on the lid gleamed under the dim light of the car, and I hesitated when Everett set it on my lap.

"Go on," he said, his voice smooth, like he was offering me more than chocolate. "Try one."

I swallowed hard and lifted the lid. Inside, rows of perfect little chocolates lay nestled in golden paper, each one a tiny masterpiece. I had no idea which to pick; they all looked like they belonged in a museum.

Timidly, I reached for one, a dark chocolate square with an elegant swirl on top. My fingers brushed the delicate surface, and for a second, I almost put it back. But I could feel his eyes on me, waiting.

The chocolate melted the second it hit my tongue, rich, velvety sweetness exploding in my mouth. My eyes widened in surprise. It was perfect—smooth and decadent, with layers that I couldn't even name but felt like magic.

"Well?" my uncle prompted, a faint smirk playing at the corners of his mouth.

"It's . . ." I searched for the right word, still savoring the lingering taste. "It's amazing."

I grabbed another chocolate and then, at his urging, a few more.

And as we drove into the airport, where the sleek lines of his private plane gleamed under the floodlights, it felt like I'd stepped into a dreamworld. The soft hum of the car, the promise of a better life whispering in every luxurious detail, wrapped around me like a warm cocoon. Maybe this was it. Maybe all the bad things I'd endured—the nights of fear, the years of nothingness—had led to this moment.

But as the plane's engines roared to life, a tiny voice whispered in the back of my mind, sharp and uneasy: *Dreams don't come without a price.*

———————

When we finally pulled through the gates of his drive almost six hours later, I had to blink twice to make sure I wasn't seeing things. The place wasn't just big—it was massive. A mansion, like the ones in movies or on TV shows. The house—no, the estate—loomed in front of us, a black structure with clean lines and what seemed like a million windows. It looked like something out of a dream, all modern and cold, with perfectly manicured lawns and a freaking pond out front where I could see koi swimming around.

"Yes, you can feed them," Everett said, an amused smirk on his lips as he watched me gape at his house.

I grinned sheepishly at him and swallowed hard as the car pulled into the circular drive, dislodging my nose from where I'd had it smashed against the window as I took in the sights. Darwin opened the door for my uncle first, and he climbed out, his black hair catching the last glint of sunlight. Then my door was opened, and Darwin waited for me to step out like this was some kind of grand entrance at a ball. I hesitated for a second, my fingers gripping the handle tight.

When I finally got out of the car, the heat hit me like a wall. The air was thick, suffocating, but it wasn't just the humidity. It was the place itself, the way it seemed to tower over me like I was something small, something . . . insignificant.

"You'll get used to it. Before you know it, this place will feel like the home you've always lived in." His voice was easy as he confidently walked away, flicking his hand for me to follow him. "Come on, I'll show you around."

The foyer was even more overwhelming than the outside. White marble floors stretched out beneath my feet, gleaming like they'd never seen a speck of dust. The walls were lined with art—huge, abstract pieces that didn't make any sense to me. There were high ceilings, chandeliers hanging down like frozen waterfalls, and everything was quiet, like the whole house was holding its breath.

I wasn't sure I liked that.

"You live here all alone?" I muttered, not really meaning for him to hear.

Everett chuckled, but it didn't sound like real laughter. "You live here now, remember?"

I followed him up a wide staircase, my footsteps echoing as I walked. The house felt like it swallowed sound, like it was waiting for something to happen. My skin prickled, but I shrugged it off.

We went down a long hallway, passing what seemed like a million closed doors until we got to the last one.

Everett grinned, his white teeth glinting under the lights, and then he opened the door with a flourish.

My breath caught in my throat. The room was insane. Like, over-the-top, "pinch me I'm dreaming" insane.

The walls were painted in soft blush pinks, but not in a little-girl way—it was elegant, sophisticated even. A crystal chandelier hung from the ceiling, casting sparkles of light over the room. There was a plush, oversized bed in the center, piled with pillows in different textures and shades of pink and gold. The headboard was tufted velvet, the kind I'd imagine you'd see in some fancy hotel, not a bedroom for a teenager. Across from the bed was a huge wall-mounted flat-screen TV, and to the side, a vanity filled with designer makeup and perfume bottles that shimmered like little jewels.

I took a step inside, my eyes darting everywhere, not sure where to focus because everything was . . . incredible.

Everett stood by the door, watching me take it all in with a satisfied smirk. "The bathroom's over there," he said, pointing to a door against the wall. "But check the closet first."

I glanced around, immediately finding the door that was slightly ajar, revealing rows and rows of clothes, all neatly hung, organized by color and style. As I skimmed my fingers across the soft fabric, my skin caught on a tag. I nearly fainted when I saw the amount of zeros on it. Just this one shirt was probably a hundred times more than the entirety of all the clothes I'd ever owned.

"I hope it's to your liking," he said, his voice smooth and confident, because he knew he'd done well.

I couldn't even find the words to respond. It wasn't just to my liking—it was beyond anything I'd ever dreamed of. In our crummy apartment I'd been too busy *surviving* to think about the condition of the four decrepit walls we were living in. And then afterward, in all of those foster homes . . . I'd just decided that was it for me. A lifetime of struggle and secondhand things, and I'd put aside all thoughts that life could actually be different.

Everett must have realized I was struggling because he smiled gently and turned to go. "I'll leave you to settle in," he said. "If you need anything, just let me know." His smile broadened. "Welcome home."

Home. The word got caught in my throat, burrowing into my chest as the door clicked behind him, and I threw myself onto the bed, sinking into the softest mattress I'd ever felt.

A squeal of pure joy slipped from my lips, and my legs kicked up in the air as I buried my face in the pillows, grinning like an idiot.

I rolled onto my back and stared up at the chandelier, the giddiness bubbling inside me. Was this what the princess felt like in the stories when she was whisked away by the prince and her fairy tale came true?

Maybe—just maybe—things were starting to turn around for me.

The first week passed in a blur of disbelief and exploration. Every corner of the house proved just how small and out of place I was.

I spent most of my time wandering around, trying not to get lost. There were rooms that seemed to have no use at all for Everett, like the libraries with shelves towering to the ceiling, filled with books that still smelled new and untouched. I ran my fingers along the spines, reading titles I'd never heard of, feeling a strange pang of disbelief inside me that I would now have the opportunity to read them all.

The house had its own home theater. Rows of leather recliners faced a screen that took up an entire wall. There was a candy bar and popcorn machine, and I spent almost every night watching movies while eating popcorn and ice cream until all hours of the morning.

There was also an enormous pool. It was sprawling, glittering under the sun like a sapphire embedded in the backyard. There were lounge chairs lined neatly along the edges, a cabana off to the side, and even a little waterfall feature that trickled into the water. I'd never seen anything like it in real life. It was the kind of thing I'd only ever dreamed about, and yet there it was, right outside the glass doors.

My uncle's rooms were on the second floor on the other side of the mansion overlooking the pool and gardens, and the first couple of days I rarely saw him because of work. He told me he was in "acquisitions and sales," but he hadn't given me any other details besides that.

School wasn't starting until the next week, so I took advantage of all the rooms, reading all the books I could, swimming in the hot Texas sun, and trying on all of my clothes like I was Cinderella herself.

Everything seemed too good to be real.

And I forgot an important lesson that I should have already learned. That sometimes, when everything feels too perfect, like a dream you're afraid to wake from, it's because the cracks were hidden just beneath the surface, waiting to remind you that nothing that good ever comes without a cost.

My uncle had set me up to attend the most prestigious school in Dallas—even though one look at my grades should have told him I had no business being there. Everyone at Smithwood Preparatory wore crisp uniforms, and the buildings looked like something out of an Ivy League brochure. It was intimidating at first, seeing how polished and put-together everyone was, but I somehow managed to make friends—quickly—for the first time in my life.

Here, I wasn't the girl with a junkyard past and a suitcase full of secrets. No one knew what my life had been like before I got here, and I wasn't about to tell them. It was easier to blend in, to let the shiny new exterior my uncle had handed me do the talking. The uniform helped—a tailored blazer and pleated skirt that somehow made me look like I belonged. It was a far cry from the thrift store finds I'd patched together back in public school.

Friends. I'd never had them before, not really. I'd had people who were nice to me in passing or sat next to me in class because there were no other options, but this was different. These girls wanted to sit with me at lunch, wanted to know where I got my hair done, wanted to tell me secrets they swore no one else knew. They asked me to join their group projects, to go shopping after school, to come to their birthday parties.

And I could say yes. For once, I could actually say yes.

The best part? I could invite them over to my house. *My house.* Not my mom's cramped apartment that always smelled like cigarettes and cheap air freshener, or the foster homes that never allowed it anyway. My uncle's house was a palace, and for the first time in my life, I wasn't ashamed of where I lived.

The first time I invited a group over, I thought I might throw up from the nerves. They piled out of their cars, giggling and chattering as they walked up the driveway, their eyes widening as they took in the mansion. The house looked even more extravagant from their perspective, and I saw it through fresh eyes—the sprawling gardens, the shimmering pool in the back. It wasn't just a house; it was a statement.

"Sloane, this is your house?" Claire asked, her voice dripping with awe.

I smiled, trying to act like it wasn't a big deal, even though I was literally beaming inside with pride. "Yep. Home sweet home."

Home. The word still tasted strange on my tongue, but it felt good to say.

We spent the afternoon lounging by the pool, sipping Diet Coke from crystal glasses my uncle's staff brought out on silver trays. The girls gushed over how amazing everything was, complimenting every detail of the house. I couldn't stop smiling, basking in the feeling of being . . . normal. For the first time, I wasn't the girl hiding where she lived, making excuses for why no one could ever come over. I was part of something, part of a group that wanted me there.

By the time they left, hugging me goodbye and promising to do it again soon, I felt lighter than I had in years. I closed the door behind them, leaning against it and letting out a deep breath before I slowly sank to the floor.

———

A few blissful months later, I was walking to the kitchen when the faint hum of music and muffled conversation floated up the grand staircase. I made my way down, curiosity tugging at me with each step. My uncle had had a few meetings since I'd been here, but this sounded different. Bigger. The sounds were too lively, too vibrant, too full of something electric to be the kind of dry business meeting I'd seen him host.

At the base of the stairs, I hesitated, clutching the banister as the low rumble of voices and the clink of glasses grew louder. The source of the commotion was obvious—the ballroom doors were cracked open, a warm golden light spilling into the dim hallway. The flicker of chandeliers and the faint scent of expensive perfume filled the air, and I had to see more.

I crept closer, careful to keep my steps light, and peered through the opening. My breath caught in my throat.

The room was filled with men in perfectly tailored suits, the kind of suits that screamed old money and whispered power. They moved in clusters, their conversations animated, their laughter polished and practiced. Each of them held a drink in hand, swirling amber liquid in crystal glasses as if it were part of the performance. Their faces carried that air of effortless confidence that came with knowing you owned the world—or at least enough of it to not care about the rest.

But it wasn't the men who stole my attention.

Scattered among them were women, draped in gowns that shimmered under the light of the chandeliers. They were glamorous in a way I'd only seen in magazines, their hair perfectly styled, their makeup flawless. Diamonds glittered at their throats, their ears, their wrists, catching the light every time they moved. They looked like they'd stepped out of a dream, impossibly elegant and stunning, and the men, the much older men . . . they were enthralled. Hanging on their every word, leaning in too close, their eyes greedy and admiring all at once.

One of the women laughed, a soft, musical sound that drew the attention of everyone around her. She tilted her head, her fingers lightly brushing the arm of a man who looked like he belonged on the cover of *Forbes*. He leaned closer, captivated, his gaze never leaving her face. Her smile widened, the diamonds at her throat catching the light like tiny fireworks.

They looked like they were having the time of their lives.

I couldn't tear my eyes away. The scene was intoxicating—sparkling, seductive, and dripping with wealth. The gowns, the jewels, the effortless grace of the women as they charmed the room . . . it was mesmerizing. They were the kind of beautiful that didn't feel real, the kind that made you question if you were looking at actual people or some kind of fantasy brought to life.

My hand tightened on the edge of the doorframe, my pulse quickening. It wasn't just their beauty or their gowns or the way they commanded attention. It was the way they seemed to *belong*. They moved through the room like they owned it, like they belonged among the men and the money and the power.

And for a moment, just a moment, I wondered what it would feel like to be one of them. To wear the diamonds, to command the room, to be admired instead of ignored. To have that kind of power.

"They're breathtaking, aren't they?" Everett's voice floated behind me, making me jump.

"Oh, hi. I'm sorry. I heard something on my way to get a snack," I told him, worried he'd be mad at me for being nosy.

He grinned at me, his smile making him look younger . . . more carefree.

"Nonsense. This is your house. And I'll keep telling you it's your house until you believe it."

I smiled shyly, my gaze flicking back into the ballroom.

"Who are they?" I asked.

He studied me for a moment, his gaze unreadable as he brought his highball to his lips and took a long drink. "They're masters of their own fate," he said, his tone smooth, practiced. "Businesswomen, if you will. Women who know how to control a room, how to navigate power and wealth with ease."

I frowned slightly, his answer only raising more questions. "What kind of business?" I asked.

His smile widened, but there was something cold in it. "The kind that requires charm, intelligence, and a certain . . . finesse."

That didn't clear anything up. If anything, it only made me more confused.

"Those women command attention. They know what they want, and they know how to get it. It's a skill few possess, but those who do . . . they thrive."

I nodded slowly, trying to piece it together. There was something about the way he spoke, the deliberate way he chose his words, that made me feel like he wasn't telling me the whole story. But I didn't dare press further.

"I see," I said quietly, even though I didn't.

"Do you?" His tone was amused, almost mocking, as he leaned against the doorway. "Good. You should pay attention to women like that, Sloane. They understand the world in ways most people never will."

My gaze went back to the ballroom.

"You know, I could see you being like them, strong and beautiful and in charge of your destiny."

"Really?" I asked, blushing. After six months I still wasn't used to praise, and my uncle was generous with it.

"Oh, yes. I'm quite sure that someday you'll possess all the same traits."

He patted my shoulder. "You'd better get to bed, though. You'll be exhausted at school as it is."

I nodded, saying good night and wandering back to my room without the snack I'd come down for in the first place.

I couldn't stop thinking about those women while I walked to my bedroom. About the way they carried themselves, how they seemed to own the room. It wasn't just the wealth or the beauty; it was something deeper, something magnetic.

My uncle had given me so much, and now he'd shown me even more. I didn't want to let him down, and I didn't want to lose the chance to be like those women. Because more than anything, I wanted to be in charge of my destiny, just like he'd said.

CHAPTER 1

SLOANE

Seventeen Years, Eleven Months, and Twenty Days Old

My knock on Everett's office door felt heavier than usual, like my knuckles already knew something I didn't. He called me in, but his tone was crisp; it was the voice he used for business meetings . . . and it made me even more uneasy.

I stepped inside, and he looked up from his desk. The room smelled of leather and something smoky, like his cologne or the cigars he sometimes enjoyed after dinner. Everything in here screamed power: the bookshelves lined with unread leather-bound books, the polished desk that reflected the soft glow of the desk lamp, even the chair I sank into across from him.

"You wanted to see me?" I asked, my voice steady, even though my palms felt clammy for some reason.

He'd never given me a reason to be nervous before. I didn't know why I was now.

Everett leaned back in his chair, folding his hands over his stomach. He studied me for a moment, his eyes sharp and almost . . . calculating, before he finally spoke. "Sloane, your birthday's coming up. The big eighteen."

I nodded, unsure where this was going. I knew Everett had his staff planning a huge party for me, but besides that, I didn't know what was happening.

"We need to talk about next steps," he said, his tone smooth, as if he were discussing a quarterly business review.

"Next steps?" I echoed, a nervous laugh slipping out. "Like . . . graduation?"

Everett tilted his head, the corners of his mouth twitching in what might have been a smile, but it didn't feel like the amused kind. "Not exactly. You'll be graduating soon, and as an adult, it will be time for you to start life on your own."

I blinked, not understanding. "Wait . . . what?"

He sighed, like he was explaining something obvious to someone who should've known better. "You'll be moving out after graduation. I've given you every opportunity to succeed—this house, your school, everything you could possibly need. Now it's time for you to stand on your own two feet."

My stomach dropped like the floor had disappeared beneath me. "But . . . I don't have a plan yet. My grades—" I swallowed hard. "They're not good enough for most colleges. I don't even know what I want to do."

"That's something you'll need to figure out," he said simply, as if this was a puzzle I could solve by next Tuesday. "You've been given the tools, Sloane. What you do with them now is up to you."

I stared at him, waiting for some kind of punchline. Some indication that this was a test, or a joke, or anything other than the cold truth settling over me like a weight I couldn't carry. But his expression didn't waver. He leaned forward, placing his hands flat on the desk, and looking me in the eye.

I couldn't believe this was happening. I'd thought he'd let me stay after school while I got a job or an internship or even took classes at the local college until I figured out what I wanted to do with my life. Never in my wildest dreams did I imagine being cut off the second that I graduated.

"You'll be fine," he said, his tone final. "We'll discuss it more after the party . . ."

I barely made it back to my room before the panic hit. My legs felt like jelly as I shut the door behind me, the sound of the latch clicking echoing in my ears. I stumbled toward the bed, my chest tightening. Maybe I should have expected this, but it felt like I'd just gotten here, and I was still getting my feet under me. Like I was still trying to dig out of a hole created by years of poverty and a spotty education. He'd never mentioned this once, that I would have to move out. What happened to this being my *home*?

Eighteen. Out. On my own.

The words swirled in my head, overlapping with memories I hadn't let myself think about in years. The tiny apartment with peeling paint and a refrigerator that barely worked. The foster homes with their cold beds and even colder rules. The times I'd gone to school wearing the same clothes for a week because there wasn't anything else. The days I hadn't eaten a single meal.

I clutched the edge of the bed, my fingers digging into the comforter as my vision blurred. I'd thought I'd escaped that life. I'd assumed that Everett's house, with its countless rooms and glittering chandeliers, was my fresh start. But now . . . now it felt like the rug was being ripped out from under me, and I was falling back into the life I'd barely survived.

I'd be alone again. Even with Everett working all the time, I'd still had someone around. I'd had a family, even if it was small.

Pressing my hands to my chest, I tried to force the air back into my lungs. My breaths were fast, shallow, and sharp. My mind was racing, a flood of worst-case scenarios crashing over me. What if I couldn't find a job? What if I lost everything I'd been given and ended up right back where I started?

The room felt too small, the walls suddenly closing in. I sank to the floor, my back against the bed, and pulled my knees to my chest, trying to stop the trembling. The panic gripped me tight, refusing to let go, until I couldn't tell if I was crying or gasping for air or both.

I pressed my forehead to my knees, squeezing my eyes shut. *This can't happen. I can't go back. I can't.*

But no matter how hard I tried to push the fear away, it lingered, clawing at the edges of my mind, whispering that everything I had now was temporary. That I was just a visitor in this life, and soon, I'd be thrown out into the cold.

Again.

Eighteen.

It was my eighteenth birthday, and I'd woken up feeling like I'd reached my death sentencing day. Celebrating at the enormous birthday party my uncle was throwing me felt like celebrating the end of my life instead.

The grounds around the estate were alive with music and laughter, the kind of noise that should've made me feel like I was at the center of something spectacular. Balloons floated in clusters, tied with silver and gold ribbons, glittering under the chandeliers. There were tables stacked with foods I couldn't even name and a massive cake that looked like it had been plucked straight out of a magazine. It was everything anyone could dream of for their eighteenth birthday.

But I wasn't really there.

I smiled when someone called my name, nodding at their comments and laughing at jokes I didn't hear. I accepted every hug and compliment like I was on autopilot. The noise around me blurred into a hum as my mind kept drifting to the conversation with Everett. His words looped in my head like a broken record.

You'll be on your own.

I stood near the edge of the room, watching as my school friends crowded near the DJ, dancing and taking selfies. They looked so carefree, like they didn't have a single worry in the world. I envied them at that moment, the ease with which they threw themselves into the night. Their futures were probably mapped out with scholarships, internships, and safety nets. They didn't know what it felt like to be standing on the edge of a cliff, staring down into uncertainty.

"Sloane, this party is *insane*," Marissa gushed, pulling me into a quick hug. She smelled like expensive perfume, and her sequined dress sparkled as she moved. "Seriously, this is the best party I've ever been to."

"Thanks," I said, forcing a smile. "I'm glad you're having fun."

"You're not?" she teased, tilting her head. "It's your night!"

"I am," I lied, my cheeks aching from the effort. "Of course, I am."

She didn't seem to notice my hesitation, her attention already pulled toward the tray of drinks being passed around. I'd learned since moving here that underage drinking was an acceptable part of rich people's lives, and there were bars set up all around the room tonight.

Letting out a slow breath, I glanced at everything again, trying to see it from Marissa's perspective. The decorations were perfect. The music was perfect. Everyone was having the time of their lives.

Everyone except me.

I wandered outside to the patio, needing a moment to breathe. The pool glowed under the soft lights, filled with people swimming and drinking. Voices and laughter were everywhere. Leaning against the railing, I stared out at the manicured lawn.

What was I supposed to do? I'd spent the last couple of years convincing myself that Everett's house, his resources, had changed my life. That I'd left the chaos and uncertainty behind. I spent the last few years convincing myself I was safe . . . that I had a home.

But now, it felt like I was about to lose everything all over again.

"Sloane!" someone called from behind me. I turned to see one of my friends waving me over, a wide grin on her face. "Come take pictures with us!"

"Be right there," I called back, forcing another smile.

They were just photos, but even the thought of posing felt exhausting. I straightened my ridiculously expensive dress, fixing my face into something resembling happiness, and headed back inside.

The rest of the night passed in a blur of forced smiles and shallow laughter. The gifts piled up on a table, each one more extravagant than the last. I thanked everyone, nodding and smiling until the words felt meaningless. The music grew louder, the crowd more animated, but I felt like I was moving through it all underwater, disconnected and heavy.

As the party wore on, I found myself sitting on the edge of the pool in the bikini I'd changed into, nursing another glass of something fizzy and sweet as my friends laughed and splashed in the water. I stared at the crowd around the deck, watching as everyone else danced and lived in the moment.

That should be me, I thought. *This is my party.*

But no matter how hard I tried, I couldn't shake the anxiety twisting in my stomach. Every laugh, every cheer, every flicker of happiness around me felt like a reminder of everything I was about to lose.

I was already feeling like I wasn't a part of their world.

And soon, when graduation came, that would be true.

A copious amount of alcohol was clouding my head as I walked down the outdoor path when the party had *finally* ended. The pebbles of the walkway bit into the bottoms of my feet with every step, and my discarded party dress was gripped in my hand.

Turning the corner, I stumbled when Everett was suddenly there. "Sorry," I whispered. Things had been strained between us since that talk a few days ago. I needed to work on that. He'd already done so much for me. I needed to not be a brat. It wasn't his fault that I was useless.

"There you are." He smiled, but it was a different smile than he normally gave me. "I've planned an after-party for you. It starts in an hour."

"An . . . after-party?" I asked, trying to keep my voice steady. My pulse was suddenly throbbing in my neck, and it felt like there was a charge in the air, an energy filled with something I couldn't quite name . . . but it made the hair on my arms stand on end.

His smile deepened. "Yes, a more . . . exclusive gathering." He tilted his head slightly, studying me with those eyes that always knocked me off guard with how much they resembled my mother's. "There's a new outfit waiting for you upstairs. It's on your bed. Take a shower and put it on. I'll be waiting."

My throat tightened, I nodded, unable to form words. I was moving on autopilot as I climbed the stairs, feeling Everett's gaze follow me until I was out of his sight. Was this going to be more bad news? Was this where he told me that I actually *couldn't* stay until graduation and he was kicking me out *now*?

Although why would I wear a new dress for that news?

I really shouldn't have drunk so much. It was hard to think clearly about anything.

As I pushed open the door, the first thing I saw was the dress. It lay neatly on my bed, draped across the blankets. A thin, black slip dress. The fabric shimmered under the low light, silky and delicate. I was still holding the white lace dress that I'd worn to the party. Was it . . . intentional that the dress on the bed was the exact opposite of the one I had worn today?

Maybe this was a fancier party.

That could be it.

My gaze flicked to the silver slingbacks and the small black lipstick tube next to the dress. Slowly I walked to the bed and picked it up, undoing the cap and staring at the color.

The bright pink color wasn't something I usually wore.

I stared at the dress for a long time until Everett's voice echoed in my mind: *I'll be waiting.*

Forcing myself to the shower, I washed the chlorine out of my hair and then dried it until it lay straight against my shoulders, applying light makeup after that. By the time I reached for the dress, my hands were trembling.

The fabric was cold against my skin as I slid it on, the thin straps resting softly on my shoulders. The front dipped down, leaving my cleavage exposed. I stepped into the heels, and then I picked up the lipstick and applied it, turning to the mirror.

There was a stranger in the reflection. That couldn't be me. The pink-stained lips stretched across my face, seeming to mock me cruelly.

I turned away and took in a deep breath. Whatever he had to say, or whatever this was—I would accept it gracefully. Everett had done so much for me; he'd *saved* me. It was stupid for me to feel nervous.

The mansion was silent except for the distant thump of music. I followed the sound, each step feeling heavier than the last. The music grew louder as I walked down the staircase, a slow, pulsing, dragging beat that did funny things to my insides. Everett had had the occasional party with work associates before, like the one he'd caught me watching last year, but I'd never been allowed to go. Who had he even invited to the party tonight? All of my friends had left.

When I reached the living area, I stopped dead in my tracks.

The room had been transformed. The lights were low, casting long shadows over the sleek furniture. The air smelled faintly of something sweet and smoky, unfamiliar. And the guests—there were men everywhere, all dressed in tailored suits.

But that wasn't what stopped me, a scream building in my throat, my blood running cold in my veins.

It was the fact that every single one of the men was disguised, dark and featureless, hiding their faces completely behind red masks. It was like I'd stepped into some kind of twisted masquerade.

I turned to run, but the doors had closed. When I looked around to find somewhere I could escape to, Everett was there, his mask in hand, a smile playing upon his lips.

"Everett?" I whispered in a scared, timid voice.

"Welcome to your after-party," he purred, his voice low and smooth, almost too casual for the tension that filled the room. His eyes gleamed as he looked at me, and bile rose in my throat.

The men in the room shifted slightly, and I felt their eyes on me— beneath those crimson masks, watching, waiting. I swallowed hard, my skin prickling with the undeniable danger. My fingers were clenched into fists at my sides, but I was frozen, like a butterfly trapped in a jar.

"I don't understand," I breathed.

Everett took a step closer, his smile never wavering. "Don't be nervous," he said softly, although his tone held something deeper, something darker. "Tonight is . . . *special*."

I glanced around the room again. The alcohol was still messing with my head. I folded my arms in front of me protectively, but when some of their eyes went to my chest, I immediately dropped them, realizing the movement had made my breasts stick out even more.

"This is it, Sloane," Everett said. "Your moment."

I turned to look at him, my stomach knotting. "What moment?"

He smiled faintly, the kind of smile that never reached his eyes. "To take control. To decide what your future will be."

My brow furrowed.

He gestured toward the room, to the men still watching me like I was prey. "This is your chance," he said, his voice like velvet. "If you choose to participate in the auction, you won't have to worry. About anything. I know you've been terrified about what's to come. You don't have to be. I came up with a solution for you. I'm giving you another chance."

The word *auction* hit me like a slap, and I took a step back, my pulse quickening. "What kind of auction—" I asked quietly, still trying to grasp what he meant.

"You'll be entering a world of privilege, of wealth, of security," he interrupted smoothly, his hand coming down to tighten on my shoulder. "Where *you're* in charge. You won't have to worry about money or your future. You'll have everything you've ever dreamed of and more."

I shook my head, the words refusing to settle. "I don't—" I stammered, but he cut me off again.

"Remember the women you've seen at my parties? I know you've always admired them," he said, his tone insistent now, coaxing. "Remember how they looked? How they moved through the room commanding attention, respect? They made the choice to be masters of their destiny, and now that you're an adult, you can as well."

My mouth went dry as I stared at the glittering scene before me, my mind flashing back to the way those women had seemed untouchable, powerful, radiant. But now the illusion cracked under the weight of my uncle's words, the edges of their perfection fraying in my memory.

"Do you mean . . . those women are paid by those men? To . . . be with them?" I asked, finally starting to connect the dots.

"They know the power their beauty wields," he said, his voice growing softer, like a whisper that wrapped around me. "And your beauty, Sloane . . . it's even more magnificent than all of theirs."

Everett's words sent a shiver down my spine, his compliments and flattery hitting their mark. Even after two years, I still soaked it up like a dying flower desperate for water.

"You could be pampered. Wealthy. Never have to worry about supporting yourself. You can be one of the elite. Not many women get this chance."

I looked up at him, searching his face. He looked completely confident, like he believed this was my only option.

"I . . ." My voice faltered, my heart pounding so hard it felt like the room might hear it. "I don't know. You . . . you want to put me up for sale in an auction?" I clarified, the words too horrifying to really be true. He had to mean something else.

I waited for him to deny it. To tell me I was putting his words together all wrong.

He didn't.

"Me? No. *I* wouldn't be doing anything. You would be *choosing* to put yourself in the auction. You're an adult, Sloane."

I shook my head, my ears thudding in time with my heart. "I couldn't . . ."

"You don't have a plan, Sloane. You have no job, no acceptance letters, no place to live. Once you graduate, you could end up on the streets. I'm giving you an incredible opportunity, and it's just for the night."

He smiled again, but it was victorious this time, like he already knew what my answer would be. Like he'd planned for every possible reaction, every protest. "You do know," he said. "You're just afraid. But fear is temporary. Power, Sloane . . . power lasts."

I swallowed hard, my eyes darting back to the room. The men were watching, their gazes sharp even behind their masks. And somewhere in the middle of it all, I felt myself shrinking, folding in on the edges of who I thought I was.

Was this really control? Or was it the most beautiful lie I'd ever been told?

My uncle's question hung in the air, heavy and unrelenting. "What's it going to be, Sloane?" he asked, his voice smooth and patient, like he had all the time in the world. But the weight behind it felt anything but patient. He was waiting for me to decide, his hand still resting lightly on my shoulder, anchoring me in place.

The room around me seemed to be shimmering at the edges. The laughter, the soft clink of glasses, the hungry looks of the men—all of it swirled together, threatening to drown me. Everett's words played on a loop in my head. *Privilege. Security. Control.*

"What's it going to be?" he repeated.

I looked at him, his face as calm and unreadable as ever, and then back at the glittering scene before me. My pulse pounded in my ears as the memories came flooding back, unbidden and overwhelming.

Again, I thought of my mother's apartment, of the nights I'd gone to bed hungry because there hadn't been enough food to go around. I thought of wearing the same clothes for days at a time, of the embarrassment when kids at school noticed. I thought of the foster homes, of being handed secondhand scraps and told I should be grateful.

The hollow ache of those memories clawed at my insides, filling me with a fear I could taste. I remembered the sting of shame, the bitterness of being powerless, of having nothing, of knowing there was no one in the world who cared whether I sank or swam. It would be like that again if I had to leave. I would have nowhere to live, no job . . . no car.

I swallowed hard, my throat dry as sandpaper. My uncle's voice pulled me back to the present, soft and insistent. "You don't have to go back to that, Sloane," he said. "You don't have to live that life. Not if you make the right choice."

The right choice. I hated how his words sounded, like the decision had already been made, like I'd be a fool to refuse. But the truth was, I *was* afraid. I was terrified. Of being poor again. Of struggling, of never having enough. Of falling back into that pit I'd spent so much time trying to climb out of.

My hands trembled as I clenched them into fists, my nails biting into my palms. I stared at the room again, thinking of those women, at the way they seemed untouchable, invincible. I thought of how my uncle had described them: *masters of their fate.*

I grasped onto that. Because they *had* looked powerful. Beautiful. Like they were enjoying every glamoured second. It was a far cry from my other option of having nothing. I couldn't go back to that. I just couldn't. So even though my heart was pounding so hard I was having trouble breathing, I knew what I needed to choose.

My throat felt tight as I gave my answer. "Okay."

"What was that?" my uncle asked, tilting his head slightly.

I forced myself to look at him, my voice trembling but a little louder this time. "Okay. I'll do it."

His smile was subtle, almost smug, as he gave a small nod. "Good girl," he said, his tone smooth and satisfied, like I'd passed some kind of test. I couldn't help but feel relieved that I'd pleased him. "You've made the right choice, Sloane. You'll see."

I didn't feel right, or powerful, yet. Right now, all I felt was hollow. But that would change. One day, when I wasn't so scared, I'd be more like those confident women . . . I hoped.

"Gentlemen, shall we begin?"

I glanced up at him, but he was staring around the room, a challenge in his gaze. "Sloane turned eighteen today. She is a certified virgin. Let's start at three million," he said casually, as if he were talking about stocks or cars or artwork . . . and not me.

Three million.

The words took a second to filter through my consciousness. *Certified virgin?* I squeezed my eyes closed in embarrassment as I thought about the gynecologist appointment I'd had last week. I'd been having terrible cramps, and Everett had set me up with an appointment. The doctor had questioned me about my sexual history, but I hadn't thought anything of it. I'd thought that was how they were supposed to go. I'd never dreamed the doctor would tell Everett.

The bodies shifted around the room, and there was a beat of silence. I wanted to run, but I made myself stay still. I'd made my choice.

"Three and a half," one of the masked men said, his voice deep and calm, like this was just another night for him. Another game.

My skin felt too tight, like it didn't belong to me anymore.

"Four." Another voice called from across the room. It was a slow, deliberate drawl, tinged with amusement, like he was savoring the moment.

"Five million," said a third. My legs shook beneath me, and I thought I might collapse. The numbers kept climbing—six, seven, eight million—and with each bid, the air grew heavier, suffocating.

Everett leaned in closer, one of his hands sliding from my shoulder to the small of my back. I flinched but still didn't move, my pulse fluttering like a trapped hummingbird, its tiny wings beating faster and faster, desperate to break free. But I still couldn't get myself to move. I was paralyzed.

He whispered in my ear, his voice smooth and almost affectionate. "It's all for you, Sloane. You should feel honored. This . . . this is power."

It didn't feel like it. I felt like I was being torn apart, like everything inside me was breaking, unraveling with each new bid. This felt like something else. Like something dark and twisted that I couldn't even begin to comprehend.

But I wanted to be safe. I didn't want to be homeless and penniless and alone. This was the only way.

"Ten million," a voice called out, louder than the rest. The room stilled, completely silent except for the sound of someone gasping.

Oh, that was me. It was *my* ragged breaths filling the room. It was *my* heart racing so fast that it felt like it might burst out of my chest.

Everett's grip tightened, and I could feel the smile on his lips, even though I couldn't see it. He took a step forward, guiding me along with him. The masked men watched us, most of them leaning forward slightly, hungrily.

My knees buckled, and I stumbled forward, barely catching myself before I hit the ground. Everett grabbed my arm, his hand holding me tight.

"Going once," Everett announced, his voice calm and controlled, like I hadn't almost collapsed, like I wasn't trembling under his touch. "Going twice."

I sucked in a breath, forcing myself to stand straighter, even though my legs were shaking beneath me.

"Sold."

The masked man who'd won stepped forward, grabbing my hand and immediately pulling me through the door into another guest suite. The door closed behind us, and the monster licked the side of my face as I was crowded against him, one arm wrapping around my chest as his other hand dragged up and down my body, cupping my core through my silk dress. Hot tears splashed on his arm, and he laughed cruelly.

"I'd easily pay twenty to have you, my sweet. It's always better when they cry."

And I did cry.

I cried when he ripped my dress from my shaking frame. I cried when he roughly violated me with his fingers and his mouth, and I cried when he pushed inside me.

When he was done with me, I stayed in that room, in that bed, and I stared out the window at a cloudless sky that was once again mocking me like it had that day my mother had been lowered into the ground.

All my tears had dried.

In the quiet aftermath of that terrible moment, when the world had finally gone still and the wreckage of everything I once knew lay scattered around me, I felt something inside me die. It wasn't sudden, like the snap of a breaking bone; it was slow, like a flame choking beneath too much ash.

I'd been split open in ways I couldn't even name, and the pieces that were left just didn't fit anymore. My soul, once vibrant and full of those small, fragile hopes that had kept me moving forward through my mother's addiction and death and the year of being passed from home to home like errant trash . . . it had dimmed to a flicker, barely there. It was as if the core of who I was had turned to glass—fragile, empty—and with every breath, more of it slipped away, leaving me hollow. The person I used to be was gone, lost in the quiet where there had once been life.

Now, there was only the ghost of who I had been, the power Everett had mentioned, nowhere to be found.

Maybe I hadn't taken matters into my own hands and saved myself.

Maybe I'd destroyed myself instead.

But I'd chosen this . . . and there was no going back now.

CHAPTER 2

SLOANE

Four years later

I sat on the floor, cross-legged, sipping my French latte. The steam from the cup curled up toward my face as I stared at the painting I was working on. The strokes across the canvas felt dark and heavy, the moody blues and blacks swirling together in a way that felt suffocating, even to me.

The woman in the painting sat alone on an old pier, her back hunched, shoulders slumped under a cloudy night sky. The pier stretched out into an endless sea of dark, churning water, the whole scene drenched in shadows. It felt like looking into the heart of despair.

And that was the point.

I took another sip of my latte, the rich flavor tasting like ash on my tongue. The painting wasn't supposed to be this way. It had started with a photograph I took in Majorca. That day had been . . . as close to perfect as I could get in my life. Sun shining, the water sparkling in the light, the sky a clear, endless blue. The woman in the photo had been a local girl smiling, the sunlight bathing her skin and the pier in a warm glow.

But of course, when I'd started painting, the picture had shifted. The happiness in the photograph had drained away with every brushstroke. Now, all that remained was a version of the scene that felt like it had been submerged in grief. It was as if I'd taken the original image and dunked it in anguish, letting it drown in the emotions I was careful not to let myself feel.

I set the cup down on the floor beside me, my fingers stained with paint from hours of work. I studied the brushstrokes—heavy, uneven, almost angry. The woman in the painting felt lost, isolated, grieving.

Like me.

I shook my head. All my paintings seemed to end up like this. I eyed the stacked canvases strewn all over the room, all of them macabre versions of the photos they'd been based on.

"What the hell am I even doing?" I muttered to myself, running a hand through my dark brown hair, smudging a streak of paint across my temple.

I reached for the brush again, not ready to give up on it, but not sure what else to add. What else was there to say? The painting already screamed everything I didn't want to admit.

My phone rang, and I knew who it was before I picked it up. It had been a week since my last job, and I'd been on eggshells the last couple of days, wondering when I'd get my new assignment. I stared at the screen, the familiar number flashing like a warning.

Everett.

The only other calls I got were from telemarketers—although those calls were much more welcome than his.

I took a deep breath and swiped to answer, steeling my emotions for what would come next.

"Sloane." His voice crackled through the line, cold and impersonal, just like always nowadays. "Tyler Miller has requested you for the Stanley Cup Finals coming up."

My stomach twisted. Tyler Miller. The cocky asshole who booked me every time he was in town for a game. He acted like he was God's gift to women and liked to stare at himself in the mirror while he fucked me, pumping his muscles and changing positions if he didn't like how he looked. I hated him.

But I guess he wasn't as bad as some of my other clients.

Not that it mattered if I liked him or not. I didn't have a choice.

"For this contract, you'll be traveling to attend all of his games during the series. You'll stay at whatever hotel he's staying at, in a room he can visit."

"You want me to go to his games?"

I bit down on my lip, going through the logistics. Tyler played for Tampa Bay. Not a terrible place to travel to for work, considering how close that arena was to the beach. Going to his games had never been part of the job, though. That sounded . . . almost like it could be fun—especially watching Tyler get hit.

As long as I didn't think about what would happen *after* the games.

"He's offered up a large sum for your services. So I'm allowing it. I've advised him that I don't want any undue attention on you, though.

No cameras focusing on your face, no press, and no media. He's not one of their star players, so I don't think there should be any issues," my uncle continued, his tone clipped, efficient. "He just wants you hanging on his arm, making him seem like the up-and-coming star who's already scored. You'll need to sell it to his teammates and the spectators. Make him seem desirable. Wanted. A sex symbol. Get people interested in him. And then, you'll wait in the hotel and fuck him however he wants. You know what to do—keep your mouth shut and remember this is a job. Is that clear?"

That was always the reminder he gave me. As if it was possible for me to catch feelings for the assholes who paid him to have my body for a night or two.

I bit my lip harder, hard enough that the taste of iron and salt flooded my mouth. Oops. I tried to relax my body—my hand was gripping the phone so tight my knuckles had turned white. "Of course," I muttered, already feeling the familiar numbness creeping in.

"And, Sloane?" His voice dropped to that concerned tone he liked to use whenever he felt like I was acting too . . . sullen. "Make sure you have a checkup with Dr. Jennings before the first game—we can't let any slipups happen."

There was a beat of silence as I choked back the pain that sliced through my chest. We were both on the same page about making sure my birth control was up to date. Perhaps the *only* thing we were on the same page about at this point in our relationship.

I forced myself to let out a bitter laugh, the sound hollow in my ears. "Of course."

"Good. His payment will replenish your accounts. You'll be good for several months after this." He hung up without another word.

I stood there for a moment, staring at the phone, as I began to mentally prepare myself for the next week and for Tyler's *touch*—when every second would feel like I was crawling out of my own skin. Realizing I was still clutching my paintbrush in my free hand, I set it down and walked out quickly.

I wouldn't be back in that room until after the job was done.

Painting was when I allowed myself to *feel*. I couldn't have that happening now.

Walking into my bathroom, I stared into the mirror in front of me, studying my reflection. My face was the same as it always was—perfect, composed, blank. And inside? Inside I felt nothing. Not anger, not sadness, not fear. Just . . . *numb.* Like I was floating above it all, detached from my own body, like it wasn't mine anymore.

Although wasn't that the truth? It *wasn't* mine. It hadn't been for a long, long time.

I leaned forward, my hands gripping the edge of the sink, examining the . . . emptiness.

My phone buzzed again, and I glanced down, already knowing what it would be. A text with my appointments over the next few days to prepare for my assignment. A list of providers and times.

There would be my eyebrow wax, my hair appointment, and my facial. Another appointment was for laser hair removal on my entire body. Whatever I was doing at those appointments was already chosen for me. I would show up to do my hair, and they would tell me if it was going to be highlights or lowlights, or even to dye my hair a different color if it was what a client had requested and Everett approved it. I would have no say in the matter.

The words blurred together on the screen as my chest tightened. Staring back into the mirror, I had the urge to break it, shatter it into a million pieces just so I didn't have to see myself like this. More of a shell than a person.

I closed my eyes, pushing down the flicker of anger that threatened to break through. Anger was dangerous. Feeling was dangerous. I couldn't afford to let either one in. Not now.

Not ever.

I took a deep breath. I could do this. I knew how to survive this, how to detach, how to make myself disappear into the role I was forced to play.

It was the only way to get through it.

Pushing away from the counter, I walked into my large closet, trying to decide what I was going to wear today—the last day I would have a choice for a while. The tags were all still designer, luxury that had only increased as the years had passed. Everett ensured I had everything I needed in order to take on more high-profile clients, so he could charge them more. So more money could go into his accounts, and the account he kept for me that paid for everything in my life.

What I wouldn't give to have told myself that first day, as I'd wandered through my closet in Everett's mansion, that those tags and those fancy clothes, they were just a trap. That I should have been happy in that rundown apartment with my dying mother. That those foster homes had actually been havens.

Because they were so much better than anything I would have after that.

I picked out a pair of tailored black shorts and a muted tan blouse that wouldn't earn me any attention while I was out. People liked to stay in the dark about what was happening right under their noses. They didn't want to be confronted with the darkness that permeated polite society.

At first, I thought the auction would be enough. I'd get a percentage of what the man had paid and I'd move on. I hadn't understood what I'd chosen that night. Not at all.

But a month later when I'd had to dress up in a slutty schoolgirl costume to service a senator who liked them young, I'd finally gotten the message—this was my life now.

I was twenty-two, and I'd lost track of all their faces. Their touches haunted my nights, though.

And I never felt clean.

The phone buzzed again, letting me know what my account balance was after Tyler's deposit, but I couldn't have cared less; it wasn't like I had access to withdraw the funds.

I lived in an expensive penthouse. I drove a black Mercedes, and the account to pay for my life was full of money.

And I would give every single bit of it up.

Shoving the phone into my pocket, I left the closet to head to the first of my appointments.

I had work to do.

And whatever I felt—it didn't matter.

Because my life wasn't mine, and it never would be.

But as I always reminded myself when my thoughts got too dark.

I'd chosen this.

CHAPTER 3

LOGAN

Staring at the phone, I debated texting him for the millionth time today.

Your dad should want to come to a fucking Stanley Cup Finals game, right?

I felt like a fucking fool when I typed out my message and actually hit send.

> Me: You coming tonight? I'll have a ticket for you at the box office.

Tapping my fingers on the counter, I stared at the phone, wondering if the *great* Grant York was going to deign to answer me.

I was a tough motherfucker ninety-nine percent of the time, but when it came to my father . . . well, he was excellent at reducing me to feeling like a sniveling little kid again.

After five minutes, he still hadn't answered, even though the message clearly showed that it had been read. Sometimes I wondered if he left that setting on specifically for me, just to be sadistic. To let me know that I was so unimportant he couldn't find time to answer me promptly . . . about anything.

My buzzer went off, signaling that someone was in the lobby waiting for me, and I frowned . . . a little, stupid spark of hope flickering inside me. Maybe it was my dad.

I pressed the button.

"Socks, can you let me up already? There's a chick taking pictures of me through the glass doors. She's got the glint."

I smirked, a sense of fucking relief filling my chest at the sound of my best friend's voice.

At least there would be one friendly face in the crowd cheering me on tonight.

"Get up here before she starts crying and pounding on the glass," I teased, proud of myself for not sounding emotional at all.

A minute later, there was a hard knock on the door, and I barely had time to get it halfway open before Asher barreled through like a freight train. "Socks!" he shouted, grinning like a kid on Christmas. And then his arms were around me in one of his infamous bear hugs that could probably crack my ribs if he wanted to.

It had been a few months since I'd seen him, but Asher hadn't changed a bit. His dark brown hair was a little longer, but still that messy "I don't own a comb" kind of look that seemed to drive women crazy. His green eyes were still their usual mix of mischief and genuine excitement, the kind that always made it impossible to stay mad at him. I could already see the gleam of trouble brewing there.

"Dude, I'm about to play in the Stanley Cup Finals, not a wrestling match," I grunted, though I didn't bother trying to push him off. It was Asher. If he didn't greet you like a golden retriever who hadn't seen you in years, something was seriously wrong.

He finally let go, stepping back with that wide grin still plastered on his face. "First game of the finals, man! I wasn't gonna miss it. You really think you could get through this without me here?"

I rolled my eyes, pretending I wasn't all emotional at the sight of him.

He cackled and pounded my back one more time before releasing me and immediately heading to the kitchen.

If there was anything I could count on with Asher, it was his appetite.

"You must be the luckiest asshole in the whole fucking world," Asher commented a few minutes later with a mouth full of chips as he somehow stuffed in another handful in the same breath. I wrinkled my nose when he winked. He looked like a demented chipmunk.

Wait a second. Those weren't just chips. Those were *my* fucking chips. My Flaming Hot Cheetos!

What a fucking bastard.

"Give those to me," I growled, snatching them out of his red-stained fingers. "You know that I have to eat Flaming Hot Cheetos every game day. That's my last fucking bag."

He grinned and chewed slowly, really driving it home that he'd managed to down half of the bag before I realized anything.

"And do *not* wipe your fingers on my couch," I ordered, shaking the bag at him because despite the fact that his mama had taught him manners, he always seemed to forget them when he was at my house.

Or anywhere, actually.

There was a reason Mama Matthews considered me her favorite child. Her *real* son was a giant pig.

Asher sighed and made a big show of wiping his hands on a towel before he grabbed my Gatorade and took a big gulp. It was a good thing that I'd gotten used to sharing with him ever since the day he'd hit me in the head with an errant baseball when our Little League teams were playing each other. As I'd stared up at the sky and wondered if I was dead, a grinning brown-haired boy with freckled cheeks had leaned over and told me I was an embarrassment to baseball players everywhere and I needed to "man the fuck up."

We were eight.

We'd also been best friends ever since.

"Why am I the luckiest bastard on the planet?" I asked, popping a delicious ambrosia-of-the-gods Cheeto in my mouth. I could already feel my super hockey powers building.

"Stanley Cup Finals as a rookie? Even Lincoln Daniels didn't manage that," Asher said as he strolled over to my fridge.

I mentally added a "King" to the front of Lincoln's name. Not that I was ever going to tell a single soul that I did that.

Wouldn't want to be labeled a "simp."

The team already had one too many of those. *Cough* *Walker Davis* *Cough*.

"To say I'm a prime reason for that would be a lie. The team is literally made of superstars at this point," I told him, even though inwardly I was preening. Up for Rookie of the Year. Stanley Cup Finals. It wasn't a bad gig to be me.

Asher raised an eyebrow. "I'm just saying, the Venom didn't even make the playoffs last season. I think they booed us every inning last game."

"An appropriate response to seeing your ugly face," I said with a grin.

He had the nerve to chuck *my* Gatorade bottle at me.

Last season, Asher had spent exactly one game in AAA before he'd been brought up to the majors. He'd set the single season batting average record for a rookie and was set to be the next All-Star of MLB. He was already breaking all the records this season.

In other words, he was doing just fine himself.

"So, you nervous?" he asked, opening my fridge and reaching in toward—

"I *will* cut off your hand."

He grinned, turning around with one of Mrs. Bentley's burritos in his hand. "This is it, isn't it? The deliciousness you've been bragging about all season."

I held up both hands as I approached him slowly. "Just put it down."

"You can't have both. Cheetos or burrito. What's it going to be?"

It felt like I was being asked which I liked better, tits or ass.

An impossible decision.

"I need that for the game," I told him, making my best puppy-dog face as I prepared to tackle him.

It was universally known that baseball players were major wusses. I could definitely take him.

Asher unwrapped the burrito with a demonic glint in his eye and before I could pounce . . . he bit into it.

And then spit the huge bite out.

"What the fuck?" he growled, dropping the burrito and clutching his throat as he threw himself toward the sink.

I watched, flabbergasted, as he turned on the water and frantically started washing out his mouth.

"What the hell is wrong with you?" I asked, leaning over to pick up the burrito and examine it.

It took me exactly one second to realize what had just happened.

Something, either sand or kitty litter, was coating the inside of the burrito.

And there was only one person who could be responsible for such an appalling crime, and it wasn't Lincoln's housekeeper.

Ari Fucking Lancaster.

As Asher continued to make noises like he was dying, I pulled out my phone and opened the latest group chat.

Me: This means war.

Ari: I just laughed out loud.

Lincoln: ?

Me: I'm serious. I needed that burrito.

> **Camden:** I don't think I've ever been this lost in a conversation.

> **Lincoln:** I doubt that, Hero.

> **Camden:** Insert middle finger emoji.

> **Walker:** I doubt that as well.

> **Ari:** You would, you simp.

I eyed the sink, where Asher was now lying on the counter, outstretched under the faucet, his mouth open as he continued to dramatically gulp down water. Sniffing the burrito, I threw up a hallelujah for Asher's gluttonous, thieving ways. The kitty litter was obviously coated with hot sauce—so spicy that my eyes were watering just smelling it.

> **Me:** As enthralling as this is, can we get back on topic?

> **Lincoln:** Yes, please inform us what the hell you're talking about.

I grinned, typing out a quick *Thank you* to him because it was good to be polite.

> **Me:** I'd like to report the desecration of a burrito.

> **Camden:** Why didn't you say it was this serious?

Hmm, I wasn't quite sure if he was being sarcastic or not.

"Why are you grinning like a loon?" Asher asked, creeping up and scaring the living shit out of me.

"You look like you've recovered," I drawled as I pocketed my phone.

He glanced at the burrito and shuddered. "I don't know if I can eat for at least twenty minutes after that," he told me. My eyes widened. That was big news coming from him.

"Maybe ten," he amended.

That was more like it.

"Glad to see you weren't scarred for life."

"Glad you were so concerned for me," he quipped back.

I snorted, shaking my head, and feeling much more relaxed than I had before Asher had shown up at my door, surprising me for the first game of the Stanley Cup.

My phone buzzed in my pocket, but before I could look, Asher decided to ruin my good energy. All it took was him saying one name.

"Tyler Miller."

I growled just hearing it.

"Still not his biggest fan?" Asher asked . . . as he picked up an apple, obviously recovered from his "near-death experience." In far less than ten minutes, I might add.

"That's the understatement of the century, Matthews. Literally the century."

"You didn't even like Clarissa that much," he commented, biting into the apple.

Clarissa had been my girlfriend sophomore year of college, and her cheating on me with Tyler Miller still burned years later. I mean, you would have thought I'd have picked someone with better taste than that.

I scoffed. "I'd been dating her for a year, and the bastard slept with her for half of that."

"You weren't going to marry her."

"I could have! He got her pregnant, and she tried to say the baby was mine!"

"That was bad," Asher said with a full mouth. He swallowed and straightened up from the counter. "You're right, let's kill him."

I raised an eyebrow at how serious he sounded.

But also, I appreciated the support.

Sighing, I shook my head. "Moral of the story, I fucking hate the dude. And the fact that he's in the series fucking sucks."

Asher clapped me on the back. Hard. "Man up, get your head in the game, and fucking win. Think of it as a gift that he saved you from eighteen years of misery." Asher gave me a pointed look as he started singing the second verse of "Gold Digger" . . . terribly.

"Please, don't ever do that again," I said seriously.

He grinned, flashing the pearly white teeth that had been all over the television thanks to him being paid to be the face of a famous toothpaste company.

My alarm rang on my phone, signaling it was time to get to the arena. Unnecessary, since there'd been a countdown blasting in my head all fucking day.

Asher pounded on my back again and then raised his fists in the air, jumping up and down like he was a fighter about to walk out to the ring. "Let's fucking go," he yelled, and then next thing I knew, I was also jumping up and down like a lunatic too.

If there was one person that could hype me up, it was my best friend. And yes, I was well aware of how sappy I was being today. I blamed it on the fact that I was about to play the biggest game of my career.

Feeling much better than I had earlier, I danced my way down the hall to get ready for the game and to kick Tyler Miller's ass.

I walked into the locker room, noting the intense air in the room. Fuck, I didn't usually get nerves. But this? This was the big time.

"Rookie," Lincoln said with a nod, as he sat in front of his locker, wrapping tape around the handle of his hockey stick.

I nodded back, trying to look chill, cool, nonchalant, so to speak.

Lincoln Daniels was just a few years older than me, but he was *the* man.

I'd fucking wanted to be him for years. MVP almost every year, led the league in scoring, and had a million endorsement deals. Who wouldn't want to be him?

Another thing I was never going to admit, obviously.

"Well, you don't look like you're going to faint, that's a start," Ari, the burrito violator, remarked as he eyed me, looking cool as a cucumber leaning against his locker, already fully dressed.

Glancing around the room, I could see that most of the team was already dressed. Fuck, how early had everyone gotten here? We'd been doing practice, press conferences, social media videos, and about a million other promotional things since we'd won the conference finals. No one had told me that getting to the arena four hours early was a thing, too!

"Ah, there it is, the panic is properly settling in," Camden, our other star defenseman on the team, tossed out.

"On a scale of one to ten, how badly are you shitting your pants right now?" Walker Davis asked, sounding way too casual as he strapped on one of his goalie pads.

"Since when are you so concerned with the state of my briefs, Disney?" I asked. "Not that I'm wearing any."

Ari groaned in disgust, but all four of them were still eyeing me as I slowly walked to my locker.

Alright . . . this was suspicious; my eyebrows rose because . . .

"What's the fucking bet?" I growled.

Almost identical blank stares appeared on their faces. My jaw dropped. "I can't believe you bet on me. Which of you were on my side?"

"Who do you think?" scoffed Ari, rolling his eyes so hard I was surprised they didn't get stuck there.

I made the mistake of staring hopefully at Lincoln, and it was a mistake I paid for immediately.

Ari jumped up, his finger waving at me. "I knew it! I knew you were just like him!" His finger moved to Walker, who was *also* staring hopefully at Lincoln.

This was a fucking disaster. So much for my plan of playing it cool.

"When are any of you going to give me the proper respect I deserve? I need simpage, people. And lots of it," Ari snarled.

I shook my head in disgust . . . and amusement as I turned to my locker and started to get ready.

"So, Rookie, I don't think we ever finished our texts this morning . . . how was breakfast?" Ari asked, his voice becoming innocent as he came up beside my locker.

"It was great," I responded mildly. "Best I've ever had."

Ari looked confused for a minute, before a big grin spread across his face. "Someone else ate one first, didn't they?" He snorted and then began laughing so hard that he about fell over.

"I could have died," I said indignantly, all my good intentions of acting cool going completely out the window.

"No one's died because of a little kitty litter and hot sauce, Rookie," Ari said, ducking the water bottle I'd just thrown at his head.

"Yeah, Rookie, stop being so dramatic," drawled Camden.

"That was excellent simpage, Hero. Ten gold stars for you," Ari said approvingly.

Camden preened, even though I knew he had no idea what the stars even meant. There seemed to be a moving target in this group as we worked to get into the Circle of Trust. Sometimes it was points, sometimes it was stars. Sometimes it was—well, it was a lot of things. This reward system was very confusing.

But it also worked *very* well. I was almost at the point where I'd do any-thing to add to my bank of rewards.

Hence, how I'd ended up posing in my briefs for Camden's eighty-something-year-old friend Geraldine one night.

"Someone could have died," I continued . . . as a terrible thought hit me. "Please tell me that was fresh kitty litter," I begged, horrified at the alternative. I mean, Asher was still alive and not throwing up as far as I knew—and he'd eaten almost an entire rotisserie chicken after that—but still.

"What do you think I am? A monster?" Ari said, looking affronted.

"Wait . . . that's what your inane text was, Rookie? Ari desecrated one of Mrs. Bentley's burritos?" Walker suddenly asked in a horrified voice.

I waved at him. "*That* was the proper response. Horror. Dismay. All the things!"

"Something like that could mean Mrs. Bentley cuts off her supply," Lincoln said as he glanced at his phone, a video of Monroe—his wife—playing on the screen.

Ari stared at him, looking like he'd just been brutally betrayed. "You wouldn't."

Lincoln glanced up from his phone, his lips curled in amusement. "I would."

I saddled up next to Lincoln and crossed my arms in front of my chest. "He would," I said sternly.

Ari grinned, shaking his head. "Remind me never to include you in a joke, Rookie. Your presence gives it away immediately."

I growled, but before I could say anything, music began to blare over the speakers.

Fuck, if T-Swift was already playing . . . I needed to get ready.

As I hurried back to my locker to finish getting my uniform on, the locker room erupted with dance moves that would have been embarrassing in most cases.

But we were the Dallas Fucking Knights.

So that was obviously not the case.

DALLAS #9 KNIGHTS

CHAPTER 4

LOGAN

There's a moment when you step out onto the ice, where the world seems to fall into slow motion. I'd never felt that out on the football or baseball fields as a kid, that moment of rightness, where the crisp air seeped into your lungs and you felt like you were at home. It's how I could tell a good game from a bad game, whether I had that one perfect moment or not.

Unfortunately for me, I wasn't finding any sort of perfection right now. Which was really bad timing since out of all the games I'd played in my career, this one was the one where I needed to be my best.

I skated along the boards, trying to center myself, trying to find that moment . . .

And then there was Miller. The fucker. Grinning at me like the absolute asshole that he was.

"What's it like jacking off with those tiny hands, Miller," I called out as the dipstick in question slid to a stop a foot away from me, showering me with a sheet of ice.

"Not a lot of that going on with *her* around," he said cockily—his inference clear, even though any woman who willingly got within five feet of him definitely had something wrong with her.

I rolled my eyes and glanced at the stands as I headed toward a puck . . . only to almost trip over my skates.

Holy fuck.

I watched as a literal goddess walked down the steps toward the glass. Blinking a few times, I wondered if I was having a hallucination.

Long brown hair with gold streaks in it, she was styled like she'd just walked out of a magazine. She wasn't wearing a jersey or anything remotely related to hockey. Instead, she had on this sleek, fitted coat like she was at some ritzy event. Everything about her screamed sophistication.

I couldn't stop staring, I didn't *want* to.

"Now *that* girl knows how to make an entrance," I muttered, forgetting all about Miller as I stared at her as if I had been hypnotized.

"I'm sure you want to become very familiar with her entrances," mused Ari, skating up next to me. I reluctantly glanced at him, because that was actually funny, but he wasn't even paying attention to the goddess. He was staring at Blake, his wife, like usual.

"That was a good one," said Camden right before he smacked a puck at the net.

Ari snarled, his eyes going wide as he stared at Camden in shock. "Why do you sound surprised at that, Hero? If anyone is funny in this group, it's me." He shoved past Lincoln, who was staring at Monroe, and Lincoln growled at him.

See, that was why I aspired to be like Lincoln Daniels. He just had it.

"Golden Boy, tell them how funny I am," demanded Ari as he started stretching.

"It seems like you're doing a good job of that yourself," Lincoln muttered, rubbing at where Ari had hit him.

As amusing as they were, I had to look at her again. It was like she had a beacon inside her that was pulling me in.

"I think I'm in love," I murmured pitifully.

Camden laughed at me, but I wasn't sure why. He couldn't stop staring at his girl in the stands. He shouldn't be laughing at my new obsession.

I'd heard Anastasia call him "Daddy."

"Tell me I'm not seeing things," I said, elbowing him so he had to pay attention. Was there a glow around her? It felt like there was, like she was literally shining out among the sea of people.

He ignored me, of course, grabbing a puck and sending a shot at Disney's head in the goal.

I glanced back at the girl, almost tripping over my skates again.

Miller.

The all-consuming pussy magic around this girl had distracted me for a moment that he still existed.

Miller was standing near the boards, just below where she was now sitting. Like a fucking nightmare unfolding in slow motion, I watched as he leaned an arm against the glass, grinned that smug, shit-eating grin of his, and blew a kiss at her.

The world went silent for a moment and then an unhinged buzz filled my ears. I gripped my stick so tight that I heard a crack. My pulse was hammering, louder than the crowd, louder than the skates cutting across the ice.

"Fuck," I snarled. "Fuck, fuck, fuck."

I had to literally use all of my willpower not to go after him.

Okay then. So she had really bad taste in men.

I'd just have to fix that for her.

I could feel eyes on me, but I wasn't in the mood. I forced myself to skate off, shooting at the net with all my pent-up rage.

"What the fuck, Rookie?" Walker snarled as I pegged him in the face mask. He hit the goalpost, the clang barely registering with me.

Don't look at her. Don't look at her, I chanted over and over.

I needed to focus. I would find her later. I would *keep* her later.

Fuck, this was going to be a long game.

From the second the puck dropped, I was skating with a purpose that had nothing to do with the game plan.

Tyler Fucking Miller. Of all people, why did it have to be *him* with her? I kept seeing it—the image of him leaning toward the glass, his lips forming a kiss. It dug into my mind like a knife, twisting with every shift, every glance in his direction. Fuck. If his blowing her a kiss affected me this much . . . what was I going to do when he *actually* kissed her?

And what the fuck was wrong with me? Why was I having such a violent reaction? I didn't even know the woman.

It must have been because she was saddled with the biggest douchebag on the planet. That's what this was. I was just being a good citizen, concerned because she had such terrible taste.

I was a guy. When a girl looks like that, you're going to get hard.

The fact that I'd gotten an erection in front of an arena full of spectators meant nothing. Or at least it only meant that my testosterone levels were doing well.

I refused to think about the fact that all these thoughts and excuses felt like the biggest lies I'd ever told.

The first time Miller had the puck, I didn't think. I just acted. I hit him into the boards, harder than I should've. The crowd roared, and for a second, I felt immensely better . . . until he skated by the girl, placing his hand on the glass in front of her while she gave him an enthralled look.

I wanted to throw up.

I was faintly aware of the ref's whistle, warning me, but I couldn't find it in myself to care.

"What's your problem, York?" Miller said with a grin after he turned his back to the glass.

I snapped, slamming into him again, this time even harder, driving him against the boards with enough force to make the glass rattle. His smug face smashed up against the hard surface.

"What the fuck was that for?" he spat, shoving me as he pried himself off the glass and turned toward me.

I grinned, and before I could answer, his gloves and helmet were off. His fist came flying, and I barely ducked in time. I straightened and threw a hard punch that connected with his jaw, sending him stumbling back. We were tangled up within seconds, fists flying, our bodies crashing back against the boards as the refs scrambled to break us up.

"Fuck you, York," Miller spat, his teeth bloody as he tried to swing again. I grabbed his jersey and yanked him down, throwing another punch to his ribs.

Adrenaline was roaring in my ears as the refs finally pulled us apart, dragging me toward the penalty box as I tried to shake them off. I could still hear Miller chirping from the ice.

I slammed down on the bench, breathing hard, my fists clenched beside me. My knuckles were throbbing, but it was the good kind of pain.

Lincoln skated by and banged on the glass. "Get your fucking head on straight," he roared, his eyes locked on me with a fury I hadn't seen directed at me before. "We're in the fucking Stanley Cup Finals, Rookie, and you're playing like a fucking *idiot*. What the hell is wrong with you?"

He shook his head and raced toward the puck as I gritted my teeth and hissed in frustration. Next door, Miller wiggled his fingers at me from his own penalty box.

Fucking asshole.

I shouldn't have done it. I tried not to. But I couldn't help but look over at her. She was sitting there serenely, with no idea that I was out here losing my mind over her.

It felt weird, that I could be feeling so crazy . . . and she didn't even know I existed.

She was going to know that I existed soon enough, though . . . if I kept telling myself that, maybe it would come true.

Maybe.

Fuck. Stop thinking like that.

I groaned when the puck slipped past Disney, and then the buzzer was going off, signaling the end of the first period.   ＇

We were down by one. Mostly because of me.

I raced out of the penalty box toward where the team was gathered.

"I'm coming for you, York!" Miller bellowed over the din of the crowd, and all my good intentions went out the window. I was going to kill that prick.

"Fucking hell," I snarled, resisting the urge to lunge at him right then.

"Hey, Rookie, is there a reason you keep checking number forty-five? And was that fight really necessary?" Ari spat as we walked back to the locker room. "I'd rather not be one man down the entire fucking game."

I gritted my teeth, feeling the insane urge to lunge at him at the moment too. "That was fucking Tyler Miller. The biggest motherfucking asshole you will ever meet. We played together in college." I began pacing the locker room, stomping as I went. I was sure I looked like a lunatic, but I couldn't get myself to stop.   ·

"As enthralling as this story is—get your fucking head on straight, Rookie," Walker snarled as Coach Porter threw open the door and stalked into the room.

"This is the fucking Stanley Cup Finals, gentlemen," he sneered. "How about you start fucking playing like it!" His cheeks were red with anger, and I was pretty sure there was a new tic in his right eye.

Walker and Ari chewed me out for the rest of the break and all the way onto the ice for the next period.

I wish I could say that their "pep talk" worked, but it was like that girl had rewired my brain. I'd gone from a mostly sane, mostly disciplined player, to a completely unhinged one.

It was really bad timing, honestly.

Miller came at me as soon as the buzzer started the period. I had just finished a pass to Camden when I felt the hard crack of his shoulder slamming into mine, driving me into the boards. The impact rattled through my body, the breath knocked clean out of my lungs. I blinked and shook my head, trying to pull myself together. He grinned at me, all teeth, and gave me a fucking thumbs-up as he began to skate away.

Once again . . . I had lost my mind. I dropped my shoulder and rammed into him with everything I had, sending him crashing into the glass so hard I heard one of the fans scream. There was a satisfying crunch as his body folded in on itself, and then he sank to the ice. I went for him again, but before I could get in another shot, Lancaster was on me, grabbing the back of my jersey and yanking me off him.

"Fucking chill," Ari hissed, his grip tight as he shoved me back toward the bench before the refs could get involved. "If you end up in the penalty box again . . ."

"Would you chill if it was fucking Soto?" I snapped, seeing the light come on in Ari's eyes. Soto was a player with the L.A. Cobras who was also Ari's nemesis. I wasn't sure of all the details, but I knew Soto was now sporting full-on dentures after a fight with Ari . . . and that was from when they were playing on the same team.

"Touché," Ari muttered, letting me go and pushing me toward the bench.

I couldn't sit down; instead, I stood, bouncing anxiously as I wiped the sweat from my forehead. My gaze ping-ponged from the play on the ice to Miller to *her* and then repeated the cycle.

Right before I got back on the ice, I glanced at her one more time, but this time . . . she was watching me.

And just like that, my mood shifted. A grin pulled at the corners of my mouth, and I couldn't help myself. I gave her a little wave, playful-ish, like I hadn't nearly broken her boyfriend against the boards a few seconds ago.

For a brief second she smiled. Just a hint of it crossed her pretty lips, but it was enough to make my dick hard in what was once again the most inopportune moment possible.

Well, actually, a woody at Geraldine's would have been worse. She would have taken it as a sign.

I shuddered at the thought.

As I reluctantly moved my attention from my dream girl back to the game, I saw that Miller was watching me, an angry snarl on his face because he'd obviously seen the entire interaction.

Good. He needed to get used to disappointment and loss real quick.

Once I was back on the ice, Miller snarled, shoulder-checking me as he skated by. Hard enough to make a point, but not enough to get called for it. He was even more pissed now.

Good.

For the rest of the game, the gloves were off—figuratively at least. I didn't care what the score was, didn't care about anything but getting Miller every chance I got. Every shift, every time he had the puck . . . I was there. Slamming him into the boards.

"How's Clarissa these days, York?" he said at one point, after he spit what I believe was his tooth out onto the ice.

I passed the puck to Lincoln and then went after Miller again, shoulder-checking him so he went sprawling.

The ref's whistle blew.

"Fuck!" I growled as the ref signaled me to the penalty box . . . for the third time this game.

"Shame, shame, shame," Tampa Bay's fans screamed as I made my way to the bench.

I plopped down dejectedly, throwing off my helmet and running my hands through my sweaty hair, trying to catch my breath. I could feel the eyes on me—the coaches, the fans . . . her.

Tampa Bay scored again, and I raced back on the ice. But we were done. They got back the puck almost immediately, and we spent the rest of the period just making sure they didn't score again.

The final buzzer echoed through the arena like a death knell, and my senses came back enough to feel the burning disappointment—and shame—that came with the loss. Tampa had taken Game One on our home ice. All the anticipation for tonight . . .

My chest heaved as I stared at the scoreboard, blinking away the sting of sweat dripping into my eyes.

The noise around me was deafening, but it felt distant, muffled under layers of frustration and rage.

They were letting what looked like Tampa family members onto the ice like this was fucking Game Seven, flooding the surface with their obnoxious cheers. Security? Nowhere to be found.

"Unbelievable," Camden muttered next to me, his face mirroring my disappointment and disgust as we made our way back across the ice to go to the locker room.

I stopped in my tracks when I saw the girl come out, a small, almost amused smirk on her lips as she tried not to slip in high heels that had no business being on the ice.

They made her ass look amazing, though. My head dipped to the side as I watched her walk.

If the guys thought that I'd lost it already, it was no match for how I lost it right then.

I skated straight toward her, not thinking, not caring. The crowd didn't matter. The loss didn't matter. I had one thing on my mind.

She looked up, her eyes wide as I reached her, and before she could say a word, I grabbed her by the waist and pulled her into me.

"Wh—at," she gasped.

Without a second thought, I dipped her back dramatically, my hand firm on her lower back as I kissed her, right there in the middle of the ice, in front of everyone. It wasn't just a kiss. It was a statement. A middle finger to Miller. A claim.

I'd thought that the moment on the ice when everything faded was as close to perfect as life could get.

But I'd been wrong.

This was what perfection felt like, her warm body in my hands, her lips against mine.

The crowd roared, some cheering, some gasping, but I didn't hear any of it. All I could focus on was her—how she froze for a second, then melted into the kiss, her hands grabbing at my jersey for balance. For that brief moment, it felt like we were all alone in the most perfect moment known to humankind.

Until I heard Miller's fucking voice.

"What the fuck?"

I barely had time to react before I felt his hands shove me hard, knocking me off-balance. I let go of her, staggering back, and I saw her slip on the ice, her arms flailing as she went down. Miller didn't even notice, his eyes locked on me, looking like he wanted to kill me. But I noticed.

Something inside me flared white-hot.

I reached out to help her up, but before I could do anything he was lunging toward me.

"You son of a—"

My fists flew before my brain even caught up. The first punch landed hard, right on his jaw, sending him stumbling back. But he came at me fast, his shoulder driving into my chest as we both crashed to the ice, fists flying. I got in another hit, square in his ribs, before he managed to swing wildly, his knuckles clipping my lip.

The crowd exploded. The sound was deafening—cheers, screams, gasps— but it didn't matter. I could barely hear any of it over the rush of adrenaline. Miller's fists were everywhere, but I was faster, stronger, and the next punch I threw hit him square in the nose, blood splattering across the ice.

"Logan!" Walker's voice broke through the chaos, but I couldn't stop.

Teammates from both sides rushed in, grabbing us, pulling us apart, but I was still fighting, still throwing punches even as Lincoln grabbed me by the jersey and dragged me backward.

"You're fucking dead, York!" Miller screamed, his face splattered with blood as he was held back by two of his teammates. His voice was shrill, desperate, but it only made me grin.

"Bring it, asshole!" I shouted back, wiping the blood from my lip with the back of my glove. Out of the corner of my eye, I saw my girl walking off the ice in the other direction.

Lincoln shoved me toward our bench, his face red with frustration. "Get your head out of your ass, Logan! You're not getting suspended over that idiot!"

I barely heard him. My eyes were locked on Miller, who was still trying to get at me despite all the people trying to hold him back.

I flipped him off with both hands, a maniacal grin splitting my face. "I'll see you in Game Two, motherfucker!"

Lincoln pushed me toward the tunnel, shaking his head. "You've lost your fucking mind."

I grinned through the blood, my pulse still racing. I *had* lost my mind. And I had a feeling this was only the beginning.

Bring it on.

CHAPTER 5

SLOANE

Walking into the arena felt like stepping into another universe. The crowd was a sea of jerseys, blues, whites, and greens with numbers on the backs of players I'd never heard of—their names echoing through the halls as fans shouted and laughed. There were huge smiles on everyone's faces, a lot of them already halfway to drunk by the looks of it. I watched a group of couples, all of them shouting over each other, so eager to talk. They suddenly held their beers up and all yelled at once.

Definitely a different universe. I couldn't have felt more out of place if I tried.

I fidgeted with my coat, suddenly very aware that I was one of the only people not wearing a jersey. I'd thought about buying one at the shop outside, maybe blending in a little, but that idea died quickly. If that had been something that Tyler wanted, he would have communicated it to Everett. It wasn't like he had forgotten the specifics of my outfit for *after* the game tonight: four—not three—inch strappy black heels and black lingerie that "showed a lot of boob." I figured if he could specify that, he would have specified if he'd wanted a certain outfit at the game besides "for me to look hot." Tyler hadn't hired me for my deep understanding of slap shots and power plays. He didn't expect a thrilling conversation about his job—or anything else. He just wanted me to play the part of the perfect girlfriend for the cameras during the series and entertain him after.

It was unfortunate that the idea of what came after made my stomach twist.

I mulled over our interaction before the game and how I was already annoyed by Tyler.

He tugged me closer, his grip tightening. "You ready to make me look good?"

I swallowed hard and nodded. "Always."

"That's my girl," Tyler said, his voice low and possessive, like he was proud of himself for owning me for now.

I bit the inside of my cheek, forcing another smile. I could play the part. I could pretend. But inside, I was already counting the minutes until it was over.

Narrowly missing being taken out by a woman's long ponytail as she whipped around, I shook off my thoughts and walked up the tunnel that led to my seat.

I hesitated at the top, watching the players warming up on the ice. Some of the Dallas players were standing by the glass, talking to a group of gorgeous women in the front-row seats. I watched as the Dallas goalie held up his glove, and a woman who looked strangely familiar held up her hand on the other side to match him.

It was corny, but adorable, and there was a strange ache in my gut as I watched the group.

Having a partner in life, what did that feel like?

I couldn't even comprehend it.

Taking a deep breath, I tried to steady the nerves rattling in my chest. This was just another job. Another game.

And I had chosen this.

That's what I had to tell myself when the nights became long, and I wanted to throw up just from their touch, and it didn't feel like I could continue.

I had chosen this.

And I deserved everything that came with it.

All I had to do was get through the series, act the part, and keep my head down.

I spotted Tyler leaning against the glass near where I would be sitting, his arms crossed, his gaze sweeping over the arena like he owned the place. Maybe that was an epidemic among NHL players, being full of themselves. As far as I knew he wasn't a huge star—that would have made Everett balk at the job for sure—so Tyler was just one of those guys full of themselves for no apparent reason except he had been born. He noticed me coming down the stairs and flashed me a smirk as I approached. "You look hot," he mouthed.

I forced a smile in return, trying to channel my role. I'd obviously never been a devoted girlfriend, or a girlfriend at all, but swooning seemed to be a requirement for the job title, right?

I could pretend to swoon.

He lifted his chin at me and winked before pushing off the glass and skating away.

I swallowed the bile creeping up my throat and pasted on a smile, even though no one around me seemed to have noticed the interaction.

Absent-mindedly scanning the ice, I blinked when I saw one of the Dallas players . . . staring.

Thinking he must be looking at someone else, I glanced behind me, but there was no one. When I turned around, he was still looking.

Why was he staring at me?

And then . . . he took off his helmet. I wasn't prepared for the jolt of lust that hit me the moment his face came into view. The rough edge of his jawline, sharp enough to cut through ice. The mess of blond hair, damp with sweat, falling haphazardly around his forehead. His eyes—bright, intense, dark green, like the forest at dusk, dangerous and consuming. Even from my seat, I could feel the intensity behind them, like he saw through everything and everyone. Like he could see me.

I couldn't look away.

For a split second, everything around him seemed to blur, the noise of the arena fading into the background as I took him in. His expression was serious, focused, but there was something about the way his lips tugged at the corner in a small smirk that made him impossibly hotter to me. He wasn't just good-looking—he was gorgeous, the kind of face that made everyone else pale in comparison.

He wiped a tattooed hand across his forehead, shaking out his hair, and I realized now *I* was the one staring. Not just staring—gawking. My pulse quickened, a flutter of nerves and something else—something I didn't want to acknowledge—rising in my chest.

I yanked my gaze away, finding Tyler on the ice skating toward me. He leaned against the glass and smirked. Pinning my practiced, plastic smile to my lips, I pretended I was madly in love as he blew me a kiss.

So much for trying to stay under the radar.

Heat rushed to my cheeks—not the good kind, but the kind that made you want to crawl under your seat and disappear.

For some reason I found myself glancing at the Dallas player again.

He was a few strides away, near the edge of the ice, his stick gripped tight in his hands. Even with the helmet on, I could see the fury radiating off him. His entire body was coiled, his jaw clenched so hard I thought he might snap his mouthguard in half. Dark green eyes burned under the shadow of his visor, locked directly on Tyler with a ferocity that made the air feel ten degrees hotter.

Well, that was interesting. He looked like he wanted to kill him.

I glanced between the two of them, trying to piece it together. I was sure I would hear about it from Tyler later.

I hadn't been sure of what to expect for my first hockey game.

But it certainly hadn't been this.

Hockey, it turned out, wasn't boring at all.

I'd also found out the name of the Dallas player I'd been drooling over— Logan York—and that the glare I'd seen him give Tyler . . . was because they hated each other.

"Fight! Fight! Fight!" the crowd chanted as Tyler and Logan dropped their gloves and went after each other for what felt like the millionth time of the game. Fists were flying, bodies slamming into the boards, helmets scattering like loose change on the ice. I couldn't stop staring, a grin sliding onto my lips as Logan landed a vicious punch that sent Tyler reeling. Blood sprayed from Tyler's mouth, dotting the ice like red confetti. The crowd went wild. That was what I liked to see.

"Wow," I muttered as Logan shoved Tyler into the boards once more with enough force to make the plexiglass rattle. Tyler snarled something at him—something I couldn't hear, but could guess, judging by the murderous look on Logan's face. The ref tried to separate them, but Logan landed one last jab before being dragged away, his eyes still locked on Tyler like he wanted to murder him in front of the entire arena.

I bit back a laugh. Tyler, sputtering and furious, skated toward the penalty box, blood dripping onto the ice. Logan followed him moments later, slamming himself onto his bench with a grin that looked downright feral.

"They're both insane," I whispered, half to myself, as the game resumed.

It didn't take long for them to get into it again. Tyler tripped Logan with his stick, and Logan retaliated by body-checking him so hard it sent him sprawling onto the ice. The refs blew their whistles, but the crowd ate it up, roaring with approval as the two of them shouted at each other, their voices drowned out by the chaos.

Logan ended up in the penalty box again, shaking his head like he couldn't believe he was stuck there while Tyler smirked at him from across the ice. The animosity between them was palpable, crackling through the air like static electricity.

By the time the game ended, Tampa had won, and I was genuinely surprised I cared about the outcome. Not because I wanted Tyler to win—I didn't—but because I had wanted Logan to. The thought caught me off guard, and I quickly shook it off as the crowd erupted into a mix of cheers and boos. I stood, brushing imaginary lint off my sleek coat, ready to leave. But then I noticed a Tampa Bay employee gesturing wildly at the fans in our section, motioning toward an open gate that led onto the ice.

What?

I froze, confused, until I realized he wanted us to go out there. People started filing down the stairs, chatting excitedly as they made their way down to the ice.

I hesitated.

"Miss, are you coming?" the employee asked, snapping me out of my thoughts.

I nodded, forcing a polite smile. "Of course," I said, not feeling like I really had a choice.

My heels wobbled precariously as I stepped onto the ice, the cold biting through the thin soles of my shoes. The surface was slick, impossibly smooth, and I immediately regretted the decision I'd made to wear these death traps. I felt like a newborn foal, my legs trembling as I worked on not falling flat on my face.

Other fans seemed to be doing just fine, posing for pictures and taking selfies. Meanwhile, I clutched at the boards for dear life, cursing Tyler and the universe for putting me in this ridiculous situation.

"Just walk normally," I muttered to myself, trying to channel every ounce of grace I didn't have.

I was almost to the crowd of players and fans . . . when he was there.

Logan York.

He was standing in front of me, blocking my path. His skates dug into the ice with a casualness that felt deliberate, but it wasn't his stance that stopped me. It was the look on his face.

Yearning. That was the only word that came to mind. Like I was something he'd been searching for and finally found.

It caught me off guard, that look. It made me falter, one foot sliding slightly on the ice, and I reached out instinctively for balance. My eyes locked on his, wide and unblinking.

"What—" I started, but the word barely made it out before he moved.

One second, he was standing there, staring at me like I was the answer to every question he'd never asked. The next, his hands were on my waist, strong and sure, pulling me forward. I stumbled, my heels slipping again, but his grip steadied me. And then his lips were on mine.

It wasn't gentle. It wasn't hesitant. It was a claim, bold and unapologetic, like he'd been waiting his whole life for this moment and wasn't about to waste it. His hands tightened slightly, anchoring me against him, and for a heartbeat, I forgot to be shocked. I forgot everything.

I should've pushed him away. I should've said something, anything. But my brain short-circuited, leaving nothing but the feeling of his lips moving against mine, the faint taste of adrenaline and mint on his breath. The noise of the crowd swelled around us, cheers and gasps blending into a deafening roar, but I couldn't process any of it.

What the hell was he doing? What the hell was *I* doing?

Somewhere in the chaos, I heard someone yell, "What the fuck?" But it barely registered until I felt Logan pulled away from me abruptly, his hands dropping from my waist. My lips tingled, still warm from the contact, and my mind struggled to catch up as I stumbled back, only to remember my heels had no grip. My arms flailed for balance, but the inevitable happened—I went down, landing hard on my ass with an unceremonious thud.

Logan's eyes darted to me immediately, a flicker of anger . . . and guilt crossing his face. He reached for me, but a second later, Tyler was there.

And then all hell broke loose.

I pushed up from the ice, slipping and sliding my way back to the opening in the sides. I was desperate to get away before a camera got a clear shot of me amid the melee I was leaving behind.

But as I frantically tried to get away, I considered it a very bad sign . . .

I wanted to go back.

Just so I could see Logan York again.

CHAPTER 6
SLOANE

Being in the hotel room with Tyler felt all wrong. He was currently pacing the length of the room like a caged animal, his face twisted into an ugly scowl, the veins on his neck bulging with every angry word that burst from his lips. His dark hair, usually perfectly gelled when he wasn't playing, was starting to fall out of place, strands sticking to his slightly sweaty forehead. His tie was loosened, and his suit jacket hung open, the crisp white shirt underneath wrinkled from all the movement.

Tyler's jaw was clenched so tight I could see the muscles ticcing under his skin, and his eyes were wild with frustration. The tension rolled off him in waves, and I jumped when he picked up one of the hotel's fancy wooden brocade armchairs and broke it on the floor, pieces of wood flying everywhere.

"Motherfucker!"

He'd been ranting for thirty minutes now, and I watched as he picked up a tumbler of whiskey, sloshing the drink in his glass as he raged. The amber liquid dripped out onto the carpet.

Glancing down at my nails, I idly picked at a fraying cuticle that my manicurist had missed while watching Tyler out of the corner of my eye . . . just in case he decided to take some of that anger out on me.

It had happened before with other clients.

I was feeling fairly safe, though; he hadn't even looked at me since we walked in the door.

"Can you believe that asshole?" Tyler spat, his face twisted in frustration. "Logan Fucking York. That last hit could have ended my career."

Logan. Logan York. I hadn't known his name before tonight.

But I sure knew it now.

I'd overheard people talking about him at the game—how he'd had a record-breaking rookie year, how they were shocked about him gunning for Tyler.

Then after the game, despite the Tampa win, all anyone could talk about was the *kiss*.

The kiss.

I could still *feel* his phantom touch, how his strong hands had gripped my waist, the way his lips pressed against mine, firm but almost . . . sweet in the middle of all that chaos.

It had thrown me completely off-balance. Everything else—the noise, the crowd, the tension of the game—had faded away.

But the kiss wasn't even the crazy part. The crazy part was that I'd kissed him back. Instinctively, without even thinking, I had let myself fall into that moment. It was reckless. Stupid.

Dangerous.

I couldn't stop thinking about it.

Tyler slammed his glass down on the dresser, making me flinch. "York thinks he's hot shit," he muttered, pacing again. "But I'll show him. Next game, I'm going to take his fucking head off."

I nodded, not really listening. I was still thinking about that kiss and how I'd felt turned on for the first time since . . . well, ever.

He ranted for a few more minutes, but then he threw his hands up, heading toward the door. "I'm getting drunk. Screw it. I'm not wasting my energy on that asshole tonight."

I didn't point out that he'd already wasted a whole bunch of energy on "that asshole." Instead, I just watched, relieved as he opened the door. I was suddenly feeling pretty lucky about my odds that I wasn't going to have to fuck him tonight. I'd learned in our past . . . interactions . . . that he had a limp dick when he decided to drink.

Thank fuck.

"Do whatever you want," he mumbled over his shoulder as he stormed out. "I don't care."

I didn't need to be told twice. As soon as the door had slammed behind him, I slipped off the bed and headed for the bathroom, closing the door softly behind me and clicking the lock. Leaning against the door, I let out a breath I didn't realize I'd been holding as I glanced around the bathroom.

Tyler had sprung for a suite, and the hotel bathroom was luxurious, with a huge tub that looked like something out of a spa.

If Tyler was going to be drunk and ranting all night, I was going to take a bath.

I started filling the tub, the sound of water echoing softly in the marble room. Slowly peeling off my clothes, I took a few deep breaths, trying to let out some of the tension from the eventful evening. I sank into the warm water, letting it envelop me all the way for a second.

But that was a mistake. Because as soon as I closed my eyes . . . I saw *his* face.

Logan York.

The guy was hot. More than hot. He was the most beautiful man I'd ever seen—and I'd stopped thinking of men as anything but pigs a long time ago.

He was beautiful in a way that felt dangerous, like he could ruin you with a single glance, and you'd thank him for it.

Huffing in annoyance at my thoughts, I splashed some water in my face, trying to distract myself.

It didn't work.

Kissing wasn't something I did if I could help it. It was too personal. Most of the time I could think of sex as a transaction, but a kiss meant something more.

I'd had a crush at the fancy high school Everett had sent me to when I'd first arrived in Dallas. Jared was tall and cute and a star soccer player. When he'd kissed me at seventeen, I still remembered the butterflies I'd had, even though he'd used far too much tongue.

Maybe that was what had started it. The unfortunate romantic attachment I had to the meaning of a kiss.

Logan's kiss had been what I'd used to dream about. It made me feel something. It had shaken me, pulled me out of the numbness I was so used to.

And then when I'd fallen to the ground after Tyler had pushed him and I'd slipped . . . it had almost seemed like he was defending me.

What had that been about?

I leaned back in the tub, staring up at the ceiling. The steam curled around me, softening the edges of the room.

And I couldn't stop myself.

My hand slipped down my stomach, in between my legs, until I was softly stroking my clit. Thinking about him.

His thick, hard length slowly pushed inside. His gaze was half-lidded as he stared down at me, his tongue sexily licking his bottom lip as he slid in, inch by inch.

"That's my good girl," he rasped, *his thumb coming between us to massage my clit. "I have to be inside you, baby."*

My hips tilted, and my body softened around him, allowing him to push in those last few inches. He captured my gasp with his lips, our tongues tangling together as he stayed still for a moment, letting my body adjust around his huge dick.

"You're going to fucking kill me," he groaned as he slid a few inches out before slamming back in.

"Yes," I cried as he moved, fucking in and out of me like he was desperate. Like he couldn't stop himself if he tried.

"That's it, sweetheart. Choke my dick. Give me what I want."

I whimpered into his mouth, loving the taste of him just as much as I loved the punishing pace of his cock.

"Come for me, Sloane. Be my good girl."

My body obeyed immediately, the combination of his praise and his dick and his tongue too much to withstand.

"Logan," I cried as pleasure surged through my insides.

Holy fuck.

I came back to my bath, my pussy clenching tightly around my fingers, the orgasm coursing through me. Crying out, I let my head fall back as I free-fell into euphoric bliss that was so good I couldn't tell you my name if I was asked.

Wave after wave of pleasure slid up my spine until I was gasping for breath, a low moan filling the room as I came back down to Earth.

My eyes flew open, and I blinked in amazement at the wall as I withdrew my fingers out of my still-pulsing core.

I couldn't believe that had happened. I'd never gotten off with a partner, and I rarely was able to get off by myself—I was never in the mood.

But that . . . two minutes of daydreaming about Logan York, and I was coming like I never had before.

And I was still turned on. I could slip my hands back between my legs and be ready in just a second.

Squeezing my eyes closed, I suddenly felt the urge to cry. I couldn't afford to lust after someone. Because lust could lead to more.

I opened my eyes, but I could still see him in my mind, like he was right there, and how he'd looked at me right before our lips had met out on the ice . . . like he'd been waiting for that moment his whole life.

Sinking under the water, I tried to drown out my thoughts. I wasn't allowed to want anything. That wasn't part of the deal I'd made that night.

But I couldn't stop thinking about him.

And how for the first time since my eighteenth birthday . . . I felt alive.

CHAPTER 7

LOGAN

I hadn't slept for more than an hour last night. I'd been so amped up on adrenaline, pure lust, and want that the best I could do was stare at the ceiling, trying to plot my next move.

Unfortunately, all I could come up with was Googling *Tyler Miller's girlfriend* and seeing if anything came up.

It didn't.

No one cared about Tyler Miller. Satisfying, but not helpful for my current predicament.

My phone buzzed on the desk next to me, and I sighed as I picked it up, ready for what I knew was coming from the guys.

> **Ari:** So, Rookie. You still auditioning for an episode of "Days of Our Lives"?

> **Walker:** I was thinking more Broadway? The dramatic kiss? The brawl?

> **Lincoln:** . . .

> **Camden:** "As the Ice Melts" starring Logan York.

> **Ari:** That was really bad, Hero. I'm disappointed in you.

Me: It could have been worse.

Ari: You kissed someone's girlfriend in front of a whole arena and got into like ten fights. How could it have been worse? There's probably an indentation of your ass in the penalty box.

Walker: I did like the dip. Personally, I would have added a twirl. But it gave good energy.

Ari: You would say that, Disney, you simp.

Me: I was making a point, okay?

Camden: Oh, we got the point. The point was: "I'm a lunatic." Loud and clear.

Ari: Pot meet kettle, Hero. My big toe is never going to recover from your antics for Anastasia.

Camden: . . .

Me: Can we admit that the last bit was awesome?

Lincoln: . . .

Ari: Are we talking about the dramatic double bird flip? Because was it really necessary? Although I'm grateful you didn't moon him for the grand finale.

Camden: And let's not forget the Joker grin at the end. I had a nightmare about that last night.

I preened at that revelation.

Me: Really?

Ari: I just scoffed out loud. Blake just gave me the look. The idea that you could be the stuff of nightmares is hilarious.

I frowned.

Me: I can be scary! And I definitely got under his skin. Did you see his face? I was in his head.

Lincoln: You are also inches away from being out of the lineup for Game 2.

Well, yes, that was unfortunate.

Ari: Is this a "just the tip" joke?

Ari: Honestly, I don't know what's worse— your unhinged behavior or the fact that you didn't even get the girl.

Me: It's early, my dude. The good ones always take more than one try.

Camden: Did you just call him "my dude"?

Walker: Disappointed in you, Rookie. Very un-circle-of-trust-like behavior.

Me: . . .

They were almost making me feel bad. *Almost* being the operative word.
While I didn't want to let down the team, the feel of her lips . . .
I'd gotten off three times today just remembering them.
Better not tell them that, though.

Me: No more grand gestures. Noted.

Camden: I think, and correct me if I'm wrong, gentlemen, that we're saying get a better grand gesture. One that doesn't leave us a man down for a majority of the game.

Ari: Or Geraldine's dogs. I would like those wild beasts kept out of all future grand gestures.

Lincoln: It wasn't that bad.

I raised an eyebrow.

Ari: I almost died, Golden Boy! I could have frozen to death.

Camden: Would that have been before or after you lost your big toe?

Ari: I feel like you're mocking me right now. And I don't appreciate that since you owe me for the rest of your life.

Me: Which is significantly less than the rest of us.

I gave myself a mental high five. I always liked when I could get a good grandpa joke in on Camden.

Walker: That was a good one, Rookie.

Ari: You still aren't forgiven.

I scoffed.

Me: Can I remind you all of the sacrifice I made that night! I stood there posing in my briefs, in her living room, for hours.

Camden had come up with a plan to get his now-wife, Anastasia, to move in with him. Long story short, I had been left behind to entertain his eighty-something-year-old neighbor, Geraldine, in exchange for the use of her dogs. I still didn't know all the details of what had happened that night—and why they'd needed the dogs—but I did know they'd gotten the better deal. Geraldine was . . . well, she was something.

> Camden: . . .

> Ari: . . .

> Walker: Why did I miss that night again?

> Ari: And I still want to know what you were posing for.

Well, I wasn't going to tell him that.

> Lincoln: Regardless, don't fuck up tonight. Monroe likes me better when I'm holding a Stanley Cup.

I snorted at that. I was pretty sure Monroe's obsession with him had nothing to do with Stanley Cups.

> Me: Got it. Don't show up with roses and a boom box.

> Ari: I feel like we've taught you nothing.

Setting down the phone, I shook my head. I was pretty sure I could do almost *anything*, and it would still be better than the tidbits I knew about what they'd done to get their girls.

Drumming my fingers, I came up with my next plan.

Security tapes.

There were all kinds of facial recognition software, right? I could get some tape of the game from the security guys—who loved me, by the way, since I always brought them treats. After I'd almost gotten mauled by a group of crazy girls who were nuttier than a bowl of Cheerios, I had made sure that I was *always* in the good graces of the security team. I shuddered to think of the state of my balls if they hadn't pulled that one chick off me.

Picking up my phone again, I called Ernie, who was one of the managers of the security team.

"Ernie, my man, how are you?" I asked as soon as he picked up.

"What do you need, Logan?" he drawled.

Right to the point, I liked it. It was like he could sense the urgent chaos whirling around inside me that demanded I find out who that girl was. Now.

"I need some security tape from last night."

"Of your five billion fights?"

I snorted. That was a little bit of an exaggeration.

"As great for posterity as that would be, I actually need it of a certain portion of the crowd."

He paused for way too long, and I started to get antsy. "We have privacy laws, I could get in trouble," he finally muttered.

"Need I remind you I brought some of Mrs. Bentley's burritos to you last week out of my limited stock?" I answered sternly. Sternly because I would have much rather eaten them myself if I knew he was going to give me trouble.

There was another long pause. This guy had to be the king of them.

"Two batches next week?"

I thought hard about it. I'd have to convince Lincoln of that since Mrs. Bentley was technically *his* housekeeper and not my personal chef . . . but that was probably doable.

"Deal."

There was no pause this time.

"Alright, where do you need video of?"

Twenty minutes later I was staring at her image on the screen, zooming in so I could try and get the full experience. Everything on the ice had happened so fast, I hadn't gotten time to savor her.

Was she doing alright after her fall?

Finally admitting to myself that staring at her on a screen wasn't going to get me any closer to my goal, I tried ticketing next. They weren't any help because Tyler Miller had purchased those seats, and he hadn't assigned names to them.

I was actually going to have to use facial recognition software after all. That was going to be a stretch of my capabilities.

I picked up my phone and texted the group.

Me: I need some software.

Ari: I find it unreal that you're asking for favors right now.

I sent a picture of Geraldine's dog Fluffy.

Me: Need I remind all of you that the Circle is in debt to me. Perhaps forever.

Lincoln: So an old broad took some pictures of you, when are you going to get over this?

Ari: Don't call my bestie an "old broad." Have some respect.

Ari: But also . . . Fifi's balls literally hit my face. I almost got them in my mouth.

Lincoln: . . .

Camden: This is the first time I'm hearing this part of the story . . . and the dog's name is Fluffy.

Ari: The rest of the story was bad enough. It's hard for me to talk about that part.

Walker: Once again, I'll state for the record that I'm going to forever mourn the fact I wasn't there that night.

Me: Lamaze class does come with a price.

Ari: Why did we move on from my trauma so fast?

I huffed out a laugh.

Me: Can we focus? I need facial recognition software.

Walker: Why do all of our conversations in this group make me worry that the FBI is going to burst through my door at any moment and take my phone and computer?

Ari: Don't say FBI! That triggers something in the algorithm. That's when they start stalking you.

Walker: You literally just said FBI.

Ari: You did it again!

Me: Focus! We have to be at the arena in like three hours.

Lincoln: Surprised you remembered that, Rookie.

Me: . . .

Lincoln: I'll send a program over.

I whooped, because if anyone was going to have that kind of program, it was going to be him. Besides being a star hockey player, he'd inherited an insane amount of wealth thanks to his father's hedge fund and some wise investments with his trust. He also seemed to "always have a guy." Also why I aspired to be like him. He was very useful . . . and terrifying.

Ari: Anyone else think Golden Boy epitomizes "Spooky Sexy."

Lincoln: . . .

My email showed a message from him, and I grinned when I clicked on the program he'd attached and it immediately started loading.

Lincoln Daniels was a fucking king.

——————

After some trial and error, because I sucked at technology . . . it came up.

Sloane Calloway.

A pretty name for the fucking most gorgeous girl on the planet.

But that was it.

Unlike with the other faces around her, the software program didn't have any extra details on Sloane. No address, no occupation . . . nothing I could use to find out more about her. I could find out all I wanted about the woman who'd been sitting two seats down from her—seventy-five-year-old Dorothy, who'd previously worked as a bank teller if you were wondering—but nothing on Sloane.

Groaning in disappointment, I stared at her face on the screen, resisting the urge to grab my dick because I was so hard I was a little worried it was going to explode.

I would just have to move to the next stage of the plan . . . using Lincoln's PI. Surely he'd be able to find out some information on her.

If not, I'd just have to ask her. Something that, ironically, was not the easiest part of the plan.

CHAPTER 8

LOGAN

I was sitting in the locker room, staring at my phone. It was almost time to go out on the ice, but I'd texted Lincoln's PI an hour ago, and I was feeling fucking impatient. My phone buzzed, but the text I'd just received wasn't from who I wanted.

> Asher: Why do hockey players have such bad fashion?

I grinned, thinking of what I'd worn today for my arena entrance. Usually the front office made us wear suits, but they'd relaxed the rules for the playoffs, thinking it would bring more publicity to the team if we showed our personalities more.

My outfits happened to be fan favorites . . . because I was a fucking baller like that.

> Me: Take that back.

> Asher: I'm just saying, I felt like you were trying to audition for a boy band.

That could have been a fair characterization of what I'd worn today . . . but I was pretty sure "boy band" was back in style. Or at least that was what my stylist had told me when she'd brought me the outfit.

> Me: That jean vest I wore today was iconic.

Asher: I believe the lady on TV called it "tragic."

Me: I thought you had better taste than this.

Asher: Socks, you looked like the lost member of NSYNC. All you needed was frosted tips.

Me: I'll have you know that frosted tips are making a comeback. I'll also have you know that I didn't hear any complaints from the fans lining the hallway, cheering me on. So there's that.

Asher: They were probably blinded by the amount of denim you were wearing. Denim vest, denim jeans . . . no shirt. It was a lot of . . . denim.

Me: It's called high fashion. Look it up.

Asher: Did you mean highly questionable? I wouldn't usually question you on typos, but . . .

Me: Says the man who wore cargo shorts to a wedding.

Asher: First, it was my ex's wedding, so it seemed appropriate. Second, they had five pockets. And everyone knows five pockets is key. Do you know how many jello shots I fit in there?

Me: . . .

Me: You looked like you were ready to pull out a flashlight and compass at any moment and join Dora the Explorer on her adventures.

I gave myself a mental high five on that burn. It was a good one.

> Asher: Hey, I was navigating myself to an open bar. At least I didn't look like I just walked off the stage after performing "Bye, Bye, Bye."

> Me: You'll see, next time we go out, I'll wear that vest. And then you'll see.

Obviously, the only person I wanted to look at me was Sloane. But I wasn't prepared to inform Asher of that. He might take issue with the fact that the only thing I knew about her was her name.

> Asher: ...

My eyebrows rose, and I growled.

> Me: Hey, none of that.

> Asher: What do you mean?

> Me: I mean, no ...

> Asher: I still don't get it ...

> Me: I've worked too hard to get in the COT for you to just adopt our ways willy-nilly.

> Asher: See, this is why I'm pretty sure you're not in the "COT." You just said "willy-nilly." And literally no one says that anymore.

> Asher: I also have doubts that Ari Lancaster allows Circle of Trust abbreviations. Doesn't seem official enough, ya know?

> Me: 🖕

Asher: . . .

Asher: Kick ass tonight.

I was grinning as I tossed my phone into my locker and pulled on my gloves.

"Does that smirk mean you aren't going to suck tonight?" Ari asked innocently as he continued taping his stick.

"Or does it mean that you are preparing for *more* suckage?" Walker added. "Because it feels like that smirk could go either way."

I scoffed and shook my head.

"Because in that case, we should just kill you now."

That comment was from Lincoln. I side-eyed him . . . because honestly you never knew with him. He might not be joking.

Which would be unfortunate in this case since I'd only just found my new reason for living.

Lincoln clapped me on the shoulder, and I breathed a little sigh of relief—not that I would be admitting that. "Rookie, I have complete faith in you. There's no way you're going to fuck up like you did last game."

His words seemed a little like a warning . . . but that might be fair in this case with how ridiculously bad I'd played last game. Everyone in this locker room wanted a Stanley Cup. Figuring out how to win that while also getting the girl who happened to be dating my sworn enemy was just going to be a little bit of a challenge.

I glanced at Camden, who was wearing a scary-looking smile on his face, and I gulped.

"I'm going to be so good tonight, boys. It's going to be like the last game never even happened."

Lincoln's grip on my shoulder tightened one more time before he finally let go. "You do that."

I stood up, still feeling very confident. In both my plan for Sloane and the game.

One of the assistant coaches came in and started giving us a pregame speech.

I didn't need one of those tonight, though. I was fully pumped up.

I'd never been more motivated to go out and kick ass in my life.

———

Sloane

The arena buzzed with pregame energy as I sat in the stands, my eyes focused on the ice. Tyler was out there somewhere, warming up. Every so often I'd glance over, and Tyler looked as if he was . . . posing. Like he was trying to give fans a good angle for their pictures. Which was weird.

I really wasn't paying much attention to Tyler, though.

I couldn't stop staring at *him*.

Logan.

I'd come to the game with good intentions. I really had. I'd kissed Tyler in the hallway before the game. I'd sat in my seat like a good girl, smiling and clapping or waving every time he skated by.

But as soon as Logan skated out on the ice, all of those good intentions had disappeared. All of my focus was on *him*—the way *he* moved, all power and control. He had that intensity, that raw focus, that I couldn't tear myself away from. I could just imagine how all that focus and intensity would feel like if he centered them on . . . me.

The game hadn't even started, but something in me had shifted. I wasn't just acting anymore. I was . . . watching.

I was mentally cursing myself out when all of a sudden there was a commotion behind me. I glanced up, and before I knew it, a line of women, all dressed in Dallas Knights polos, were making their way down the stairs toward me. Each of them carried something—a bouquet of flowers, a basket, and . . . a jersey.

A *Logan York* Dallas Knights jersey.

"Excuse me, miss," one of the women said with a bright smile, holding out the red roses. "These are for you, from Logan York."

My brain stalled. "What?"

Before I could even process it, another woman handed me the basket—snacks and even more flowers. Then came the jersey, Logan's number 42 emblazoned across the back, with *YORK* stitched across the top in bold letters.

I blinked, staring down at the jersey in disbelief. What the hell was happening?

I looked back toward the ice, still stunned, and there he was—Logan. He was standing there, holding his stick, his helmet pushed up on his head, grinning like a cat who'd just caught a canary.

And looking way too hot.

When he caught my eye, he winked and blew me a kiss.

Heat flushed my face instantly, and there was a strange fluttering feeling in my chest. I could feel my skin burning. I tried to keep my expression neutral, but I knew I was blushing. Badly.

"What the fuck is this?" I heard Tyler's voice, full of anger, from the ice. I whipped my head back to see him skating toward Logan, his face twisted in fury.

Logan didn't even flinch. He just stood there, watching Tyler approach like he had all the time in the world. That same grin still on his face, daring Tyler to make a move.

"You think this is funny, York?" Tyler shouted, his voice carrying across the ice. His teammates noticed the tension and started to hover, probably knowing what was about to happen. "Are you really hitting on my girlfriend?"

Girlfriend. That was a joke. I knew that was what we were pretending . . . but the fact that he could call me that with a straight face was laughable.

I ignored the fact that a part of me didn't want him calling me that in front of Logan lest he get the wrong idea . . .

Logan didn't move. He just shrugged, that grin widening as he casually waved in my direction. "Just thought she needed some snacks and a jersey. She's looking a little out of place in the crowd."

Tyler's face turned a shade of red I'd never seen before. His fists clenched, and I could see it in his eyes—he was ready to snap. He charged at Logan, his skates cutting into the ice with fury, but before he could get close enough, two of his teammates grabbed him by the arms, pulling him back.

"Not now, man!" one of them said, trying to calm him down. But Tyler wasn't having it.

"You're dead, York!" Tyler shouted, still straining against his teammates, his face flushed with rage.

Logan just smirked, unfazed. He turned and gave me another sexy wink, like this whole thing was just a game to him.

I dragged my gaze away, staring at the jersey in my lap like my life depended on it. My hands were trembling, my nipples were hardened into points under my bra. My heart was pounding so hard I could hear it over the noise of the crowd.

I couldn't stop the feeling creeping up inside me.

I wanted him.

And that was terrifying.

Logan

The second game had a completely different feel to it. The moment I stepped onto the ice, my mind wasn't consumed with rage toward Miller like it was in Game One. This time, I wasn't out to settle some stupid score or get caught up in whatever bullshit rivalry we had going on. No, this time was about *her*.

I could feel Sloane's presence, even from across the rink. I knew exactly where she was sitting—front row, just behind the glass. The memory of the way she'd looked when I sent those flowers and the jersey was burned into my mind, the way her cheeks had flushed when I blew her that kiss. And now, all I wanted was to see that look again.

And again.

And again.

Preferably when she was writhing underneath me in my bed.

Forget Miller. Forget everything else. Tonight, I was playing to impress her.

The puck dropped, and we were off. I could feel the electricity in the air, the tension of Game Two thick in the arena. Tampa was fast, but we were faster. Every shift, every pass felt like we were locked in, and I could feel it building—the pressure, the anticipation.

Midway through the first period, we got a power play. I took the face-off, locking eyes with their center for a brief second before snapping the puck back to Lincoln. The play moved fast—Ari fired it toward the net, but the goalie kicked it out, the rebound landing right in front of me.

I didn't hesitate. I crashed the net, scooping the puck up with a quick flick of my wrist and burying it in the top corner before the goalie could react.

The red light flashed, and the crowd erupted.

But I wasn't listening. I wasn't celebrating with the guys. I was already skating toward the boards, straight toward Sloane's seat. I slammed my fist against the glass, grinning like an idiot as I blew her another kiss, knowing full well the entire arena was watching.

She blushed again. That same look of surprise, like she couldn't believe what I was doing—making her the center of attention. I felt that surge of satisfaction hit me like a shot of adrenaline.

"You need at least five more of those this series to make it up to us," said Lincoln, patting my helmet as he skated by.

"You've got it, Daddy," I said. It was only the bemused look on Lincoln's face as we got off the ice that made me realize what I'd just said.

"Kill me now," I muttered as Camden almost fell from laughing so hard. "I obviously didn't mean that. It's because you idiots are always joking about that. It was just in my head."

"This better not ruin it for me next time Anastasia says it," Camden finally said when he was able to form words, wiping his eyes because he was an asshole.

I dared a peek at Ari, because I definitely didn't have the nerve to look at Lincoln.

Ari was scowling at me. He pointed a finger as he pushed through the gate and out into the action. "I knew it. I fucking knew it. You're an even bigger simp than Disney! This is an outrage."

He was still shaking his finger right before he slammed Miller into the ice, and I lifted a fist in victory.

"Any way we can forget that happened?" I finally muttered to Lincoln, side-eyeing him because I wasn't brave enough to look him in the face.

"Not a fucking chance," he answered with a smirk, his attention glued to where Walker had just made a save.

As the game went on, we kept pressing. The intensity on the ice was ramping up, but my head was clearer than it had been in Game One. No stupid penalties, no getting sucked into Miller's crap. I had one goal in mind— score again and make sure Sloane was impressed.

Late in the second period, we got another break. Lincoln passed it up the boards to Camden, who fired a stretch pass right to my tape. I broke free, flying down the wing with a Tampa defenseman on my heels. The goalie came out to challenge, but I snapped the puck over his blocker, top shelf, right where Grandma hides the cookies.

The horn blasted, and I felt that rush again.

I didn't even think about it. I skated straight to where Sloane was sitting, banging on the glass again. The noise was deafening, but all I saw was her— her wide eyes, the way she couldn't stop watching me now.

Another kiss blown through the air. Another blush from her. And another victory for me.

"Three more," Lincoln yelled, his fist raised in the air.

Evidently, scoring goals was much more effective than fighting when it came to getting under Miller's skin. I'd outscored him five to one in college, but he'd always had the misguided notion we were competitors. Currently, his face was beet red under that helmet, and I could tell he was just waiting for an excuse to snap.

I gave him one.

Late in the third, with the score still tight, I saw my chance. Miller had the puck and was skating up the ice, trying to make a move. I was on him in an instant, sticking close. He didn't see it coming when I reached out, subtly clipping his skate with my stick, just enough to send him tumbling forward, arms flailing as he face-planted onto the ice. The crowd gasped, and I could feel the laughter bubbling up from the bench.

He looked like an absolute idiot.

I couldn't help but laugh, catching the look of fury on his face as he scrambled to get up. His teammates were losing it.

"You're not very good at this," I chirped, smirking as I passed by him.

"Fuck you, York," he spat, but I just waved him off.

Miller could hate me all he wanted. I'd already won. I didn't need to throw punches tonight to get under his skin. This was better—way better.

As the clock wound down, I felt the satisfaction building inside me. I'd done my job. I'd scored twice, humiliated Miller, and, most importantly, I'd made sure Sloane couldn't take her eyes off me. Every time I passed her section, I could see her watching, her expression torn between shock and something else.

Something that made my chest tighten in a way I wasn't used to.

The final horn blew, and the game ended with a win for us. The arena roared in celebration, but I was already skating toward the glass, toward *her*. I banged my fist against the boards one last time, my eyes locked on hers, and blew her the biggest, most obnoxious kiss of the night.

This time, she smiled. She tried hiding it immediately behind her hand, but it didn't matter. She'd definitely smiled.

And I swear, that smile was worth every second of the game.

As I celebrated with my teammates, I had a big grin on my face. One step closer to making that girl mine.

CHAPTER 9

SLOANE

Tyler was supposed to be walking into the locker room, but instead he was gesturing for me to come over to where an employee was opening the door that led down to the ice again. Taking a deep breath, I quickly walked over, dread filtering through every step. As soon as I was at the entrance, Tyler's hand gripped my arm tightly, pulling me toward him before I even realized what was happening. "Don't forget who owns you this week," he growled.

I barely had time to blink before his lips crashed down on mine.

The kiss was all wrong. His mouth was cold, his grip possessive. It wasn't soft, it wasn't tender—it was a claim, a message to the world.

A message to Logan.

I tried to pull back, but Tyler's hand tightened around my waist, forcing me closer. My heart raced, panic threading through my veins as the crowd around us seemed to go still. I could feel them watching, the weight of their stares pressing down on me like a suffocating blanket. Whispers started behind me.

Logan had already brought unwanted attention to me . . . and now Tyler was making it worse.

I could only imagine what everyone was thinking.

Whore. Slut. Tramp.

With each second, my stomach twisted tighter. This wasn't supposed to happen. I wasn't supposed to be the center of attention.

When he finally pulled away, my skin was crawling. I could still feel the weight of his hands on me, like a stain I couldn't wash off. He leaned in, his voice a low, mocking whisper only I could hear. "Looks like York's watching. Let's see how much he likes that."

I didn't respond. I couldn't. My throat felt tight, and the taste of him still lingered on my lips—bitter and wrong. My mind was racing, my body frozen in place. As Tyler walked to the locker room, smirking like he'd won, I realized I wasn't just scared of what he'd done.

I was scared of what would happen next. I couldn't even begin to think about what Everett would say. How disappointed he'd be.

Doing my best not to meet anyone's gaze—especially Logan York's—I hustled up the stairs, pushing through the crowd to get to the exit.

I hadn't even made it to the hallway when my phone was buzzing, the sound cutting through the haze of my panicked thoughts. I fumbled to pull it out of my pocket, my hands shaking. The moment I saw the name flash across the screen, my stomach dropped.

Everett.

"Sloane," he said coldly through the phone the second I answered. His voice was sharp, furious. "What the fuck is going on?"

"I—" I started, but he cut me off, his voice seething.

"You're drawing too much attention to yourself. What do you think you're doing? Tyler's already called me. He's not happy with your performance. Said you've been too focused on that Dallas player."

My heart hammered in my chest, the panic rising as his words sank in.

"You wouldn't happen to be doing anything behind my back now, would you? Because you know the rules." Everett's voice was perfectly calm, and somehow that was way more terrifying than when he sounded mad.

"I'm not—" I began, my voice weak.

"Don't lie to me," he snapped. "You're playing with fire, Sloane. You think you can afford to be careless? You think you can afford to let people notice you? I've worked too hard to keep you under the radar, and now you're screwing everything up."

The anger in his voice made my blood run cold. I could picture him on the other end of the line, pacing, his face twisted in that familiar look of disgust.

"I'll fix it," I whispered, my voice trembling. "I promise . . . I don't even know Logan—"

"You certainly know his name," he said—cutting me off once again.

There was an awkward, terrible silence as I waited for him to speak. Nothing I said was going to convince him.

"I don't want to hear another word about this," he finally said. "Do your job and stay invisible. Got it?"

"Yes," I whispered, my chest tight with fear and shame. "I've got it."

He hung up without another word, the silence on the other end of the line like a slap in the face.

I sat there for a long moment, staring at the phone in my hand, my mind racing. All of the fear, the anxiety, the panic—it twisted together in a messy knot in my stomach. Tyler was furious, my uncle was furious.

I had to stay away. I had to.

My whole future depended on it.

Logan

I was never going to watch Tyler Miller kiss Sloane again.

I hadn't even spoken to her, and I'd only just learned her name.

But I did know one thing.

And that was the fact that I wanted her.

My stomach churned, a wave of nausea hitting me hard as I watched. I had the urge to take my stick and drive it through his brain; it was all I could do to stop myself.

He kissed her like he was marking his territory, like he owned her, and she . . . she looked miserable.

Of course she did. She felt the same thing I did.

Or at least that was what I was telling myself.

By the time I hit the locker room, I already had a plan.

A crazy plan.

It wasn't the kind of plan I'd ever envisioned for myself, but I didn't care. I needed Tyler out of the picture, at least for tonight.

I'd focus on forever after that.

Later that night I sat in a corner booth in the hotel bar where the Tampa players were staying, my hat pulled low over my eyes as I watched Miller at the counter, getting hammered.

I mean, fuck, he was making this way too easy. We were in the fucking finals. He couldn't just drink water for a few days?

And where was Sloane? If I had her, you can bet I wouldn't be spending a second away from her if I could help it.

Just further evidence Tyler Miller was a fucking idiot . . . and that he didn't deserve her.

Miller was leaning closer and closer to the bartender like a vulture circling its prey. She was young—midtwenties, maybe—with sharp, dark eyes and a no-nonsense air about her. But even her best efforts to stay polite weren't enough to keep Miller at bay.

"You're really gonna pretend you don't know who I am?" he slurred, flashing her a grin that probably worked on puck bunnies but looked ridiculous now. "Come on, sweetheart. Take a guess."

She didn't even glance at him, just poured another drink for someone else and slid it across the counter. Her lips were pressed into a tight, professional smile, but I caught the subtle roll of her eyes as she moved to the other end of the bar.

Tyler, however, wasn't the kind of guy who took being ignored lightly.

"Hey," he called, rapping his knuckles on the bar. "Hey, I'm talking to you."

She paused, her shoulders stiffening as she turned back to him. "What can I get you, sir?" she asked, her voice polite and flat.

"You can start by telling me your name," he said, leaning forward with a smirk. "And then maybe we'll talk about what time you get off tonight."

Her expression didn't falter, but the faint flicker of annoyance in her eyes gave her away. "I'll get you another drink," she said, turning away again.

Miller laughed, the sound loud and grating. "You don't know how lucky you are, do you? This is a once-in-a-lifetime chance, babe. Tyler Miller doesn't waste his time on just anyone."

The bartender's hand froze for a split second before she grabbed a glass and began pouring. I watched her closely, saw the way her fingers gripped the bottle just a little too tightly, like she was trying to channel her frustration into something constructive instead of chucking it at his head.

I couldn't blame her. Miller had a way of bringing out the worst in people.

That murderous urge was hitting me hard again. I couldn't believe he was actually trying to cheat on Sloane. He deserved everything he had coming.

She slid the drink across the bar, her smile thin and forced. "Here you go."

Miller took a long sip, never taking his eyes off her. "You don't talk much, huh? That's okay. I like the quiet ones."

She turned away without responding, busying herself with the register. Miller's grin faltered, and his tone shifted, taking on an edge. "You think you're too good for me? Is that it?"

The bartender didn't respond. Instead, she stepped back, busying herself with another customer. But Miller wasn't one to take a hint. He reached for the bartender's wrist, his grip too tight, and I saw the flicker of fear in her eyes before she yanked her arm back.

"Please don't touch me again," she said, her voice low but firm. She muttered something under her breath to the guy working next to her—a tall, gangly kid who looked like he wanted to melt into the floor—and then untied her apron, tossing it onto the counter.

Without another word, she walked toward the back exit, her head held high, but I didn't miss the way her shoulders tensed. Miller watched her go with a smirk.

I glanced at my glass, pretending to take a sip, but my eyes tracked her every move. When the door swung shut behind her, I set my drink down and stood, crossing the room quickly, weaving through the crowded bar with my head down. I pushed open the back exit, stepping into the dimly lit alley behind the building.

The bartender was leaning against the brick wall, her arms crossed tightly over her chest, a tear sliding down her cheek. She jumped when she saw me, her eyes narrowing in suspicion. "What do you want?" she asked, furiously wiping at her face.

"Busy night?" I asked, my voice casual.

Her eyebrows raised as she stared at me. I could see her trying to figure out if she recognized me or not. Finally she nodded. "Always is when a team's in town," she said, her voice flat.

I nodded, keeping my tone light. "You get a lot of the players in here?"

"Some," she said, her eyes narrowing slightly. "Why? You a fan?"

"Not exactly," I replied, a smirk pulling at the corner of my mouth. "Bet it gets exhausting, though."

"What?"

"Dealing with assholes all the time," I answered, leaning against the brick and trying to look unassuming—kind of difficult when you're a six-foot-four, tatted-all-over hockey *star*.

I liked to refer to myself as such because it was good to manifest greatness.

"Are you another of those *assholes*?" she asked, wiping at her face again as more tears fell.

"I try not to be," I said honestly. "I'd like to help."

She snorted, shaking her head. "Guys like you don't help."

I held up my hands, palms out. "You've had a rough night, and I've got a solution."

Her brow furrowed, but she didn't move. "A solution?"

I pulled the vial from my pocket, holding it up between two fingers. "For that guy. Just a few drops in his drink, and he'll be out of your hair for the rest of the night."

She stared at the vial, her expression unreadable. "What is that?"

"Nothing dangerous," I said smoothly. "Just enough to give him the shits until morning."

That was a lie, it was going to make him sicker than that, plus get him suspended when the NHL drug tested him. But it wouldn't kill him, so really that was all the information she needed.

"You're seriously asking me to drug a professional hockey player?"

I shrugged. "It will make you feel better."

Her lips twitched like she wanted to smile, but she crossed her arms tighter. "Why should I trust you?"

"Because you don't deserve to deal with assholes like him," I said, staring at her. "And because if anyone asks, you had nothing to do with it."

She hesitated, her eyes flicking between me and the vial.

"Don't you want to take back some of your power? Finally get back at the idiots you have to deal with all the time. And he's just getting started," I told her, nodding to the door. "Who knows what he'll do next."

Her eyes widened at that thought, and the look of fear returned. She was silent for a few seconds, but I saw when the light in her eyes changed, when she went from prey—to a would-be predator.

She reached out and snatched it from my hand. "Fine. But if this comes back on me—or if something really bad happens . . ."

"It won't," I promised. "He won't even remember where he got the drink."

She studied me for a moment. "What's your name?" she asked.

"John Soto," I said immediately, thinking that would earn me a few gold stars if I ever told Ari about this. Or whatever the Circle of Trust was handing out on that particular day.

I personally would have asked for more information, a lot more, but she'd reached the desperation stage. Assholes like Tyler Miller could get you there fast. She walked back inside without a look back, and I stayed there for a minute before I followed her inside to where Miller had somehow managed to get even more drunk while we'd been outside.

I slid into my booth again, watching as she moved to Miller's side of the bar. I couldn't see her hands, but I did see her hesitating for a second—right before he opened his asshole mouth once again and sealed his fate.

"So, do you like to be fucked in public, or am I going to have to take you to my room?" he slurred.

That same look I'd seen in her eyes outside, the one that said she was sick and tired, came back, and her movements were sure and determined after that. A few seconds later she was handing him another glass.

"Here you go," she said, her voice neutral.

Miller didn't hesitate for a second. He grabbed the glass, downed half of it, and slammed it back on the counter. The bartender shot me a glance, her expression a mix of satisfaction and wariness. I nodded, raising my glass in silent thanks before I grinned and slid out of the booth.

Miller was about to be very incapacitated . . . and now, it was time to try and find Sloane.

I wandered through the lobby, trying to come up with a plan to get her room number, when I saw her.

Sloane was sitting at a table in the corner of the hotel restaurant, looking like she'd stepped off a runway. She was wearing a black cocktail dress, the kind that hugged her body just right, accentuating her curves without being too obvious. Her legs were crossed, one foot lightly tapping the floor in rhythm with the soft jazz playing in the background. Her hair was perfectly styled, waves falling just past her shoulders, but it was the red lipstick that caught my attention—a shade she'd been wearing both nights, that somehow made her look both powerful and untouchable.

She was fucking perfect.

And evidently there were a lot of people who agreed with my assessment.

Everyone was watching her. Men at the bar kept sneaking glances, some of them even standing up from their chairs, preparing themselves to talk to her. I *prepared* myself to escort them out of the restaurant if they tried.

Luckily for them, they either had no balls, or they realized that she was so far out of their league it wasn't worth trying, and they sat back down each time.

Sloane didn't seem to notice any of it. Her eyes were downcast, staring into the glass of wine in front of her as if it held all the answers to life's problems. Her fingers gently traced the rim of the glass, her posture perfect but somehow distant, detached, like she was in her own world.

She was lonely; it hung around her like a veil, hidden beneath the sophistication, the perfect appearance. She looked elegant, yes, but there was something else. Something deeper. Something broken.

I couldn't tear my eyes away.

Before I could overthink it, I was walking to her.

"Hi," I said, sliding into the chair across from her, acting like I had every right to be there.

Because I did. She was mine.

Her head snapped up, her eyes widening in shock. "What are you doing here?" she asked, her voice low but tense.

I smiled softly, my eyes greedily taking in her face. "Just passing through. Saw you sitting here alone."

"You were passing through the hotel where Tampa's staying?" she asked incredulously.

I shrugged. "Or maybe I was trying to find you."

She looked stunned at that statement, visibly swallowing her shock.

"Do you always look this serious when you're drinking, or is it just because I wasn't here?" I teased, leaning across the table and feeling like I was high from being this close to her.

She glanced up, one brow arching in perfect disinterest. "Are your pickup lines always this bad?"

"Not always," I said, shrugging. "But I figured I'd start slow. Give you time to fall in love with me."

Her lips twitched, almost a smile, and it felt like a victory. "Charming."

"I've been told. By my best friend, mostly."

That earned me a full-on smile, and I blinked because it was so fucking glorious. Her hand slid across her face, like she was trying to hide it again, and when she moved it . . . her smile was gone. "And what makes you think I want to fall in love with you?"

"Call it a hunch." I rested my chin on my hands. "Or maybe it's just that you haven't walked away yet."

She tilted her head, considering me like she was trying to figure out if I was worth her time. "Maybe I'm just bored."

"Lucky me, then. I'm an excellent distraction."

That smile was back, and she wrinkled her nose at me. Fuck, not only was she hot . . . she was cute.

A lethal combination for my currently aching dick.

"You don't even know my name."

"Sloane Calloway," I responded quickly, and her eyes widened again, an almost panicked look filling their depths before she blinked . . . and they went perfectly blank.

"And what else do you know about me?" she asked in a careful, practiced voice, glancing down at her fingertips as she went back to tracing the edge of her wineglass.

"Absolutely nothing. But I'm desperate to change that."

That had her meeting my eyes again, her lips pursing as she studied me.

"Let me take you out," I said, all that desperation I'd just mentioned leaching out into my words.

Her brow arched again, this time in surprise. "Take me out?"

"Dinner. Drinks. I could even be persuaded to dance," I said, ticking off options on my fingers. "Whatever you want."

"I have a *boyfriend*," she said, her voice firm, but there was a flicker of something—disgust?—as she said the word like it tasted rotten on her tongue.

"Do you?" I asked, raising an eyebrow. "Because I know where he is right now, and you deserve way better than that." I tapped my chin. "I mean everyone deserves better than that, actually, but the sentiment stands."

Her mouth opened, then closed again. She looked away, her hand stilling. "You're probably right on that," she whispered.

"Good. Then there's room for an upgrade."

She snorted, shaking her head. "If you won't take that excuse, then take this one. I'm swearing off hockey players."

"Calloway, that's an awful idea. I happen to know that most hockey players make the best fucking boyfriends on the planet. Just not Tyler Miller, obviously."

She grinned again, her cheeks flushing slightly. "I thought you were talking about a date. And now you're talking about boyfriends. You're moving awful fast there, buddy."

"Can I add that I'm also fun, charming, and excellent in bed?"

She scoffed, taking a drink of her wine. "All of those things are probably debatable."

I grinned, the corner of my mouth tugging upward. "You should give me a chance to prove that, then, for research purposes, of course."

"Of course," she said, a hint of laughter in her voice.

I winked at her, and she squirmed in her seat, that blush in her cheeks darkening.

Before I could say anything else, a commotion broke out near the entrance. Voices rose, a mix of horrified gasps and muffled groans. We both turned, and I had to stifle a laugh at the sight.

Miller, looking like death warmed over, was stumbling through the lobby, clutching his stomach. His face was pale, sweat dripping down his temples as he staggered forward. And then, as if the universe had finally decided to do something right, he doubled over and vomited directly onto a woman's head.

The woman shrieked, her hands flying to her hair as Miller stumbled back, his hands raised in weak apology. The entire lobby froze, everyone watching in stunned silence except for Sloane, who sat there looking disgusted but entirely unmoved to help him.

I bit back a laugh, turning back to her. "Definitely not your boyfriend, right?"

Her nose wrinkled again, her lips curving into a smirk. "Definitely not."

"That's what I like to hear. Now, should we start our date?" I asked, standing and offering her my hand.

She stared at it, her eyes narrowing slightly.

"It's just a date, Sloane," I said softly, and her answering smile may have been the saddest thing I'd ever seen.

"I wish," she murmured back, gracefully sliding out of her seat and straightening invisible wrinkles out of her dress.

"Forget you ever met me, Logan York," she called over her shoulder as she walked away.

I frowned as I watched her move out of the lobby and past where Miller was struggling to walk. She went straight to the elevator and stepped through the doors after they opened, not even giving me one look back.

"Not a chance," I whispered.

CHAPTER 10

LOGAN

I gaped at the file, my mind completely blown.

There had been a lot of different scenarios going through my head about various reasons why Sloane would date an asshole like Miller. But I had not come up with what was written in front of me.

Sloane was an escort.

"Are you sure about this?" I asked, my voice rough as I continued staring at the page in disbelief. I'd wanted information, but I wasn't prepared for this. My heart was suddenly beating really loud, and I absent-mindedly rubbed my chest, trying to calm down.

The PI, a grizzled-looking guy, nodded. "Positive. She's tied to an escort service—a high-end one. They specialize in celebrities and government officials. I traced pictures of her online with a senator and several others."

I swallowed hard and turned the page.

Each page made me a little sicker—there were so many details. The clients, the places she frequented, how many "appointments" she had a month. Tyler Miller's name stood out in bold letters, a repeat customer by the looks of it. I recognized a lot of the other names as well.

Just thinking of them touching her made me want to throw up. She was too good for all of them.

"How did you even find all this? Surely these people pride themselves on anonymity," I said, tossing the file on my desk.

"Nothing is ever a secret if you know where to look," he answered, a small, weird-looking grin on his face. And now I was officially creeped out.

"Alright, thanks." My tone was stiff.

He gave me a knowing smile before he headed out of the room. "I'll bill you."

"I bet you will," I muttered as the door closed behind him.

I stared at the file, finally picking it back up and flipping through the pages again as I scanned for more details. There was her address—a very nice condominium high-rise that was located in downtown Dallas. That was actually useful. She didn't live that far from me.

How had she started this? Did she want to be an escort? Did she like it?

Nope. She definitely didn't.

I could answer that question pretty easily because I could picture how lonely and miserable she'd looked last night. And the fact that she'd had to hook up with Tyler multiple times—there was no way she liked that.

I stared at the address again, the words blurring in front of me as I came up with a genius idea.

If she wouldn't date me, I would hire her. I'd pay whatever it took to make sure she didn't have time for any other clients.

For as long as it took . . .

Until she fell in love with me.

A brilliant plan if I didn't say so myself.

I'd remind myself of all the ways it could go wrong at a later date. If I had to see her kiss Miller one more time, I really was going to be responsible for manslaughter.

Okay . . . how did one actually *hire* an escort. Not to toot my own horn, but I hadn't exactly had a need to pay people to fuck me. I'd never understood why celebrities did that in the first place. I got wanting no-strings-attached interactions, but there were plenty of women who just wanted to say they'd fucked an athlete. They didn't actually want anything else from them.

Although there were plenty who did.

I sighed. Back to my problem . . . it probably wouldn't work to just ask her. So . . . Google it was . . .

Thirty minutes later, and I felt like an idiot as I stared at the screen, feeling more frustrated by the second. All I needed was a straightforward answer to a very specific question, but apparently, Google wasn't as helpful as I thought it would be.

How to hire an escort.

Simple, right? Except nothing useful was coming up. I scrolled through the results, my eyes glazing over as I clicked on another link, only to get more useless information about *personal companions* and *how to up your date nights.*

"This is ridiculous," I muttered, leaning back in my chair. Google was supposed to know everything, but apparently, it had limits. And I didn't know how to access that whole "dark web" thing.

I glanced down at my phone, contemplating my next move. I could keep clicking through sketchy websites or—fuck me—I could ask for advice.

I groaned, already knowing what was going to happen if I did that. But whatever, screw it.

I opened the group chat with the guys, hesitated for about two seconds, and then typed out the message.

> Me: Anyone know how to hire an escort?

It took less than ten seconds for the first response to come through.

> Lincoln: . . .

> Walker: . . .

> Camden: . . .

> Ari: Things get that desperate, eh?

I sighed, glancing at the screen, regretting my life choices already.

> Me: I'm not asking for me.

> Camden: The old "Asking for a friend." Got it.

> Me: Well, I'm technically asking for me, but it's complicated.

> Ari: This is getting good. Tell me more.

> Me: Is there any way for me to get the answer to this question without talking about it?

> Lincoln: Absolutely not.

Ari: I just laughed out loud, Rookie. I didn't realize you were so funny.

Walker: I'm on the edge of my seat here. You've finally gotten all our attention.

Me: Hey! I never said I wanted everyone's attention.

Ari: Oh right . . . that wasn't you that called Golden Boy "Daddy" the other day. I'll edit that in my journal.

Me: You didn't write that in your journal.

Ari: I did. I made a note about how I was outraged that once again I wasn't getting the attention I deserved. It says right here: "Another simp infiltrated the group."

I perked up at that.

Me: So, I am in the Circle?

Camden: Absolutely no one said that.

Walker: It's true. No one said that.

Lincoln: I see what you're doing, though. You're trying to distract us from the fact that you have to pay for someone to touch your dick.

Ari: Definitely not Circle of Trust behavior.

I huffed, impatient because I could picture Sloane with Miller right now, and it made me feral.

Me: HOW DO I HIRE AN ESCORT?

Ari: So shouty.

Camden: Are you hiring an escort for, like . . . normal escort stuff? Or . . .

Ari: Or because you want someone to call you "Daddy." Because Hero can testify that you don't need to pay for that.

Camden: It's true.

Walker: And it seems like you already have practice with that term so . . .

Lincoln: Good point.

I ran a hand over my face.

Me: You all are going to be calling me "Daddy" if someone doesn't help me the fuck out right now.

Ari: Ooh. I just got goosebumps, York.

Me: This is for an important thing. I'm trying to figure something out, and Google isn't helping.

Lincoln: Google isn't helping because normal people don't Google how to hire an escort, Rookie.

Walker: Why don't you try typing in "how to rob a bank." Or what about "poisoning your lover's husband."

Ari: Personal experience with that, Disney?

I groaned, sinking back in my chair. This was a disaster.

> Me: Never mind. I'll figure it out myself.

> Walker: Oh, no. You've opened the door, and now you're stuck with us.

> Camden: I'm still waiting for you to explain why you're asking about escorts, though.

> Ari: Maybe he's Googling "how to hire an escort" because he thinks it's code for bodyguard. Hint, Rookie, it's not.

I snorted and sighed again. I was going to have to fess up.

> Me: I may be a little obsessed with a woman who happens to have that occupation.

> Walker: Is this like that song "I'm in love with a stripper?"

> Lincoln: Sounds similar.

> Me: . . .

> Ari: That was oddly appropriate, Logan.

My phone rang, and my eyes widened. It was Lincoln.

"Hey," I said, ignoring the fact that there was a little squeak in my voice. He probably . . . hopefully hadn't noticed.

"Does this love interest belong to an organization, or does she work on her own?" he asked without any introduction.

"With an organization," I responded, looking at the page again.

"Okay," he said, talking slowly like I was dim-witted. "And did my PI get you the contact for the head of that organization or the scheduler?"

Kill me now. Maybe I didn't deserve Sloane on account of being a fucking idiot.

Good thing I didn't care about things like that.

I glanced at the paper, and there was an email address: *exxy@eholdings.org.*

"There is."

There was a long silence. "I hope you're typing out your email right now."

I was not . . . only because I wasn't sure what to say. But I wasn't about to tell him that.

"And, Logan."

"Yes?"

"Do whatever it takes," Lincoln said. And then he hung up.

I typed out an email, and a minute later I was in business—uploading all my information that would no doubt get me in a whole lotta shit if it ever got out. Which, I assume, was the point.

I kept repeating Lincoln's words in my head, though. *Do whatever it takes.*

Sloane

The sound of Tyler retching echoed through the bathroom door like some grotesque symphony that I couldn't escape. I sat on the edge of the hotel bed, staring at the muted TV, my stomach churning in solidarity. He'd been at it all night, a miserable mix of groans and curses, punctuated by the occasional thud as he probably tried to stand and failed. At one point, he'd stopped even trying and just lay on the bathroom floor, his weak shouts for water going unanswered. Not by me, anyway.

It wasn't in my job description to play nurse for my clients . . . unless that was what they were into. I shivered thinking about one of the costumes I'd had to wear in the past for a very, very old man.

Another moan from the bathroom, and I scooted back in the bed, turning up the television loud enough to drown him out so I could watch *Top Gun: Maverick* for the fiftieth time.

Morning came, and Tyler stumbled out of the bathroom looking like death itself. His face was pale and clammy, his hair sticking to his forehead in sweaty clumps. He glared at me as if his misery was somehow my fault.

"You could've at least gotten me a Gatorade," he snapped, his voice hoarse.

"You could've at least not drank yourself to death," I shot back, crossing my legs and giving him a pointed look.

His nostrils flared, but he didn't have the energy to argue. Instead, he muttered something under his breath, grabbed his gear bag, and stomped out the door, still looking like he was going to keel over.

Today's game was going to be interesting, I thought, a slow grin spreading across my face. Watching Tyler struggle . . . should be fun.

———————

Watching Tyler from the stands was actually almost painful—not because I wanted him to succeed, obviously, but because I suffered from secondhand embarrassment. I had always been that way, blushing when people embarrassed themselves in books or on TV.

But this was on another level.

Tyler looked awful out there, barely skating at half his usual speed. His cheeks were hollow, his movements sluggish, and he seemed more focused on staying upright than actually playing.

My phone buzzed in my lap. I sighed, pulling it out, half expecting some scolding message about keeping up appearances. Instead, the name on the screen made my stomach clench.

Everett.

I hesitated, knowing that another call from him in the middle of a job meant bad news. Finally, I swiped to answer, pressing the phone to my ear.

"What's wrong?" I asked, skipping pleasantries.

"Tyler Miller." Everett's voice crackled through the line, sharp and businesslike. "He's about to be suspended after this game."

The words hit me like a slap, though I wasn't sure why. "Suspended? For what?"

"Performance-enhancing drugs. The NHL had some players give samples for their 'random' tests based on a tip. The powers that be will be testing them during the game."

My brow furrowed. That didn't make sense. Tyler wasn't the type to use something like that. He was too arrogant, too convinced he was naturally superior to everyone else. "That doesn't sound like him. How did you even find that out if the NHL itself hasn't tested the samples yet?"

His silence had me rolling my eyes. Naturally, Everett had an in. He watched his company's clients closely, tracing their every move to make sure something they did didn't come back to bite him. "None of that matters. What matters is that he's done after this game. And since he's done, you're done with him." Everett's tone was cold, final.

I sat up straighter, glancing down at the ice. Tyler was wobbling on his skates, the puck slipping past him like he wasn't even there. Logan York skated by effortlessly, moving across the ice with all the ease and precision that Tyler lacked.

"What happens now?" I asked, my voice barely above a whisper as I greedily took Logan in.

"You have a new client," Everett said, his tone suddenly stern. "One who's paying a lot more than Miller ever did."

The knot in my stomach tightened. Everett usually gave me time off between clients. Although I guess I really hadn't done anything worth taking a break—he wouldn't even have to arrange for any *testing* since Tyler hadn't gotten anywhere near me.

I gripped the phone harder, my gaze drifting to Logan, who was now leaning against the boards, his eyes scanning the crowd. I froze when his gaze landed on me, piercing and unrelenting.

"Who?" I asked, the question coming out as a breathless whisper . . . a strange sense of foreboding filling my insides.

Everett paused, and I could hear the faint sound of papers shuffling in the background. "Logan York."

My chest tightened, and the world seemed to tilt slightly. I barely heard the rest of what he was saying, his usual instructions about keeping things professional, about following the rules.

Logan knew what I was.

I wasn't prepared for the shame suddenly coating my insides, for how the arena suddenly became hazy and the sharp taste of self-hatred filled my mouth.

Somehow in my head, some ridiculous, never-going-to-happen part of me had been picturing Logan and me in a real relationship—one untainted by the choices I'd made in my life. I felt that part of me was dying when I realized Logan was just like all the others.

"This job, Sloane?" Everett said, his voice slicing through my daze like a knife. "It goes against my better judgment, but it would be wrong of me to have you miss out on the amount of money he was willing to pay. His time with you starts immediately following the game."

"Of course," I whispered, only faintly aware of him hanging up on me.

My hand was trembling as I dropped the phone in my lap. My eyes darted back to the ice, to Logan, who was still looking at me. He tilted his head slightly, like he could tell something had shifted.

"*It's just a job,*" I whispered.

And I'd never hated those words more in my life.

CHAPTER 11

LOGAN

Warm-ups were supposed to be routine—stretch, skate, shoot, get loose.

Miller . . . was making them look incredibly difficult. He was barely moving, his face gray and sweaty under his helmet. Every stride looked like it was taking everything he had, and he leaned over and gagged at one point.

It was delightful.

I skated past him, grinning behind my mouth guard. Seeing him like this—sick, weak, floundering—it was better than I'd imagined. The bartender had done good work. It was too bad she couldn't see him like this, it would be poetic justice for her.

Tampa's head coach, a barrel-chested guy with a voice like a foghorn, was already on the bench, barking orders. "Miller! You gonna fucking skate, or are you just here to take up space?"

Tyler barely lifted his head, his stick dragging behind him as he shuffled to the boards. "I'm fine," he muttered, though it was obvious to everyone in the arena with eyes that he wasn't.

"Bullshit," the coach snapped. "You look like you're about to keel over. What the fuck did you do?"

I chuckled under my breath, circling back to grab a puck. Miller shot me a glare, his eyes bloodshot and watery, like he was barely holding it together. He opened his mouth to say something, but his coach cut him off.

"Move your ass, Miller! We don't have time for this shit!"

Miller turned, his shoulders hunched like a scolded schoolboy, and skated off toward the far end of the rink. If he was trying to prove he was ready to play, he wasn't doing a great job.

Satisfied, I glanced toward the stands, where the real reason for my focus—or distraction—was sitting. Sloane. She stood out like a diamond in a gravel pit, her sleek outfit and perfect posture screaming sophistication in the sea of jerseys and hats. She wasn't paying attention to Tyler's pathetic performance or even the ice. Instead, she was on a call, her pretty face looking distressed.

And then I saw it.

The moment she figured it out.

Her face went pale, her lips parting slightly. She looked up, her eyes scanning the ice like she was searching for something—or someone.

When her gaze locked on me, I knew. She wasn't guessing anymore. She knew.

She knew I'd hired her.

My heart pounded, but I didn't look away. Instead, I tilted my head just slightly, giving her a look that I hoped conveyed exactly what I was thinking. *Yeah, I hired you. And yeah, I'm not sorry, baby. It's all going to work out.*

Her face froze, and I could see the storm brewing behind her eyes, even from a distance. She turned back to her phone, gripping it tightly as though it might offer her some kind of escape.

Good luck with that, sweetheart.

The sound of Tampa's coach screaming snapped me out of my trance. Tyler was wobbling again, missing an easy pass and almost taking out one of his teammates in the process.

"For fuck's sake, Miller! Get off the damn ice!" the coach bellowed.

Tyler skated off, his helmet tilted awkwardly as he slumped onto the bench. The guys around him didn't even try to hide their disgust, scooting away like he was contagious.

I skated past the boards, my smirk firmly back in place. Warm-ups hadn't even finished, and I was already winning. And if the drug test results came back the way I expected? This was the last time I'd be playing Tyler this season.

The best part? Sloane was free now—or at least, she was free for me.

And she'd figure that out soon enough.

The second Miller's stick came down on my kneecap, I knew I was in trouble. Pain shot through my leg, hot and immediate, and I crumpled to the ice, clutching my knee. The roar of the crowd faded into the background as I gritted my teeth, trying to push through it, trying to get up. But the stabbing pain wasn't going anywhere.

He had sucked up enough energy to come after me the entire game. But a slash to the knee? That was low, even for him.

"If you get lost out there, ref, just follow the sound of everyone booing," Ari growled as he made it to me. There were a few whistles, but I couldn't muster past the pain to see what was happening to Tyler.

Ari helped pull me up, and then I limped my way to the bench, my breath coming in ragged gasps as the trainer worked on getting me patched up.

"You're out for now," the trainer said, shaking his head. "I'll see how it looks after this period."

I cursed under my breath, slamming my hand on the boards in frustration. This was Game Three. I had fucking plans.

And if I couldn't fucking perform for Sloane later . . . Miller was going to be a dead man.

I glanced over to where Sloane was sitting and caught just a glimpse of her concerned face as she peeked at me before she quickly whipped her head around the moment she saw me looking.

If that wasn't a sign she was about to be in love with me—I didn't know what was.

Miller chose that moment to skate by with that stupid grin on his face, like he'd just won something. It made my blood boil, but there wasn't much I could do except sit there, seething, as the game went on without me.

"You okay, Rookie?" Lincoln asked as he skated by the bench.

I nodded glumly, trying to look tough despite the fact that it felt like Tyler Fucking Miller had tried to remove my kneecap.

Lincoln nodded, but there was a scary energy about him that made me glad for the millionth time he was on my team. I watched from the bench as he zeroed in on Miller, his eyes locked on him like a predator about to strike. And when he did, it wasn't subtle. Lincoln came at Miller full force, driving him into the glass right by our bench, so hard that the boards rattled, the entire arena going silent for a moment.

Miller's body crumpled against the boards, his stick clattering to the ice, and I could see the pain etched on his face as Lincoln held him there for a beat longer than necessary. The refs were already blowing their whistles, but Lincoln leaned in close, his voice low and dangerous. "Don't touch my rookie again."

Miller didn't even respond, his body limp as the trainers came to haul him off the ice. He wasn't going to be playing what was hopefully his last game after all.

It was incredibly satisfying.

I avoided Ari's eyes when he skated by. "Simppppp," he singsonged, and I scoffed, because Walker was probably over there nutting in his pants right now at the display Lincoln had just put on. Why wasn't *he* getting crap?

But also . . . yes, I was possibly Lincoln's simp, as well.

We'd talk about that at another time.

Lincoln got sent straight to the penalty box after smashing Miller into the glass. I watched him skate off, his face hard as stone, not a single ounce of regret in his eyes. He wasn't getting tossed from the game, though—probably because even the refs knew Tyler had it coming. A slash to the kneecap wasn't exactly something they were going to let slide.

Lincoln dropped onto the bench in the box, glaring out at the ice like a caged animal. I could still feel the throbbing in my knee, the ache spreading through my leg, but seeing Miller get taken off the ice made it sting a little less.

When the penalty clock finally started ticking down, Lincoln looked over at me from the box, a small nod in my direction. No words, but I understood. He'd handled it.

And when I could get back in the game, I'd handle business too.

———

I couldn't play for the rest of the game thanks to my swollen knee, but the good news was the team doc didn't think I'd be out for Game Four.

Even though we lost . . . there was a small amount of solace after the game.

Miller's drug test had come back positive, and NHL officials had swooped in. The arena was buzzing with the news—Tyler Miller had been hit with a twenty-game suspension, without pay, for performance-enhancing drugs.

I was now standing at Sloane's hotel room door, holding a bouquet of flowers, my knee wrapped, and hoping that the news about Miller would soften the *complicated* feelings she might be having.

Sloane and I started *now*.

CHAPTER 12

SLOANE

A knock on the door sounded, and I smoothed my hair and glanced in the mirror one more time, reapplying my red lipstick. The color was the one thing Everett let me choose about my appearance. It was my version of battle armor.

The only problem . . . it didn't seem to be working properly. I was trying to be numb, but I kept feeling things.

I had to remind myself that he was just like all the others who'd hired me. No matter what connection I'd felt when we'd locked eyes . . . when he'd kissed me . . . when he'd asked me out at the bar . . .

None of it was real.

I had to remember . . . this was just another job. He'd made sure of that when he hired me.

Except when I opened the hotel door and saw him standing there, he was holding a bouquet of red roses.

No one had ever brought me flowers before. You didn't do that when the girl was a sure thing. Expensive gifts. Alcohol. Lingerie. Sure.

But not flowers.

The red roses were perfect, fresh, like they belonged in some romantic movie. Not in *my* life.

What was he playing at?

I tried to keep my face neutral, not wanting him to see the swirl of emotions hitting me all at once—shock, disbelief, and something else I couldn't name. I couldn't even bring myself to reach for them.

He frowned, his eyes searching mine. "Why do you look so upset?"

I swallowed hard, shaking my head. "I'm not upset."

He raised an eyebrow, clearly not buying it. "Alright," he said slowly, stepping into the penthouse and pressing a kiss on my lips like it was second nature, like we'd been doing that for a lifetime.

I froze, my lips unmoving. It took a second for me to kiss him back, and when I did, it felt like there were ants crawling across my skin. We weren't supposed to be like this. I didn't kiss my clients like they were my boyfriend.

He pulled away, studying me for a second. "You *are* upset. What did I do?"

"You didn't do anything," I snapped petulantly, turning away and trying to get a hold of myself. I wasn't supposed to snap at my *clients*.

But when I turned back around, there the roses were, the bright red petals taunting me.

"Then what is it?" he said soothingly, reaching out and trailing his fingers across my cheek. I blinked, too much emotion slithering under my skin, and I couldn't stop staring at those stupid roses.

The crazy thing was, I *wanted* to tell him what I was feeling. I wanted to give him a reminder about what this was between us.

It was just that the words felt too heavy to say. Finally, I whispered, unable to look at him, "Whores don't get flowers."

The silence after I said it was thick. I braced myself, waiting for him to pull back, to realize what he was doing—to see me the way I really was.

It wasn't like my clients were waiting at the door, desperate to woo me. Fancy hotel rooms rented for the night under a pseudonym so that no one knew what they were up to didn't play well with romance.

But instead, he stepped closer, his face hardening with something I didn't expect. He shook his head slowly. "Don't," he said, his voice firm, almost like a warning. "Don't ever call yourself that again."

My throat tightened, the shame I tried to keep hidden now out in the open. I looked down, my fingers curling into fists at my sides. I didn't know how to explain it—how could I? It was the one thing I was certain about.

"You hired me, did you not? And just so we're clear, *hundreds* of other men have hired me too."

He flinched, and my teeth clenched.

"By definition, I think that makes me a whore."

Logan wasn't having it. He tipped my chin up so I had to meet his eyes, his touch gentle but determined. "I figured we'd have to have this conversation."

I tried to shake my head, but he didn't let me look away. "I hired you because you wouldn't go out with me. And the thought of anyone else touching you made me want to kill someone. This is my solution." His voice softened, but the intensity was still there. "But make no mistake, sweetheart, the last thing I think of you is that you're a whore. I'll get you flowers every week for the rest of our lives, just so you know who you are."

"And who's that?" I murmured, blinking up at him because it felt like I'd entered some surreal universe where beautiful boys turned out to be heroes instead of the object of my worst nightmares.

"Mine," he said simply.

I could feel his words breaking something inside me, something I didn't know was fragile until he touched it. I ripped my chin away from him and walked back into the room, my hands trembling as I clutched the roses and tried to ignore what he'd just said.

Because it was insane.

"How did you even find out . . . about me?" I asked softly, trying to ignore how it felt when he came up behind me, so close that with every breath, his chest brushed my back. "Did Tyler tell you? Because he's not supposed to do that."

"Tyler is an asshole," he mused.

I shook my head. Tyler was going to pay for breaking the rules—even more than what he'd already lost with his suspension.

I glanced around the hotel room and realized I didn't know what to do with the flowers. There didn't seem to be any vases floating around.

I stared at the roses again, my fingers clenching the stems a little too tight, and one of the thorns tore into my finger.

"Ouch," I huffed, staring down where a drop of crimson blood was dripping down my fingers.

Before I could even react, he was there, his larger hand gently but firmly capturing mine.

"Careful," he hummed, his voice low, almost hypnotic. His thumb brushed over my palm, sending an electric jolt up my arm.

"I'll survive," I said, my voice coming out softer than I intended. I tried to pull back, but he held on.

Tilting my hand toward him, he focused on the drop of blood that was sliding down my finger. His lips curled into a frown, one that sent a rush of heat straight to my cheeks. "You're bleeding," he said, like it was some kind of revelation.

"Just a scratch," I replied, my words stumbling over themselves. I tried to tug my hand free again, but he didn't let go.

His eyes flicked up to mine, something unreadable swirling in their green depths. Before I could process what was happening, he lifted my finger to his lips.

My breath caught as his tongue flicked over the cut, his mouth warm and soft as he pressed a kiss there, slow and deliberate. The sensation was startling, intimate, and entirely unexpected.

"Logan," I breathed, not sure if it was meant to be a protest or a plea. My heart was pounding, a wild, erratic rhythm that matched the heat crawling up my neck.

"Relax," he said, his voice a playful rumble. He licked his lips, smirking as if he'd just done something as casual as wiping ketchup off his chin. "Just making sure it doesn't get infected."

"You know that's not how first aid works, right?" I said, my voice shaking more than I wanted it to.

"It's how *my* first aid works," he countered, finally releasing my hand but not stepping back. His eyes lingered on me, his grin widening as I tried to shake off whatever spell he'd just cast. "And admit it, I'm better than a Band-Aid."

I pressed my hand against my chest, trying to steady my breathing as I glared at him. "You're crazy."

He shrugged, utterly unbothered. "Crazy for you."

"Stop saying that!" I snapped, but there was no heat in it. "That's not how anything works in the world."

He leaned closer, his grin morphing into something more wicked, more intoxicating. "How about this . . . I'll stop when it stops being true."

My cheeks burned, and I looked away, trying to gather my thoughts . . . but he seemed to be taking up all the space in my head lately.

The thorn? Barely a sting. His smirk, plus the sweet, ridiculous words coming out of his mouth?

Those were inflicting a wound far more dangerous.

I forced myself to back up, ignoring how amused he looked at my efforts. He was underestimating me if he thought I was going to fall into his arms after a few sweet words.

Had I experienced them before?

No.

Did I trust them?

Also no.

I fidgeted with the tight black dress I was wearing before I realized what I was doing, and I plastered my hands to my sides, trying to look unaffected. Even though I felt like flames were licking at my insides as we stared at each other.

"So . . . should we do this?" I asked stiffly, everything I'd ever learned about seduction going out the window. I didn't do this with clients . . . talk to them. But for some reason it felt completely wrong to just lead Logan to the bed and go from there.

Even though he was the first client I could ever remember actually *wanting*.

It was the flowers . . . and the words . . . and the whole finger-in-the-mouth thing. And the fact that he had the face and the body of a god.

He was messing everything up.

Logan prowled toward me again, his hand loosely gripping my neck as his thumb stroked along my pulse point.

"I'm going to take you on a date, Sloane," he said in a rasping, sexy voice that slid right down my spine.

"Why bother?" I whispered.

"I meant what I said . . . the fact that money is involved is only to make sure that no one else touches you while I make you fall in love with me."

He let my neck go before taking my hand and leading me toward the door like he'd simply complimented my dress.

I pulled on his hand, and we came to a stop at the door as he looked back at me questioningly.

"You're not actually serious about all this, right? This can't go on forever . . . and there will be other clients."

He didn't blink. "If another man touches you, I'll kill him."

The words slipped out like a fact, like it was the most normal thing in the world to say. Like he meant every single one of them.

I stared at him for a second and then burst out laughing, because this was ridiculous. "You're intense, I'll give you that. I can't tell if you're being dramatic or just trying to mess with me."

Abruptly, I was against his chest, his lips melding to mine, his tongue sliding in my mouth, licking and taking and sucking . . . like he really did own me.

I was breathless and shaking when our lips finally parted, but he only pulled a breath away.

"I've never been more serious about anything in my life, sweetheart," he murmured, and then he was whisking me out the door, to where I had no idea.

I only knew one thing as we walked down the hall, my hand clasped firmly in his.

Logan could ruin everything.

And I might be alright with that.

CHAPTER 13

SLOANE

The hotel valet barely had time to hand Logan the keys before he stepped in behind me, crowding the guy out so he had to step away. Logan's truck—a massive red behemoth that looked like it ate smaller cars for breakfast—idled at the curb. Logan opened the passenger door and motioned for me to get in.

"I've got it, thanks," Logan said to the valet, who was still hovering close by, his eyes on my ass.

I hesitated, my hand brushing the edge of the seat as Logan's hand appeared, firm but careful on my lower back, steadying me as I climbed in. It was unnecessary, but . . . nice. Too nice. It made my skin prickle.

"Is your leg okay?" I asked, realizing all this walking around might be hurting him.

"I'm good," he said with a sunny grin.

Once he was behind the wheel, Logan threw the truck into drive, and we were off. The city lights blurred by as he maneuvered through traffic with the confidence of someone who thought stop signs were suggestions. His hand rested casually on the steering wheel, but his eyes—those sharp, unrelenting, *beautiful* eyes—kept flicking to me every couple of seconds.

"So," he started, his voice light but probing. "Where are you from originally?"

"Here and there," I said, keeping my tone breezy, but also not wanting to talk about my childhood. At all.

"Hmmm." He shot me a grin, his teeth white and wicked. "Alright, Ms. Mysterious. Favorite food?"

"Depends on the day," I said.

"Okay. What about music?" he pressed. "What makes you sing in the shower?"

"Again, it depends."

"You're killing me here," he said with a laugh, tapping the steering wheel with his fingers. "Fine. What's your favorite thing to do when you're not busy?"

I opened my mouth to avoid the question . . . but my mouth had a different idea, apparently. "I paint," I mumbled, crossing my arms and leaning back in my seat because for some reason that admission felt as vulnerable as if I was standing in front of him naked.

"What kind of painting?" he asked . . . actually sounding interested. He was holding my hand again, his fingers intertwined with mine like he was trying to make sure I didn't run away.

"Oil and watercolor," I answered, shifting in my seat uncomfortably.

"Well, I can't wait to see something you've painted. We can hang them all over our house."

I scoffed, trying to ignore the utter panic that came with not only his words . . . but showing him something as personal as my paintings, and tried to pull my hand away. "You didn't just say that."

He grinned at me unrepentantly. "I'm going to say a lot of things like that. So prepare yourself."

"This is all part of your master plan to make me fall in love with you?" I asked sarcastically.

He laughed softly and winked before turning back to the road. "You're catching on, Calloway. Has it worked yet?"

I scoffed and tried to bite back a smile, but it came out anyway, like he had some kind of magic that could pull them out of me when no one else ever could.

We pulled into the valet of a fancy steakhouse, and my stomach grumbled. Steak happened to be my favorite food. Logan handed the keys off, but not before making sure the valet didn't look at me for too long. His hand found the small of my back again as he guided me through the entrance, his grip light but steady.

It almost seemed like he was proud to be seen with me.

That was strange. Not just strange . . . it was weird. I wasn't used to it—being walked into a place like this, in the open, no hesitation. Where was the catch? The order that I come in from the back? The rules about keeping my head down and not making eye contact?

The hockey game had been weird enough in that Tyler had been acknowledging me in public . . . but this felt different. This felt like more . . .

As we entered, heads turned, and I shifted uncomfortably. But they weren't looking at me. They were looking at *him*.

And I didn't blame them. Logan was a sight to behold. Even if he hadn't been an up-and-coming sports star, there was something about him—a magnetism that was hard to look away from.

He glanced down at me, a small smile on his lips. I wanted to lash out, to tell him to stop staring at me like that—like I was the center of his universe. I could feel it radiating off him, that quiet pride, and it made my stomach twist.

The hostess greeted him with a bright smile, one that faded as she watched him let go of my hand and instead wrap his arm around my waist so I was glued to his side. Logan gave her our reservation name, and then he kept me close as we were led through the maze of tables to our seat near the window that looked out on the whole city.

"Do you like it here?" he asked once we were settled. His voice was soft, uncertain, like he cared way too much about the answer.

"It's good," I said, trying to sound casual.

His brow furrowed, and he leaned forward, elbows on the table. "Good? That sounds like 'fine.' We can go somewhere else if you don't like it. Seriously. I just guessed, but I should have asked. You probably don't even like steak. Fuck."

I blinked at him, thrown by how earnest he was. "It's fine, I promise," I said, more firmly this time.

"Fine isn't good enough," he said, almost pouting. "We'll go somewhere else. What do you like? Italian? Sushi? We can get tacos. Do you like tacos? Ari has this one taco place that he drags us to all the time."

I stared at him, trying to reconcile the big, intense guy who just moments ago was smirking like he ruled the world with the one now babbling about tacos like a golden retriever desperate to please.

"It's perfect," I said, my voice soft because the bastard was ripping through my defenses like they were made of paper. "I like it here. Steak is my favorite."

His grin instantly returned, bright and easy. "You just told me something else about you." He did a fist pump in the air, and a small giggle escaped my lips.

"Fuck, that's my new favorite sound."

I blushed at the look in his eyes.

And for a second, I forgot how strange this all was. I forgot the rules, the walls . . . the constant need to be on guard. In that moment, with his eyes shining as he stared at me like he'd found everything he'd been looking for in life, it felt like maybe, just maybe, this wasn't a trap.

But then again, in my experience, things that felt too good to be true always were.

Dinner with Logan was going perfectly. I could barely eat because I was so caught up in listening to him, in looking at him . . . in just being with him.

He was smiling across the table, saying something about the game, and I caught myself smiling back.

"Sorry, I have to use the restroom," he said a few minutes later, a slight blush to his cheeks, like he was embarrassed.

It was adorable.

"I'll be right back." He slid out of the booth before turning back to me. "Please don't leave."

"I won't," I murmured, surprised at how much I meant those two words.

"Good," he said, a hint of that cockiness leaking into his voice. "Because I *would* find you."

With those . . . interesting . . . words, he headed to the hall with the bathrooms.

The second he was out of sight, I felt it—a shift in the air. My stomach tightened, and before I could even look around, I heard a voice that I dreaded.

"Sloane Calloway. If it isn't my lucky day."

The voice sent a cold shiver down my spine. I didn't have to look to know who it was—Charles Spiker. A rich financier . . . and one of my regulars. My stomach rolled at the memory of the last time I'd seen him, his old, shriveled dick down my throat as he pounded into me.

I hadn't been able to swallow normally for a week.

I forced myself to glance up, and there he was.

Charles's hair was steel gray, combed back with too much product, because he thought it made him look distinguished. The navy suit he wore was expensive, but even the finest craftsmanship couldn't disguise the paunch straining against the buttons of his shirt or the way the fabric pulled awkwardly over his midsection.

His eyes—small, watery, and too close together—raked over me with a lecherous intensity that made my skin crawl. His gaze lingered far too long, his lips curling into a smile that was more predatory than polite. There was a shine on his forehead, the kind that spoke of too many martinis and too little shame, and his cologne was heavy enough to choke a horse.

"Charles," I said quietly, my voice steady. It had disappeared, that glittery, light feeling I'd been experiencing only moments before. The familiar numbness was seeping back into me.

He looked me up and down, his eyes lingering on my breasts.

I wanted to disappear.

"You look stunning, as always," he said, leaning in slightly, his voice dropping to a whisper. "I'll be contacting you soon for a little . . . *meetup*. I know how much you enjoyed last time."

His words dripped with suggestion, and I felt like I'd been punched. My throat tightened, and the best I could do was muster up a blank look as a wave of disgust washed over me. Why men like him pretended they were doing *me* a favor by fucking me—I'd never understand.

They were all unequivocally terrible in bed.

It was a good reminder, though. *This* was my life. Whatever Logan said, whatever Logan did . . . it wasn't real.

I had a stained soul. I'd traded it at eighteen.

You didn't come back from that.

I'd never be clean again.

Charles chuckled softly when I didn't respond, his gaze flickering over my shoulder as he straightened up. "You can try to pretend you're something else tonight, but we both know the truth, don't we?" He smirked, and with one final look, he turned and walked away.

I exhaled shakily, my heart pounding. A bead of sweat slid down my forehead, and I hastily wiped it away, wishing there was a way to wipe away my worthlessness at the same time.

Logan returned a few minutes later, sliding back into his seat with that easy smile. "You didn't leave." He sounded relieved, and once again I had an insane urge. I wanted to pick up my mashed potatoes and throw them at him, because there was no way he was for real.

You shouldn't play cruel jokes on people who are already broken.

It never went well.

I tried to smile, but my face felt stiff. "Yep. Still here." And as an afterthought, I added, "What you're *paying* me for."

He frowned at that, his eyes flicking to where Charles had been standing moments ago. "Who was that?"

My gaze dropped to the table. He'd seen.

My stomach knotted, and I felt the heat of shame crawl up my neck. "No one," I finally muttered, picking up my glass of water, hoping the cool liquid would calm down whatever was happening inside me.

Logan didn't press it, but the magic that had been there before he left was gone. The rest of the dinner felt strained, the conversation awkward and stilted. Logan tried to pull me back into the moment, asking questions, making light jokes, but I couldn't focus. I was too in my head, too wrapped up in this familiar, sick feeling.

Logan noticed. I could see it in the way his smile faded, the way his eyes darkened with concern, but he didn't push. He didn't ask again. He just watched me, and the weight of his gaze made me feel even worse.

By the time dessert came, I was barely touching my food, my thoughts spinning in a thousand directions. I felt like I was slipping, like the ground was crumbling beneath me, and no matter how hard I tried to hold on, it wasn't enough.

I was never going to be enough.

Logan

The second I saw him standing at the table and the scary blankness on Sloane's face as she looked at him, I'd known something was wrong.

I didn't have to be a genius to guess what had happened. She'd had a run-in with a former client . . . I said *former* because, obviously, he was never going to be a client again.

Dallas was huge, but Charles Spiker was a known entity around town. His law firm was actually one of the sponsors for the team.

And I was about to ruin him.

I texted Lincoln's PI on the way to the table.

Charles Spiker. Find me something on him. Anything.

I sat back down at the table, trying to cajole Sloane out of the shell she'd crawled into, but her walls were up. All the easy conversation from before I'd gone to the restroom was gone.

I cursed my bladder.

And then my phone buzzed.

Spiker's dirty. Skimming from his law firm. Offshore account in the Bahamas. I'll send you the details.

I stared at the message, a small grin spreading across my face.

Sloane was picking at her apple crumble when Spiker finally got up from his table, a cocky swagger in his walk as he headed toward the restroom.

"I'll be right back," I told her, remembering to shoot her a reassuring smile before I left the table.

Not that she was looking at me.

I followed Spiker into the bathroom, my pulse steady but the rage simmering underneath as I clicked the lock closed on the door.

He was at the sink, adjusting his cuff links. I glanced at the stalls, making sure we were alone before I came up behind him. He caught my reflection in the mirror, and his eyes widened.

"Logan York? Well, I'll be. Heck of a game the other night—"

That was the last thing he said before I grabbed him by the back of the neck and slammed his face into the mirror. The glass cracked with the impact, shards splintering across the sink as he let out a strangled grunt. Before he could react, I shoved him toward the nearest stall, his body crashing against the door.

"What the hell—" he cried in a garbled voice.

I didn't answer. I kicked the stall door open and slammed him into the toilet, forcing his head down into the water with a sickening splash. He struggled, thrashing under my grip, but I kept him down, his hands slipping on the slick porcelain as he tried to push back. His muffled shouts echoed in the stall, but I didn't let up.

"You made a mistake tonight, Spiker. Coming near what's mine," I growled as I lifted his head for a second, enjoying his gasping breaths before I forced his head deeper, his feet kicking uselessly against the floor.

He gurgled, trying to scream, but it only came out in choked gasps as water filled his mouth. I yanked him up by his hair, his face dripping and pale, gasping for air like a fish out of water.

"You don't get to touch her. You don't even get to *look* at her," I hissed, my fingers tightening in his hair before slamming his head into the side of the stall again. His skull made a dull, wet thud as he cried out, his body slumping against the toilet.

"Fucking hell!" He coughed, blood running down his face now, mixing with the water. "You're insane!"

"You haven't seen anything yet," I snapped, pulling him back up. His hand scrambled against my arm, trying to stop me, but I grabbed it, twisting it behind him. His scream ripped through the small space, sharp and desperate.

"Please," he cried. "What do you want?"

I smiled darkly. "I already have everything I need. You've been skimming money from your partners. Offshore accounts. You've got some dirty little secrets, don't you, Charles?"

His eyes widened, real fear creeping in. "I—what—how do you—"

I slammed his hand into the toilet tank, the bone crunching under the pressure as he screamed again. "13948209. That's your account in the Bahamas, right?"

His face went white as a sheet, blood pooling from his nose, his eyes wild with panic. "Fuck," he moaned, clutching his broken hand to his chest. "How do you know about that?"

"I know everything." I crouched down, gripping his hair again, pulling his face up to meet mine. "Now, here's how this is going to go. You're going to forget Sloane. You're going to pretend she doesn't exist. If you ever talk to her again, or even think about her, I'll make sure your little law buddies know *exactly* what you've been doing. I'll blow up your entire life, and you'll be finished. Got it?"

He whimpered, tears mixing with the blood on his face. "Okay," he gasped. "Okay, I'll—I'll leave her alone. Please, just—stop."

I let go of his hair, standing up and looking down at the pathetic mess of him crumpled on the bathroom floor. "You don't get another warning. You come near her again, and you'll lose more than your hand. I'll take everything from you."

He didn't respond, just rocked back and forth on the floor, cradling his broken hand, his face twisted in pain and terror. I stepped over him, my jaw tight, my fists still clenched.

"And the same thing goes if you say anything about this to anyone. Clean yourself up and leave out the fire exit."

"Okay. I promise. Please," he cried, looking nothing like the smug asshole he'd been just minutes earlier.

I washed my hands and then walked out of the bathroom, the sounds of his whimpers fading behind me.

Sloane finally looked up at me when I got to the table . . . and then her eyes widened. "Are you alright? There's blood on your shirt."

Oops.

I glanced down and saw that some of Charles's nasty blood had splattered onto my shirt. I'd have to burn it later.

"Just a hangnail," I told her reassuringly, holding my finger up for a second before I quickly put it under the table so she couldn't look closer. "Are you going to eat any more of that?" I nodded at the still-full bowl of dessert.

"I'm full," she lied, biting down on her plump, red lipstick–stained lower lip. "But everything was delicious," she quickly added, like she didn't want me to think she was ungrateful.

"I'll get it boxed up, and you can have it later," I told her, watching as her eyes softened for a moment at my gesture.

After I paid, I grabbed her hand again and started leading her out of the restaurant. She tried to pull her hand away, but I wasn't having any of that. As we passed the table where Charles's companions were—and he wasn't there—her shoulders relaxed.

What a fucker. I should have drowned him in that toilet. The only consolation I had was not only were his hand and nose broken . . . but there'd been urine in the toilet water I'd dunked him in.

Disgusting . . . but excellent.

"What's your address?" I asked her when we got back into the truck.

"What?" she asked, looking adorably confused. "We're not going back to the hotel?"

"It's our first date. I'm going to take you to your front door and kiss you again. Then I'm going to leave. It's a Circle of Trust policy to not sleep with someone on a first date."

A complete lie. But it *was* a policy for me tonight.

She gaped at me and blinked a few times before she had a response. "What's a Circle of Trust?"

I shook my head as I pulled away from the curb. "You have so much to learn," I said dramatically.

Her answering giggle was everything I could hope for.

The drive was quiet after she gave me her address, and I could tell by the pensive way she was staring out the window that she was deep in thought. We got to her very nice condominium complex, and I got out and walked around to open her door.

"You don't have to walk me up," she told me quickly, and I took the opportunity to smooth a piece of hair behind her ear . . . and then quickly kissed her.

"This is how first dates work, Calloway," I told her, and she may or may not have swooned from me saying that.

Sloane obviously needed love; every little thing I did, she soaked up like she was a dying, dry land getting its first drop of rain. I couldn't wait to give her everything she wanted and more.

I grabbed her hand as we walked into the high-rise, my dick hardening at the shy, wondrous look she gave me.

"You're beautiful," I said, the words blurting out of me because in that moment, I was more confident than ever that there wasn't a more stunning creature on the planet.

Sloane yanked her gaze away, concentrating on her fancy lobby like her life depended on it. "There you go again," she whispered. "Acting crazy."

I grinned and kissed the top of her head. "Get used to it."

We got into the elevator, and Sloane punched in a code to get up to her floor—which I, of course, memorized—and the doors opened up into a condo that screamed money. Sleek lines, marble countertops, and floor-to-ceiling windows that framed a killer view of the city. But amid the magazine-perfect décor, I soaked in the few little personal touches. There was a cozy throw blanket draped over the pristine leather couch and a stack of well-worn books on the coffee table. Glancing around, I spotted a small collection of framed photos on a shelf—most of them black-and-white shots of places around the world, but there was one of a little girl, grinning wide and holding a puppy in her arms.

"Nice place," I told her, genuinely meaning it. She had taste—even if I didn't want to think about how she had so much money.

I pretended to look around. "Any pets? Roommates?"

"It's just me," she said with a shrug that I could see right through. My girl was lonely.

"Are you sure you don't want to come in?" she asked.

I wanted to . . . more than anything, actually. I wanted to walk around this whole place and learn all I could about her. But I was trying to prove a point tonight—that I was in this for more than sex.

So I was going to have to pass.

The fact that I would be coming back tonight after she'd fallen asleep wasn't something we needed to discuss.

"Not tonight, baby," I told her.

"Ah yes, still holding to that little rule of yours."

"Yes." I grinned. "I'm very proper about these things."

She snorted, shaking her head. "How are second dates, though? What are your rules for that?"

I pretended to think it over. "Only one rule for that one, really," I told her.

"And what is that?"

"That they happen tomorrow, any free second we have."

Her eyes widened, and her cheeks flushed. "That's quite the rule."

"No games between us," I told her as I pulled her close and brushed a soft kiss against her lips.

"No games," she whispered, staring at me with that same wide-eyed disbelief she'd had the entire night.

"Give me your phone," I told her in a rough voice, because I was so turned on, it was hard to talk . . . or think. And I really needed to get this last thing done.

"What? Why?" she asked, her eyes a little dazed as we separated.

"I'm going to put my number in your phone and text myself so I have your number."

"Oh right," she said, pulling out her phone and handing it to me after she punched in her code. That was a good sign, she was much more trusting than I thought she'd be. I was starting to wear her down. "I'm sorry about this . . ."

"About what?" I asked as I quickly pulled up the app Ari had sent me that I could use to track her phone.

"Being so awkward. I'm not usually like this," she told me, wringing her hands in front of her nervously as she searched my face. "It's just—"

"What, baby?"

"This is a first for me—dating. Even if it's not really dating because you're paying . . ." She was rambling, and it was adorable.

I typed in my number and saved it as *Boyfriend* before texting myself. "It's definitely a date," I corrected her after I finished. "And this 'situation' between us . . . is only going to be temporary. You're going to fall in love with me. It's only a matter of time," I told her with a smirk. "I always get what I want. It's a trademark of mine."

She scoffed, and I watched as a dark thought flitted through her head and the humor in her eyes faded.

"It won't happen this time, Logan," she whispered in a solemn, devastated voice. "I promise I'm something you won't win."

I brought her close again and tipped up her chin so she had to look at me. "Why not, Sloane? Why *not* give me a chance?"

Sloane searched my face, her deep blue eyes glistening with emotion.

"I made a vow to myself that someday, no one was ever going to control me," she said. "That someday, *I* would be the captain of my own destiny." Her lower lip quivered, and my hands squeezed at my sides knowing that she needed to get this out. "So you might be the most beautiful man that I've ever seen. And you might say the prettiest words I've ever heard come out of a guy's mouth." She brushed a piece of hair out of her face and straightened her shoulders. I could see the decision in her eyes before the words had even come out of her red-stained lips. "What I'm trying to say . . . is that I may give you my body. I may be the best fuck you've ever had in your life. You might even start to think that you're in love with me.

But that would be a mistake, Logan York." She paused, her tongue peeking out to slowly lick her bottom lip. "Because I'm never going to give you my heart. That would just be another form of controlling me. And I could never do that."

I stared at her for a second, a slow grin sliding across my lips. I leaned forward and pressed a hard, long kiss on her mouth, not pulling back until her skin was flushed and her breath was coming out in gasps. "We'll see about that."

With that promise, I headed toward the elevators. "See you tomorrow," I told her as I stepped through the doors and winked as they began to close.

My last glimpse of her was her shell-shocked face.

At least until the elevator was descending and I could pull up the app on my phone. *Then* I was able to look at her through the camera as she stood there, holding the phone in her hand and staring at the doors.

I kept the app up for the entire drive back to my place, listening as she watched TV and then got ready for bed.

Later, I listened to her breathing as I drove back to her building after I was sure she'd fallen asleep.

I parked the truck a block away from Sloane's place, cutting the engine and leaning back in the seat. The neighborhood was quiet, the kind of silence that comes late at night when the world's finally asleep.

Turning the volume up on my phone, I listened to the reassuring sound of her sleeping. I'd gotten lucky that she slept with the phone by her bed.

But I'd always been a lucky kind of guy.

I glanced at the clock on the dash—just past midnight.

An hour passed, and I stared at the streetlights casting long shadows across the pavement. My knuckles still throbbed from the encounter with Charles, and so did my knee, and I absently opened and closed my fist, trying to work the soreness out as I waited to ensure Sloane was into the *deep sleep* part of her night.

When I was sure enough time had passed, I stepped out of the truck and headed toward the doors. They were locked. *Fuck.* I hadn't thought about that. I glanced around, spotting a keypad next to the glass, and I held my breath as I typed in her elevator code.

The door clicked open, and I grinned. Perfect—although I'd have to talk to her about increasing her safety measures after we were officially together. Getting into her place should not be this easy.

I made my way to the elevator and typed in her code again, anxious adrenaline throbbing through my veins.

Like always.

Fun fact, Asher and I had been hellions growing up, and something we liked to do—break into places for the fun of it. There'd been an asshole in our high school, Peter, who we both despised. We'd spent a summer sneaking into his house and leaving things in his room to scare him—like dead birds—and we'd never gotten caught.

I hadn't done anything like that in a long time, but years of breaking and entering were certainly coming in handy right now.

The elevator doors opened to her dark condo, the only light coming from the soft glow of the outside city lights filtering through the windows.

For a moment, I just stood there in the entry, listening. I could hear the hum of the fridge, the occasional creak of the building settling. But no movement. No sound from anywhere else.

After a few more minutes, I began moving through the living room quietly, my steps careful and controlled. I probably should have asked for a tour before doing this so I knew where everything was, but I'd had to make a point with her—that I wanted this for the long term, not just for the night.

Coming inside and inevitably ending up in bed would have been the opposite of that.

Although it would have been very useful right now.

A quick glance through the first door in the hallway and I saw a home gym. The second room was completely empty. The third room . . . jackpot.

Peeking through the cracked door, I saw Sloane, seemingly fast asleep, her body curled under the blanket, her breathing gentle and steady. The soft light from the windows illuminated her just enough to outline her features, casting delicate shadows across her face.

Fuck. She looked ethereal right now. Without much light, her hair was a cascade of dark silk, spilling out over the pillow, framing features that seemed almost too perfect to be real—sharp cheekbones, long lashes that rested lightly on her cheeks, and lips slightly parted, like she was waiting to be kissed. The faint rise and fall of her chest gave her an almost fragile serenity. I cocked my head, still studying her. It was an interesting thing that even in sleep, there was something untouchable about her, like she belonged to another world entirely.

Tiptoeing across the room, I made my way to a chair in the corner and sat down. I leaned back, my eyes locked on her sleeping form.

There was something calming about watching her like this, something that made the rest of the world fall away. She looked so vulnerable, so delicate, and it only fueled the possessiveness in me.

I didn't move. I just sat there, watching her breathe, listening to the soft rise and fall of her chest . . . trying to make excuses for why I'd turned into a raging psychopath since I'd seen her.

Was that what love was? Absolute lunacy, where nothing you did made sense? It would explain why my parents had been such a miserable mess—my mom had married my dad for money, and my dad had married her because she was pregnant. If they'd loved each other, everything would have been different.

What I was feeling didn't feel like love, though. It felt darker. It was a need thrumming through my insides, blocking out all rational thought. It was a need to own her, to devour her, to carve her into my skin . . .

Into my soul, maybe.

My dick was throbbing in my jeans, and the more I stared at her . . . the harder it got.

Until I came, right there in my pants. A low groan seeped out of my mouth as pleasure licked across my skin.

Fuck.

Sloane whimpered as she stirred, and I tensed, prepared to throw myself onto the floor if her eyes opened.

A minute later, though, her breath evened out, and I could sit back in the chair.

I kept watching her.

My pants would dry, but everything else about me was never going to be the same.

Sloane Calloway was mine.

CHAPTER 14

SLOANE

There was a small smile on my face the next morning as I hovered in front of the group home that I volunteered at. There had been a text waiting for me from Logan when I'd woken up. I'd been confused at first because he'd put his number in under *Boyfriend*, but I'd quickly changed that.

And the texts had continued from there.

He asked me question after question, and unlike when I was looking him in the eye . . . it was much easier for me to answer him over the phone.

I smiled as one more came in.

> **Logan:** Favorite dessert?

> **Me:** That's easy. Apple crumble.

> **Logan:** So boxing that up last night wasn't a complete miss.

> **Me:** Not at all. I ate it for breakfast this morning.

> **Logan:** Ten gold stars for me!

> **Me:** If I had gold stars, you would definitely get them.

Logan: We should decide our reward system right now so it doesn't get confusing.

Me: Do we have to have a reward system?

Logan: I like tangible awards for my achievements.

Me: And imaginary gold stars are tangible?

Logan: . . .

Logan: Good point. I'll go back to the drawing board.

Me: I can think of things I could reward you with.

Logan: Miss Calloway . . . it almost seems like you're flirting with me.

I grinned, my cheeks flushing like he was there in front of me. I was definitely flirting with him. And I never did that.

Me: . . .

Logan: Ten gold stars for you.

I closed my eyes, trying to steel myself against his charm. This wasn't something I could lose on. I'd thought that my disastrous choice on my eighteenth birthday had destroyed any part of me that had the capacity to feel.

But all of Logan's attention was teaching me that somehow . . . there was something inside me still fragile enough to be broken. Some part of me that was still dreaming of a happily-ever-after . . .

And that was something I could not deal with. Because when Logan was done with me . . .

I pocketed my phone, ignoring the next time it buzzed as I walked inside the building.

I had a love/hate relationship with this place. I loved hanging out with the children, but I hated all the memories it dug up. How different would my life have been if Everett had never shown up that day? In that imaginary life, maybe I could have deserved someone like Logan York.

These kids also deserved better than me, but unfortunately, there just weren't a lot of people out there who cared.

So I guess I was better than nothing.

The group home was always bustling with noise—kids shouting, laughing, crying—chaos everywhere. But Rome? He was different. Every time I walked through the door, I'd find him in the same spot, in the corner of the room, his tiny body folded up into itself, head down, as if he was trying to disappear.

I knew that feeling.

The sponsors of the place kept it clean, but there was still a worn-down look to it. The walls were painted bright yellow, chipped in places where tiny hands had pulled at the cracks. Toys were scattered around, some new, others with pieces missing. The air always smelled faintly of crayons and disinfectant. There was a warmth to it, a sense of care, but there was also an underlying heaviness, the weight of too many kids with too many stories not many people wanted to hear.

The first time I'd seen Rome, something had pulled me toward him. He was just sitting there, head tucked down, not speaking, not even looking at anyone. His pale blond hair fell over his face, hiding those big, sad eyes I knew were there. He was a visible representation of how I'd felt growing up—the raw loneliness, that silence that came from losing too much too soon.

Reaching into my purse, I pulled out a box of crayons and a coloring book that I had brought with me. He didn't move as I made my way over, sitting down next to him on the floor. He just stayed curled up like I wasn't even there.

"Hey, Rome," I said softly, grabbing a crayon, careful not to push him. "Want to color with me?"

At first, he didn't respond. He didn't even look at me. But I was used to that. I picked a page and started coloring, letting the quiet stretch between us. I wasn't here to force him out of his shell. I knew that wouldn't work. You couldn't rush these things. I had to wait for him to come to me.

Minutes passed in silence; the only sound was the soft scratch of crayon across paper. I kept coloring, filling in the lines with bright blues and yellows. Slowly, his head lifted, just a fraction, his eyes peeking through his hair.

Rome didn't say anything, but he reached out and grabbed an orange crayon.

I smiled, keeping my gaze on the coloring book. "That's a good color. There's far too much blue and yellow on this page."

He gave a small nod, and I felt like crying, just like I did every time when he began to open up.

We colored for a while, his small hand moving carefully over the paper. Still silent, but he was *there* with me, and that was something.

After a few pages, he dropped his crayon, taking a deep breath before he asked, "How long did it take for you not to miss your mom anymore?"

I fumbled with the crayon in my hand, caught off guard at his question, and that he'd remembered me telling him when I'd first met him that my mom had died too.

One of the employees had told me the first day I'd come that Rome had been in a car crash two years ago. His parents had both died, but he had survived. He'd been badly abused at the foster home he was put into, though, and he'd been at this place ever since while they tried to help him.

Rome was still staring at the coloring book, but his hand had stilled while he waited for an answer.

The answer was complicated, and I tried to think about how I could explain it to a six-year-old.

"I don't think you ever stop missing your mom," I said softly, wishing I had a different answer for him.

But it was the truth.

Even though I'd watched my mother fade away with her addiction . . . and then cancer . . . I still didn't stop missing her. Or at least the idea of her. I think no matter how awful your parents are, every child carries that dream of who they wish their parents could be. Sometimes missing them . . . actually means missing that dream.

If I could have figured out a way to not miss my mother, I would have done it by now, though.

Rome peeked up at me through the strands of hair that had fallen into his face. "So I'm always going to be sad?" he asked miserably, tears starting to gather in his eyes.

I wanted to cry just looking at him. If I knew he wouldn't freak out, I would have pulled him into my arms. Rome needed a big hug.

"Not always. It will just be little moments when you're doing something and you wish she was there," I whispered to him, unable to stop myself from at least reaching over and touching his hand. "But most of the time, you'll be really happy. Because you have such a good life. And because she would want you to be."

It felt like I was lying to him, but I *wanted* it to be true. It hadn't been true for me, but maybe it could be for him.

"You really think so?" he whispered, his voice small, fragile.

I nodded, my heart aching at the hope in his voice. "Yeah, Rome. I do."

He stayed quiet for a moment, his fingers gripping the crayon a little tighter. Then, barely above a whisper, he said, "I hope you're right."

My chest tightened, and I swallowed hard, unable to say anything else because my voice was too choked up.

For a long time, neither of us spoke again. He went back to coloring, and I watched him, my heart heavy. But then, slowly, he scooted a little closer to me, his shoulder brushing mine as he worked on filling in a truck with orange.

My hand shook as I tried to resume coloring. This was why I came here every week when I wasn't working. For moments like this, where it felt like maybe . . . I'd made a difference.

I smiled down at him, watching as he concentrated on the picture, and for the first time, I saw a little light in his eyes. It wasn't much, but it was a start. And I'd keep coming back, again and again, until that light grew.

"Want to color another one after this?" I asked, my voice soft.

He nodded, and this time, his eyes met mine with the smallest hint of a smile.

Later, I was packing up the crayons, putting them back in their box, when one of the staff members—Vicky, I think her name was—walked up beside me, smiling. "You're really good with him, you know," she said, nodding toward Rome, who was still quietly coloring at the table.

I glanced at him, a small, warm flicker lighting up in my chest as I watched him still focused on his drawing. But it faded as quickly as it came when Vicky added, "You'll make a great mom someday."

The words hit me harder than they should've. I froze for a split second, my heart stuttering in my chest, but I forced a smile, something practiced and easy, as I turned back to her. "Thanks," I said, my voice calm and steady.

But inside, I flinched.

The smile felt like a mask, stretched too tight, too forced. A good mom? No. That wasn't in the cards for me. It would never be in the cards for me. Not after everything that had been done to me, after everything I'd survived. My body was a battlefield, scarred and ruined in ways no one could see, in ways I couldn't fix.

A rush of memories hit me at once.

My hands were shaking as I stared at the test in front of me, two pink lines on it that stared back at me like a cruel joke. I'd been careful—as careful as I could be in this job, but it hadn't mattered. None of it mattered.

I was pregnant.

I didn't have time to figure out what to do next. Everett found the test in the trash the next morning. He didn't say anything at first. He just stood there, holding it up with two fingers, his face cold and unreadable.

"Who?" he asked, his voice like ice. Somehow he seemed to think that this wasn't a client's child. That I'd broken the rules.

I couldn't answer to defend myself, though. My throat felt like it had closed up, my entire body shaking with fear.

"Who?" he asked again, louder this time.

I still couldn't speak, the words lodged in my throat, suffocating me.

His face twisted in disgust as he threw the test across the room.

Before I could even react, he grabbed my arm, dragging me out of the house and into his car. The ride was silent, but the tension in the air was suffocating. I wanted to ask where we were going, but I was too scared. And . . . I already knew.

We pulled up to a run-down building on the edge of town, the windows dirty and the paint peeling. It didn't look like a clinic. It looked like a place people went to disappear.

Everett led me inside as if he was taking me to the mall. "This is for your own good," he said, his voice low and soothing. "I won't have you ruined because of your carelessness."

And then I was in a back room, where a man in a lab coat waited, the stench of antiseptic thick in the air.

"Take care of it," Everett had told him, his voice cold and indifferent.

The doctor didn't ask any questions. He just nodded, motioning for me to get on the table. The room spun as I lay down, my body shaking, my heart pounding in my ears. I wanted to scream, to run, but I couldn't. I was trapped. I was put under a light sedation, and then the room seemed to float around me.

The procedure was quick and impersonal. Afterward, I clenched my fists so hard that my nails dug into my palms, trying to focus on anything but the pain. But there was no escaping it. There was no escaping any of it.

"Ready to go?" Everett asked in a bland, pleasant voice as he came in an hour later. "You'll feel better once you get back home."

I couldn't move. I couldn't speak. I just lay there, staring at the ceiling, tears streaming down my face, wishing I could disappear.

I blinked as I came back to the present, bile filling my mouth as I fought the urge to throw up.

Vicky didn't notice the shift. She kept smiling, like she'd paid me the nicest compliment in the world and didn't even realize the wreckage she'd stirred up inside me. "It's not easy to get Rome to open up, but you've got a way with him. Kids need that. They need someone who gets them, someone patient."

I nodded, the fake smile still plastered on my face, but every word felt like it was driving a knife deeper.

As soon as she walked away, I let out a breath I didn't realize I was holding, my chest tightening as the mask slipped away. I pressed my palms to the table, grounding myself, trying to push down the familiar ache. It never got easier.

I straightened up, glancing over at Rome again. He looked up at me, his eyes brightening for a second, and the ache dulled just a little. This—this was enough. I didn't need more.

I couldn't have more.

I didn't deserve it.

CHAPTER 15

LOGAN

was sitting in my truck, trying to delay meeting up with my dad, when my phone buzzed. I grinned when I saw it was from Ari. I could spare a few more minutes.

Ari: Treachery, betrayal, a knife in the heart.

Lincoln: Someone give Lancaster a cookie.

Ari: Sarcasm? That's what you give me when I come to you with those words.

Camden: Is this a SOS type of situation. Or a summer ombre sausages kind of thing.

I snorted, shaking my head.

Me: Good one, Grandpappy.

Camden: . . .

Ari: As I was saying . . .

Ari: Wait, why hasn't Disney responded. We need his simpage.

Camden: Well, you're not Lincoln . . . so I'm not sure how much simpage there would be.

Lincoln: Excellent point, Hero.

Ari Lancaster removed Camden James from the chat.

This was my time to shine.

Logan York added Camden James to the chat.

Ari: Shame. Shame. Shame.

Walker: You've been watching Bridgerton again, haven't you?

Ari: Oh, now you show up.

Lincoln: We're all waiting with bated breath for what you have to tell us.

Ari: Oh, yes. THE TREACHERY!

Ari: I posted a thirst trap for Blake Baby-cakes Lancaster.

Walker: As one does.

Ari: . . .

Camden: And . . .

Ari: I'm never going to be able to finish this story if you keep interrupting me.

Camden: I was trying to act engaged.

Lincoln: A man above men, Hero.

Me: I feel like you're interrupting yourself here, Lancaster.

I found myself blocked for that one.
I stared at the phone, waiting for someone to let me back in.
I waited . . .
And I waited . . .
After fifteen fucking minutes, Camden added me back into the chat.

Me: That was cruel and unusual punishment, gentlemen.

Ari: The fact that you're back in here is cruel and unusual punishment, actually.

Me: . . .

Camden: Excellent use of that, Rookie.

I preened at the compliment.

Me: Thank you.

Ari: . . .

Ari: As I was saying . . .

Me: You still haven't told us. What have you been doing?

Ari: My finger is on the remove key . . . don't make me do it, Rookie.

Walker: My child is going to be two before this conversation goes anywhere.

I scrolled back through the messages, trying to see if I had actually missed something. But it was mostly just pictures of Disney's daughter, Isabella, the cutest child on Earth, that had somehow entered the chat. A worthy distraction.

> Ari: I posted a thirst trap. DO NOT RESPOND TO THIS UNTIL I'M DONE SPEAKING.

> Ari: And that's when I realized . . .

A minute passed, and it hit me that I was still staring at my phone in anticipation of what he was going to say.

> Lincoln: Please tell me Blake didn't give you the look right in the middle of the story.

> Ari: Oh, are you still there?

> Walker: . . .

> Me: Keeping us on our toes, Lancaster. I like it.

> Camden: Why can I picture him preening right now?

> Ari: Because that's what he's literally doing (this is Blake btw).

> Walker: Snort.

> Ari: Sorry for that interruption. Can't believe my wife did me dirty like that. Although she's a baby angel face, and I love everything about her.

> Ari: Of note, Disney, that was unladylike.

> Me: OMG. JUST TELL US THE STORY.

> Ari: So shouty, Rookie.

Lincoln: . . .

Ari: As I was saying. I posted my thirst trap. Waited for all of you to like it.

Ari: And that's when I saw it.

Lincoln: I swear if you drag this out again . . .

Ari: I would never.

Ari: Geraldine is following all of you. ALL OF YOU.

Ari: But not me.

Ari: I'm distraught. Destroyed. Hanging on the edge of the cliff.

Lincoln: . . .

Camden: . . .

Walker: . . .

Me: Shame! Shame! Shame!

Ari Lancaster removed Logan York from the chat.

I snorted and shook my head, feeling considerably better about life, even though I still hated what I was about to do. I took a deep breath and got out of the truck.

My good mood evaporated with every step I took.

Why was I doing this? That was the question of the day. When I could be stalking my new obsession, I was meeting up with the man who hadn't deigned to come watch me play in my first Stanley Cup until the *fourth* game.

But only because he had a media event he'd been invited to.

There'd been no excuses for why he'd missed the others, no apologetic phone calls or texts. I was positive he hadn't even watched the games on TV—judging by the fact that he hadn't called to chew me out about my performance after that first game.

So again, why was I doing this?

Probably because for some reason the inner kid inside me was still waiting for the day when my only living relative woke up . . . and thought I was worth something.

Pathetic.

On that note . . .

I walked into the bar, the familiar pit in my stomach tightening with each step. There he was right in the middle of it all, holding court like a king surrounded by his loyal subjects. The laughter around him was too loud, too eager, like everyone was auditioning for his approval.

And they probably were. He thrived on that.

Unlike me, who wanted to be surrounded by people I could respect and who I wanted to be like someday, a "circle of trust," so to speak. My father preferred his crowd to be the kind that tripped over themselves just to suck up to him—more like hyenas than anything else. The kind who'd laugh a little too hard at his jokes and nod a little too quickly at whatever stupid thing he decided to throw their way. His taste in friends was as deep as his taste in women. Hence his three divorces since my mom had left us.

He still looked good, though. A close reflection of the NFL star he'd been. Grant York kept himself up like he had something to prove, and even in this bar he was wearing a lean, polished suit, and his hair was perfectly styled. His smile flashed, all teeth and charm, and the group around him ate it up like they were starving for it. But I'd seen that smile too many times to be fooled.

As I made my way across the room, the anxious knot in my chest tightened. They never went well, these meetings. They always started with him throwing out some backhanded compliment, then spiraling into passive-aggressive remarks about my career or life choices. And I'd sit there, pretending it didn't bother me, while his entourage looked on like they were watching the main act at some twisted theater.

I stepped closer, feeling the weight of his presence before I'd even reached him. His head turned, eyes locking onto me. The smile didn't falter, but there was something in his gaze—a flicker of something unreadable, maybe disappointment, maybe indifference. I couldn't tell, and at this point, it didn't really matter.

"Well, well," Dad said, his voice dripping with smooth confidence as his arm lifted in that too-casual gesture, like we were just catching up after a round of golf instead of walking into another verbal sparring match. "Look who decided to join us."

I forced a smile, already bracing myself. "Hey, Dad."

The eyes around him shifted toward me, the piranhas recognizing me as someone else they could potentially leech from. Unfortunately for them, I had a no-leech policy.

Dad didn't hug me. Didn't even pretend to. Instead he leaned back in his chair, hands gesturing dramatically as he dove into a story that was so tired, I could recite it in my sleep. "So there we were, fourth quarter, two minutes left on the clock, down by six. The whole stadium was on its feet. You could feel the tension, you know? Everyone was holding their breath." He paused, like he always did, soaking in the admiration from the guys around him.

I mouthed the words as he continued, eyes lighting up like this wasn't the millionth time he'd told the story. "Coach calls a time-out, pulls us all in. Everyone's looking at me—*everyone*. It was like they knew who the ball was going to."

The group around him leaned in, nodding along like this was some new revelation.

"So we line up," he said, his voice lowering like he was building suspense. "And the ball snaps. The defense comes at me hard, but I spin right past them. The crowd goes *nuts*. I can still hear the roar."

I resisted the urge to roll my eyes. He *always* acted like he could still hear that roar.

"Then . . ." Dad said, leaning forward as if he was actually saying something important. "I see it—the gap. I go for it, full speed. Thirty yards. Twenty. Ten. Touchdown! Game over. I won the Super Bowl for them."

The guys around him exploded into applause, laughing and slapping him on the back like he was still the star of the night. "Hell of a play, man," one of them said. "Best I've ever seen."

I could even do the dramatic pause he always used right before the big moment—that was how many times he'd told that story. His friends leaned in, though, hanging on every exaggerated detail like they hadn't heard it a million times too. But that's what they were there for—to worship at the altar of Dad's past.

I sat there, fading into the background, just part of the scenery. I could have been anyone, really. He'd glance my way once or twice, just enough to acknowledge my presence without ever actually speaking to me. The conversation flowed around me, the spotlight firmly on him, while I became the invisible son at the edge of the table. I couldn't decide if it was better or worse that he'd decided to ignore me today instead of insulting me.

Probably better.

It went on like that for at least thirty minutes. Him talking, them nodding and laughing in all the right places, while I sat there pretending I wasn't counting down the seconds until I could leave. My foot tapped under the table, a slow, growing beat of impatience.

Until I finally was sick of his shit. I stood up, pushing my chair back a little too hard, the legs scraping against the floor. "I've got to get to the arena," I said, the lie easily slipping out.

Dad barely looked up. "That's all you can spare for your old man?" he said sarcastically, like I'd been the one ignoring him this entire time.

I felt the burn of the comment, harsh and familiar. But I swallowed it down and said nothing. What was the point of arguing? It was always the same with him. He was always right.

Without another word, I turned and walked out.

I had much better things to do than sit through a recitation of Grant York's glory days. I needed to continue to work on how to get my girl.

CHAPTER 16

SLOANE

The sharp buzz of the intercom made me jump, pulling me out of my thoughts. I pushed away from the bathroom vanity where I'd been finishing my makeup, and I walked over to the panel on the wall, pressing the button to answer.

"Your car is waiting, ma'am," a calm, detached voice informed me.

I sighed, leaning my head against the cool wall for a second before responding. "Thanks, I'll be right down."

Logan had asked me to go to the game tonight and arranged for a car to pick me up, and I'd been stressing about it all afternoon. "This is just work. That's all this is. He's paying you," I muttered to myself as I stared into the mirror one more time. I let the words settle, a small knot twisting in my stomach. That was the only reason I was wearing his jersey—because it was a client asking me to do something.

Shaking my head because I was a liar, I walked out into the hallway, grabbing a light jacket from the coat closet as I made my way to the elevator. It might be boiling hot outside, but it was freezing in the arena.

When I stepped outside, a sleek black car idled at the curb, the driver standing beside it in a crisp suit. He opened the door for me without a word, and I slipped inside, the smell of leather and fresh pine greeting me.

The drive to the arena passed in silence, except for the sound of my shoes tapping nervously against the floor as I crossed and uncrossed my legs, fidgeting. Every few minutes, I glanced at my phone, then out the window, then back to my phone. The knot in my stomach tightened the closer we got.

When the car finally pulled up to the arena, the driver stepped out and opened my door. I thanked him quietly and climbed out.

Logan had already sent me my ticket, and I pulled it up on my phone, skimming over the section and seat number. As I walked through the maze of the arena, I slowed when I caught sight of the section I was heading toward.

My steps faltered as I realized where I was sitting—and more importantly, *who* I'd be sitting with.

I recognized the women immediately. I'd seen them at the previous games, noticing them because some of the Dallas Knights players were always flirting with them through the glass. I was pretty sure they were wives or girlfriends of Logan's teammates.

Of course, he would have me sitting by them.

My fingers tightened around my phone as I stepped into the row. One of the women, a gorgeous redhead who looked really familiar, looked up and smiled, her hazel eyes bright. "Oh, hi! You must be Sloane, right?"

I hesitated, my throat dry, that unfamiliar warmth flooding my insides— he'd told them about me . . . in detail apparently since she'd known what I looked like. "Uh, yeah. That's me."

She patted the seat next to her. "Come on, we don't bite. I'm Olivia."

I forced a smile, sliding into the chair . . . trying not to look like I was freaking out.

"Hi," a beautiful blonde said from the other side. "I'm Blake. I'm married to that one," she said, wrinkling her nose as a tall, black-haired—very gorgeous—Dallas player stopped at the glass in front of us. He turned around and started shaking his ass at her, glancing over his shoulder to watch her reaction.

"Go warm up, Lancaster." She grinned.

"You're eye-fucking me while I skate, ma'am. A guy is only so strong when the most beautiful girl in the world is giving him the eyes."

Blake giggled, almost hysterically, as he blew her a kiss before skating away.

"I'd just like to know when you aren't 'giving him the eyes,'" a raven-haired woman on Blake's other side mused.

"You're probably right," Blake said, still watching him with a dreamy look on her face.

My gaze went to Logan, who was talking to the Dallas goalie. A weird pang of longing hitting me hard.

Because I wanted that kind of flirty ease with someone—I wanted that with *him*.

"That's mine over there talking to Rookie—sorry, Logan," Olivia said, distracting me from the thoughts I was not supposed to be having as she pointed to the Dallas goalie.

"I wish you'd brought Isabella," the ebony-haired woman said, her lips pressed into a pretty pout.

Olivia snorted. "It's too loud in here, even with those noise-canceling earmuff things. Walker wouldn't be able to concentrate. He'd be looking over here every few seconds, making sure she was alright. You can come over tomorrow to play."

"Fine, I'll try and live without her for a day." The girl huffed before shooting me a dazzling grin. "Hi, I'm Monroe. I'm married to . . ." She scanned the ice, her lips turning into a soft smile as a tall, golden-haired, very hot man skated to a stop in front of her and stared at her intensely while he made a heart sign with his hands and pointed to her. "That one," she whispered, a flush hitting her cheeks as they stared at each other.

I actually knew that player. People had been talking about Lincoln Daniels almost constantly the first three games. Being this close to him . . . were they feeding the Dallas team something different than everyone else? I'd never seen so many hot guys in one place.

"I think I'm pregnant *again* just from watching you two," huffed Olivia to Monroe. "I don't know how you aren't."

Monroe giggled and shook her head. "Don't give him any ideas. Just think of how he'd be if I got pregnant. I'd be sitting here in a full-on bubble with armed guards around me that would be instructed to shoot first, ask questions later."

A tan beauty with light blond hair giggled next to her. "I think Elaine would be offended if he added more guards," she said, nodding her head to an intimidatingly strong-looking woman who looked like she could bench-press half the arena . . . with one hand. "And hi, I'm Anastasia. I'm with number sixty-three, Camden," she said, pointing to another very attractive guy who was talking to Ari out on the ice.

"Hi," I said. I bit down on my lip . . . having so many questions. "You guys have bodyguards?" I finally asked, unable to keep in that one.

"Well, originally the guards were for this one," Anastasia said, nodding to Olivia. "She's kind of a big deal."

Olivia snorted and shook her head. "It was only a matter of time until the others cracked and got some. Did you see how Lincoln was glaring at the popcorn boy the other game? I thought he was going to leap over and grab him!"

Monroe smirked. "I'm surprised they haven't found some way to hang a suspended platform in the air above the ice where we can see, but no one else is nearby."

My eyes widened. They sounded so casual about all of these . . . crazy things.

I cocked my head, thinking. They were about as crazy as hiring someone to spend time with you, now that I was thinking about it.

It hit me then, and my jaw dropped as I glanced over at Olivia.

"Wow. I know you. You're the famous singer!" I said, a slight screech in my voice as I realized that *the* Olivia Walker was sitting next to me. "How did I not connect the dots?"

Olivia looked amused. "I am a singer."

Blake leaned forward with a grin. "And she *is* famous."

Olivia wrinkled her nose at her. "Says the supermodel."

"I'm just a student," Monroe said, raising her hand.

"And a writer working on the most amazing book," Blake retorted.

"She's an incredible principal ballerina," Monroe said, pointing at Anastasia.

I had a bemused smile as I stared at all of them. They were obviously very close and supportive of each other. I'd never had close female friends . . . not since my eighteenth birthday party. I'd been so messed up after the auction that I'd cut myself off from everyone. Everett hadn't exactly encouraged me otherwise.

Don't think about that.

I bit down on my lip, realizing what their next question was probably going to be . . .

And right on cue . . .

"What do you do?" Blake asked. "I guess the better question would be, what do you like to do . . ."

"Besides Logan, of course," Anastasia said with a straight face as Olivia snorted again beside me.

"Ana," Monroe said, elbowing her. "We don't even know if Rookie has enough game to bag a ten like Sloane. Maybe they're just friends." All of them looked at me at the same time, and I blushed.

I could just picture what their reactions would be if I told them the truth about what *I did*. They wouldn't want anything to do with me. I scrambled to think of an answer. Usually I said things like . . . consultant . . . or business.

But this time . . .

"I paint," I said softly, wanting to whack myself on the head because I had no idea why I'd said that.

"You do?" Olivia asked, looking so earnest and interested, I wanted to cry.

Before I could say anything else, Logan was in front of the glass. "Hi," he mouthed, looking all hot and sweaty . . . and delicious as he stood there. I waved because all my game was gone, evidently.

"You complete me," he mouthed, and I snorted as the girls all laughed.

"Hope you like corny," Olivia whispered. "Because these guys are full of it."

I grinned, that warm feeling spreading through my chest. "It's still up for debate," I muttered back as the game began. Even though that was another lie.

"We've all been there, girl," Blake said as Lincoln faced off across a Tampa player.

"Been where?" I asked, frowning.

"Trying to pretend we're not completely obsessed with a Knight," she said, her tone teasing. The other women laughed, and I felt my face heat.

"I'm not—" I started, but the words died in my throat as Logan glanced up from the ice. His gaze swept across the stands, until it landed on me.

His lips quirked into a grin, and my heart flipped.

Olivia raised an eyebrow, clearly amused. "Right. Not obsessed at all."

I sank lower in my seat, my cheeks burning as I stared down at the ice, wondering if she wasn't that far off.

———

Logan

That feeling was back, the one I was used to, where everything felt right when I was out on the ice.

I knew *why* it was back. It was because of Sloane, because she was where she belonged.

Watching me instead of Tyler Fucking Miller.

Sloane's presence had me feeling so good . . . I didn't even care that my father was somewhere in the stands, pretending to watch while critiquing my every move like he knew as much about hockey as he did playing football.

"A new addition to the 'Ladies of the Circle,' ehh?" Camden asked as he stole my puck and brought my head back to warm-ups.

"Ladies of the Circle? When did we approve that?" asked Ari.

"I've got some ideas!" said Walker eagerly.

"Of course you do, simp," snarked Ari.

Walker huffed as he easily stopped a puck that Dex, one of our team-mates, had shot.

"Well, we're listening, Disney," drawled Lincoln right before he smacked the puck and sent it sliding past Walker and into the back of the net.

Walker grimaced. It was a good thing that Lincoln was on our team, because Walker could rarely stop his shots. "Ladies of the Locker Room, the Sin Bin Sweethearts, the Stanley *Cup*cakes," Walker recited. "I also have the Stick Whisperers or the Hat Trick Honeys . . ."

"Ooh, what about the Trustettes?" offered Camden, obviously eager to redeem himself after the whole "Ladies of the Circle" debacle.

"None of these are deserving of Blake 'Honey Bunny' Lancaster," Ari griped as we skated back toward the bench to get chewed out one more time by Coach. "You all need to do better."

Lincoln barked out a laugh, and Ari grinned at him over his shoulder. "Liked that one, didn't you, Golden Boy?"

"Was he laughing with you . . . or at you? *That* is the question of the day," said Camden as my attention drifted over to where Sloane was talking to the girls. She had a faint blush to her cheeks and looked happier than I had seen her. The Hat Trick Honeys . . . already working their magic.

Nope, not a good one. I'd have to think of some better ones to offer—especially since Sloane was one of them now. Only the best for my girl.

The game started, and it was immediately balls to the wall. We were down by one in the series, and everything felt like it was on the line tonight. I could feel it in my bones, that tight coil of adrenaline ready to snap at any moment.

"Hey, ref, is it a penalty to breathe now?" Ari asked as the whistle blew, and Camden was sent to the penalty box for high-sticking halfway through the first period.

The ref in question, definitely a Tampa Bay sympathist based on his calls, blew the whistle in Ari's face as I skated into the face-off circle.

My eyes were locked on number seventy-five as he lined up across from me. My stick tapped the ice twice, my knees bending a little deeper.

"You look nervous," I said.

"Shut up, York," he shot back, tightening his grip on his stick.

The ref raised his arm . . . and the puck dropped.

I reacted before he could, my stick snapping down with a clean *crack* as I swept the puck back toward Ari. My body surged forward as I drove off my skates, leaving the guy cursing and scrambling behind me.

Ari had the puck now, snapping it over to Lincoln, who charged up the boards. I kept my speed, weaving into position, my heart pounding in sync with the roar of the crowd.

And then it happened.

I saw the hit coming before it connected, but there was nothing I could do to stop it. Lincoln was in the corner, battling for the puck, his focus so locked in that he didn't see the Tampa player barreling toward him. The hit landed high, slamming into Lincoln's shoulder and sending him crashing into the boards with a sickening thud.

Everything slowed down for a second. The crowd gasped. The refs blew the whistle. But all I could focus on was the sound of Lincoln hitting the ice and the way he didn't get back up right away.

"Shit," I muttered under my breath, skating toward him, but I already knew something was wrong. He wasn't moving like he normally did, his face twisted in pain as he pushed himself up.

"Golden Boy, you good?" Ari called out, his voice tight.

Trainers were on the ice in a heartbeat, helping him to his feet. He tried to shrug them off, but he grimaced as he tried to stand on his left ankle.

"Get off the ice, Linc," I said, skating up next to him, my voice quieter now. "Don't push it."

"Fuck," he muttered, shaking his head, clearly pissed but in too much pain to argue. He turned toward the bench, hobbling away with the trainers on either side of him, while the rest of us stood there, trying to pretend like this wasn't as bad as it felt.

The rest of the game felt like a blur. Without him, it was like the wind got knocked out of us. Every play felt harder, every shift slower. Tampa knew it too. They smelled blood in the water and started hammering us, taking advantage of every missed opportunity—every mistake we made.

Hockey is a momentum sport. I would argue more than any other, and the momentum had turned in Tampa's favor. We played catch-up the rest of the game. No matter how hard we pushed, we couldn't find the net.

By the time the final buzzer sounded, we were down by two goals. The crowd was quiet, a low murmur of disappointment filling the air as we skated off the ice.

In the locker room, the tension was thick enough to cut with a knife. After getting railed by the coaching staff, I pulled out my phone and saw a text from my dad.

> Dad: That was an embarrassment.

I growled and chucked my phone to the floor.

"Chin up. Linc's got a sprain, but he'll be back . . . at the very least for Game Seven," said Ari, plopping into a chair beside me.

"If we even make it to Game Seven," I grumbled, pushing my wet hair out of my face.

"None of that," said Ari, patting me on the shoulder. "It's not over till it's over."

"That's the best you've got?" I asked glumly. "Because if that was supposed to be motivating, it sucked."

"I can quote you the *Remember the Titans* speech," Walker offered.

Ari grinned at that one for some reason—probably some inside joke from before my time. I hated those.

"He's really good at that one," said Ari.

"Maybe next time," I drawled, still a Sad Sally as I got up and grabbed my bag.

"Pretty sure there's a gorgeous girl out in the hallway who'll make you feel better," Ari said with a slow grin as he wiggled his eyebrows up and down. "Hopefully she can fix your head. Give you a little *can-do* attitude, if you know what I mean."

That made me perk up. I decided right then and there that only one thing could make me feel better after a game like that.

A second date . . . that ended in my bed.

"Don't call her gorgeous," I snarled at Ari as I walked to the door.

"So touchy," I heard Ari say right before the door closed behind me.

But I forgot about everything else when I saw Sloane leaning against the wall a little down the hall, looking adorably awkward about being there.

She saw me, and a small, sexy smile slid across her lips.

"Hi, Calloway," I murmured as I brushed a kiss against her mouth. "You in love with me yet?"

She huffed. "I'm sorry you lost, Logan," she said sweetly, ignoring what I'd asked. Her voice came out breathy and sexy after our kiss.

"Mmm. Me too. But I know one thing that will make me feel better."

"What's that?"

"You," I told her. With that, I wrapped an arm around her waist and walked her toward the exit that led out to the parking lot.

It was time to *show* Sloane Calloway that she was . . . mine.

CHAPTER 17

SLOANE

Welcome home," Logan purred as he opened the door of his apartment. "Wait." He put his hand up, a weirdly determined look on his face.

"What?" I asked, grinning because we'd just had the best fettuccini I'd ever tasted . . . and a few glasses of wine.

I was pretty sure that Logan York was the most charming man I'd ever met.

"I think it's customary to carry your girl over the threshold the first time she enters her new home," he said, a lock of his blond hair falling onto his forehead as he continued to charm me.

"You're beautiful," I blurted out, because I couldn't keep the words in. It was a problem that I kept having, actually, saying everything I would normally keep locked in tight. A smug grin spread across his face, and I blinked a few times, not comprehending how someone so perfect looking existed.

"Says the world's most beautiful woman," he responded with a wink, and I actually giggled, which was definitely the wine's fault. "Now, as I was saying, *beautiful* girl. It's time to cross the threshold."

Logan swept me into his strong arms, holding me carefully against his chest as I looked up at him.

"I'm pretty sure you're just supposed to do this when you get married. And did you say 'her' new home, or am I really drunk and imagining things?"

He grinned. "I don't think it's a wedding-exclusive thing, but in any case, this is good practice."

I blinked at the easy, confident way he said the *craziest* things. And how he'd ignored what I'd asked.

"I hope you're not talking about me," I told him as we walked across his entry. "Because I'm quite confident those kinds of love stories don't involve escorts." I said it like I was joking, but the words secretly made me die inside.

"Maybe *we're* the ones actually writing the greatest love story ever told. Maybe those *other* stories are missing crucial elements," Logan shot back, leading us into a giant living room and sitting down on an oversized brown sectional.

Normally, I'd be interested in seeing his home, but I couldn't look away from his face.

The way he was gazing at me . . .

It wasn't the kind of look I was used to receiving—the greedy, predatory stares—this was different. His eyes swept over my face as if he was committing it to memory, as if I was something rare, someone extraordinary.

"Why are you looking at me like that?" I asked, my voice barely above a whisper.

"Like what?" he breathed, his voice low and thick.

"Like . . ." I faltered, heat creeping up my neck. "Like you're in awe or something."

Logan's lips curved into the smallest of smiles, and my stomach flipped. "Because I am."

I blinked, unsure if I'd actually heard him right. "What?"

His hand came up, brushing a strand of hair from my face, and his fingers lingered there, just barely grazing my skin. "You're the most incredible thing I've ever seen," he said quietly, his voice steady, like it was a fact.

My throat tightened, and I forced a laugh, yanking my gaze away from him. "You're talking crazy again." I swallowed hard, my hands gripping the fabric of his shirt like I might fall apart if I didn't hold on to something. "Logan . . ."

Before I could say anything else, he leaned in slowly, his movements deliberate. His breath brushed against my lips, warm and steady, and then his mouth was on mine.

The kiss wasn't rushed or frantic. It was soft, slow, like he was savoring the moment, savoring *me*. His hand cupped my jaw, his thumb grazing my cheek as his lips moved against mine, and I melted into him, every nerve in my body sparking to life.

"Sloane," he sighed against my lips as my fingers played with the buttons on his shirt.

Maybe I'd known this was inevitable, from the second I'd seen him out there on the ice—his mouth on mine, me straddling his lap, and him looking at me like I was the only thing in the world worth wanting. His hands were everywhere—strong, sure, tugging me closer as though he could pull me inside him if he tried hard enough. And fuck, I let him, because I didn't want distance. Not right now. Not from him.

"It's the second date, Logan," I murmured, beginning to slowly unbutton the dress shirt he was wearing. His breath hitched, and my fingers trailed across his chest as I revealed inch by tattooed inch of perfect skin.

I couldn't do *feelings*. But I could do sex. If he meant everything he was saying—which was highly doubtful—I'd never be able to give him any words like that back.

But I *could* give him the best orgasm he'd ever experienced.

His lips left mine, trailing along my jaw, his breath warm and ragged as he kissed a path across my skin. My head tipped back automatically, my fingers digging into his shoulders as I tried to breathe through the storm raging inside me.

"Are you sure?" he asked, his voice low and rough, like gravel coarse at the edges.

I had the sudden urge to cry because I'd never had a man ask me something like that.

It had always been assumed.

His lips hovered there, just below my ear, his hands still moving—one running up my waist, the other steady on my hip.

I began to kiss my way down his chest, wanting to taste every inch of him. The rich men who hired me weren't always attractive, so when I had an actual work of art in front of me . . . I wanted to worship him.

I was suddenly scooped up, and Logan was walking us down a hallway.

"What?"

"Our first time is going to be on *our* bed. I've been jerking off thinking about this moment since the first time I saw you."

"No you didn't—" I laughed, my breath whooshing out as he tossed me on the mattress before kneeling on top of it, beginning to prowl toward where I was lying.

"I'd lie here—and let's be clear, I pride myself on how long I can last—and one thought of you . . ." He made an explosion movement with his hands. "Best orgasms I ever had."

"Well, hopefully the reality of me lives up to the one in your head, Mr. York," I told him in a raspy voice as I slid my dress up my thighs to reveal black lace thigh-highs he had no idea I was hiding. His eyes widened, a red flush appearing on his cheeks as he hungrily took me in.

"How's this? Does it live up to what you imagined?"

"Better. Much better," he groaned, finally reaching me and helping me slide my dress up all the way until I was lying there in nothing but my black lace bra, matching underwear, and thigh-high set. "Holy fuck. Are you even real?"

I didn't tell him how this body came to be. A strict diet, an hour at the gym every day, and weight loss drugs when Everett thought I was looking too "fluffy," as he called it.

Wouldn't want to ruin the fantasy.

"Come back to me," he murmured, and I blinked, his dark green eyes boring into me.

"I'm here," I breathed.

"Good girl," he said with a sexy grin.

"So, in this fantasy . . . what happens next?" I asked him.

"In my fantasy—which I'm just going to reiterate is nothing compared to what I'm seeing right now—I get . . . to taste."

"Taste," I whispered, rubbing my thighs together. "I like the sound of that."

———

Logan

Sloane was stretched out on my sheets like some kind of goddess, all long lines and soft curves, her black lingerie clinging to her like it had been made just for her. The lace barely covered anything, teasing me with glimpses of flawless skin and the delicate dip of her waist. My breath caught as my eyes trailed down the sheer fabric, the way it hugged her hips, the thin straps of the garter that disappeared against her thighs. It was stretched tight across her slit, dipping between her pussy lips . . . she was a fucking feast.

Her hair was a mess—wild and dark against my pillow. Her lips were parted just slightly, painted a shade of red that had me desperate to see them stretched around my dick, staining my skin with that color. Her eyes were hooded as she watched me enjoy myself, a half challenge, half invitation in their blue depths.

I continued to gape at her, trying to remember how to breathe. "You know, you could've warned me," I said finally, my voice rougher than I intended.

Her lips curved into a slow, dangerous smile, the kind that made me forget every coherent thought in my head. "Warned you about what?"

"That you were about to ruin me," I said, shaking my head like I was trying to snap myself out of whatever spell she'd cast. It didn't work. Nothing would've worked.

I reached back and brushed my hand against her ankle before I ran it up her leg, slow and deliberate. Her skin was warm, smooth, and when she shivered under my touch, I grinned . . . and then trailed my hands up to the edge of her panties until I was tracing the edge of the scraps of lace.

"Remind me to buy you a hundred more pairs of these," I growled, before I ripped them off her body, revealing a pussy that I was going to worship until my dying day.

"Fucking hell. You're perfect," I said, leaning forward because if I didn't taste her . . . the day that I died was going to come quick.

"Logan," she said, reaching out and stopping me before I could get between her legs.

"Yeah, baby?" I answered, my voice coming out feral . . . crazed as I desperately stared at her pussy. I was surprised I wasn't drooling . . . that's how badly I wanted her.

"I—I'm clean," she whispered.

I blinked, caught off guard, and for a second, I didn't understand what she meant. But when I did, my gaze snapped to hers. She looked away quickly, her cheeks flushing with embarrassment as her fingers twisted in the edge of the sheet.

I sat back slightly, trying to catch her eyes again. "Sloane," I said, my voice low and steady. "I didn't doubt you for a second, baby."

Maybe I should have asked about something like that, but I kept forgetting what she did for a living . . . I kept forgetting there was money leaving my bank account weekly to pay for every minute I spent with her. Hell, I kept forgetting everything except for the fact that I was confident she belonged to me.

She shook her head, her hair falling in front of her face like a curtain. "I just . . . I didn't want you to think . . ." Her voice trailed off, her hands gripping the sheet tighter.

I knelt down and parted her folds with my tongue, holding her gaze the entire time as she sucked in a sharp breath. "Most delicious thing I've ever tasted."

"Logan," she moaned, her hands fisting in my hair. I might be bald after this, but it would be worth it.

I pushed my tongue into her cunt, desperate for more.

She moaned again. So sexy that it took me a second to realize there was something off about the sound.

I did my best flicking trick, and she moaned again . . . and again, and each time I became more and more convinced.

She was faking it.

That was not going to fly.

I pulled my mouth away and frowned as I assessed her perfect face. No rosy cheeks, no glossy eyes. The sound had been right, she'd been writhing against my face . . . but she was definitely faking it.

"What's wrong?" she asked, her lips pursing as she studied me right back.

"How did that feel?" I asked her, and a look of confusion spread across her face.

"What do you mean?" Her voice was cautious . . . almost nervous-sounding, which rarely happened with Sloane. I lived for the moments when her walls came down and I saw past the tough-girl exterior she wore like a shield.

"Tell me how that felt," I ordered calmly.

She palmed my cheeks and tried to bring me back to her core. "Amazing, keep going," she said soothingly.

I licked her once more, because I couldn't help it, and then pulled back again.

"You're faking," I said matter-of-factly. "You're not enjoying this at all."

She opened her mouth and then closed it before a *fake* laugh erupted from her lips.

"It feels so good. I love it," she lied.

I leaned over and pressed a soft kiss on her thigh. "Those sexy little moans and those sweet words coming from that perfect fucking mouth may have fooled the assholes you've been with before. But they're not fooling me. Tell me what you like. We're not going to stop until it feels so good you're screaming and riding my face *and* begging for more."

She turned her head to her side, her white teeth biting into her plump bottom lip.

"I don't know what you're talking about."

"Here's a little thing about me, baby, my favorite thing about sex is pleasuring my partner. And since I'm positive that sex with you is going to be the best thing I've ever experienced, I want to make sure it's the best thing *you've* ever experienced as well."

She was quiet for a long moment, and I took the time to skim my fingers down her smooth thighs, trying to think up my best tricks to get my girl going.

I was in it to win it.

"I've never been able to . . ."

I waited for her to finish the sentence. I was obviously slow in the head since it took me more than a second to realize what she was talking about.

"You've never?" I asked. It wasn't a stretch to say that my girl was very . . . experienced. The idea that she'd never gotten off with all of those pathetic fuckers was . . . I don't know that I'd ever been more shocked . . . and pissed off.

She was still averting her eyes, staring at the wall like it held the secrets of the universe.

"I've gotten myself off, I just . . ." Her words were halting, and her cheeks were the flushed color I'd been hoping they'd be while I was eating her out. "No one's ever been able to make me come. I don't think it's possible."

My fingers were still making small circles on her skin as my mind raced with ideas.

"Oh, it's possible, Red."

"Red?" she asked, sounding amused.

"Yep, because those *red* lips torture me every time I look at you—I love them so much."

Her blush deepened.

"You've just never had someone with the right touch. Your body obviously has standards," I continued.

She finally met my gaze, a small smile on her lips that I could tell she was trying to hide. "You sound very cocky, Mr. York. You should know, no one's even come close."

"Not cocky, just confident, baby. And along with my superb skills, I also happen to be the most determined motherfucker on the planet. So it feels like I have everything going for me," I replied, feeling like perhaps I'd just discovered my purpose on this Earth. I'd always thought it was hockey, but obviously I'd been wrong. It was to take care of Sloane Calloway—physically, emotionally, and spiritually. Not sure what that last one meant, but I was quite sure that this girl was the closest thing to heaven I could get, so it seemed to fit.

I sat up, determination sinking down my veins as I searched the room for a pen and paper.

"What are you doing?" she asked as she sat up and watched me search the room.

I got lost for a second staring at her bare skin. It was sort of an out-of-body experience looking at her. You started to think that maybe you had died or something or she'd been created by an alternate being than the rest of us—she was just that perfect-looking.

She stretched her arms above her head, fully taking advantage of all that perfection as she smirked at me. "Come back to bed," she pouted.

I shook my finger at her, finally finding a pad of paper. "Nope. I can see right through you. You think it's not possible, and you're trying to distract me with all of that."

Sloane slowly opened her legs, revealing the prettiest pussy I'd ever seen as she slid her hand down her body. "Are you sure you don't want to come over here?" she purred.

I had to shake my head to keep a clear head. Because in fact, yes, I did want to go over there. Badly.

But it would be much easier for her to keep her distance from me if she didn't connect with me during sex.

I'd meant what I'd said.

I was in it to win it. I wanted her body. Her heart. Her fucking soul. I wasn't going to let her keep anything from me, no matter how hard she tried. Sloane was mine, and I would settle for nothing less than owning *all* of her.

Watching her touch herself did give me an idea, though. I brought the pen and paper with me as I grabbed the desk chair and dragged it over to the edge of the bed.

"What are you doing now?" she asked, an edge of exasperation in her voice since she couldn't get me to do what she wanted.

"I'm going to watch you touch yourself. You said that you can get yourself off. Well, I want to watch, study what you like, memorize everything you do so that I can do it too," I said smugly, feeling very good about my plan. Her mouth was open as I got up and adjusted my chair so I had the perfect viewing position. "Proceed," I said magnanimously, gesturing for her to continue.

I'd truly shocked her. She had no idea how to proceed. It was obvious that Sloane thrived on control. She didn't have any in very important facets of her life, so what she could control, she did with an iron grip. It was my goal to give her back control in all the things she'd lost and to take over in other ways she would enjoy. My poor girl had no idea how to proceed.

I watched as determination filled her gaze. "Fine. You can watch me. But you're not allowed to touch," she said brattily, as if I was going to say no to that. Her fingers began to slide through her folds as she locked eyes with me challengingly. "Do you think you can do it?"

Grinning, I dropped the pad of paper on the floor and undid my dress slacks, pulling my dick out. I'd have to take mental notes because there was no way my hands could do anything but play with my dick during this. "As long as I can touch myself while I watch, I think I can manage that, Red."

Sloane resembled a cartoon character as she stared at my dick, her eyes wide, her mouth dropping open even more . . . a blush spreading across her chest that I was certain was my new favorite color.

Yeah, baby, you're going to have all of this.

Still staring at my dick, she worked herself, sliding one finger and then another into her core as her other hand pulled at her nipple. I studied her movements in a way that would ensure me perfect grades in school, taking note of every brush of her hand, every push against her clit, every way she touched her breast.

Holy fuck, I was turned on.

Gripping my dick like it was a lifeline, I yanked my fist up and down, pinching my head every few seconds so I didn't embarrass myself and blow all over my hand before she was done.

I'd never seen anything as hot as her hands gliding over her hips and thighs, cupping her breasts and pushing them together as her hips thrust forward like I was fucking her. She pushed three fingers inside herself, her thumb desperately rubbing against her clit.

And through it all, her beautiful blue eyes were locked on my dick, her tongue sliding across her lips like she was imagining taking me into her mouth.

"That's it, baby," I said hoarsely. "Touch that pussy, show me what a good girl you are, make yourself come for me."

A low moan slid from her lips—that sounded nothing like her earlier fake attempts.

I grinned as I pinched the tip of my head again, because fuck, knowing she was feeling good could be my kryptonite.

"Is that a fourth finger, my dirty girl? My cock is going to make you feel so good. I can't wait to feel that tight cunt. Listen to that sound. You're so fucking wet right now."

She cried out, and a trickle of pre-cum fell on my hand. Fuck, I was close.

"Can I taste you, is that allowed?" I begged, feeling like I might die if she didn't say yes.

"Yes. Fuck. Please," she gasped, holding out her fingers to me like an offering from the gods.

Eagerly lapping at the essence on her skin, I groaned as I tasted her. This was it. This was what I wanted to live on for the rest of my life. She had to give it to me.

I sucked her finger harder when she tried to remove it, my tongue stroking her skin and making sure I got every drop of her flavor. She rasped out a laugh at my desperation, like she was well aware of the spell she had cast on me with just one taste.

"I'll give you more if you're a good boy," she teased, throwing my words back at her. I reluctantly let her go, determined to be a very, very good boy—forever—if that was what the reward was.

Her hand went back to her pussy, and I soaked in the sight. She was so wet that her thighs were glistening. It was all I could do not to feed directly from the source. But this was a learning expedition, I had to remember that.

"Keep going," I urged, sounding more like I was begging than anything else. My hand had a mind of its own at that point, gripping my dick, hard, as I imagined pushing inside her.

She circled her clit with one hand while massaging her breast . . . and then there it was, her back arched off the bed as her whimpers filled the room and she fell off the edge.

A few more tugs, and I was coming, harder than I could ever remember, my groans joining her cries as rope after rope of my cum coated my hand and the floor. I'd clean it up later, I decided, as I slumped back into my chair, still mesmerized by the sight in front of me. Sloane was a glowing, glorious *mess*, her breasts rising and falling enticingly as she came down from her orgasm.

That was what I wanted to see. It was what I would look for in the future when I needed to make sure she was telling me the truth. The memory of tonight would be the star of every future wet dream, any time I jacked off.

Fuck. She was divine.

My new religion.

And I intended to worship her every day.

"So, did you learn anything?" she finally asked in a sexy raspy voice that had my dick ready to go all over again. She sat up, her arms behind her, breasts jutting out in a way that had my mouth watering.

I wondered how much of her movements were a result of practice, or if she was naturally that sensual. Either way I didn't care.

"So much. I'm going to get an A-plus next time . . . that's a promise."

Sloane grinned, watching me as I got up and walked into the bathroom. I cleaned myself up before I stripped off the rest of my clothes and came back into the bedroom.

"What are you doing?" she asked as I slid into the bed and pulled her close to me.

"We're cuddling, Sloane. It's an epic love story kind of thing."

"Oh," she said, her body stiff at first as I curled myself around her, my already hard cock poking into her skin. "You need help with that? Or we could have sex," she suggested, pressing back and torturing me as she moved against me.

Yes. I definitely wanted help with that. And I definitely wanted sex.

But not tonight.

"Go to sleep, Sloane," I murmured, memorizing what had to be one of the best moments of my life.

"And when we wake up, I'm going to make you come."

"I think I might believe you," she whispered.

I squeezed her. "I'm going to keep going until you do."

Between the game and the epic orgasm, my eyes were already sliding closed, but I was pretty sure the last words I heard before I fell asleep—

"That's what I'm afraid of . . ."

CHAPTER 18

SLOANE

I woke up, orgasming. Logan was braced on his forearms in between my legs, licking and sucking my clit.

"Ohhh," I whimpered, pleasure surging through me as I writhed against his tongue.

I was gasping for breath as I came down, and he looked up at me with hooded eyes, his lips shiny with my arousal as he smirked at me.

"Good morning," he groaned. "Hope this is okay . . . I had to taste you. I've been thinking about eating this sweet pussy all night." He licked slowly up my slit, circling my clit as two of his fingers pushed inside me.

It felt . . . so good. How had he done that? And while I was asleep?

I stared at him in amazement . . . and a little awe . . . as his fingers lazily slid in and out. Like he was just playing with me.

"Round two." He hummed, withdrawing his fingers and pushing my thighs farther apart as he suddenly sucked on my clit.

"I can't wait to get inside this gorgeous pussy," he growled, holding me still as I squirmed against his mouth. His tongue pushed inside my core, and I whimpered as he hit that perfect spot I'd heard about but never experienced for myself.

This was some kind of witchcraft. Last night had been hot, but I hadn't really believed he could do it.

But he definitely was.

Logan shoved one of my legs over his shoulder, moaning into my slit as his mouth moved back to my clit, and he slid three huge fingers inside me.

I thrashed underneath him, and he groaned. "Fuck. You taste so fucking good." His tongue licked through my folds, circling my clit, while his fingers continued to move. I tried to rock against his mouth, but he held me tightly so I couldn't move.

My insides were clenching . . . just a little more. I locked eyes with him and that was it, another orgasm tore through me, and my cries filled the room. His expression was so possessive . . . so hot as he continued to lick and suck. Goose bumps broke out on my arms. My pulse quickened, my breath caught, and I closed my eyes, my head falling back into the pillow as wave after wave of pleasure surged through my insides.

This was so much better than any orgasm I'd ever given myself.

Ugh. Why did he have to be so perfect?

Logan lowered my leg and crawled up my body, pressing a deep, rough kiss against my lips that had me tasting myself. I loved that. I wanted him to carry me with him everywhere, a sign to everyone that he belonged to me.

The idea of that made me want to cry, because it was far-fetched . . . so out of reach.

I could feel his hard length between us, and my mouth watered just thinking of how amazing it was going to feel if he was this adept of a student with his tongue.

"That's so good," he whispered against my lips, his hands rubbing up my sides. "So good, sweet girl . . . you're incredible."

I soaked in his praise, liking it for the first time. Wanting to please him—not because it was my job, but because it was him.

My lips quivered against his, and he paused. "I know, baby. I know. Me too," he murmured. "Me too."

I wrapped my arms and legs around him, holding him as close as I could. Later, I'd use this memory when I was alone and he was gone, when it was business as usual. I'd use it to remember I had one bright, sparkling moment in my useless life.

"I have something for you," he said, rolling off me to grab something out of his closet.

"You got me something?" I asked, a strange, light feeling spreading through my veins.

He reappeared, holding up a box, a warm gleam in his eyes. Biting down on my lip, I studied it for a second. I'd gotten gifts before from my clients, but this felt different.

A present from him felt like *more*.

"Open it." He grinned as I finally took it. "And don't be so scared. You're going to have to get used to this. Presents all the time. It's a *boyfriend* thing."

I steadfastly ignored the fact that he'd just called himself my boyfriend, and I cracked the box open, my breath catching when I saw what was inside. Nestled on black velvet was a necklace—thin, delicate, with a teardrop-shaped diamond at the center that caught the light like it was made of magic. It wasn't just gorgeous—it was overwhelming.

"Logan . . ." I trailed off, unsure of what to say.

"Do you like it?" he asked, his tone casual, but his eyes sharp, watching my reaction like a hawk.

"Like it?" I laughed nervously, shaking my head. "This is . . . I mean, it's stunning, but—"

"No 'buts,'" he interrupted, sitting up and taking the box from my hands. He pulled the necklace out and let it dangle from his fingers, the diamond swinging slightly. "I want you to wear it."

My chest tightened. "Logan, it's too much."

"It's not," he said firmly, his voice brooking no argument. He leaned closer, brushing my hair to the side as he reached around to clasp the necklace around my neck. His fingers skimmed across my skin, sending shivers down my spine.

"There," he said, pulling back to look at me. "Now, you'll wear it all the time, and you'll know I'm always thinking about you."

I swallowed hard, my fingers brushing against the diamond that now rested against my skin. "That's . . . really sweet," I admitted, my cheeks heating.

"Do you really like it? Because if you don't, I can get something else," he said, leaning in, his lips brushing mine in a way that was soft but insistent.

"I love it," I murmured as he pulled back, leaving me breathless and more flustered than I cared to admit.

I opened my mouth to respond, but before I could say anything, Logan swung his legs off the bed and stood up, stretching like a cat and showcasing a set of abs that I wanted to lick. I took in the sight of him shirtless, wondering if he would notice if I grabbed my phone and took a picture.

"Now, I'm making you breakfast," he announced, walking toward the door.

I blinked, still clutching the necklace like I couldn't quite believe it was real. "You cook?" I called after him, the disbelief evident in my voice.

He turned, flashing me a devilish grin. "Mrs. Bentley cooks. But I'm very good at heating things up."

"Who's Mrs. Bentley?" I called after him, but he didn't answer me. He disappeared from the room, leaving me alone with a necklace that was far too beautiful and a heart that was beating far too fast.

Logan had tried to convince me to stay at his apartment while he was at practice, but I'd refused. That felt too close to a "girlfriend" thing.

So now I was trying to find distractions back at my place, which suddenly felt cold and empty . . . and lonely. I ended up in my studio, which I never visited while I was in the middle of a job. But I was here, and I was feeling . . . strangely inspired. This piece was different from my others, more hopeful. Even when I was painting landscapes of places I'd traveled to, I tended to drown the paintings in dark colors, sunny days becoming stormy nights.

But not today.

Today I was painting a field of ranunculus flowers I'd seen at Carlsbad Ranch when I was visiting San Diego last year. And *today*, the sky was staying sunny.

The elevator out in the entry dinged, and I stiffened, all the sparkles Logan had given me disappearing like they'd never existed at all. The only one who had the code to get up here . . . was Everett.

Fuck.

I set my paints down and wiped off my hands, knowing that I wouldn't be in the mood to paint anymore after finishing with him. Walking out of the room, I took a deep breath as I caught sight of him, sitting on my couch like he owned the place.

Which I guess . . . he did.

In his tailored suit and crisp white shirt, he looked every inch the powerful man he was. His eyes swept over me, calculating as ever, and a familiar chill crept up my spine.

"Everett," I said, trying to keep my voice steady. "What are you doing here?"

"What a way to greet your uncle. Want to try again?" he asked, raising an eyebrow as he continued to eye me.

I smoothed my hands down my top, wishing that I was dressed appropriately for one of his visits.

"Uncle, what a pleasant surprise," I said obediently, pasting a practiced smile on my face.

He stared at me unnervingly for a second. "Better." Everett glanced at his watch. "It's been a few days, Sloane," he said. I bit down on my lip. Everett liked to keep a close eye on his . . . girls. "Why haven't I heard from you?"

"Just busy with . . . Mr. York." For some reason it tasted wrong on my tongue to talk about Logan with Everett.

"I've been worried about you, Sloane. Something's different. Anything you want to tell me?" He was using his voice that usually succeeded in getting information out of me. But today it wasn't making me want to give him . . . anything.

My skin felt clammy, and I clasped my hands in front of me, trying to steady myself. "Nothing new."

He continued to study my face, and I was terrified he could see all the chaos of my thoughts.

Everett stood up, glancing around like he was assessing how I'd been taking care of the place he'd provided for me. When he finally turned back, his expression was unreadable. "You've got another job."

I fell back a step and then quickly recovered, cursing myself for having a reaction. My throat tightened, and I swallowed hard, forcing my features to relax. "Another job?" I echoed, my voice quieter than I wanted it to be.

"Yes." He straightened his cuffs, his movements deliberate. "Tonight. Eight o'clock sharp."

My stomach churned. *Logan.* His voice was in my head again, low and certain. *If another man touches you, I'll kill him.*

"I—I thought that I was booked with Logan for the whole week."

There was a long pause, and I knew I'd just shown my cards. Fuck.

"It almost sounds as if this other job is a problem for you," Everett said coldly.

"No. That's not what I—"

"Do I need to remind you that everything you have is because of me?"

I held up my hands. "Everett—"

"Do I need to remind you that without the opportunities I've given you, you'd be out there struggling, working yourself to the bone just to have food on the table? Do you want to go back to how you grew up, Sloane? Is that what your tone means?"

I bowed my head. "No, Uncle."

His footsteps were slow and methodical as he approached me, and then he was tipping up my chin until I was meeting those brown eyes of his, the ones that always reminded me of my mother.

And how much she would hate what I'd become.

"Remember, you chose this . . . and remember, this is all you're good for."

With those words he released my chin and walked to the elevators. I didn't bother to watch him leave.

All you're good for.

It was the reminder I needed to dig out the tendril of light that Logan had infected me with.

Maybe a better woman would have cried. Maybe she would have screamed. Instead, I sat on the couch, staring at nothing, as the reality of my life closed in around me.

My phone buzzed in my pocket, and I slowly pulled it out, not surprised to see the instructions on the screen.

Everett: JS. 8 PM. Plaza Hotel.

For a second—just a second—my mind drifted to Logan. To that one perfect moment this morning.

And then I stood up and went to my bedroom to get ready.

Walking into the closet, I grabbed one of the dresses—black, fitted, something that showed off my body in all the ways it was supposed to. My hands moved on autopilot, slipping the fabric over my skin, zipping it up without thinking. I sat down at the vanity, brushing out my hair, applying my makeup, covering my heartache with just the right amount of concealer.

My phone buzzed again. This time, with a call from Logan.

The brush trembled in my hand as I stared at his name on the screen, the weak part of me wanting to pick it up, to hear his voice . . . just one more time.

I silenced the call, ignoring the tear falling down my cheek. He wouldn't want anything to do with me after this.

But it was better this way—to ghost him. It would be torture now to hear his voice and see his face.

I already missed him.

Setting down the makeup brush, I stared at my reflection. My heart felt heavy, but I shut the feeling down, putting the image of him in a vault I wasn't going to think about again.

Standing up, I smoothed out my dress, and grabbed my purse. The Plaza Hotel. Eight o'clock.

I wasn't allowed to be late.

CHAPTER 19

LOGAN

JS. 8 PM. Plaza Hotel.

Thanks to the app I had installed on her phone, I could see all of her incoming and outgoing text messages. I read the text she'd received two hours ago over and over in disbelief, my stomach twisted into a knot so tight it felt like I couldn't breathe. A dark, burning sensation filled my veins as I stared at the message, the words branding into my mind. I didn't need to guess what it meant. I'd looked through enough of her messages to know how she was informed about clients.

I'd missed catching the text when it came in thanks to practice, so I frantically turned on the video feed for the tiny camera that was in the necklace I'd given her this morning.

Fuck. She'd taken it off. The feed showed her ceiling, and the recorder wasn't picking up any sound.

I hit her number immediately, pacing the locker room with the phone pressed to my ear. It rang, and rang, and rang—then went straight to voicemail. I gripped the phone tighter, so tight my knuckles turned white, and I forced myself to take a deep breath. She was shutting me out. It was her instinct—to push me away.

This was just another test for me to show her I was all in.

I wasn't going to let any guy but me touch her ever again.

"See you guys later," I told Walker and Camden, ignoring their questions as I stalked out of the locker room. I'd have to catch them up later, because this needed to be handled. Now.

Dialing the number for the PI, I breathed a sigh of relief when he picked up after the second ring. "I need you to find out who's on her client list for tonight, eight p.m. at the Plaza Hotel." My voice was tight, barely controlled, fury lacing each word.

"You got it," he said, no hesitation, no questions. My kind of guy. I'd never had a need for a PI in my life before Sloane, but I was fucking grateful for him now, or at least for Lincoln. It's not like the PI was doing any of this out of the kindness of his heart.

Waiting around for him to call me back was something I couldn't do. Not when every second felt like I was one step closer to losing her forever. I stormed out of the practice facility and drove straight to the hotel.

The Plaza looked pristine, gleaming . . . like luxury wrapped in glass and steel. It didn't look like the kind of place where something like this could happen. But that was the whole point, wasn't it? Things like this didn't happen in seedy motels. They happened in high-end hotels, where the rich could pretend they weren't doing something filthy.

I parked around the corner and got out of the truck, pacing the block like an animal trapped in a cage, my phone in hand as I waited for the info to come in. Every second stretched out painfully long, my mind racing with what could happen tonight. I wanted to punch something, anything, just to release some of the fury bubbling beneath the surface.

Finally, the phone buzzed. I snatched it up, and the investigator's message came through.

Politician. Big name. Family man. Campaigns on values.

Of course it was. The hypocrisy of it hit like a slap to the face, but it made perfect sense. These guys always did this. They built their reputations on being the perfect husbands, the perfect fathers, all while dipping into the darkest parts of the world.

His disgusting hands weren't going to touch my girl.

I read through the guy's information as I entered the hotel, keeping my head down just in case someone recognized me, my jaw clenched tight as I walked into the lobby. The place was buzzing with guests, people moving about like it was just another day. They had no idea what was really happening beneath their oblivious noses, how many lives were being twisted in these hallways.

I booked a room on the same floor she was supposed to be going to, knowing I wouldn't be able to use the elevator without a room key. Finally making it to the elevator, I was pretty sure it was the slowest elevator that existed on Earth. "Fuck," I muttered as I pulled out my phone and looked at

Sloane's location. Based on the tracker on her phone, I only had ten minutes to make this happen, so everything needed to go smoothly.

The elevator doors dinged, and I stepped out, grinning when I spotted the maid's cart near an open room. They really should have better security up here.

I strode over and grabbed the universal key off the top, slipping it into my pocket as I moved down the hallway, my eyes scanning the room numbers until I found the one I was looking for. I didn't bother knocking. I swiped the keycard and pushed the door of the suite open, revealing a fancy living area with a couch and a television. I could hear the faint sound of moans and grunts coming from the next room, and I braced myself for what I was about to see. Striding across the carpet, I stopped when I reached the doorway of the bedroom.

Fuck. I was going to have to bleach my eyes after this. Jared Stroople, one of the most esteemed congressmen from Louisiana, was lying on the hotel bed, butt naked, his dick already ready to go. Porn was playing on the television, and there was an array of dildos on the bed.

And I doubted they were all for Sloane . . . I wanted to throw up thinking of this fucker anywhere close to her.

The huge grin on his face fell fast when he saw me, his eyes widened in shock, his entire body freezing up like he couldn't believe someone had just barged in on him.

"What the hell—" He was struggling off the bed when I pulled out my phone and snapped a series of pictures, each one capturing him in that moment of panic.

He shot off the bed, stumbling over himself as he tried to straighten up. "What are you doing? You can't be here!" His voice cracked with the fear I could see all over his face.

I took a step forward, my voice low and controlled. "Says who?" I asked with a grin. I snapped another picture, the flash bright in the dim room. "Here's what's going to happen. You're going to walk out of this room, and you're never going to contact that service again. You're never going to come near Sloane or anyone else involved in this mess. You're not going to complain. You're not going to make a single sound. Because if you do—" I held up my phone, showing him the photos I'd just taken. "These go to every news outlet in the country. Every. Single. One. Missy would be really interested in this situation . . . don't you think?"

The blood drained from his face at the mention of his wife of twenty-five years, his mouth hanging open as he stared at me like I was holding a loaded gun to his head. "You can't . . . you wouldn't . . . I have a family . . ."

"And that's your problem," I snapped, cutting him off. I wasn't here to listen to excuses. "You didn't think about that family before you came here, did you?"

He stumbled backward, his hands trembling as he tried to cover his tiny dick.

I wasn't done, though. I swiped through my phone, pulling up the list my investigator had sent me—every time this guy had used the service, every girl—and guy—he'd requested.

"Let's see . . . April 3 you met Dolly in room 378. On April 7, you met Felicity in room 492. And Todd was on April 12." I raised an eyebrow as the congressman whimpered, and then I huffed out a laugh. "Interesting . . . that was your ten-year-old's birthday. Just couldn't keep it in your pants, could you?" I held the phone up, making sure he saw the list in full detail. "This is a history of all the times you've dipped your tiny dick into this well. I know who you've seen, when you've seen them, how much you've paid . . . and I'll make sure the world knows, too."

His face was the face of a dead man, gray and haunted.

If he ever touched Sloane again . . . he would be a dead man. So this experience was probably good for him.

His legs nearly gave out beneath him as he threw on his boxers, grabbed his suit, and bolted for the door. His whole body was shaking as he tried to get out of the room as fast as possible. "You forgot your dicks," I called after him, but he didn't look back, struggling to put on his pants as he turned the corner. A man running like his ass was on fire.

I stood there for a moment, breathing hard, trying to let the adrenaline settle. It wasn't over yet.

I walked to the chair by the window and sat down, my hands steepled in front of me as I waited. Sloane would show up soon, and she wouldn't be expecting me. She wouldn't want to see me, but I didn't care. She needed to know that this was the line in the sand. When I'd said no one else . . . I'd meant it.

———————

Sloane

The hotel was immaculate, as usual. High-end hotels always had a certain coldness to them, everything too perfect, too sterile. I paused just outside the door, smoothing down my dress as I mentally prepared myself for the night ahead. I was used to this by now, the careful masks I had to wear depending on the client. Tonight was no different—I knew exactly who I was meeting and how to play my part.

So why did everything feel . . . wrong?

I used the key to open the door.

The silence hung heavy in the air, thicker than usual. Jared wasn't in the living room . . . but that wasn't a surprise. He tended to be . . . more eager than some of the others. I strode across the room, a part of me—like always—wishing that the intricately carved ceiling would cave in and stop all this before it began.

Pasting on a smile, I walked through the entryway—

Logan.

He was sitting in a chair in the corner, one leg casually draped over the other, his hands folded in his lap. The dim light caught on the sharp angles of his gorgeous face, highlighting the calm, deliberate intensity in his expression. He didn't move, didn't say a word. He just stared, his eyes fixed on me like a predator assessing its prey.

My pulse spiked, embarrassment and adrenaline flooding my insides. "What are you doing here?" I managed to ask, my voice tighter than I wanted it to be.

"Waiting for you," he answered coolly.

I glanced over my shoulder at the entry, tension beading down my spine as I imagined the door opening and Jared seeing Logan in the room. The congressman was going to be here any minute. Logan couldn't be here. "You need to leave. Right now." My voice was frantic and pleading.

He didn't move from the chair.

His posture was deceptively relaxed, but the intensity in his gaze belied the casual way he sat. "There's no hurry," he said, his voice low, almost soothing. "Congressman Stroople isn't going to be joining you today."

My stomach churned, and the air in the room seemed to thicken. How had he found out? "What do you mean?" I whispered, my gaze darting away from him in embarrassment. It wasn't a secret that Jared held himself out to be a devoted family man. It was a secret, however, that he enjoyed escorts on a regular basis . . . me being one of them.

Logan tilted his head slightly, his expression unreadable. "I mean, he had other . . . matters come up. You won't be seeing him tonight. Or any other night."

Anxiety surged through me, overriding the tension that had gripped me moments before. "How did you—"

"We had a deal, Sloane," Logan interrupted, his voice sharp now, cutting through the room like a blade. "No other man was going to touch you again."

I let out a bitter laugh, the sound harsh even to my own ears. "That's not the reality of my life, Logan," I shot back. "It's not even an agreement I can make. Obviously, you weren't paying enough if I was sent here."

His jaw tightened, and for a moment, the room was silent except for the steady thrum of my pulse pounding in my ears. Then, slowly, he stood, the chair creaking slightly as he pushed himself up. He moved toward me with deliberate steps, each one making the space between us feel smaller and smaller. My breath hitched, but I couldn't seem to make my feet move.

"You don't have a choice?" he asked, his tone deceptively calm. "Well then, I'll just be taking over from now on. This . . ." His hand gestured vaguely, encompassing the room, the situation, my entire life. "Isn't going to happen anymore."

"It's not up to you!" I snapped, my voice rising despite the tremor in it. "You're a fool if you think you can walk in here and—"

Before I could finish, he grabbed my wrist—firmly enough that I couldn't pull away. In one swift motion, he was sitting on the bench against the bed and pulling me down across his lap. My heart jumped to my throat as I realized what he was doing.

"Logan, don't you dare—"

The first swat landed on the curve of my ass, hard enough to sting but not enough to hurt. My breath hitched, and my hands scrambled against the fabric of his pants as I tried to push myself up, but his arm pinned me in place.

"What the hell are you doing?" I snarled, my voice muffled as my hair fell across my face.

"Teaching you a lesson," he said, his tone maddeningly calm. Another smack followed, sharper this time, and I felt the heat rise in my skin. "Next time you get an . . . assignment. You will let me know, and I will take care of it."

"You'll take care of it?" I spat, twisting against his hold. "You're insane—"

Another swat silenced me, and I gasped, the sound more out of shock than pain. "I'm not letting anyone else touch you," Logan growled, his voice low and dangerous. "Not ever again."

The words sent a shiver down my spine, though I couldn't tell if it was from anger or something far more confusing. My fists clenched at his pants as I tried to push myself up again, but he didn't budge.

"You're out of your damn mind," I hissed, my voice trembling now.

"Maybe," he said, his hand hovering over me for a moment before resting lightly against the fabric of my dress. "But I'm not wrong."

I squeezed my eyes shut, trying to block out the whirlwind of emotions raging inside me—anger, humiliation, something that felt precariously close to longing . . . and lust.

Another swat and then another. Until tears were streaming down my face, and my core was achy and hot.

When he finally let me go, I scrambled to my feet, my cheeks burning as I glared at him.

"This isn't something you're going to win," I said, my voice shaky but firm.

Logan leaned back on the bench, his gaze steady as he looked up at me. "I'm not going anywhere, Sloane," he said, his voice quiet but resolute. "When I said you were mine, I meant it."

"You barely know me!" I hissed, angry, frustrated . . . turned on, tears still streaming down my face.

I hated him in that moment. Hated the way he looked at me like he could see every scar, every wound I tried to hide. Hated how his words made something inside me ache with the kind of hope I'd long since buried.

And most of all, I hated that . . . it was impossible for him to win.

Logan

I watched as the anger seeped out of her, slow like dripping water from a faucet. Her eyes were glued to the carpet as her shoulders lowered and defeat settled over her skin.

"How can you stand to look at me?" she finally whispered.

I pushed up off the bench. "I have the opposite problem, Sloane, I can't seem to take my eyes off you."

"Do you know how many men and women have touched this body? Do you know how many mouths have been on this skin, how many dicks have been inside my cunt, how many cocks have been inside this mouth?" she cried.

"None of that matters to me," I told her, taking a step forward.

She finally looked at me. "I'm a mess," she said brokenly, desperately, like it was a matter of life or death that she convinced me of this. "My past, my present . . . it's going to make you bleed, Logan York. It's going to cut you open and leave you with *nothing*."

I gathered her in my arms. "I don't mind a little blood, Red."

"What if I can't ever give you everything, what if—what if they took too much of me? And I can't ever get it back?" She stared up at me, and I watched, entranced as another tear slid down her smooth cheek.

"Then I'll love what's left of you." I watched as the words sank into her skin. "I'll love whatever you can give me, and it will be enough. Because, Sloane," I murmured, pushing a piece of her hair behind her ear. "Even a single piece of you is worth more than anything anyone else could give me."

A harsh sob burst from her lips as she buried her face into my chest.

Scooping her up, I glanced once at the bed before shaking my head in disgust and striding into the other room. Settling onto the couch, I kept her tucked tightly against me as her sobs eventually faded and her soft breaths filled the room.

I let myself rage then. I let myself feel all the hatred I was capable of as I thought about what had been done to her. I still didn't know much, but I knew enough to imagine ripping their metaphorical dicks off and shoving them down their own throats so they would know what it was like.

Right before I killed them.

As I lay there, holding her, a darkness seeped into my veins, destroying any semblance of the good guy I'd once thought myself to be.

And as her soft breaths caressed my skin, I decided . . .

I was perfectly alright with that.

CHAPTER 20

SLOANE

I was barely aware of Logan getting up from the couch and moving me toward the door. I stayed in a daze as he led me through the lobby and down the sidewalk until he was helping me into his truck.

He didn't try to talk to me as we drove.

I didn't wake up, so to speak, until we were pulling into a parking garage, and I realized that Logan hadn't taken me back to my condo—he'd brought me to his place.

"What are we doing here?" I asked, still not understanding why he wasn't kicking me out of his truck in front of my apartment and shouting "good riddance" as loud as he could.

He glanced over at me with an unimpressed look. "Obviously I'm not leaving you alone tonight," he told me matter-of-factly, like that was something I should have known.

Logan parked and came around to let me out of the truck and then grabbed my hand as he led me toward the elevator.

The door clicked shut behind us, the sound echoing in the quiet entryway of his apartment. Shadows stretched along the walls, the dim light catching the sharp angles of his jaw and the faint stubble that made him look rougher, hungrier. Logan stood there, still as stone, his eyes locked on me, and for a moment, it felt like the entire world had shrunk to just this hallway. Just him.

I should have been thinking about how to get out of this—how to disentangle myself from whatever this was. Instead, I found myself studying him. The way his blond hair fell slightly over his forehead, the way his broad shoulders filled the space, and the way he seemed so utterly untouchable for a girl as tainted as myself were all overwhelming to me.

He shifted, his hands clenching at his sides as though he was trying to keep himself in check. "I *should* give you a chance to leave," he said finally, his voice low, the words almost hesitant.

There was a pause, and then his mouth twisted into something that might have been a smile if it weren't so full of frustration. "But I can't," he admitted, his voice raw. "I won't even pretend that I can."

My chest tightened, and I dropped my gaze to the floor for a moment, as if that might shield me from the intensity of his confession.

I didn't move.

Instead, I looked back up at him, my pulse racing as I searched his face, trying to find an answer that wasn't there. His expression was raw, unguarded, and it unsettled me in a way I wasn't prepared for. I tried to think of all the reasons I shouldn't be here, shouldn't stay. There were plenty of them, an endless list of warnings I should heed.

I should leave.

But . . .

My gaze traced the line of his collar. I could feel the weight of his stare pressing into me, grounding me and making me want to run all at once. But my feet stayed rooted to the polished floor.

I blinked, continuing to study him. "I think my life has shown that maybe I shouldn't be given any big choices. I'll always choose the wrong one."

A faint flicker of a grin slid across his lips, but then it slipped away.

"I want you," he said roughly. "I want you more than anything I've ever wanted in my life. I want you more than hockey, more than money . . . more than fucking air. Tell me I can finally have you, Sloane." He took a deep breath. "Tell me that you're mine."

I stared at him, admiring his face for a moment as I told myself one last time all the reasons why this wouldn't work.

And then I forgot them all.

I stepped back, keeping my eyes on his as I slowly slid the strap of my dress down my shoulder.

One side and then the other. His eyes sparked as he watched me, like his very life was tied to every move I made.

"You're beautiful," he murmured, his voice a sexy rasp, his dark green eyes glittering as he focused on me.

I'd had many men watch me as I undressed, but none of them had watched me like this, like a man dying of thirst.

I slid my dress down my body until it pooled at my heeled feet, and I was standing there in nothing but my lingerie and heels.

"Logan York," I whispered. "I don't know how any of this can last. I don't know how anything you say can be true . . . but for however long it can . . . I'm yours."

He stood there for a long moment, so long I started to wonder if he'd changed his mind . . .

And then he snapped.

Logan grabbed my arms and spun me around, his firm chest against my back. His hand drifted to my breast, softly kneading it as his other hand slid down my stomach, down my thighs, and then up again.

"Mine," he growled, and I shivered at the sensation of his breath caressing my skin.

His arms tightened around my waist, and then he was lifting me up, moving me so that his hard cock could rub against my ass.

I whimpered as he set me down, leaning over me as one of his hands slid between my legs, caressing my clit through my already soaked panties. He rubbed harder, and I squirmed as the pleasure consumed me. His other hand went back to my breast, pinching my nipple beneath the thin lace.

"Logan," I gasped.

"I couldn't make up this body, even in my wildest dreams, Sloane. I'm convinced you were made just for me," he said. I melted against him, loving the feeling of him surrounding me. I cried out as his fingers continued to work my breast, kneading and pulling at my nipples while his other hand applied just the right amount of pressure to my clit.

"I want you. Take me to bed," I whimpered, feeling out of my mind as an orgasm built inside me.

"I thought you'd never ask," he bit out, scooping me into his arms and walking down the hallway to his bedroom. My heels fell to the wooden floor with a clatter as we moved.

"Wrap your legs around me," Logan ordered as he stopped halfway down the hall and shifted me so I could obey. He slid me down his abdomen, his huge dick sliding against my core.

"Ohh," I panted as he started walking again. His cock was rubbing against my clit with each step as his tongue slid down my neck.

"Logan. This is—" I tried to say, but every step felt better, until I was on the verge of coming just from the movement.

I was almost over the edge when we reached the bed, and I whined when he stopped walking.

"Look at me," he ordered, and my eyes flashed to his as he stared at me unwaveringly, something that almost resembled madness lurking in his gaze.

Or maybe . . . that was just love.

Since I met him, I was starting to understand—the two could feel the same.

He pulled me against his dick, rolling his hips in a way that showed exotic dancers evidently had nothing on hot hockey players. Like he had the ability to read my mind, he somehow stopped each time I was about to climax, until my cries were filling the room because I was so desperate for him.

Considering I'd never had a partner who could make me come . . . this felt far too easy for him. I was starting to think that Logan York had magical powers.

"Please," I begged, my voice desperate and needy.

I want you more than anything I've ever wanted in my life. His words echoed in my head, a mimicry for how I was feeling.

He slowly slid me down his body until my feet hit the floor. Still staring, he ripped his shirt off, leaving me momentarily stunned as I gaped at him.

I'd never get used to this level of perfection. Every time I saw him, it felt life-changing.

Smooth, taut skin stretched over sculpted, tattooed, chiseled muscle. As I stared at his defined abs, I remembered that I'd wanted to lick them the first time I'd seen them.

Now seemed as good a time as any.

He watched, his hands slowing at his belt as I leaned forward, pressing a soft kiss to his chest before my tongue dipped out and slid across his skin.

"Sloane," he breathed.

"I want to *taste*," I told him, and his eyes glimmered.

"Just for a second. I *need* to be inside you." There was a feral edge to his voice that had me dripping for him.

My tongue dipped down his chest, and I traced each ab, just how I wanted, worshiping every inch of his sculpted form.

"My turn," he purred, picking me up and dropping me on the bed. A second later, my bra was snapped, my panties were gone, and I was spread out before him, completely naked.

"Fuck," Logan swore, pushing a tattooed hand across his face. "Fuck. Fuck. Fuck."

I smiled, and he lunged forward, his mouth capturing my nipple as he sucked hard. I arched beneath him, my core tightening as his talented, perfect tongue set my body on fire.

I was faintly aware of his hands moving between us as he pushed his pants down, but then his rough fingers were trailing through my folds, pushing inside me as his mouth teased my breasts.

My head thrashed back and forth, my cries filling the room as he added another finger . . . and then another.

"I want you," I breathed. His mouth worked its way up my chest, and then my neck, before he was kissing me again, his lips hard and desperate.

My hips moved against his fingers, trying to get more friction, but he was determined to be in charge. His movements were agonizingly slow, his fingers sliding out of me in a sedate pace that wouldn't allow me to come.

"Please," I begged in between filthy, possessive kisses. "Please. Please. Please."

A tear slid down my face when he removed his fingers, and he briefly pulled back.

"Shhh. Baby. I'm going to give you what we both need," he murmured.

He slid me back on the bed and crawled over me, and my eyes greedily took in his tattooed chest. He was completely covered with ink. And I couldn't wait to discover every mark on his body.

Logan pushed my thighs apart, and a moment later his cock was sliding through my slick folds.

I glanced down and almost passed out.

Holy fuck.

His dick was a monster.

"Thank you," he said, and I realized that I'd said that out loud.

I'd seen a lot of dicks, but nothing held a candle to what was in front of me. How did he walk around all day with that in between his legs?

"Lots of practice," he assured me, and I slapped my hands over my mouth because I obviously couldn't be trusted to speak right now. "I'm going to make you feel so good," he said as he moved my hands away from my face. "Now kiss me while I make you mine."

My lips met his, and he sucked on my tongue as he pushed in slowly . . . gently . . . like I was made of glass instead of a whore.

I gasped against him, trying to adjust to his size as he stretched me, inch by inch.

There was an awestruck look in his eyes, like we were teenagers, fumbling around in bed, and this was the first time he'd ever felt a woman's cunt.

Or maybe it was something more.

A hiccuped sob burst from my mouth as he surged all the way in. It *was* more. Definitely more.

"Red. You're doing so good," he breathed as he pressed kiss after exquisite kiss across my face.

"It's too much," I told him, and a tear trickled down my cheek.

"I know," he said simply, before his hips tilted and he pulled back slowly.

Our eyes were locked as he slammed into me hard, and my cry met his deep growl.

He kissed me softly as he expertly moved, his dick hitting every perfect place inside me.

His arms caged me in, and I was consumed by him.

His scent, the sound of our bodies moving together, the way his hair fell in his eyes.

I love you, I wanted to whisper to the world.

But I think he already knew.

"You're perfect, Sloane Calloway," he breathed as his huge cock fucked in and out of me, his muscles flexing under my fingers as I held on and enjoyed the ride with every fiber of my being.

He was transforming me.

"I didn't know it could be like this," I sobbed as an orgasm ripped through my veins, the pleasure almost agonizing in its intensity.

He buried his face in my neck, groaning as we moved together.

"You're so fucking tight," he growled. "Fuck."

My nails bit into his skin as his hips moved faster. He was too big for me, and every push of his hips carried a bite of pain with it.

But I loved it.

My insides clenched as his finger found my clit between us. "Come with me, Red. Squeeze my dick and give me what I want."

A few thrusts later, and his movements became erratic.

My cry was almost a scream as I came again, emotion and euphoria surging through me as he groaned, and I felt his hot seed deep inside.

"My perfect, magical girl," he whispered as he pressed kisses against my skin. I sobbed again, my emotions too much to be kept inside.

Magical.

I'd never been called that before.

Amazing. Good. Incredible. Sexy.

I'd gotten all of those.

But I hadn't gotten that.

I let the word spread across my skin, sinking into my veins until there was a warm feeling everywhere.

Until a thought hit me.

"I'm on birth control," I said hurriedly, as I'd grasped that I'd just let him come inside me. Birth control was unnecessary since I couldn't have children, but going bare was still something I *never* did given my occupation . . . and my history.

Surprisingly, though, I wasn't panicking like I normally would have. And not just because it was impossible for me to have kids. But because it was him, and I . . . loved having a part of him inside me like that.

Logan lifted up, a strange look in his eyes as he stared . . . almost like he was disappointed. "Okay," he finally murmured before breathing a kiss onto my lips and rolling so his full weight wasn't on top of me.

"What happens now?" I asked as we lay on our sides, staring at each other only inches apart. His breath was my breath as we breathed in, like we were in our own *magical* world that only included us.

"Now you let yourself love me and trust me to catch you," he responded, reaching up to smooth a piece of hair from my face.

"Okay, Logan."

The words slipped from my lips, and I didn't hate it when they did.

He smiled, and it might have been the most beautiful thing I'd ever seen.

"Good girl."

I tried to stay in that moment; a part of me worried it was another perfect piece of time that would slip away . . . but my eyes still closed.

And I was so exhausted that I forgot to ask before I fell into a deep, dreamless sleep . . . how had he known where I was tonight?

CHAPTER 21

LOGAN

My phone buzzed over and over again until I was forced to turn away from Sloane's warm, sleeping body to see what was happening.

I scrolled through the texts, noting that, although it was chaos . . . it was in fact, not an emergency.

> **Camden:** Wake up, Rookalicious.

> **Ari:** No. Absolutely not.

> **Camden:** Not a winner?

> **Ari:** I shouldn't be the only one saying this. Why aren't more people speaking up?

> **Walker:** I bet Geraldine calls him that.

I grimaced at that thought.

> **Camden:** That's actually why I'm texting.

> **Lincoln:** Because Geraldine calls him that? I could have lived without that knowledge.

I nodded my head, because I agreed with that statement.

Camden: Geraldine has requested our presence tonight for dinner after practice. She claims it will be good luck because "we've been sucking something awful."

Ari: She specifically mentioned me, right?

Camden: . . .

Ari: Get it together, Hero. That's not the proper usage of that right now.

Ari: And why was Logan the first person you thought of in this scenario? How does that make any sense?

Camden: . . .

Lincoln: I actually thought that was the perfect usage.

Ari: Betrayal. The cold slice of betrayal. That's what I'm feeling right now, Golden Boy.

Walker: As head of the Circle, it does seem like Linc can confirm the rules.

Ari: Listen, simp. I don't think that we ever said that Lincoln Daniels was the head of the Circle. If it even exists, might I add.

Camden: See, I don't think the leader of the Circle would pretend like it didn't exist.

Ari Lancaster removed Camden James from the chat.

I was struggling not to laugh and wake up Sloane.

Lincoln Daniels added Camden James to the chat.

Ari: Apparently you chose violence this morning, Golden Boy.

Ari: I don't like how this is going, gentlemen. Maybe I'm the leader of the Circle, and you've just gotten yourselves kicked out. Or maybe I'll go and start a group called the Trust Tree or the Cone of Silence. Maybe the Mutual Mischief Club!

Lincoln: All of those are unequivocally terrible, Lancaster.

Walker: It's true. No one will want to join those clubs.

Camden: . . .

Camden: Wait . . . we're a club?

My body was shaking, and Sloane stirred next to me. Fuck. She needed her sleep. I'd worn her out, unable to stop myself from taking her multiple times throughout the night. Even now, I wanted her, although my dick was probably rubbed raw at this point.

Me: Alright, alright. No need to be so shouty. Rooka-licious has entered the building.

Camden: Knew you would like that one.

Ari: I'm not talking to anyone. You guys are lucky my angel-poo wifey is next to me, because she's the only one who could stop my rage at this point.

Lincoln: As we were saying . . .

Camden: Dinner. Tonight. 7:30 at Geraldine's. She said to dress to impress.

Ari: You still haven't answered me. She included me in that invitation, right? Like she said specifically, I can't wait to see Ari again?

Camden: . . .

Camden: I think the main invite was actually for Logan, which I was very offended by, if that makes you feel any better, Lancaster.

Ari: . . .

Me: Good use of that, Ari.

Ari Lancaster removed Logan York from the chat.

A second later, Walker added me back in.

Me: It's good to be back.

A soft sigh had me setting down the phone and turning toward the woman I was . . . in love with.

Holy fuck, I was in love.

I'd known I was obsessed . . . I'd known I was attracted . . . but this? This feeling inside me, like the sun rose and fell with her presence, like I couldn't live without her . . . it had to be love.

My eyes widened as I took her in, devouring her perfect features. Asleep, she looked so peaceful, and a sense of pride hit me that she trusted me enough to relax like this. She was still just stirring, coming out of her deep sleep, and I took the opportunity to just . . . watch her.

———

Sloane

Sleep had always been my enemy. Nights were the worst—long, endless hours of tossing and turning, my mind a storm of memories and fears that wouldn't shut off. The darkness felt suffocating, like it was pressing in from all sides, and no matter how hard I tried to escape it, I couldn't. I hadn't slept through a night in years. I'd almost forgotten what it felt like to rest, to wake up without that fog of exhaustion dragging me down.

But after being with Logan, everything felt different.

I didn't realize it at first. It crept up on me, slow and subtle, unlike the way he'd forced his way into my life. I woke up, tangled in the sheets, the sunlight streaming through the window, and for the first time in as long as I could remember, I didn't feel like a zombie.

I'd slept.

I'd actually slept.

I blinked, sitting up, rubbing my eyes like I couldn't believe it. My heart pounded as the realization hit me—my mind had been quiet. For once I wasn't haunted by nightmares, by the weight of everything I'd been running from.

Maybe Logan York did have some kind of magic.

The bed was empty next to me, the sheets still warm, though, so he must have just gotten up.

I stretched my arms above my head, loving the delicious soreness in every muscle of my body after the night we'd just had.

Swinging my legs to the side, I moved to get out of bed. And then I paused—

I didn't want to leave. I was afraid that once my feet hit the floor, the magic of this world Logan had built around us . . . it would disappear.

The door creaked, and a second later Logan was coming into the room, shirtless, holding a tray filled with delicious-smelling food.

A different kind of hunger was stirring inside me as I took in his tattooed chest.

"You can have all of that you want as soon as I get food in you," he teased with an easy smile.

And something inside me cracked.

The tears came before I could stop them, hot and sudden, and I wiped at my eyes, embarrassed.

"Hey," he said softly, setting down the tray, his brow furrowing with concern. "What's wrong, baby?"

I shook my head, the lump in my throat making it hard to speak. "I—" My voice caught, and I had to swallow hard before I could get the words out. "I slept. Logan, I *slept* last night."

He frowned, not understanding. "You slept?"

My voice was shaking as I explained. "I never sleep. I—my mind doesn't shut off. I haven't had a night without insomnia, without nightmares in *years*." The tears kept coming, my heart on full display. "But last night . . . after being with you . . . I actually slept."

His eyes softened, and he sat down on the bed, pulling me into his arms. "Sloane," he said gently, his voice low, calming. "Maybe your body is finally believing what your mind doesn't yet—that you're safe here. Safe with me."

The tears spilled over, and I shook my head, overwhelmed by the weight of it all. "I'm not used to this. I'm not used to feeling like this. I don't even know how to *be* like this."

Logan's grip tightened slightly, his thumb brushing over my skin. "Then let me show you. Let me show you what you deserve. Let me take care of you—take care of everything."

I collapsed into his chest, the sobs breaking free, my hands clutching his arms like he was the only thing keeping me from falling apart. And in that moment, I realized that maybe—just maybe—I could trust this. Trust him.

For the first time in a long time, I wasn't fighting the dark. I wasn't running away.

I was running straight toward it.

———————

Logan slowed down as we approached the front door of Geraldine's penthouse. His pace went from brisk to suspiciously sluggish. I raised an eyebrow, watching him shuffle forward like a man on death row.

"What's wrong with you?" I asked, my heels clicking on the tile floor.

"Nothing," he said, a little too quickly.

He shot a glance at the door ahead, then back at me. There was a twitch in his jaw, and his hands were jammed into his pockets like he was resisting the urge to bolt.

"Logan?" I pressed. "Are you . . . nervous?"

His shoulders tensed, and he muttered something under his breath that sounded suspiciously like *You'll see*.

Before I could demand clarification, the door flew open, and a woman who could only be described as an eccentric hurricane of chiffon and sequins swept into view. Logan had told me Geraldine was pushing eighty, or possibly there already . . . but the woman in front of me didn't look like any eighty-year-old I'd ever met.

She was draped in a glittering gold gown that seemed to cascade like molten metal, its high neckline offset by a daring thigh slit. Her oversized earrings were shaped like chandeliers, swinging with every dramatic gesture she made, and a feathered capelet in deep emerald perched on her shoulders like she was ready to take flight.

Evidently, she hadn't been kidding when she'd ordered us to "dress to impress," as Logan had mentioned. I glanced down at my black cocktail dress . . . feeling wildly underdressed.

"My favorite boy!" she crowed, pulling Logan into an embrace that seemed more like a full-body tackle. She smacked a dramatic kiss on his cheek, leaving a crimson lipstick mark that he immediately tried to wipe off, his face a shade of pink I'd never seen before.

"Good to see you, Geraldine," Logan murmured.

"And who is this lovely creature?" Geraldine asked, nonplussed at Logan's awkwardness as she turned her sharp gaze to me.

Logan straightened up, his hand moving to my back as he pushed me forward like a sacrificial lamb. "This is Sloane," he said proudly.

"Oh-ho!" Geraldine said, eyeing me like she'd just uncovered a delightful secret. "The infamous Sloane. I've heard so much about you."

I raised an eyebrow at Logan, who looked like he was about to spontaneously combust. "All good things, I hope."

"Oh, darling," Geraldine said with a wicked grin. "Good things are boring. Come in, come in!"

She stepped back, waving us inside with a flourish, and Logan grabbed my hand, pulling me along like his life depended on it. A few steps in, he moved me strategically in front of him, using me as some kind of human shield between himself and the eccentric older woman in front of us.

Geraldine glanced back at us as we walked, her eyes twinkling like she knew exactly what was going on.

The entryway was what you'd expect from a woman like Geraldine: massive, opulent, and dripping in luxury. But it wasn't until we could see into the living room that I understood why Logan had been dragging his feet.

I stopped dead in my tracks. The room was filled with sculptures—most of them the same man . . . posing nude. But right in the center stood one that was unmistakably . . . Logan.

And it wasn't just that it was him—it was him in nothing but a pair of briefs, his muscular form captured in excruciating detail. The pose was heroic, his chin tilted up as if he were surveying his kingdom, but the whole thing was so ridiculous that I couldn't hold it in.

"Oh my gosh," I gasped, doubling over in laughter. "Is that . . . is that you?"

Logan groaned, running a hand over his face. "Can we just—"

"Isn't it fabulous?" Geraldine interrupted, her voice dripping with smug amusement as she pointed at the sculpture with an exaggerated flourish. "It captures him perfectly. Even my Harold would have thought so," she said, pointing to the man featured in her nude collection.

"That's her late husband," Logan murmured in my ear, still sounding completely mortified.

"How did you manage to make the list for her . . . art?" I whispered back.

The doorbell sounded, and Geraldine began to walk back to the front door. "Go in and make yourselves comfortable, darlings. I'm sure that's the others."

"Kill me now," Logan said as we walked into the living room. "I'm never going to be able to live this down."

The sound of laughter erupted from behind us, and the rest of the crew walked in. Camden was hunched over, looking like he was about to fall to the ground, Ari was clutching his stomach, and Lincoln—who I'd never seen look anything other than composed—was leaning against the entryway like he'd lost the ability to walk. Walker and Olivia were staring at everything with their jaws wide open, and the rest of the girls were giggling.

"I can't believe it," Camden choked out between laughs.

"Your clothes were on when we walked in that night," Ari said, wiping a tear from his eye. "You left out some pretty big details, Rookie."

"Shut up," Logan grumbled, his ears turning red. "You have no idea what that night was like. It was the purple drink. I blame *it* completely."

"It's so nice that we can gather together like this," Geraldine said, clapping her hands as she walked up from behind the group.

Ari suddenly put his hand over Blake's eyes.

"What are you doing?" she squealed, trying to bat him away.

"Geraldine? Those proportions are exaggerated, right?" Ari asked, his gaze dipping to the . . . ginormous bulge in Logan's briefs on the statue.

"No," she chortled delightedly. "Everything is completely accurate."

There was a beat of silence, and then Lincoln began pushing Monroe toward the other side of the room. "Appetizers are in the dining room, Geraldine?" he called behind him as he made sure that Monroe was faced away from the statue.

"Oh, well, I was thinking we could enjoy hors d'oeuvres and drinks in here but . . ." Geraldine began.

"Dining room sounds great," Camden said, gliding Anastasia toward the archway that Lincoln and Monroe had just disappeared through.

"I could pose for you," Ari suddenly offered, his hands going to his waist like he was going to start undressing right here.

"That's alright, dear," Geraldine said, almost dismissively, as she swept dramatically toward the dining room. "I think my collection is complete."

Ari's jaw dropped.

"How is she not noticing how hot I am?" he complained.

Blake patted him on the chest, a wide grin on her face. "You're hot to me, Lancaster," she cooed reassuringly.

Ari's eyes grew hooded, and he smirked at her, pulling her into his chest. "Good, because you're stuck with me, angel face," he said, and I looked away, because it was suddenly getting *very* hot in here.

Geraldine stopped Walker before he and Olivia had made it to the dining room. "You know . . . *you* would make an excellent addition to my collection, Walker dear. I could make an exception for you."

Walker was turned away from me, but I could see the tips of his ears turning red, even from where I was standing.

Logan was cracking up next to me, burying his face in my neck.

Ari stiffened and pointed a finger in the air as he kept Blake plastered against him with his other arm. "This is an *outrage*," he hissed.

Blake started giggling.

"This is not funny."

"Sorry," she said, her giggles turning into hysterical laughter. "But it kind of is."

"Traitor," he grumbled, letting her go and hustling after the eccentric woman. "Geraldine, have you been watching my thirst traps lately?"

She ignored him as she disappeared from the room, but it took Logan a second before his laughter calmed and he could hold himself upright.

We passed his sculpture, and I stopped in front of it. "You know, I don't think it's quite as big as you are," I commented.

"That was the nicest thing you've ever said to me, Red," Logan said before he pulled me into a deep kiss. I was breathless when he released me, my body ready to desert this dinner party and head home for another round in bed.

"Soon," he commented, his eyes growing hooded and his dick stiffening as he pulled me close.

"Logan, darling. Are you two joining us?" Geraldine asked, popping her head out. "I want to talk about your tattoos."

"Coming," Logan answered in a choked voice, looking very afraid all of a sudden.

"Pssh. You talk a big game, Logan York, but I think you actually like how Geraldine fawns over you."

His cheeks flushed. "I don't know what you're talking about."

I leaned in close as we started to walk. "After we're done *talking* about your tattoos . . . I think I want to hear about what happened that night."

Logan gulped and muttered something unintelligible under his breath.

Dinner was as extravagant as you'd expect—long table, crystal chandeliers, more silverware than was necessary—and the chaos didn't stop once we sat down.

Ari, clearly desperate for Geraldine's attention, kept trying to chime in with witty comments, only to be ignored as she focused on Logan or Walker. Every time Ari opened his mouth, Geraldine waved him off like an annoying fly.

"Geraldine," Ari said finally, his voice taking on an exaggeratedly dignified tone. "If you don't acknowledge my brilliance soon, I may take my talents elsewhere."

Geraldine didn't even look at him. "Yes, dear, you do that."

The table erupted in laughter, and Ari threw up his hands in exasperation. "You're all dead to me."

"You'll survive," Lincoln said dryly, raising his glass in a mock toast.

As the night went on, the banter flowed as freely as the nonalcoholic wine, and I couldn't help but notice Logan relaxing beside me, his earlier tension melting away. At some point, Geraldine leaned over to me, her sharp eyes twinkling.

"He's different with you," she said quietly, nodding toward Logan.

I glanced at him, my chest tightening at the softness in his expression as he laughed at something Camden had said. "Different how?"

Geraldine smiled knowingly. "Happy."

For a moment, I couldn't find a response. Instead, I just squeezed Logan's hand under the table, feeling a warmth I hadn't expected. Maybe Geraldine was right. Maybe he was different.

And maybe, just maybe, so was I.

CHAPTER 22

SLOANE

The sleek black car came to a stop, and the driver stepped out, opening the door for me with a polished smile. "Here you go, ma'am," he said, handing me my suitcase as I stepped out into the humid morning air. The private plane loomed ahead, gleaming against the runway lights. I swallowed hard, gripping the handle tightly. Logan had insisted that I fly with his friends' wives to the next game, and somehow . . . I'd agreed. Despite the fact that they'd been overwhelmingly warm and kind at the last game and also at dinner the other night, I was still trying to not be an anxious mess.

Taking a deep breath, I climbed the stairs, each step echoing faintly in my head. As I reached the top, the door opened, and I was greeted by the last thing I expected: a gray-haired woman with spectacles, who had to be at least seventy, dressed in a cat sweater that said *I'm feline fine*. She was wearing orthopedic shoes, and her warm smile radiated grandmotherly energy.

I glanced back and helplessly watched the car I'd arrived in drive away. He'd dropped me off at the wrong plane.

"Hi, dearie," she chirped. "You must be Sloane. My name's Mabel. I'm so glad you're here."

I blinked. Once. Twice. Or maybe I wasn't in the wrong place. "Uh . . . thanks," I said slowly, my voice trailing off as I tried to piece together what was happening.

"Have a cookie while we wait to take off," Mabel said, holding out a tray piled high with what looked like homemade chocolate chip cookies. "We'll have all sorts of good stuff for you once we're up to cruising altitude."

"Thank you," I said, my voice trailing off as I hesitantly took a cookie from the tray. I stepped inside, blinking at the sight of another older woman ahead of us with a pitcher of lemonade. Did her name tag say . . . Edna?

The sweet smell of freshly baked goods followed me into the plane, and I glanced into the cockpit as I passed by. There, to my utter disbelief, were three more older women—all with silver hair—fiddling with switches like they'd been flying planes since World War II.

What was going on?

I kept moving, the cookie halfway to my mouth, as I began to make my way down the narrow aisle. My focus was still on the bizarre setup I'd just seen, so much so that it took me a second to realize everyone else was already here.

Monroe, Blake, Olivia—holding the cutest baby I'd ever seen—and Anastasia were lounging in plush seats, looking perfectly at ease as they sipped what appeared to be lemonade from crystal glasses. Their faces lit up when they saw me.

"Sloane, you're here!" Monroe said excitedly, patting the seat next to her.

"Hi," I said awkwardly, her enthusiasm catching me off guard.

"Take a bite of that cookie. It's life-changing," Blake urged, gesturing to the warm treat in my hand.

"Oh, right." I bit into the cookie out of politeness . . . and then moaned. It was warm and gooey, melting in my mouth. "Holy fuck, that's good."

"According to Mabel, she's been working on that recipe her entire life," said Anastasia, happily snacking on her own cookie.

"Mabel and Edna . . . are the flight attendants?" I asked hesitantly. "Are they like Lincoln's grandmas or something?"

Olivia snorted, and a second later, all four of them were laughing.

"Welcome to Grandma Airlines," Blake said, throwing up her hands and giving me jazz fingers like she'd just gotten done with a big reveal on a game show.

"I can't tell if you're joking or not," I snorted.

"No, seriously. That's what we call it," said Monroe, taking a sip of her drink. "It was Lincoln's way to ensure that no guy would talk to me, and then the others joined in."

I gaped at her. "He bought this so other guys wouldn't talk to you?"

She smirked, like she was amused by my reaction. "Yep. He's a little obsessed."

"I think calling Lincoln Daniels a little obsessed is like saying Texas is only a 'little' hot during the summer, Monroe," teased Blake.

"Says the girl whose husband has a ring on his—" Blake slapped her hand over Monroe's mouth so she couldn't finish her sentence.

"Shhh. You can't show our crazy yet. We have to make her love us first before you start talking about that," she hissed.

I giggled, and Blake winked at me. I could see why she and Ari were together, both of them were ridiculously charming.

"So . . . I'm assuming you've discovered if Logan's tattoos cover . . . all of him." Olivia grinned, rocking her sleeping baby in her arms as she munched on a cookie.

I blushed at that reference because there was actually only one place Logan didn't have a single tattoo, and I'd had that monster dick all up inside me just this morning before he'd left for the team plane.

"I knew it," Anastasia huffed. "You *luvvvv* him."

"What does that have to do with her seeing his tattoos?" asked Monroe, raising an eyebrow.

"Tattoos aren't important with these guys?" Blake asked innocently.

"Oh my gosh, you guys are the worst," Monroe practically screeched, and then the others all burst into laughter.

I was so lost.

But I loved it.

Feeling like maybe I was becoming a part of their group.

They wouldn't be acting like this if they knew who I was . . .

The thought popped into my head, and the smile that had been on my face died. I pulled out my phone, suddenly wanting to create a wall between myself and the others.

The plane began to taxi down the runway. While the girls continued to tease each other, I pulled out my phone, reading Logan's latest text as I set the cookie down on the table in front of me.

> Logan: Red. I beg of you. Bring me some cookies.

> Me: Oh, do you mean the cookies made by the women in cat sweaters that you failed to warn me about—who exist because your friends are a little crazy.

> Logan: . . .

Me: So you don't deny it?

Logan: Listen, Sloane. Baby. Love of my life. I have been trying to get a hold of these cookies since I first heard about them. They told me that I couldn't have them until I had a lady. You are my lady. You have to get me one.

A little flutter built up inside me at the fact that he'd just said *love of my life*. Who knew you could swoon this much from a text.

Me: Almost sounds like you're using me for cookies, York.

Logan: I would never . . .

Logan: PS This is a matter of life or death.

"What's Logan saying over there?" asked Monroe with a smirk.

I blushed. "He was saying he wants some cookies."

"I bet he wants your cookies," said Blake innocently. There was a pause, and then we were all laughing.

"That was a good one, Lancaster," Olivia said. She pressed a kiss to her daughter's forehead, and there was a sudden pang of longing inside me as I watched them.

I blinked, wishing I could just be . . . normal for once.

We made it to cruising altitude, and soon the cheerful bustle of Edna and Mabel filled the cabin. Edna refilled our lemonade glasses with military precision, and Mabel beamed as she carried another tray of cookies down the aisle.

Across from me, Monroe raised an eyebrow, watching me as I stared at the flight attendants, bemused. She was clearly trying not to laugh. "Something wrong, Sloane?"

"This is really all because your guys don't want men flirting with you?" I asked.

Olivia grinned, bouncing her baby gently on her knee. "You know those red flags they tell you to stay away from when you're growing up."

"Yeah?" I asked, confused.

"Well, it turns out . . . they're actually very green once you get to know them."

I blinked at her, and then the four of them were bursting into laughter.

I took a bite of my second cookie, shaking my head in amusement. "This is one of my weirder experiences," I told them.

"It's only weird if it doesn't work," quipped Anastasia.

"Good try," said Blake, snorting.

"Hey, that was a good one."

"It was better than usual," Monroe said soothingly.

I realized there was a big, goofy grin on my face as I watched them.

"If Logan isn't showing any red flags yet . . . it'll just be a matter of time," Blake said, some cookie crumbs falling out of her mouth as she talked.

I went to shake my head again . . . and then stopped.

"Oooh . . . Rookie's already showing his game, isn't he?" Anastasia asked.

I smirked, miming zipping my lips.

"We'll get your secrets out soon, Calloway," Blake teased, getting up from her seat and walking over to a box on one of the empty seats. "Speaking of secrets, evidently the guys had something made for us, but I wasn't allowed to open the box until we were on the plane."

Blake opened it and pulled out a blue T-shirt with the Dallas Knights logo on it. "They want us to wear these instead of jerseys?" she asked, sounding confused as she turned it around.

A bark of laughter reverberated through the plane as she stared at the shirt.

"What is it?" Monroe asked, craning her neck to see.

Blake's smile was huge as she turned the shirt around to the back where *Stanley Cupcake* was written on top of Ari's number.

"I guess we finally have a name, girls," Monroe laughed as Blake began to pass out the shirts.

There was even one for me.

I'd never been more proud to be a part of something as I pulled on my *Stanley Cupcake* shirt and snacked on chocolate chip cookies and lemonade for the rest of the flight with the girls who might actually be . . . my friends.

CHAPTER 23

LOGAN

I grabbed her tits, pushing them together, nice and tight around my dick. My hips thrust in a frenzied, frantic rhythm as I fucked her breasts.

We had just a couple of minutes before I was due on the bus that would take us back to the team plane. But there was no way my dick could handle waiting to celebrate a Game Six win for when we got back to Dallas. Two straight wins meant we were going to Game Seven. So, celebrations were in order. Her cunt was my favorite part of her, but seeing her breasts in that tight T-shirt . . . well, I'd found myself doing this.

"Touch yourself," I growled. "Make yourself come." I forced my brain to connect enough that I could play with her nipples the way she liked as I slid back and forth between her breasts. Pre-cum was dribbling all over her chest, and I groaned as I made her skin a sticky mess.

As I watched, she dragged her finger through it, gathering some on her finger before she slid it sensually into her mouth and sucked it all off.

"Oh, fuck," I groaned. "Baby, make yourself come. This is . . . this is too hot," I hissed.

She grinned, but I could feel her movements below me as she touched herself like the good girl she was.

"Please come," I begged, watching her closely to make sure she didn't fake it.

Her tits were made for my dick, I decided. *Everything* about her was perfectly made for my dick. I felt like the luckiest bastard alive that I was getting to touch her, that I was able to do this.

My balls drew up, and I groaned again. I didn't want this to end. But there was nothing I could do. It was too good. Too fucking good.

Sloane's gaze was half-lidded and lust-drunk as her breath quickened, and the rosy blush spread across her skin.

"Talk to me," she begged, and it felt like a victory, that she wanted my voice to help her come. A perverse part of me wanted more than that, though. I wanted her to *need* my voice to come.

Baby steps.

"Come for me, sweet girl. You're so fucking hot I can't even stand it."

My hips thrust a few more times, and then my body tensed, my cock pulsing as spray after spray of my cum streaked across her breasts, her neck, and her chin.

"Ahh," she moaned, crying out as her body trembled underneath me, and she climaxed.

A small spurt of more cum flew from my still-hard dick at the sight of that, and I huffed out a laugh, because obviously my dick could not be stopped.

"Feed me," she begged, and my eyes widened when I realized what she wanted.

I grabbed her hand, gathering up more of the cum coating her skin before I brought it to her lips, making sure to spread it across her mouth before I pushed my fingers inside.

"You can have as much as you want, baby. Such a good girl, begging for my cum."

She preened under my praise, and I fed her more from my fingers until her chest and neck were almost clean. After she swallowed, I reluctantly let her breasts go, moving down her body so I could give her a rough kiss, enjoying our combined tastes on my tongue.

"Wow," she breathed. "That was quite the celebration."

I smirked, helping her slide her bra and shirt back on. "Just wait until we win the Stanley Cup."

"That confident, are you?" she grinned. I pressed another kiss on her lips, because I couldn't stop myself. She was too perfect.

"I just have one of those feelings, Red. Like it's going to happen. You're my lucky charm, I've decided."

A wistful look crept into her expression. "I like that," she whispered. "I've never been someone's good thing before."

I could tell it was hard for her to admit those words, and I groaned as I pulled her even closer to me. "You're *my* good thing, baby. The best thing I've ever had."

She buried her face into my chest. "You're doing it again, Logan York."

"What's that?"

"Talking crazy."

I snorted. "Kiss me some more," I ordered, and she obediently lifted her face and gave me what I wanted. Any more words were lost in a haze of kisses and exchanged breaths.

Bang, bang, bang.

I lifted my head, blinking as I came back to the present, where I'd pulled Sloane into an empty office down the hall from the visitors' locker room.

"Hate to break up the . . . party, party people. But Rookie needs to get on the bus." Ari's voice floated through the door, sounding amused.

I groaned, and she giggled.

"I'll be counting down the hours until I see you again," I murmured as I reluctantly pulled away so we could walk to the door.

"Me too," she said back as I adjusted her necklace one more time, to make sure I got as good of footage as possible for when I needed my fix of her on the way back.

"I—" I began, before stopping myself. *I love you* was bursting from my insides, but since I was getting on a plane and unable to calm her down if she got scared, I decided to wait to say it. "I'll see you soon," I said instead.

I would only be able to wait a little longer, though, I decided, taking one last look behind me as I pushed through the door that led to the outside.

Some words just needed to be said.

Sloane

I was sitting next to Olivia, listening to the soft coos from her baby, Isabella, as we flew back to Dallas. The table in front of us was covered with colorful toys and a baby blanket as we tried to keep her occupied. I was trying to focus on the moment, trying to savor the innocent joy of watching a baby discover the world, but . . . I couldn't help but think of the fact that I would never have this. The weight of it clung to me like a shadow.

Olivia gently bounced Isabella in her lap. She smiled down at her daughter, a soft, genuine smile that made her whole face light up. It was the kind of smile I wasn't sure I was capable of anymore. The kind of smile that said everything was right in her world, even if I knew it wasn't.

"She's such a good baby," I crooned.

"She's my little miracle," Olivia said, her voice full of warmth.

I nodded, forcing a smile, but I couldn't shake the heaviness in my chest.

Olivia turned to me, her eyes softening. "Do you want kids some-day, Sloane?"

The question hit me harder than I expected. My breath caught in my throat, and for a moment, I couldn't speak. I stared down at the baby toy in my hand, twisting it absently as the silence stretched on. Finally, I swallowed and looked away.

"Nobody like me should ever be a mother," I said quietly, the words tasting bitter on my tongue.

Olivia didn't say anything at first, just watched me, her brow furrowing in concern. "Why do you think that?"

I let out a harsh breath, shaking my head as I set the toy down on the table. "Olivia." I sighed, just deciding to get it over with. Logan would probably be mortified, but it was better that these girls knew now, rather than finding out later after I'd gotten even closer to them.

It would hurt more then.

"I'm an escort," I whispered. "Or at least I was." I shook my head, realizing how up in the air everything was at the moment. "My past? It's too messed up. I'm too damaged. I would ruin any child. Just like . . ." My voice faltered, the truth too painful to finish. *Just like I've been ruined.*

Olivia's baby reached up to grab her hair, and Olivia gently untangled her tiny fingers, her expression thoughtful. When she spoke, her voice was steady and calm. "You're not ruined, Sloane. None of us are."

I scoffed, looking away. "You don't understand."

Olivia's voice softened, but there was an edge to it, something deep and raw that made me glance back at her. "You think I don't understand?"

I didn't answer, not at first. But something in the way she was looking at me made me realize she wasn't just saying the words to make me feel better. There was something else. Something *real*.

She adjusted her daughter on her lap and took a deep breath. "I used to think the same thing, you know? I didn't think I deserved this—this family, this baby, this life. I thought I was too broken to be a mother." Her eyes flickered with something I hadn't seen before, something vulnerable.

I frowned, not sure where she was going with this.

"I was addicted to prescription drugs for years," Olivia said quietly, her voice trembling slightly. "And that's not even the worst of it. My manager—he raped me. And my mom? She knew. She betrayed me. I felt like I had nothing left, like I was too damaged to ever be whole again."

Her words hit me like a punch. I stared at her, stunned. I'd had no idea. I'd seen the headlines in the past about her being in a conservatorship, but I'd never paid much attention to celebrity gossip, so I hadn't known any details.

"And for a long time, I thought that made me unfit to be a mother," Olivia continued, her voice thick with emotion. "I thought all of those terrible things I'd been through made me incapable of giving my daughter the love she deserved. But Walker . . . he helped me realize that those experiences didn't make me less. They made me *more*. Because now, I know what I want for her. I want her to have the kind of life I never had. And I'll do whatever it takes to make sure she gets that."

I could feel the tears building in my eyes, but I didn't wipe them away. I just listened, her words piercing through the wall I'd built around myself.

Olivia looked down at her daughter, her eyes filled with love and fear at the same time. "Sometimes, I'm still scared I'll fail. I'm terrified, actually. But then I look at her, and I think about how much I love her, and it changes everything. Love . . . it's bigger than the pain. It's stronger than the past."

I didn't realize I was crying until I felt the tears slip down my cheeks. I blinked, trying to pull myself together, but I couldn't. Olivia's words had hit me straight in the heart, breaking open something I'd kept buried for so long.

What if . . . Everett was wrong? What if there was more for me in this life?

A deeper thought hit me.

What if I wasn't ruined after all?

"I don't know if I can do that," I whispered, my voice cracking. "I don't know if I can be . . . enough. For anyone."

Olivia reached over, gently placing her hand on mine. "You're already enough, Sloane. You just don't see it yet."

I stared at her, my throat tight with emotion. I wanted to believe her. I wanted to believe that maybe, just maybe, I wasn't as broken as I thought. But it was hard. So damn hard.

Olivia squeezed my hand, her voice soft but firm. "I don't know you well yet, but sometimes you just know. You can see a kindred spirit—that you've survived things most people couldn't even imagine. Just like me. And just like me . . . you're still here. That means something. And if you ever do decide you want kids, they won't be ruined. They'll be loved. Because you *know* what it's like to hurt, and that means you'll fight harder than anyone to protect them."

I couldn't speak. The tears kept coming, and I didn't try to stop them this time. I just nodded, my chest aching with a mixture of pain and hope.

Maybe she was right. Maybe I wasn't beyond saving. Maybe, just maybe, I could learn to believe that.

What was it with Logan . . . with his group of friends. Every time I was with them . . . I felt something other than fear.

CHAPTER 24

SLOANE

Everett had been quiet. Too quiet. He usually checked in on me almost daily, *especially* when I was in the middle of a job.

But I'd heard nothing.

I'd thought there'd be hell to pay after Logan ruined my appointment with the congressman, but there'd also been *nothing* since that night.

I could have called him, explained that the congressman had bailed before I'd even gotten there . . . but I couldn't bring myself to do it.

I also hadn't talked to Logan about the fact that he was still paying for my time. I wasn't sure how much Everett was charging . . . but even for a professional athlete, it had to be expensive.

I needed to tell Everett I was done.

But . . . I was scared.

What if Logan changed his mind? We were moving at the speed of light, and I'd always been extremely skeptical of meteoric rises.

And that's definitely what this was.

"What do you think about Thai food?" Logan mused, scrolling a menu on his iPad. "Or what about steak?" He grinned. "Although if you want some meat, I already have some for you."

I scoffed, pushing away my worries about Everett for a later date. "That was uniquely terrible, Mr. York. Even for you."

"I know you say that . . . but I don't think I believe you." He winked, tangling his fingers in my hair as he brought me in for a kiss—

"Fuck, where is my best friend, and what have you done to him?"

We jumped at the sudden voice, and Logan groaned as he let me go. "I'm sorry in advance for him," he told me as I glanced confused at the entryway, where a gorgeous dark-haired man was lounging against the wall . . . eating a sandwich.

"I need to put bells on you," Logan griped, standing up from the couch and pulling me with him. "Or take away your key."

"Sounds dangerous. What if I need to borrow your awful clothes, Socks? What will I do then?" His gaze turned to me, and a charming grin slid across his face. "Who do we have here? She can't be yours, she's far too pretty."

Logan snorted.

"Sloane," Logan said quickly, stepping between us before I could take Asher's outstretched hand. "This is Asher. My . . . friend."

"Best friend. No need to be so modest," Asher corrected with a wink. "Nice to meet you, Sloane."

"No winking," Logan griped. "And no touching."

Asher's grin widened at Logan's behavior. "This is going to be fun."

"Why are you here again?" Logan asked.

"I wanted to see your pretty face," Asher replied, dropping onto the couch like he'd been invited as he continued to snack on his sandwich. "Also, I'm coming to your last game. And I wanted dinner. So there's that."

Logan growled, batting at his hand as Asher tried to grab the iPad. "Are those my pickles? You know I have a limited amount."

Asher made a show of taking a huge bite of his sandwich.

"Just for that, I'm going to ask for extra spicy yellow curry. You'll be shitting all night, and it will serve you right."

Asher looked at me, grinning like he'd just won an award. "He's so happy I'm here. Can't you tell?"

Dinner was chaos, mostly because *Asher* was chaos. He'd unpacked the takeout like he hadn't eaten in weeks, talking a mile a minute while Logan looked like he was reconsidering every life choice that had brought him to this moment.

"So," Asher said innocently, between bites of his hopefully not spicy curry, "has Logan told you about the time he accidentally glued his hand to his hair?"

I grinned into my water. "No. As a matter of fact, he hasn't . . ."

Logan groaned, dropping his head into his hands. "Everything he's about to say is a lie."

Asher rubbed his hands together . . . gleefully. "Picture it. Little Logan, about ten years old, with a bottle of superglue and the bright idea to fix his hockey stick. Only the glue he grabbed from his dad's drawer was some kind of *crazy* superglue, and he got it all over his hand and then . . . the idiot decided to push his hair out of his face."

I bit my lip, trying not to laugh as Logan muttered, "I was a child."

"It gets better," Asher continued, undeterred. "My mom had to take him to the ER, and they had to cut the glue off with this tiny scalpel. The whole time, Logan's sitting there with his hand stuck to his hair, insisting it wasn't a big deal. They had to cut a huge chunk of it off, and he had a huge bald spot for half of fourth grade."

I giggled, and Logan shot me a betrayed look as he pushed a hand through his blond hair, like he was making sure there were no bald spots to be found. "You're supposed to be on my side."

"I'm sorry," I said, still laughing. "But I'm picturing it, and I can totally see it."

"Thank you," Asher said, raising his glass in a mock toast. "But don't worry, I defended his honor. They stopped making fun of him after I punched John *Butkiss* right in the nose."

"First, I don't think his name was *Butkiss*. I'm pretty sure that was a made-up name you gave him. And second, that didn't happen until *halfway* through fourth grade, because you were the one making fun of me along with everyone else before that."

"Even then I was worried about you getting too big of a head," Asher said benevolently as he bowed. "I've always taken care of you." He tapped his chin. "And I really *do* think that was his name."

"Really? You've *always* taken care of me?" Logan said dryly. "Was it *you* taking care of *me* when you decided to have sex with Claire Mulligan in front of her ex-boyfriend's locker?"

Asher huffed. "You weren't even that helpful in that situation. I almost died anyway."

Logan's smirk was wide when he turned to me. "Claire's ex happened to walk in as they were going at it, but he wasn't actually an ex . . . and he was *maaaad*. She got scared, tried to spray the guy with pepper spray, but accidentally got Asher instead. He's naked, running out of the basketball locker rooms, screaming about water. I find him outside the athletic building, his head in the snow, ass and balls out for all the world to see."

"So how did you save him?"

"I told him I had extra clothes in the locker room," Logan said proudly.

"You didn't go get his clothes for him?" I asked incredulously.

Asher looked like some kind of maniacal clown, his eyes bouncing from the two of us as he slowly raised a fist in the air.

Logan blinked and thought about it. "Huh, maybe I wasn't that helpful in that situation after all," he mused.

Asher's fist made it all the way up. "The truth is finally free," he yelled. "Now it's my time to tell embarrassing stories again."

And he did. Over the next hour, Asher regaled me with story after embarrassing story—like the time Logan fell off a house trying to sneak into a girl's bedroom or when he accidentally set off the fire alarm at school because he thought it was a light switch.

Logan stoically sat there, only occasionally threatening Asher under his breath. But there was a faint smile tugging at the corners of his mouth, and I got the sense he wasn't annoyed at all.

I'd never laughed so much or so hard.

We were lounging on the couch when Asher looked at me, smirking. "You probably should keep this one, York. People might want to start hanging out with you for once in your life."

Logan shook his head, but his face softened as he stared at me. "That's the plan."

There was a weighted silence as we gazed at each other.

"*And* that's my cue to go. You're giving her *the look*," Asher snorted, hopping off the couch.

Logan *was* giving me the look. And suddenly I was *very* eager for Asher to leave.

"I'll see you at the game on Monday. I'm going to see Mama Matthews tomorrow."

"Do you think you can convince her to make pie?" Logan said eagerly as we stood up and started walking with Asher to the front door.

I realized as we were walking that this was a very girlfriend thing to be doing, walking someone to the door like I lived here too.

I really liked the thought of that.

It also terrified me.

"I'm definitely going to use your name to get the pie, but can I promise you'll get a taste of it? No. Absolutely not."

Logan scoffed. "I let you eat my lucky burrito that day!"

"Oh, you mean the one that I stole from your fridge and was almost poisoned by?" Asher spat, raising an eyebrow.

Logan snorted.

I glanced between the two of them, not understanding what they were saying, but amused nevertheless.

"See ya, Socks," Asher finally said with a little salute before bowing and winking at me. "Sloane, it's been a pleasure," he told me with a sexy wink before he ambled out the door and out of sight.

Logan shook his head, a blindingly beautiful smile on his lips as he closed the door and led me into the kitchen. He sat me down on a stool and started getting everything out to make my favorite tea. I watched, as if entranced, as the tattooed god moved around, making my tea just how I liked it before setting it in front of me.

"He liked you," he commented as I lifted the mug to my nose and inhaled the sweet orange and cloves of the tea.

Perfect.

I blushed, something that had nothing to do with the steam hitting my cheeks. "He did?" I tried to ignore how happy that made me. I shouldn't care whether his friends liked me or not.

That's how far this had escalated from being more than a job.

Logan was staring at me like he knew exactly what I was thinking.

I took a sip of the tea, looking everywhere but at him.

"He seems like the kind of guy who likes everyone," I commented, clearly fishing for more information.

"It comes across that way, but he's got some major tells. When he doesn't like someone, he's got this fake smile he gives them. He's nice, but he doesn't give them the full Asher charm." He cocked his head. "He was definitely giving you that," Logan grumbled, sounding almost . . . jealous.

"You guys have quite the bromance," I said wistfully.

"He's a good guy," Logan agreed, setting his hands on my shoulders, his touch sending sparks cascading across my skin.

"Why exactly does he call you Socks?" I blurted out, trying to distract him.

A smirk curled my lips at the blush that suddenly rose up on his cheeks. Nothing like seeing a six-foot-four tatted man blushing like a schoolboy.

"I don't know what you're talking about," he answered, suddenly staring at the ceiling.

I huffed out a laugh. "You should just tell me, get the burning secret off your chest. I know it's killing you," I teased.

He crossed his arms across his chest, and I got a little distracted for a second at the sight of his muscles. He was just so fucking . . . pretty.

"I have no secrets. I'm an open book. Oh look, that's a cool bird," he commented, pointing out the window behind me.

Lifting an eyebrow, I pushed a finger into his abs. "You're not old enough to have developed into an avid bird watcher, York. Give me the deets."

"Why is it so sexy when you last-name me?" he groaned, reaching out and pulling me from the chair and into his chest as he pressed a kiss against the side of my neck. "And is that something I have to look forward to in our old age—bird watching?"

I tried to keep my head on straight as his lips moved down my skin. But it was freaking difficult. He was way too good at this.

"Socks," I gasped, pushing against his chest. "I want to hear about socks."

He growled and bit down gently on my shoulder before pressing his forehead against my skin. I had the insane urge to cry. This was intimacy, wasn't it? This was what it felt like to be close to someone, to feel their soul and not just their body when they held you.

I wanted to push him away. The closeness would just make me weak, and life had never gone well for me when I was weak.

Maybe just a second more, though . . . a second more of him holding me like I was worth something.

"In high school I got black-out drunk and then somehow ended up walking around a party with nothing but a sock on."

I giggled, and he lifted his head to smirk at me. "You think that's funny, do you?"

"I mean, I hate the thought of everyone seeing your perfect dick, but it is a funny visual," I snorted.

His grin widened. "Oh, the sock wasn't on my foot . . ." He winked as my jaw dropped.

And that did it for me. Just imagining him walking around with a sock hanging off his dick was too much. I laughed hysterically as he smiled down at me with a sort of dazed look in his eye.

"I love that," he murmured, gently pushing a piece of hair out of my face.

My laugh abruptly stopped as I blinked up at him, a warmth sliding down my skin. "What do you love?"

He stared at me knowingly, and my hands slid to his chest like they'd been possessed. I could feel the words he wanted to say like they were a tangible thing. Suddenly I was panicking, my heart racing, my fingers curling into his shirt as if I could ward them off.

"The sound of your laugh," he finally said gruffly, and a sliver of relief slid down my spine.

Along with a hint of disappointment. But I wasn't going to think about that.

"I hope someone got pics," I mumbled, trying to break whatever spell he seemed to be always casting over me.

"If they exist, I'm never showing you them."

I huffed out another laugh, which instantly turned into a sigh when he pulled me farther into his arms, so that my head was resting against his firm, muscled chest.

His heart was racing too.

I blinked as I struggled not to tear up . . . again.

"Whatever you say, *Socks*," I whispered as his hands stroked down my back.

Every day I was letting this thing between us grow. Rapid heartbeats and sweaty palms.

And feelings.

"How about now, Red? You fall in love with me yet?" he asked.

I squeezed him tight, and like usual, he chuckled at my inability to respond to him.

Although I was pretty sure he knew the answer to that question already.

I should pull away right now. I should leave and run for the hills.

But, of course, I didn't do that. Instead, I nestled into his chest and soaked in his touch like a dying flower soaking up the last drops of rain.

One more minute, I told myself . . .

Just one more.

CHAPTER 25

LOGAN

Turns out, hiring an escort full time was pretty expensive—even for a professional hockey player.

Sloane was worth every penny, though, while I waited for her to feel comfortable enough to leave the industry. Which was the only reason I had accepted this offer when my agent presented it to me.

A fast-food commercial advertising a burger. Didn't seem too difficult. He'd been a little vague about the details, but they were paying a shit ton . . . and I really liked burgers.

So win-win, really.

My phone buzzed as I waited in the dressing room for the makeup and wardrobe people to come in.

> Ari: Left the locker room pretty fast after practice, Rookie. Whatcha doing this afternoon?

My eyebrow rose.

> Me: That seems oddly suspicious.

> Ari: It would only seem suspicious to some-one trying to hide something . . .

> Walker: I agree.

I waited for Ari to call him a simp . . . but it was crickets.

Me: Did Blake give you the look or something . . . because that was a golden opportunity you just missed, Lancaster.

Ari: What are you talking about?

Walker: Yeah, what are you talking about, York?

Ari: Good one, Disney.

Me: Okay. Now this is getting weird. Walker is clearly simping. The worst case of simpage I've ever seen.

Ari: I don't think that's a word—simpage.

I blinked at my phone. Had I entered an alternate reality?

Me: You use that word on a daily basis.

Ari: Oh, well I use it correctly. How you just used it was clearly incorrect.

Me: . . .

Ari: Walker's simpage is proper when it involves agreeing with me. I'm the obvious choice in this group to worship.

Me: You just used that word.

Ari: What word?

Me: I'M GOING TO LOSE MY MIND.

Camden: So shouty.

> Ari: Here, Rookie, let me dumb it down for you. Worshiping me=good. Worshiping Golden Boy=bad. Get it?

> Lincoln: I'd like to voice an objection.

> Ari: Overruled.

The door opened, and the director's assistant, a brunette wearing a tight black suit, came in. "We're so glad you agreed to do this, Mr. York. I think you're going to be *so* pleased with how it turns out."

I set my phone on the table and stood up.

Her eyes greedily took me in like I was a slab of meat, and I shifted uncomfortably as two more people filed into the room. "This is Joan and Carla. They're going to be doing wardrobe and makeup for you today." She slowly licked her lips before shaking her head and backing out of the room.

"If you can just change into these. We'll be waiting outside. Just holler when you're done," Joan . . . or maybe Carla said to me. I probably should have paid better attention to their names.

Whoever it was set a neatly folded pair of black briefs on the table in front of the room and then left.

I blinked at my *wardrobe*.

"Briefs?" I muttered, panicking as I picked them up with two fingers like they might bite me. "They didn't mention briefs."

Nope. This wasn't happening. I'd never live it down. I fired off a text to my agent, Tucker.

> Me: You didn't tell me the premise of this ad was for me to be eating a burger in my underwear. Explain. Now.

It took less than a minute for the dots to pop up.

> Tucker: Logan, buddy, just breathe. This is an easy gig. You're going to look amazing. Everyone loves abs.

Me: Easy? How about you eat a burger in your underwear on TV. I swear this wasn't mentioned in the offer you sent me.

The dots stopped, then resumed. I could almost feel the panic in his response.

Tucker: I'm eating a burger in my underwear right now, Logan. It's not a big deal. But it was in the fine print—the fine print that I told you to read.

I didn't have an answer for that, because I probably had skipped some of the contract, trusting that *my agent* wouldn't have me do something like this. A mistake I wouldn't be making again.

Tucker: You're a professional, Logan. Just think of the zeros. Lots of zeros. Think vacation home zeros.

I groaned, throwing my head back against the wall. More like paying-for-Sloane zeros, but either way, just as expensive.

"You okay in there?" A cheery voice came from the doorway. One of the wardrobe people, the bubbly redhead one, peeked her head in. She glanced at the briefs in my hand and raised an eyebrow. "Need help?"

"Nope," I snapped. "Got it covered."

She didn't get the hint to leave. "Just making sure. Some guys get weird about this part. You'll be fine. And don't worry—we're not going to need to stuff those briefs." Her gaze bounced from the briefs . . . to my dick. I was regretting my life choice of wearing my gray Dallas Knights sweatpants . . . but Sloane was a big fan of them.

Now I knew why.

I froze, slowly turning to glare at her. "If you mention my dick again, you're going to regret it."

She burst out laughing. "Relax, Mr. York. Just trying to break the ice."

"Consider it broken," I muttered. Her smile died when she realized I probably hadn't been joking, and she quickly left the room.

I had no tolerance for women hitting on me that weren't named Sloane Calloway.

Sliding off my sweatpants, I changed into the briefs, staring at myself in the mirror.

That girl hadn't been wrong about how these things would fit—my cock did look enormous.

FML.

Although maybe I could keep them after the shoot to show to Sloane. She would definitely like them.

And at least I wasn't posing for Geraldine. This had to be way better than that.

Right?

Think of the zeros, Logan. Think of the zeros, I told myself as I opened the door and gestured for the makeup people to come in and start working on me.

———

When I finally walked onto the set, I was greeted by a pristine white table, where a monstrosity of a burger was sitting on a tray. It was stacked with cheese, bacon, and lettuce—and dripping with enough sauce to drown someone.

The director, a tall guy with a man bun and an accent I couldn't place, was hyped like he was directing the next Oscar-winning film. He clapped his hands together. "Logan, darling! You look stunning. Absolutely perfect. This is going to be iconic. Sensual. Revolutionary."

All of those attributes seemed to be a stretch, but he seemed so excited about it, I couldn't burst his bubble.

I grunted, crossing my arms, well aware of everyone in the room staring at me as I stood there, practically naked. "Thanks. So, uh, what's the game plan?"

He smiled, holding up his hands like he was directing *The Godfather*. "Simple. You and the burger. Chemistry. Seduction. Make it sizzle."

"Sizzle," I repeated flatly, even though I had no idea what that meant. "Got it."

He waved over the cameraman, who was adjusting his equipment. "And Logan, darling—don't be afraid to use your body. The briefs are working *wonders*."

I ignored the urge to punch something and went to stand where the director pointed. The lights came on, the burger gleamed under the spotlight, and I prepared for the most humiliating hour of my life.

And then it happened. I was just about to pick up the burger when a door opened, and in strolled my worst nightmares.

Ari and Camden.

Fucking Tucker. He was Camden and Walker's agent, too, and there was no way he hadn't spilled the beans.

Traitor.

Before I could even process the fact that I was going to hear about this for the rest of time, it got even worse.

"Let's see some passion!" the director called. "You're not just eating the burger—you're *in love* with it. Take a bite. Slow. Sultry."

"You heard the man. Love on your burger, York," Ari called out as they got to the edge of the set.

"Who let you guys in?" I growled, feeling like a man walking to his execution.

The director perked up, somehow mistaking what I'd just said for genuine enthusiasm. "Ah, your friends! Wonderful! They can help set the mood."

"Definitely no need for stuffing," I heard someone say, and I glanced over to see the assistant and some of the other crew staring at me.

It was official. I had to be dreaming. Because there was no way this was happening right now.

I pinched myself just in case.

Nope. Completely real.

Camden froze mid-laugh, his eyes lighting up with mischief. "Oh, absolutely. Mood is key."

Ari nodded solemnly. "Logan here is all about passion. You should see him with a stick. It's art."

The director gasped, placing a dramatic hand on his chest. "A true artist! Logan, darling, you must channel that energy. Make love to the burger. Become one with it."

"Are you fucking kidding me?" I muttered under my breath, glancing at Ari and Camden, who were barely holding it together.

"Logan," Camden said, leaning against the table like he was part of the crew. "The burger deserves your best. Think . . . Romeo and Juliet, but, you know, with meat and cheese."

"Thanks for that, Shakespeare," I deadpanned, stepping into position in just my briefs. The lights were blinding, the grease smell overwhelming, and my dignity? Long gone.

"Hold it gently," the director instructed, miming a cradle. "Like it's the love of your life."

Ari whistled and whispered mockingly. "That's it, York. Look at the burger like it just scored the game-winning goal in double OT."

The director practically swooned. "Yes! That intensity! Logan, darling, you're a *vision*."

I bit back a groan and picked up the burger, its weight ridiculous in my hands. I leaned in, trying to "connect" with the damn thing, while Ari's and Camden's whispers made it impossible to concentrate.

"Do you think he's gonna kiss it?" Camden muttered, barely audible over the hum of the lights.

"The sauce is at least going to get some tongue action," Ari replied.

"Logan, darling," the director interrupted, oblivious to their antics. "Take a bite. Slowly. Passionately. Let us feel your desire."

Camden let out a snort so loud the sound guy turned to glare at him. "You heard the man, York. Seduce that burger."

I shot them both a murderous look before leaning in and taking the most humiliating bite of my life. The sauce dripped onto my chest, and the director gasped like I'd just discovered fire.

"More! Give us more!" he cried, waving his hands. "This is *art*! You're in love with the burger, Logan. Show us!"

"I can't do this," I mumbled around a mouthful of grease.

"You can," Ari encouraged, his face serious even as his eyes gleamed with laughter. "Think of the burger as your soulmate. Your one true love."

Camden chimed in, "Yeah, York. Whisper sweet nothings to it. Tell it how much it means to you."

The director's eyes widened. "Yes! Talk to it, Logan. Communicate your longing."

I set the burger down, and immediately there were two people there, wiping the sauce off my face. "I'm going to kill both of you," I snarled.

"You'll thank us when this wins an award," Ari said solemnly, snapping a picture with his phone. "For, uh, culinary excellence."

"Aka food porn," Camden added.

"No phones on set," I snapped as Camden also started taking pictures.

"That was a funny joke," said Ari as the director called for me to pick up the burger again.

"Please don't send it to Lincoln," I hissed as I grabbed the burger and slowly brought it to my mouth. I was probably never going to be able to eat burgers after this. I was going to be too traumatized.

Ari got a weird glint in his eye at the mention of Lincoln. "Just for that, I'm taking more." And he started snapping away. Fuck, I shouldn't have brought him up.

I bit into the burger and chewed. At least it didn't taste terrible.

"Magnificent," the director drawled, his voice going up an octave.

"I can really feel your passion," Camden called out. I flipped him off when the director turned his back.

It continued like this for the rest of the session. Me pretending to make love to a burger, while Ari and Camden destroyed me.

The director clasped his hands together when he was finally happy with the session. "Logan, darling, you were *transcendent*. Your friends were right—your passion is palpable."

"Thanks," I muttered, not sticking around as I all but ran back to the dressing room, Ari and Camden's laughter following me the whole way.

The next day at practice—our last one before Game Seven, might I add—I walked into the locker room, where the whole team was gathered around the big screen, laughter echoing off the walls.

My stomach dropped. Fuck no.

There, playing on a loop for everyone to see, were the pictures Ari and Camden had taken of me in all their glory. I grimaced as one popped up of me leaning in, eyes half-closed, like I really was trying to make love to the burger.

"There's our star now!" Camden called out, barely able to get the words out between his laughter. Ari was doubled over, clutching his sides, while Walker had actually fallen to the floor, tears in his eyes.

Lincoln leaned against the wall, grinning. "You really gave it your all, Rookie. Didn't hold anything back."

"Look at the way he caresses it!" Ari said between his hysterical *giggling*, pointing at the screen. "Such a gentle lover!"

I groaned, running a hand over my face. "Kill me now."

Lincoln clapped me on the back, still chuckling. "I hope it paid *a lot*."

"It did," I muttered, although with everything I'd had to go through, I'd decided it wasn't nearly enough to pay for the dignity I'd lost.

"Next time you need money, York," Lincoln said, still grinning, "maybe just ask one of us instead of making out with a cheeseburger on national TV."

"Noted," I said, shaking my head. "But hey, at least I looked good," I said hopefully.

"I'm sure Sloane will think it's very sexy," Ari agreed mockingly.

I growled at him before moving to get dressed for practice. My only solace was that my bank account was now filled and ready to continue making *payments*.

Sloane really needed to fall in love with me soon.

DALLAS #9 KNIGHTS

CHAPTER 26

LOGAN

The phone buzzed in my pocket, and when I saw the name on the screen, I didn't want to answer. But I'd learned over the years, that only made my father more aggressive—when he didn't feel like my first priority. I pressed the phone to my ear, already feeling the tension tightening in my chest.

"Logan." My dad's voice came through the line, smooth and commanding, as if he were about to announce something that everyone should stop and listen to. "I'll be at Game Seven with a television crew. They're making a documentary on me, and they want to capture this moment."

I clenched my jaw, feeling the familiar knot of frustration build in my gut. I bet the cameras were on him right now. He always found a way to make everything about him. Of course, he'd be using *my* Stanley Cup Final for his own spotlight. I took a breath, steadying myself before I responded.

"Don't come," I said flatly.

There was a beat of silence on the other end, and then his voice sharpened. "Excuse me?"

I could picture his expression—probably the same cold, shocked look I'd seen a thousand times. Like when I'd gotten suspended at school for fighting. Or when I'd gotten that first tattoo without his permission. Or after he found out I quit football to pursue hockey.

But this wasn't the same as before. This time, I didn't care about what he thought.

"All my life," I started, my voice tighter than I intended, "I wanted you to be proud of me. You never were. It was just the two of us after Mom left, and I spent every second of my life hoping you'd look at me the way other fathers looked at their sons. But you never did. You ignored me. You used me to brag to your friends. And now, you want to show up to *my* Game Seven and claim a piece of it? You don't get to support my legacy for yourself when you've never supported me a single day of my life."

There was another long silence on the line. I could hear his breath, the tension creeping in, the way it always did before he lashed out. But this time, I wasn't afraid. I wasn't a kid waiting for him to tell me I wasn't good enough.

"Who do you think paid for your hockey all those years growing up?" he snapped, his voice low, defensive. "I paid for every damn thing you ever needed on the ice. Your equipment, your travel, your coaching."

I laughed bitterly. "Did you even notice the money coming out of your account, or did you think of it as a type of nanny, so you didn't have to deal with me? You were off living your life. Remind me . . . how many games of mine did you go to growing up?"

There was another beat of silence as I waited for him to answer, but we both knew what the number was.

Zero.

"Don't act like you did something noble. You never cared about me."

The words hung heavy between us, and I could hear his breathing, sharp and angry. But he didn't say anything. He never had an answer when it came to the truth.

"If you show up to that game," I continued, my voice cold, "you'll be escorted out. You're not going to stand there with your cameras and act like you've been the reason for any of this. Because you haven't. You don't deserve to be a part of everything now."

He sputtered, starting to say something, but I didn't wait to hear it. I hung up, tossing the phone onto the couch beside me, my pulse pounding in my ears.

Sloane came out of my bedroom, fiddling with the earring she was trying to put in her ear.

"Everything okay?" she asked. "Why were you yelling?"

Someday I would tell her about my dad, but not today. After all, she was the main reason I'd just gotten the courage to tell him off like that for the first time in my life. Because more so than even how I felt about my best friends—she made me feel like I had my own family now. She was my future.

"It was nothing," I murmured when I realized I was just staring down at her.

"You're going to be amazing," she whispered.

"No doubt about that," I grinned, and she huffed, like she didn't think I was sexy.

"What about now, Sloane? You in love with me yet?"

She flushed and started for the door, glancing back at me with a gorgeous smile. "You're still talking crazy, Logan York."

"But I'm getting close, Calloway."

She didn't tell me any different.

I ignored the buzzing in my pocket, no doubt a barrage of texts from my father telling me off for daring to disrespect him like that.

And I was smiling as we walked out the door to get to my game.

"I can't even make a joke right now," Walker said, running his hand down his face. There was a green tinge to his skin, like he was going to be sick.

Ari stared at him incredulously. "What does that even mean? When do *you* make jokes? Of the five of us, you're literally the *least* funny."

I preened at the idea that I was funnier than at least one person in the group—even though I was very aware that wasn't exactly high praise—*not* being last. It only took a second, though, for me to remember that I was also nervous as fuck, and I couldn't be funny right now if I tried.

Walker gaped at him. "You take that back right now, Lancaster. I *am* funny. And certainly funnier than Hero and Rookie."

Ari cocked his head, wrapping the tape on his stick for the second time of the evening. "Are you, though, are you?"

Walker glanced at Lincoln, his eyes like a little puppy dog's as he waited for Lincoln to step in.

Lincoln wasn't listening; he had a . . . terrifying look on his face that told me he was getting in the zone. His ankle seemed to be all healed up. He had ended up being able to play for a period last game and had even scored a goal. That made me feel a little less nauseated, that we had him on our side.

Ari snorted. "Golden Boy is being spooky sexy right now. He's not going to help you with this one, Disney."

Walker's fist went to his lips, and from the looks of it, he'd just thrown up in his mouth.

Fuck. It was one thing for me to be nervous . . . but quite another for our goalie to be feeling it this bad.

I cleared my throat. "Um, Linc?"

He glanced over, seeming unimpressed that I was daring to interrupt his . . . whatever he was doing. I nodded at Walker, although I was really referring to myself. "Maybe a speech or something would be good."

Lincoln eyed Walker like his nerves were contagious and shook his head. He moved to the center of the locker room, though, his skates clacking softly on the floor. "Alright, boys," he started, his voice low but steady. Everyone immediately stopped talking and turned their attention to Lincoln like he'd actually yelled.

"Tonight—it's different. Tonight, everything we've fought for, everything we've sacrificed, comes down to *this* game. One shot. One chance to write our names into the history books."

His eyes swept over us, and the tension in the room shifted. It wasn't anxiety anymore. It was focus. Raw, burning focus.

"They'll tell you it's just another game," he continued, his voice hardening. "But we know better. This is *the* game. The one we've bled for all season. You've got bruises from the last six games? Good. That means you've been fighting. You're tired? Hell, I *hope* you're tired, because that means you've been giving everything you've got. But let me tell you something— tired doesn't matter. Pain doesn't matter. Not tonight."

I swallowed hard, feeling my heart thump harder in my chest.

Lincoln clenched his fists, pacing in front of us now. "We know what's waiting for us out there. We've seen it. We've *felt* it. But none of that matters. What matters is this room, right here. *Us.* The Dallas Knights."

He stopped in front of Walker, those sharp eyes locking on him for just a beat.

"We've been in the trenches together. We've crawled out of every damn hole they've tried to bury us in. And now? Now we're here, with the Cup hanging right in front of us." His voice grew harder, every word hitting like a punch. "They don't think we can do it. They're waiting for us to fold. But we're not folding. Not tonight. Tonight, we show the world who we are."

He stepped back, eyes blazing. "You've got sixty minutes to play the game of your life. Sixty minutes to leave everything you've got on that ice. You're not skating for yourself. You're skating for the guy next to you. You're skating for every bruise, every hit, every fucking moment that got us here. *This* is our night."

I felt the fire surge through me, the same fire I could see in every other guy in that room. It was like Lincoln had struck a match, and we were all ready to burn for that Cup.

Lincoln's voice dropped again, the final edge of intensity hanging on every word. "So, let's go out there, and let's take what's ours."

With that, he slammed his stick against the floor, the sound echoing through the room like a gunshot. One by one, we stood, the energy boiling up, the tension snapping into something sharp, something deadly. This wasn't just a game anymore. It was a battle.

I locked eyes with Walker, who looked slightly less green. He gave me a tight nod, his eyes gleaming with the same fire that was roaring through my veins.

Ari raised his stick in the air. "And now . . . we dance."

We all glanced at him, right as "Shake It Off" started blaring through the locker room speakers.

Lincoln huffed and rolled his eyes.

"Hell of a speech, Golden Boy," Ari said, his eyes gleaming. "I'm feeling inspired. But tradition is tradition."

"Kill me now," Lincoln groaned.

"Not happening, Cap. We're *shaking it off.*"

I started with my "moonwalk," and Camden grumbled about me stealing his move.

Within seconds, the room devolved into chaos. Walker, evidently devoid of his previous nerves, jumped up onto the bench, pumping his fists in the air and yelling the lyrics like his life depended on it. Camden was doing some kind of interpretive dance that looked more like he was trying to dodge invisible punches, and Ari . . . had taken center stage, belting out the words like he was auditioning for *The Voice.*

"Play, play, play, play, play!" Ari shouted, pointing at Lincoln, who was trying very hard to look disinterested but was tapping his foot anyway.

"Stop pretending you don't like it!" Ari hollered at Lincoln, who rolled his eyes but finally cracked a grin.

"Fine," Lincoln muttered, starting to shake his ass.

Ari grabbed Lincoln's hand and spun him abruptly around like they were in a ballroom competition. Lincoln stumbled, his face turning red, but instead of yelling, he actually laughed—a rare sound that made everyone pause for half a second before bursting into cheers.

The door opened.

Coach Porter stepped in, clipboard in hand, and froze mid-step. The music was still blasting, and Ari had just attempted a jump-split that ended with him sprawled on the floor.

Coach surveyed the room like a general inspecting a battlefield, his face utterly blank. Finally, he pinched the bridge of his nose and sighed. "This is the team I'm taking into Game Seven?"

"Yes, sir!" Ari shouted from the floor, offering a thumbs-up.

Coach shook his head, muttering something about "fucking embarrassments."

Lincoln straightened up, smoothing his jersey like he hadn't just been twirled across the room. "We've got this, Coach."

Coach's gaze swept over us, his lips twitching like he was trying not to laugh. "Let's fucking hope so."

The intensity of the room suddenly snapped up, like the combination of Lincoln's speech and Ari's . . . stress reliever had magical powers. We were all ready to go.

"As my darling angel-poo of a wife says, 'It's only weird if it doesn't work,' Coach," Ari offered as we lined up to walk down the tunnel.

Coach Porter shook his head.

"I don't think she was the one who came up with that," Camden muttered.

There was a smile on my lips as we headed toward the ice. And my nerves . . . they were nowhere to be found.

CHAPTER 27

LOGAN

The roar of the crowd surrounded us, overwhelming and all-encompassing. I glanced over at Sloane to distract myself from the fact that I was about to play the biggest game of my life. You dream about making the Stanley Cup Finals when you're a little kid. But doing it in my first year in the league . . . I'd never imagined this.

She was wearing the *Stanley Cupcake* shirt again, and despite my nerves . . . and where I was at . . . my dick tightened just remembering what we'd done the last time she'd worn that shirt.

I definitely needed a repeat of that.

"You complete me," I mouthed to her, grinning as she blushed.

"Crazy," she mouthed back.

We lined up for the opening face-off, and I shot a glance at Lincoln. His eyes were locked in, laser-focused.

Sixty minutes to leave everything on the ice.

I could do this.

"Let's go, boys," Lincoln muttered, gripping his stick tighter. "This is our night."

The puck dropped, and we took off. Every shift felt like a fight for survival—scrambling for space, clawing for control. Tampa was quick and aggressive, but we matched them step for step. Ari and Camden were our anchors on defense, fucking wrecking balls. They didn't just block shots; they demolished any Tampa player that dared to take one.

One of their top guys came streaking down the wing, obviously thinking he had a clear lane. Ari leveled him into the boards with a hit so brutal, a ripple of "oohs" swept through the stands.

"Hey, Tony, my left nut dangles better than you," Ari quipped as Tampa's forward staggered back to his bench.

Midway through the first period, they started to find their legs. Their top line came at us hard, pushing into our zone. Camden, always steady, threw himself in front of a blistering slap shot, the puck bouncing off his leg as he winced but didn't flinch. He got right back up, fighting through the pain, clearing the puck out of the zone.

"Atta boy, Hero!" I shouted over to him as he skated by, his face twisted in determination.

The period ended scoreless, and Walker was buzzing as we got back into the locker room. The energy was intense. No one spoke much—we knew what was at stake. Lincoln stood at the doorway when we headed back out.

"Finish," he told all of us as we bumped fists.

The second period was chaos. Both teams were pressing harder, the stakes growing with every passing second. Their team caught a break when one of our defensemen, Peters, slipped, sending their top forward streaking toward Walker, on a clean breakaway.

Walker? Calm as ever. He tracked the guy's every move, following the puck like it was a magnet. The forward snapped off a quick wrist shot, aiming for the top corner, but Walker's glove flashed out, snagging the puck midair like it was nothing.

"That's my goalie!" Lincoln shouted, skating over and banging on his mask.

I was pretty sure that Disney busted a nut over Lincoln's compliment.

Third period and the clock was ticking down, one minute to go before the game ended. We were cycling the puck in their zone, the pressure building as we tried to break through their defense. Lincoln won a key face-off, sending the puck back to Ari at the blue line. Ari, his eyes locked on the net, unleashed a rocket of a slap shot. The puck flew through traffic, and for a split second, I thought it was going in.

Their goalie made the save, but the rebound kicked out hard. Lincoln swooped in, firing a quick shot, but it was blocked again.

The puck landed right in front of me, bouncing in the blue paint. I didn't hesitate. I lunged forward, my stick connecting with it just as the goalie scrambled to cover the net. Time seemed to slow as the puck slid under his pad, disappearing into the back of the goal.

For a second, I didn't hear anything. The arena went silent, like the entire world had frozen. Then, the explosion.

The noise hit me like a wave, the crowd roaring so loud it felt like the building was shaking. I fell to my knees on the ice, my heart pounding out of my chest

Fuck. I was going to faint.

Lincoln slammed into me from behind, knocking me forward.

"Fucking Rookie!" he yelled, his voice lost in the chaos as the rest of the team piled on. Camden, Ari, Walker—they all crashed into me, laughing, shouting, their faces lit up with disbelief and pure joy.

"We're the fucking champs!" Ari screamed, grabbing my helmet and shaking me like I wasn't already dazed.

Camden screamed right in my ear. "That Cup's coming home, baby!"

I could barely breathe, crushed under the weight of the team, their shouts and cheers echoing around me. I felt like I was floating, the reality of what had just happened slowly sinking in. We'd done it. We'd won the Stanley Cup!

The arena was still shaking as I struggled to break free from the pile, my legs wobbling beneath me as I skated toward the boards. The noise was deafening, the crowd chanting, screaming, and waving flags. But I wasn't looking at them. I was looking for *her*.

Family members of the team were flooding the ice, and I scanned their faces, my chest heaving as the exhaustion started to settle in.

And then she was there, throwing herself into my arms, her eyes wide, her face a mix of disbelief, pride, and something else I couldn't quite place.

I kissed her, pouring everything I had into my girl.

She gasped when I let her go, her lips curving into a smile that made my heart race all over again.

"What about now?" I shouted over the noise, grinning like an idiot as I stared down at her because this series had literally changed my life.

Her smile widened, her eyes bright and shiny like she was about to cry. For a moment, the mayhem of the arena faded away, and it was just the two of us, caught in the moment, everything else falling into place.

Slowly she nodded, and a strange buzzing filled my ears as she leaned in close.

"Yes, Logan York. I'm falling in love with you."

The words echoed in my ears, and I wasn't ashamed at all as a tear slipped down my face.

"Fucking finally, Calloway," I groaned, my lips crashing down on hers once again.

I was barely aware of anything when I later lifted the trophy over my head and took my turn skating around the ice.

We might have won the game, but Sloane had just made it where . . . I'd won at life.

CHAPTER 28

SLOANE

We were drunk.
                  And horny.
                  Very horny.
Or at least *I* was. I couldn't seem to keep my hands off him.

It was like telling him had freed something inside me, and now after telling him verbally what he meant to me . . . I wanted to physically show him too.

The after-party had gotten out of control. At one point I'd gulped beer from the Stanley Cup and then tried to do snow angels in the middle of the ice with Monroe.

We were back at Logan's place, though, and I was bound and determined that part two of the after-party was about to begin.

"Who cares about championships," he growled. "You're the only thing I need." We stumbled into his entryway, practically attacking each other's lips as we tried to walk.

"I would say that was corny, but it just sounds hot," I panted as his lips trailed down my neck.

"I want to fuck you in my jersey," he begged. "Can we make that happen since I was such a good boy and scored the game-winning goal?" His hands slid down and gripped my ass.

"Don't get any ideas that will always work," I said as he moved back to my mouth. His tongue slid between my lips and tangled with mine, deep, long licks that had me moaning into the kiss.

"But it can work this time, right?" he asked, and I whined as his hand pushed between my legs, massaging my clit through my leggings as he continued to destroy me with his kiss.

"Yes," I groaned, my hands running over his neck and shoulders as I arched against his touch.

Suddenly he moved away, and I whimpered, my body a live wire of need. It was still amazing how fast he could take me to the edge every time.

"Be right back. I'm not going to miss out on this," he said. "It's important to reward yourself."

I snorted at him and grinned. "Or I could follow you so we aren't having sex on the hallway floor."

He groaned like I'd said something amazing.

"Add that to the list. Hallway sex," he muttered as he suddenly scooped me up and walked us down the hall and into his room.

He was always adding things to this imaginary sex list we evidently were keeping. And all of his suggestions were very hot.

Logan almost fell over as he set me down on the bed, and I was giggling as he straightened and pressed a kiss on my nose before practically running to his closet.

A second later, he appeared with a Dallas Knights jersey. Swinging it above his head, he stalked toward me.

"Get naked, baby," he ordered, tossing the jersey at my chest.

"Only if you beg," I told him. I'd never felt powerful having sex before, but with Logan, the way he wanted me, it was impossible not to.

Logan smirked and slowly slid to his knees. "Please, baby. Strip for me."

I slid off the bed and then began working my leggings and T-shirt off until I was standing there in nothing but my bra and underwear.

"Take those off too," he said, a hint of red staining his cheeks as he took me in.

I raised an eyebrow.

"Please, Sloane. I want to see you. So, so bad."

"Only because you asked so nicely," I said, my voice coming out breathy as I undid the front clasp of my bra, and my breasts sprung free.

"Holy fuck," he groaned, licking his lips as he stared at my chest.

I took my time taking off my underwear, snapping it at his face when I was done. He caught it and brought it to his nose, breathing in as he groaned.

"*Fuuuuck*, I need you," he said, pushing his sweats down. His giant dick sprung free, and my mouth literally watered. He wrapped the lace panties around his cock and began thrusting. "Now put on the jersey."

My eyes were locked on his dick, but somehow I managed to slide it on, my nipples brushing against the rough fabric as I pulled the jersey all the way down.

He groaned again, closing his eyes for a moment as he squeezed his dick before he slowly got up off his knees.

"Turn around," he demanded, stalking toward me.

I immediately obeyed, glancing at him over my shoulder as I watched him strip off his shirt and sweats until he was standing there in all of his naked, tattooed glory.

Fuck. I'd never seen anything hotter.

"Bend over," he ordered as he slowly lowered himself to the floor once more—this time right behind me. I fell forward, my face pressing against the mattress as he slowly moved the jersey up so my ass was bared to the cool air. I could feel his breath against my skin, and then his hands worked my cheeks, massaging and kneading them.

There was a pause and then *thwack*. Logan spanked me, his lips soothing my skin when I yelped.

He separated my ass cheeks, and then his tongue was dipping in between my folds, touching everything, including my asshole.

"Logan," I cried as I thrust backward.

He laughed wickedly before his mouth moved back down, his thumb pressing against my asshole as he licked my core.

His stubble scratched my thighs, and the sensations were too much. Logan's tongue pressed inside my slit at the same time as his finger pushed into my ass.

"Fuck," I cried out.

"This pussy. I want to die eating it," he growled.

Right as I was about to come, he once again withdrew, and I squeaked as he flipped me over.

His eyes were heavy-lidded as he stared down at me, his tongue peeking out from his mouth as he slowly slid it across his bottom lip.

"Holy fuck. Best celebration present ever," he whispered, sounding dazed, like he couldn't believe what he was seeing.

I blushed, my head spinning from the champagne and his touch and the way he made me feel.

"Say it. Say it to me, Red," he demanded.

"Please fuck me, Logan," I begged.

"That's my good girl," he said, sliding his tip through my wet folds. "That's my good fucking—"

He surged inside me.

"Fuck," he moaned, his head falling back for a second as he took a deep breath.

He was the picture of erotic perfection, his tattooed muscles straining as he held himself there. Logan took a deep breath and then stared down at me again. "It's so good, Red," he purred, leaning over to kiss me, his tongue thrusting in my mouth as he groaned.

"Love you, baby," he murmured as he dragged himself back, stopping when just his tip was inside me. My insides fluttered at his words. I wondered when that would stop. When I would get used to the fact that someone in the world said that they loved me.

His hands pushed my thighs wider as he slid all the way in until he was seated deep inside me. My pussy squeezed him in response.

"Fuck," he huffed. "You're always so tight." It *was* a tight fit, every time. He was just a little bit too big, but the feeling of him was the best I ever had.

He slowly withdrew again, his face burying into my neck as his hand slid between us, beginning to work my clit.

Logan took deep, shuddering breaths against my skin as he fucked into me, my moans joining the sound of him moving in and out of me.

"I'm so close," I gasped. "Please."

He pulled up, somehow continuing his perfect rhythm as he pushed his jersey up over my breasts. His green eyes were blazing as he stared down at me.

"Come for me, baby. Choke my cock," he swore roughly as he bent over and licked at my nipple.

That was it. I came hard, my whole body shaking as searing pleasure rushed through me.

"Yes," he growled, his lips moving to my mouth as his pace picked up. "One more."

I wasn't sure that I ever came down from the orgasm. His dick slid against the perfect spots inside me, over and over again, making my climax more of a never-ending, rolling wave.

"Logan," I hissed, my hands reaching up and tangling in his hair as I kissed him over and over, feeling like I might die from how good the pleasure felt.

He jerked against me, groaning as his rhythm faltered. He came with a strangled moan, his cum filling me in hot bursts, on and on until it was dripping out, wetting my thighs and the bed underneath us.

His big body surrounded me as he continued to slowly move in and out, both of us gasping at the sensations.

"It gets better every time," I murmured, an edge of wonder to my voice.

"It's because we were made for each other. Twin souls, Red. I think I've been looking for you my whole life, and it's like I can breathe now, because you're finally here."

A tear slid down my face as I gazed up at him.

"How did we get here?"

He brushed a kiss against my lips before he licked up my tear. "Luck, I guess."

I blinked at that idea. I'd considered myself unlucky my entire life.

But suddenly, I wondered if he was right.

Because anyone who had Logan York telling them he loved them had to be at least a little lucky.

Right?

Logan

The sunlight streaming through the shades sliced through my pounding head like a knife, pulling me out of a restless, alcohol-soaked sleep. My mouth was dry, my body aching in a way that wasn't just from the Stanley Cup Finals. My dick had been some kind of superhero last night—I'd fucked Sloane for hours after we'd gotten back.

I groaned, dragging a hand over my face and squinting against the brightness. Sloane was still asleep next to me, her body half-wrapped in the sheet, her dark hair spilling across the pillow. She looked peaceful, her lips slightly parted. My dick twitched as I stared at her, but I held myself back. No doubt she was going to feel like I did when she woke up, so it was good to let her sleep as long as possible.

Carefully, I pushed myself out of bed, every muscle protesting as I stumbled toward the bathroom. The tiles were cold against my bare feet, a sharp contrast to the heat radiating from my skin. I flicked on the light, immediately regretting the blinding brightness, and turned the shower knob. Even the sound of water sputtering on was almost too loud. Fuck. This was going to be a fun day.

I dropped my briefs, ready to step into the shower, when something in the mirror caught my attention. A smear of color. Red.

I froze, leaning closer to inspect the reflection. It wasn't just red—it was the unmistakable imprint of lips. Bright, perfect, and a fucking sexy souvenir from the night before.

Sloane. The memory of her mouth, her touch, how she'd given me the best fucking blow job of my life—all of it came flooding back in vivid detail.

I exhaled, pressing my palms against the edge of the counter, my head dipping forward as the memory hit me like a slap to the face: her laughter low and teasing, the way her eyes sparkled as she'd sunk to her knees.

I straightened and took a step to the shower . . . when something stopped me. An idea. Maybe it was the hangover talking—or the remnants of the champagne-fueled haze—but I reached for my phone on the counter.

Turning on the camera, I framed the image, angling just enough to capture the mark in all its glory. One quick snap and I had it: the perfect picture.

Fuck the Stanley Cup, I'd just gotten my trophy.

Still staring at the screen, I grinned and headed to the shower, extremely pleased with how my life was going.

CHAPTER 29

LOGAN

This was a really good idea," I said dreamily as I stared at the ceiling, idly stroking the Stanley Cup as it sat on the floor next to me.

"Oh Stanley Cup, oh Stanley Cup, how lovely are your . . ." Ari belted to the tune of "Oh Christmas Tree" as he put his hand over his heart.

"Please stop," Lincoln groaned, not actually sounding annoyed by it. "It's not even Christmas."

It was probably hard to be annoyed at anything when you were this drunk. Everything was happy, happy, happy.

"What's happy, happy, happy?" Camden asked, plopping down on the other side of the Cup.

Oops, I'd said that part out loud.

"Everything," I answered. "Absolutely everything."

"You know what we need?" Ari said suddenly, cutting off his song mid-verse.

"Are you going to tell us?" Disney asked, when at least three minutes had passed.

"I was just making sure all of you were paying attention," he said, holding on to the wall.

"What are you doing?" Lincoln muttered.

"Does the room seem to be spinning? Or is it just me?" Ari asked.

We all were suddenly looking around the room.

"I think it's spinning," I told him, shaking my head and making the *spinning* worse. "Hold on to the Cup, Hero," I drawled. "We can't let it get away."

Camden grabbed it with both hands. "Wait, you forgot to tell us what we needed," Camden said. "I can't hold on to Stanley forever."

"It's been three seconds," Walker said, shaking his head.

"Tacos! We need tacos from Maria's!" Ari said, pointing his finger.

"Do you think Maria's will also be spinning?" I asked, not sure how that would work.

"Definitely not. This place is the problem," Ari said. Walker and Camden both nodded their heads in agreement.

"My place is not the problem," Lincoln said as he tossed another shot back. "Monroe loves this place."

"Well, she ended up with you. So her taste is questionable, don't you think?"

Lincoln gaped at him . . . as did Walker.

"You take that back!" Lincoln growled. "Monroe has excellent taste. The best, in fact."

"Take me for tacos, and I might consider it, Golden Boy," Ari mused, not sounding scared at all.

"Fine, we're leaving right now," Lincoln said, stalking . . . or rather stumbling toward the elevator. "Fuck, maybe the room *is* spinning."

"It is," I agreed, trying to get off the floor. "Help, I'm stuck!" I called out when I couldn't stand up.

"You're just lying there. You haven't even moved," said Camden.

Oh. He was right.

I pushed myself off the floor and somehow managed to stand.

"Good job, Rookie," Camden said, clapping me on the back and almost sending me to the floor again.

"What are you guys going to call me next year?" I asked as I also stumbled to the elevator.

"What do you mean?" asked Walker.

"Well, I can't be 'Rookie' when I'm not a rookie, right?" I held on to the elevator as we began to descend, wondering if that last shot had been a good idea.

"Oh, that's your name. Forever," Ari commented. "Just like they call me 'Chosen One.' I'm just stuck with it now. It's a part of me."

I gaped at him. "There's a big difference between 'Rookie' and 'Chosen One,' Lancaster," I scoffed.

"Why are you smiling like that?" Walker asked, suddenly poking me in the cheek.

"I'm smiling? I'm not trying to smile. I'm trying to make a point," I said, reaching up and touching my face. Hmm. I was smiling. Fuck. "Help. Something's wrong with my face!" I screeched.

"Nothing's wrong with your face, Rookie. You just need another shot," Ari said as he pulled a full shot glass out of thin air and thrust it against my lips.

That sounded weirdly sexual.

I took the glass and drank it down, wincing at the burn.

"Why did you guys already get all the cool nicknames?" I whined. "Even your dicks have a better nickname than I do."

Ari nodded. "That is true. Maximus 5000 is very cool. But we're born how we're born, Logan."

Everyone nodded like he'd just said something groundbreaking.

"Well, my dick should have a cool nickname. I have a cool picture of it." I told them proudly, thinking of the shot I'd gotten of Sloane's lipstick stain.

"Why do these conversations always go to dicks? I want to talk about tacos," Lincoln griped as we walked out to the Uber someone had ordered.

"I want to hear more about this picture. Is this something . . . tattoo-worthy?" Ari mused.

Walker nodded. "Definitely sounds like it."

"What? No! Tattoos don't belong on dicks. That's why I don't have one," I told them, right as I slid into the SUV.

The driver, a stern-looking man with bushy eyebrows, coughed.

"Ignore everything we say in this vehicle," Lincoln said, sliding him a hundred dollars.

"I didn't hear anything," he answered.

"Look at Golden Boy, thinking he's in the mafia again," Camden whispered.

Lincoln shot him a look from the front passenger seat. "I heard that."

"Wasn't trying to hide it." Camden smirked.

"I have an idea," Ari announced.

"We're still trying to do your first idea," I said, feeling hungry all of a sudden . . . for tacos.

"Go to Inked on Main Street," Ari ordered.

"This is actually a good idea, Lancaster," Lincoln said with a grin.

"What—what's a good idea?" I asked, looking between them.

"We're going to make a man out of you, Rookie," Walker said, and there was a weird, evil-looking grin on his face.

"Maria's. I want Maria's," I squeaked as we turned down a street downtown.

"Trust me, you'll be thanking us later," Camden told me, patting me on the back. "I haven't had any regrets."

"And he has virgin blood tattooed all over his dick," Ari casually remarked.

The driver made a choking sound and started coughing loudly. Lincoln handed him another hundred.

We pulled in front of Inked. "Drink this," Lincoln ordered, giving me another shot.

I threw it back immediately. "I don't think you're supposed to drink before getting inked, and I'm way beyond drunk," I gasped.

"Eh, they see everything at this place," Ari said happily as he jumped out of the car.

I suddenly seemed to be stuck to my seat, so Walker helped me by pushing me out of the vehicle. Camden caught me right before I landed face-first on the concrete.

"Hero, I think you need another tattoo as well," Lincoln said as he began to corral us toward the door.

Camden's eyebrows shot up in surprise. "Am I finally getting . . ."

Lincoln grinned back.

"Come back," I whispered as the Uber sped away from the curb.

"Maximus 5000 probably intimidated him," Ari said, staring after it.

"Probably," Lincoln drawled.

Ari glared at him. "I'm going to pretend I didn't sense any sarcasm in that answer, Golden Boy."

Lincoln winked at him. "You've always been good at pretending."

Ari's glare turned into a grin. "Good one."

"Can we please focus on . . . I don't know what we're focusing on. But this seems to be a terrible idea," I groaned as I was shoved inside the tattoo shop.

"It will all be over before you know it," Walker assured me, shoving a full bottle of vodka into my chest.

"Where are you guys keeping all of this?" I asked, momentarily distracted as I took a big gulp.

"What can I help you boys with?" the front desk girl asked us, eyeing everyone . . . hungrily.

"We're here for a dick tattoo," Lincoln said, his voice blank and disinterested as he casually examined his fingernails.

Her eyes widened.

"And a butterfly tattoo," Camden added excitedly.

Her gaze bounced around us.

"Well, okay then. Let me show you back."

I was feeling faint as Ari pushed me forward. "Help!" I called out . . . to no one.

The guys all had the nerve to snicker at me.

"We *are* helping, Rookie." Lincoln grinned as we made it to a back room. "You aren't going to chicken out on us, are you?"

I stared at the equipment laid neatly on a table and gulped imagining that anywhere near my dick.

"For the Circle," I muttered to myself.

And then suddenly, all of them had shot glasses in their hand and they were toasting. "For the Circle!"

Fuck. This was really happening.

"Is this some kind of weird sex thing?" the tattoo artist asked as I went to pull my dick awkwardly out of my pants.

"Alcohol. I need more alcohol," I said loudly, looking around for help. Lincoln, Ari, Camden, and Walker were watching a replay of Game Seven on ESPN and not paying attention—despite the fact that this situation was all their fault.

"You're not supposed to be drunk when you do this, man," the artist complained, keeping his gaze averted from my dick. "Fuck, maybe I need alcohol too. I did not think there would be this many dicks in this job."

"You're not allowed to drink!" I squealed, my voice at least three octaves higher than usual in my panic.

"Yeah, you're right," the artist grumbled, nodding his head at what should have been already obvious.

I glanced around. Was this a joke? Like, were there hidden cameras focused on me right now, and any minute they were going to pop out and say "Surprise!" or something like that?

"But is it?" he pressed.

I glanced down at him. I'd obviously been around a lot of tattoo artists in my life—my skin was practically made of ink at this point. But I decidedly liked this particular artist the least.

"Is it what?" I snapped, wanting to yank the tattoo gun from his hands and throw it at the wall. Tattoo guns should not be this close to dicks. I'd tried to tell the guys this over and over again.

How the fuck had I ended up here?

Oh right, obsessive, crazy love. That was how I'd gotten here. And the four worst friends on Earth,

He started cleaning the area, and I wanted to curl up in a ball.

"A sex thing. Like are y'all . . . all together?" He glanced at the guys. "Which one of them is Monroe?"

I barked out a crazy-sounding laugh that almost turned into a wail when the gun touched my skin, the edges of my vision going dark.

Look, as a fucking NHL hockey player, I was tough. I'd had teeth knocked out of my head, multiple bones broken, and I'd once skated an entire game with a broken kneecap in college.

But having a needle on your cock was on a whole other level.

"No, this is not a sex thing," I finally muttered, once I was convinced I was not going to pass out.

"Hmm," he answered, clearly not convinced as he stared hard at my dick as he worked.

"Alcohol!" I all but screamed as Camden gave me an amused look over his shoulder.

"I thought you said you shouldn't be drunk for this?" Lincoln asked casually. I growled. Of course, it had to be Lincoln who said that. And, of course, it made me straighten up.

"Just do it," I snarled.

"How ya doing over there, Rookie?" Ari asked, taking a swig of his beer without offering me any because he was an asshole.

"Just dandy, Lancaster. Never knew a needle shooting ink into my *stick* could feel this good."

Ari snorted, and the tattoo artist guy twitched, his face growing uneasy. He obviously hadn't gotten my sarcasm.

"Which one of them did this to you?" he finally muttered, gesturing to the red lipstick stain design he'd transferred on my skin to trace. His cheeks were bright pink.

"None of them did that to me," I snapped indignantly. "That's from my future wife!"

He held up his hands. "Okay, okay. I believe you."

He definitely did not believe me.

The needle touching my dick again made me flinch.

"No moving," he said, and it was all I could do not to punch him. But then I'd just have a weird red outline on my dick, and Sloane wouldn't think *that* was hot. I needed the whole shading effect to really impress her.

Camden appeared next to me with a shot glass. "Here you go," he said.

I yanked it out of his hand and threw it back, the burn hitting me just right. "Just for that, I'm not going to call you Grandpappy anymore," I told him seriously.

"Really?" Camden asked suspiciously, raising an eyebrow.

"At least, not for a day," I amended, because it was important to tell the truth. I wasn't going to give up the years of happiness I'd get from calling him that for one shot.

Alright, judging by my train of thought, the alcohol was already kicking in again.

"You really aren't supposed to drink," the tattoo artist grumbled. So, I took another shot just to spite him and myself. Because I obviously couldn't be trusted to make good decisions under peer pressure when I was drunk.

I only cried one tear during the process, something that Lancaster only mocked me for . . . a little.

"Alright, done. Hopefully your . . . girl . . . likes that."

"Why do you keep saying *girl* like that? It *is* for a girl."

He shook his head. "Of course it is," he answered soothingly, like I was crazy for saying it. "Now you said something about a butterfly? Is that also on a dick?" He winced when he said it, and Ari snorted.

"This is the weirdest conversation I've ever had," the artist mumbled under his breath.

Camden sat on the table and lifted his shirt. "Let's do it right on this shoulder blade," he told him, practically beaming as he pointed it out.

"It needs to look like this," Lincoln added, pulling up his shirt and revealing the giant butterfly tattoo that stretched across his entire chest and down to his abdomen.

The tattoo artist's eyes bounced from Lincoln's chest, to Camden's back . . . then to me. "Are you sure this isn't a weird sex thing?"

I glanced at Lincoln—just to make sure I was allowed to answer. This was secret COT stuff, after all.

Lincoln shook his head as he took another draw from the bottle of tequila he'd procured from . . . who knows where.

"Not a weird sex thing," I confirmed. "I'm allowed to get it . . . right?" I asked Lincoln.

Ari waved his hand in front of Lincoln's face. "Don't look at him. Look at me. What if I said no?"

"Are you saying no?" I asked, moving my head to try and look at Lincoln around Ari's arm.

"You can have one too," Lincoln said, but the words were muffled because Ari's hand had gone over Lincoln's mouth.

"What was that?"

"*I* said, you can have one too, Rookie," Ari said primly.

Lincoln rolled his eyes and then nodded, with Ari's hand still pressed against his mouth.

I did a fist pump, wincing as a sharp pang went through my dick.

"Definitely a weird sex thing," the artist whispered, his ears red as he started on Camden's chest.

CHAPTER 30

SLOANE

Where are you going?" Logan asked, his voice rough with sleep, not to mention alcohol, since he'd slipped into bed around three this morning after a night out with the guys celebrating winning the Cup. His blond hair was a chaotic mess like my fingers had tugged at it all night, and his green eyes were tracing my curves, a lazy heat in their depths as I got dressed.

I gulped as I stared at him, missing the leg of my jeans because he was very distracting. The sheets clung to his hips, low enough I was blushing, since I was very familiar at this point at what the bulge under the sheets could do.

"Ignore him. He can't help it," Logan rasped as his dick rose under the sheet. He winced all of a sudden and shifted, and I focused on his chest, but that was also distracting. Hard planes and sharp angles . . . covered in tattoos—

Fuck, he was delicious.

"You're staring," he said, one muscular arm bent behind his head like a cocky, tattooed Greek god who'd been summoned just to torment me.

"Wishful thinking," I teased, pulling my zipper up a little too fast, like that would somehow help me escape his orbit.

Logan smirked, the corner of his mouth curving just enough to make me want to throw something at him—or kiss him. Probably both. "I'm always wishfully thinking of you, Red."

I snorted. "That was corny."

"You still haven't answered my question. It's almost like you're avoiding it."

He shifted, and I tried not to notice how the movement made the muscles in his stomach ripple before I did something stupid, like cancel my plans and crawl back into bed with him.

"I volunteer at a group home on Tuesdays," I murmured. "It's just something I started doing last year."

His gaze softened. "Of course you do, because you're fucking perfect."

And then suddenly he was getting out of bed . . . completely nude, of course. I blinked, and wiped at my chin because there was no way I wasn't drooling.

That ass . . . and dick.

Wait . . . what was that?

"Did you hurt yourself last night?" I asked, looking at the bandage wrapped around his cock.

He blinked, his cheeks turning suspiciously red. "Um . . . kind of. But it was also *kind of* voluntary?"

"I don't know what you're saying," I said, watching him walk into his closet. "And what are you doing?"

"Going with you," he called.

I followed him into the closet. "I'm still looking for answers, buddy."

He stiffened and slowly turned around. "Now listen, I don't want you to get freaked out. It's actually very tasteful."

"Logan York, what did you do?"

He slowly unwrapped the bandage from his dick and revealed a . . . tattoo?

"You tattooed your dick?" I asked. "I mean, it's not surprising since the rest of your skin is covered, but why now?"

"I—I was feeling inspired," he said as I leaned forward to look.

"No," I whispered when I realized what it was. "That's my—"

"Your lip marks in *your* lipstick shade? Why yes, yes it is, Red," he said proudly.

I gaped at him.

"Nothing says you're in love more than a dick tattoo," he told me with a wink, sounding like he was quoting someone.

My gaze went from his dick to his face, and then back to his dick.

He grabbed a Dallas Knights V-neck and slipped it on along with some briefs and a pair of sweatpants.

I was still gaping at him when he finished getting dressed, so he grabbed my hand and led me out of the room.

Logan stopped and then turned around, looking much more relaxed as he tapped on my chin to close my mouth.

"You, me . . . my dick. It's forever, baby."

"Right," I finally murmured, still in shock over his tattoo . . . and how absurdly pleased I was about it.

Maybe I wouldn't tell him that part, though.

But he was right . . . what could say forever better than . . .

An inscription on your cock?

―――――――

"Are you sure you want to come in? I thought you wanted to relax today. Being around a bunch of sad kids is definitely not relaxing," I told him as we pulled into a parking spot outside the group home. I wanted him to come in with me, but I also wanted to give him an out. This place could be a lot.

"I happen to love kids. And maybe I can help make them a little less sad. I brought some signed pucks with me. You think they'll like that?" he asked, sliding on a backward hat as he opened the truck door because his goal was to torture me today.

"They will love that," I said softly, feeling strangely emotional.

"Don't look so shocked, baby. There's not anything I wouldn't do for you." He pressed a kiss against my lips before he walked around and helped me out.

When I walked into the group home with Logan by my side, I could already feel the tension building in Rome's small frame from across the room. He was sitting in his usual spot, huddled in the corner of the play area, his knees pulled up to his chest, his blond hair falling over his face like a shield. The moment he saw Logan—this tall, broad figure next to me—I watched his shoulders tighten, his body curling in on itself even more.

I couldn't blame him. Logan, with his size and presence . . . and tattoos could be intimidating, especially to someone like Rome, who had learned to associate new people with hurt, with loss. He'd been through so much, more than any little boy should have to bear. And even though I trusted Logan completely, I knew this was going to be hard for him.

I knelt down beside Rome, speaking softly, trying to make my voice as gentle as possible. "Hey, Rome. I brought someone to meet you today."

His eyes flicked up to me, wide and cautious, before darting to Logan. He didn't say anything, just stared at him, his tiny body still folded tight. My heart ached watching him.

The monsters who had hurt him should be destroyed.

Logan crouched down beside me, his presence suddenly much smaller, softer, as if he could sense the fragility of this moment. "Hey, Rome," he said, his voice calm, gentle in a way that surprised even me. "I've heard a lot about you. Sloane says you're really good at coloring."

His eyes shifted toward the coloring book on the table but didn't move. Rome was still watching him, wary and waiting. I could see the fear in his eyes, that instinct to shut down, to close himself off. I knew it all too well.

Logan stayed where he was, not pushing, not getting closer. He didn't try to force himself into Rome's space, and I was grateful for that. He just sat there, a safe distance away, giving him time.

"You know," he continued, his tone light, "I'm not great at coloring. I tried once, but Sloane said I couldn't stay inside the lines."

I smiled, because he was talking about some doodling he'd done on a piece of paper—hardly coloring. But I loved that he was trying. I glanced at Rome, hoping he'd pick up on the same ease, the same warmth he was offering him now.

For a moment, Rome didn't move. Then, slowly, his eyes flicked to me, and I gave him a small nod, trying to reassure him. "It's okay," I whispered. "Logan's really nice. I promise."

He didn't speak, but his tiny hands loosened their grip on his knees just a fraction. It wasn't much, but it was something.

Logan smiled. "Can I sit here?" he asked, gesturing to the floor a little closer to him.

Rome didn't respond, but he didn't shake his head either. Logan took that as permission, moving carefully, like he was trying not to spook him. He sat cross-legged on the floor.

"Sloane says your favorite color is orange," Logan commented, his voice low, almost conspiratorial. "That's my favorite color too."

Rome hesitated, his small fingers inching toward the crayon box in front of him. He didn't look at him directly, but I could see the way his body was slowly uncurling, like he was starting to trust him, just a little. He grabbed an orange crayon and hesitated before slowly rolling it toward Logan.

We both froze. "You're going to share your favorite color with me? That's awesome, bud."

A small smile peeked across Rome's lips. "There's another one in the box."

It took us a second to respond, because we were both gaping at the little glimpse of Rome's personality.

"Oh, well, I'm still going to think I'm special if you gave me orange," Logan said with a laugh. "I'll just imagine it."

Rome finally met Logan's eyes. His hand hovered over the crayons before he carefully plucked out the other orange he mentioned. He still didn't speak, but I could see the tension in his shoulders easing, just a little.

"Okay," he finally said with a shrug.

My eyes were glassy as I stared wide-eyed at Rome. This was the most I'd seen him interact with anyone aside from me.

Rome turned toward me . . . and handed me the crayon, his small fingers barely brushing mine as he did. It was a tiny moment, one that would have seemed insignificant to anyone else, but to me, it felt monumental.

"So you can feel special too."

And there was no hiding the tears that fell down my face at that one.

Logan took over while I was falling apart, his smile never faltering. "Okay, show me what to do. Maybe you can teach me how to color, Sloane was a terrible teacher."

Rome snorted—which made my tears come even faster—and then he picked up another crayon, blue this time, and started coloring quietly, his movements slow and deliberate. Logan followed his lead, staying inside the lines, though I noticed him purposely slipping outside them sometimes, just to make Rome smile.

"You are pretty bad," Rome said quietly after a moment, freezing as soon as the words came out, like he was scared of Logan's reaction.

Logan pretended not to notice. "Ouch," he cried softly, pressing a hand to his chest like he'd been wounded. "You got me with that one. We all can't be talented artists, though, Rome. Some of us have to be good at other things."

Rome's shoulders relaxed, and then there was another faint smile on his lips.

"What kind of other things are you good at?" Rome asked a few minutes later. "Cooking?"

I snorted, because that was also not one of Logan's skills. Rome glanced at me, confused.

"I'm not good at cooking either, unfortunately. I'm good at hockey, though," Logan said, his voice sliding into a whine. "Sloane, tell him I'm good at hockey."

I smiled, my chest tightening over the small grin that had appeared on Rome's face at Logan's theatrics. "He's very good at hockey, Rome," I said in a patronizing voice.

Rome's smile widened. "I don't think she means that," he said softly.

Logan huffed. "She *totally* means that. I even brought pucks with me today, because I'm that good at hockey. Do you want to see?"

Rome glanced back at his coloring page, like he was debating. Then he shyly nodded.

Logan kept his movements slow as he pulled a puck from the duffel bag he'd brought and slowly showed it to Rome.

"Wow," Rome whispered. "Is this a real one?"

"Yep," said Logan, waggling his eyebrows at me because he was so proud that his "puck" plan seemed to be working. "Next season you should totally come to a game."

Normally if someone had said something like that, I would have told them not to make promises to a little boy that they weren't going to keep.

But I didn't even have that thought with Logan.

I was learning . . . there wasn't a promise he wouldn't keep.

"That would be awesome," Rome breathed, looking genuinely excited for the first time since I'd met him.

By the time we finished, Logan had earned more than just his trust. He'd earned a piece of his heart, the way he always managed to with people. And as I watched him sitting there beside Rome, gently teasing him about how his picture wasn't nearly as good as Rome's, I realized how lucky I was to have someone who could be this kind, this patient, with the people I cared about most.

Rome finally looked up at him, his small voice breaking the silence. "Maybe you're not that bad."

Logan chuckled, reaching over slowly and ruffling his hair playfully. "That's the nicest thing anyone's said to me all day."

I watched for Rome to react to Logan's touch, but he went back to coloring, seemingly unaffected by it.

"Not that bad at all, York," I murmured, and he winked at me.

CHAPTER 31

LOGAN

The streets were already packed with fans, waving banners and wearing every piece of Dallas Knights gear they could get their hands on. It was loud—*really* loud. The air buzzed with excitement, the whole city ready to party. But here I was, pacing in the hotel room I'd rented, trying to convince Sloane to come with me to the championship parade. Despite the fact that I'd told her I loved her, despite the fact that I'd been all over her at the hockey games, she still was nervous about being with me on such a public stage . . .

"I'm not going, Logan," she said, arms crossed as she leaned against the door. Her eyes flickered with a mix of nerves and something else I couldn't quite pin down. "Dinners, yes. Hanging with your friends, yes . . ."

"Front row at the hockey game?"

"No one was looking at me!"

I smirked, and she stuck out her tongue at me. "No one was looking at me until you decided to act crazy."

I snorted. "I hate to tell you, Red, but everyone is *always* looking at you."

She side-eyed me, like that was the craziest thing I'd ever said. Her fingers fidgeted with the hem of her shirt. I wasn't used to seeing Sloane be so visibly nervous. She usually did her best to hide how she was feeling.

I took it as a good sign that she was letting her walls down right now.

"Come on," I said, taking a step closer. "It's a once-in-a-lifetime thing. You *have* to be there with me."

She raised an eyebrow.

I grinned, an idea sparking in my head. "Okay, how about this—we make a bet."

Her eyes narrowed, a hint of curiosity peeking through the nervousness. "A bet?"

"Yeah. If I make you *come*, you'll come with me."

She raised a shocked eyebrow, obviously not expecting that. "And if you don't?"

"If I don't, you don't come and I don't go."

Her mouth dropped. "You don't go—of course you're going. This is a huge moment for you. You can't miss it."

"Nope. I don't want to go if you won't be with me." I grinned. "Admit it, this is romantic."

"I'm not going to fake it," she said, completely ignoring what I'd just said. "Since that would violate your little rule."

Snorting, I shook my head and began to walk her toward the bed. "I'm such a tyrant, telling you that you're not allowed to fake orgasms with me."

A grin briefly split across her lips, and I worshiped the rare glimpse of it like the sun peeking through the clouds.

She stood there, pretending to think about it, but I could see her faltering. Finally, she let out a dramatic sigh. "Fine. You've got yourself a deal."

I snickered. "That was a remarkably hard sale considering it was over an orgasm."

"Well, this doesn't feel like it's a fair deal since inexplicably you make me orgasm every time."

"Something I'm very proud of," I said with a smirk.

Sloane fell back on the bed, and I got lost for a second just staring at her. *Marry me* was insanely on the tip of my tongue, but I choked it back.

Baby steps, Logan.

"Well, get to work," she said haughtily, pretending like this was such a burden for her, even though I could see the slight tremble of her hands at her sides.

"Mmm, just building up the anticipation," I purred, my gaze taking her in.

"Let's get those shorts off you," I said, finally starting to stalk slowly toward the bed.

She watched me, her navy-blue eyes glimmering in the light. There was a blush to her cheeks already, and her breath was already quickening.

I was definitely going to win.

———

Sloane

"You're soaking wet already, aren't you?" Logan rasped as he slid my shorts down my legs.

"Maybe you should check," I teased, knowing what he would find. Of course, there was already heat building inside me, just from his gaze stroking across my skin.

He threw my shorts over his shoulder, and I held in my shiver as his green eyes gleamed at me.

"You're beautiful," I blurted out, wondering if he thought it was weird that *that* was what came to my mind every time I looked at him.

He smiled, though, and that weird, glittering feeling I got around him spun around in my chest.

His gaze slid down to my legs, and I let my thighs fall open. Logan slowly lowered himself to his knees, his hands massaging my inner thighs as he pushed them even farther apart.

"I love your cunt," he breathed, his nose skimming through the lace as he inhaled me like I was a decadent treat.

"So you've said before," I whispered, feeling embarrassed about how breathy my voice sounded. It would have been one thing if this was me faking it, but it was definitely a hundred percent real.

I tried to shore myself up, wanting to make it at least a little hard for him, but then he licked through the lining of my panty-covered slit, and I was back to gasping like I'd fallen into heat.

"Pull your knees up to your shoulders," he growled. "I want to see all of you."

Locking eyes with him, I slowly pulled my knees up to my chest and then let my legs fall open farther. I was *so* going to lose this bet. He'd proven every time this wasn't a fluke.

"Such a good girl," he purred, and I nearly whimpered in response. His gaze was a mix of possessiveness and hunger . . . and a little bit of awe as well.

Reaching out, he tore off my panties like they were nothing. Liquid heat gushed out of me, dripping down my ass.

"You like that move, Red?" he asked with a grin.

I gave him my best unimpressed look, even though the evidence of my arousal was impossible to hide.

"Are you going to make me come or not?" I snapped, and he laughed at me like I was a playful kitten trying its best to be big.

Why was the sound of his laugh so freaking sexy?

Logan rubbed his fingers through my folds, lightly at first, as he began to tease me. I tried to rock against him, trying to get more friction.

"Sweetest cunt," he murmured before he slowly lowered to the floor. His tongue licked once through my folds. "Sweetest girl," he continued.

A moan slipped from my lips, and I stiffened. Because that had been too easy for him.

Logan softly rimmed my slit with one finger before sliding it inside me.

I loved his fingers. They felt so fucking good. His other hand went to my breast, massaging it just how I liked it. I'd never admit that to him, obviously, but he may have been some kind of genius, capable of mimicking what I liked perfectly just from watching me that one day.

I tried to close my eyes, because the intensity of his stare was making all of it feel even better, but he wasn't going to have any of that.

"Eyes on me," he commanded, and I forced my gaze back to him as if his words held secret powers. As I watched, he slid in two more fingers, rubbing against that one spot and making my back arch up from the bed, a mewling cry sounding around the room.

"You and I both know it's impossible for me to lose this bet. I've made it my mission in life to worship you every chance I get. Of course I'm going to make you come."

"Logan," I whispered, feeling his words deep in my chest.

And they were making me *ache*.

His tongue sucked hard on my clit, and a fourth finger pushed in. It felt *almost* as good as his dick.

"That's it, baby. Come for me," he said roughly, before his lips were torturing me again.

"Fuck," I cried out as I came with a strangled gasp. Wave after wave of pleasure floated through me, and it took me a second to realize that the screams ricocheting around the room . . . were from me.

I was having trouble remembering my own name as I came back down.

Logan stood up from the floor and then leaned over me on the bed. His lips were shiny from my cum, and I reached up and rubbed it into his skin, wanting to mark him the way it felt like he marked me.

"Fuck, Calloway. You acted like that was going to be hard," he said with a sexy grin.

I huffed and rolled my eyes before I focused on how his dick was literally trying to burst from his shorts. Reaching out, I was shocked when he slid away.

"Unfortunately, my dick is still a little out of commission," he said, a bashful note in his voice.

Ah, right. His tattoo. I licked my lips because something about him marking himself like that got me ready to go all over again.

"Maybe I should have just whipped out my dick for you to look at," he commented.

I pretended to think about it for a moment. "Maybe," I agreed.

My smile faded as he gazed down at me with a serious look in his eye.

"Tell me why you don't want to go to the parade today. I know you love my friends . . . and I know you love me. So what is it?"

I looked away from him, suddenly feeling like I was going to cry.

"What if someone recognizes me," I whispered. It had happened the other day; we'd been out to dinner, and one of my former clients had stopped at our table. Logan and I had immediately left. "I don't—I don't want to embarrass you."

His body flinched like he'd been shot. "Baby, is that what you think? That I was embarrassed the other night?"

I bit down on my lip. "Who wouldn't be? I bet some of my . . . clients will be out there in the crowd. It just feels like it's always going to happen."

"I'm not embarrassed, Red. I was just trying not to end up in jail because I'd killed a guy. It makes me crazy thinking of anyone else touching your perfect fucking body. Because you're mine. It would have been the same no matter who it was. A former high school boyfriend, someone you caught jacking off to your picture—I would have acted the same."

I studied his face, looking for the lie.

But as usual . . . I couldn't find it.

"Okay, I'll go," I finally murmured, watching as his face lit up. "But you're talking crazy again."

"If it isn't a little crazy . . . is it even love?" he asked as he pulled me up from the bed.

Logan

The energy at the parade was electric—fans packed every inch of the streets, shouting and cheering, losing their minds. The noise was deafening, but in the best possible way. We were on top of the world, rolling through downtown Dallas on a float, passing the Stanley Cup back and forth. Sloane was glued to my side, her fingers gripping my hand like I might disappear in the chaos. Even though I could sense her nerves, she was loosening up, smiling more, her eyes wide with the madness unfolding around us.

Ari, already tipsy before we even hit the first turn, climbed up on the edge of the float, balancing a beer in one hand and waving wildly with the other. "I'm king of the world," he yelled, ripping off his jersey and doing a weird shimmy that had the crowd screaming.

His wife, Blake, was trying—*failing*—to get him to get off the railing. "Ari, for fuck's sake, you're gonna fall off!"

"Angel face, baby lover, I'm invincible!" Ari roared, lifting the beer to his lips and chugging it like a man possessed. The crowd erupted, cheering him on. Blake threw her hands up in defeat, laughing.

"Dallas Knights! Dallas Knights!" Camden and Walker were waving their arms to get the crowd hyped, their wives rolling their eyes but grinning like they'd seen this show before.

Ari jumped off the railing, making a grabby motion with his hands, and he was immediately handed two beers. He nudged me with an elbow. "Think you can handle this?" he asked, nodding at the Cup, gleaming in the sunlight next to us.

"Are you kidding? I've been waiting for this my whole life," I shot back, grabbing one of the beers from him. We lifted our bottles and clinked them together, then poured the beer straight into the Cup. The crowd went wild.

"Let's do this," Ari said, lifting the Cup and tipping it back while he chugged the beer. He finished with foam dripping down his chin, grinning like an idiot, and handed it to me. I followed suit, the beer ice cold and somehow sweeter than it had ever tasted before.

And then—because Ari was Ari—he looked at the float behind us, also loaded with members of the team, and shouted, "Heads up!" before *tossing* the Cup over to the next float like it was just some casual object instead of a priceless relic.

Knights staff, standing on smaller floats around us, collectively lost their minds. One of them even screamed, "WHAT ARE YOU DOING?"

The Cup sailed through the air for a terrifying split second before Dobbins, one of our wings, caught it, laughing hysterically while the staff members nearly fainted in the background.

I doubled over, laughing so hard I almost spilled the rest of my beer. Ari gave a dramatic bow like he'd just pulled off the greatest stunt of his life, which, knowing him, he probably thought he had.

Sloane tugged on my sleeve, her eyes wide, but there was a smile there now—a real one. "You guys are insane," she said, her voice half laugh, half shock.

I grinned, feeling the buzz of the beer and the adrenaline from the crowd. "Yeah, but you're having fun, aren't you?"

She bit her lip, trying to suppress a smile. "Maybe a little."

"*Maybe*?" I teased, pulling her closer as another roar went up from the crowd. The guys were still at it—Walker had found a microphone and was trying to lead a round of terribly off-key singing, while Lincoln had his arms wrapped around Monroe, and he was now attempting some kind of wobbly slow dance on top of the float.

Sloane laughed, shaking her head as she leaned into me, finally letting the excitement of it all take over. "Alright, fine. I'm having fun. So much fun."

I gave her a look, one eyebrow raised. "What was that?"

She rolled her eyes. "*I'm having fun*, Logan."

I smirked. "Told you. Now, kiss me before Ari tries to throw me off the float next."

Sloane rolled her eyes but let me kiss her. I even slipped some tongue action in because I knew it would make her laugh. When I finally released her, we stayed holding hands while she started talking to Olivia.

"Whatcha looking at so hard with those binoculars, Colt?" I asked one of my teammates as he leaned over the railing, on the verge of falling out.

"My future wife," he murmured, and I blinked, not expecting anything like that from him. Colt was one of my quieter teammates, but he was a fan favorite. Something about his black hair and blue eyes combined with his air of mystery . . . it made our female fans crazy.

"Sorry, what?"

"My wife," he said simply, as if he hadn't said anything crazy. "I'm pretty sure I've just found her."

I glanced at Ari, who was on Colt's other side, grinning at him like a loon as Colt pulled out his phone and zoomed in on a girl with dark hair with pink streaks that was about two rows back in the crowd.

"Total COT moment," he mouthed to me over Colt's shoulder.

I nodded.

Indeed.

Sloane

The parade had been a moment I would remember for the rest of my life. I hadn't expected to enjoy it as much as I did, but the energy was contagious. Logan's grin was wide, infectious, and I found myself caught up in the thrill

THE PUCKING WRONG ROOKIE 247

of it all—cheering fans, confetti flying everywhere, and the sun beating down in that perfect, golden way that makes everything seem brighter than it is. I felt like I could actually let go for a moment. I laughed, I cheered with him, I even let myself dance on the float as the crowd roared for the Dallas Knights.

But then I saw him.

At first, it was just a blur, a figure on the sidewalk, another face in the sea of cheering fans. But then my gaze locked on him—Everett, standing there, staring straight at me. My chest tightened instantly, the familiar chill of fear crawling up my spine. His eyes were dark, cold, the same look that had always made me feel small. My heart lurched. It didn't matter how much fun I'd been having; seeing him there, in the middle of the celebration, ripped me right out of it.

I froze. For a second, the noise of the crowd faded, drowned out by the thundering of my pulse in my ears. He didn't move, didn't wave—just stood there, watching. And that was worse. So much worse.

Because that couldn't mean anything good for me.

I clenched my fists, forcing myself to look away, trying to plaster a smile back on my face. Logan was next to me, laughing, oblivious to the shift inside me. I had to keep it together. He couldn't know. I couldn't let this ruin the day for him.

But it was like the air had changed around me, everything suddenly too bright, too loud, too much. The float kept moving forward, but I was stuck in my head, trapped in the knowledge that my uncle was there, watching. Waiting.

I tried to fake it—tried to keep smiling, laughing when Logan cracked a joke, nodding when he said something to the crowd. But my chest felt tight, like I couldn't get a full breath.

Logan caught my eye at one point, his grin fading as his gaze sharpened. He knew me too well. He could tell something had shifted.

"You okay?" he asked, his voice soft but concerned, leaning in so I could hear him over the noise.

I forced a smile, hoping it was convincing enough. "Yeah, I'm fine. Just . . . tired."

His eyes stayed on me for a beat too long, and I knew he wasn't buying it. But he didn't push. Instead, he just nodded, but there was something behind it, something quiet but steady. "You know," he said, his tone almost casual, but not quite, "someday I'm gonna earn your trust enough to know your secrets."

The words hit harder than I wanted them to. I bit the inside of my cheek, forcing myself to look away, pretending to be caught up in the crowd again. But I couldn't shake what he said.

He'd already earned my trust, more than anyone else ever had. But there were things—things too deep, too painful—that I didn't know how to share. Things that I wasn't ready to let go of. Not yet.

Because they would ruin everything.

CHAPTER 32

SLOANE

The ceiling above me was a familiar sight. I stared at it, my eyes tracing the same cracks in the plaster I'd memorized over countless sleepless nights before I'd met him. It was always the same. Hours would pass, and I'd lie there, my body restless, my mind refusing to quiet. I hadn't had a decent night's sleep in years—not until Logan.

I'd tried to come back to my place alone last night, but he'd insisted on coming with me, sensing something was wrong. I was acting crazy, but I couldn't help it.

I tried turning on my side, then back again, bunching the pillow under my head, hoping the change would help. But nothing worked. What was Everett thinking? Why had he been there?

I should go talk to him. Cut the cord. I knew that.

Why was it so scary?

Logan was promising this wasn't just a short-term fling . . . but a part of me thought—what if he decided he was done?

How could I go back to my old life?

After what felt like hours of staring into the void, I gave up. I slipped out from under the covers, a pang of longing hitting my insides when Logan rolled over and reached out his arm, like he was searching for me. I swung my legs over the side of the bed, my feet hitting the cold floor. The chill sent a jolt through me, but it wasn't enough to shake off the weight pressing down on my chest.

I padded across the room, my bare feet making soft sounds against the floorboards, and made my way down the hall to the room where my art supplies were set up. The smell of paint and turpentine greeted me as I stepped inside. Canvases were scattered everywhere, leaning against walls, piled in corners, each one of them a glimpse of my tortured psyche.

I stood there for a moment, taking it all in. Half-finished paintings, smeared palettes, and brushes that hadn't been cleaned properly. It was a mess, unlike the rest of the condo. But in this mess, I found a strange kind of peace. Here, I didn't have to pretend. I didn't have to play a role or wear a mask.

I picked up a brush, my fingers closing around the familiar handle, and pulled a fresh canvas onto the easel. The brush moved almost on its own, instinct taking over as I dipped it into the paint, the strokes flowing in a way that felt both effortless and necessary. Each swipe of the brush felt like an exhale, a release of everything I couldn't say out loud.

The room was quiet, save for the soft sound of the bristles against the canvas. I tried not to think about Logan or our ending. I tried not to think about anything but the colors—the way they blended together, the way they formed something that wasn't quite whole but was still *something*.

I painted until my hands ached, until the colors blurred and the shapes bled into one another. But even then, the weight didn't lift. It never did.

I glanced around at the paintings littering the room, each one a piece of me that I kept hidden, locked away. They were the only things that made sense when everything else was falling apart. But no one would ever see them. They were mine. My private rebellion against the world that owned me.

With a sigh, I set the brush down, stepping back from the canvas. It was unfinished and dark. A reflection of me. Unfinished. Fractured. I stared at it for a long time, wondering if I'd ever feel complete. Or if I'd be stuck like this forever—just pretending, just surviving.

I didn't have an answer.

I slipped back into the bed where Logan was still peacefully sleeping, and finally fell into troubled and restless dreams, telling myself no matter what happened, I would still be me.

Even if I didn't know who that was anymore.

Logan

I didn't know what had woken me up. Sloane was curled up on her side, her body finally still after hours of restless tossing. Last night was the first time she'd done that. The way she'd slept—like she was constantly bracing herself for something—I didn't like it. I watched her for a minute, the rise and fall of her breathing, trying to reconcile the fragile way she slept with the way she carried herself during the day.

I tried to go back to sleep, but it wasn't happening. Finally, I slipped out of bed, careful not to wake her, and moved quietly through the condo, aimlessly wandering.

There was a door slightly ajar down the hall. She probably wouldn't like me exploring her place without her, but it felt like there were layers of her I hadn't even begun to see yet. I wanted to know all of her. Pushing open the door a bit more, I stepped inside.

The first thing that hit me was the smell of paint—rich and sharp, mixed with the subtle scent of something else, like turpentine. It was a studio, or at least it looked like one. Canvases were stacked haphazardly against the walls, brushes scattered on the floor, on tables. And in the middle of it all, a half-finished painting sat on an easel, of a sailboat tossing on a stormy sea. I walked over to it and realized the paint was still wet.

She'd done this at some point during the night.

I was frozen for a second, taking it all in. I'd known there was more to her than she let on, but this—this was something else. Each painting was a different piece of her, raw and visceral, like she'd poured every emotion she couldn't express into the canvas. The colors were dark, layered, the strokes aggressive but deliberate. There was a sadness to every picture, a sense of devastation she was trying to express that I could actually feel as I studied them.

I pulled out my phone, snapping a few pictures before I could stop myself. This wasn't the kind of manufactured art you saw on postcards. It was real, and it hit me right in the chest. I couldn't stop myself from capturing it, like I needed proof that this part of her existed.

I moved to the next canvas, one leaning against the wall. It was half-hidden, but when I tilted it up, I felt my breath catch. The image was haunting—a silhouette of a woman standing alone, her arms wrapped around herself as if she were trying to hold herself together. Her face wasn't visible, just shadowed, but the sadness in the image was palpable. It was like she was crumbling from the inside out, but still standing. Barely.

I took another picture, then another, my fingers moving faster as I tried to capture the details. I'd never seen anything like this. It was like she'd taken every part of herself she tried to hide and poured it into these paintings. It was mesmerizing, and I couldn't stop.

And then I heard it—the soft creak of the floorboard behind me.

I turned, my phone still in hand, and there she was, standing in the doorway, her eyes wide with shock.

"What are you doing?" Her voice was sharp, filled with something I couldn't quite place—fear, anger, betrayal . . . maybe all of it.

I froze, and for a second, I felt like an idiot. "I was just . . ." I started, but I didn't know how to finish. What was I doing digging through her private world without asking, like I had any right to be here?

She stepped into the room, her expression hardening. "You were just what? Going through my stuff?"

There was a tremble in her voice, something she tried to hide, but it was there. I could see it—the crack in her armor.

"Sloane, I wasn't—" I said, stepping toward her. "It's just . . . these paintings. They're incredible. I've never seen anything like them."

"Incredible?" she repeated, her voice thick with disbelief. "You think this is incredible?"

I nodded, taking a step closer, trying to bridge the distance between us. "Have you tried to sell these? You could—"

"Sell them?" Her reaction was immediate, visceral. She stormed past me, grabbing one of the canvases and turning it to face the wall, like she couldn't stand to look at it. "Sell them?" she repeated, her voice rising. "You don't get it, do you?"

I blinked, completely thrown by her reaction. "What do you mean? Sloane, these are—"

"I'm not an artist," she snapped, cutting me off. "I'm not someone who gets to sell things."

I stared at her, completely confused. "Why not? You're obviously talented. You could—"

"I'm a *whore*, Logan," she spat, the word slamming into me like a freight train. "Whores don't sell anything but themselves."

The room went silent, her words hanging in the air like a cloud of smoke, choking the life out of everything. I stood there, frozen, the weight of what she said sinking in.

"Sloane," I said softly, stepping closer, my heart aching. "What can I say to—"

"Don't." Her voice was trembling now, filled with a pain that I couldn't begin to understand. "You don't get to stand there and act like this is something beautiful. It's not. *I'm* not."

I didn't understand where this was coming from. I'd thought we were fine until something had happened at the end of the parade, and then she'd been completely different. The last few days I could feel her withdrawing, until last night she'd finally asked to sleep back at her place.

Her shoulders shook, and I saw the tears start to well up in her eyes. She tried to blink them away, trying to hold on to the anger, but it was slipping through her fingers. "This—this isn't who I am," she said, her voice break-ing. "I don't get to have this. I don't get to be anything but what I am."

Fuck. I felt sick. She wasn't just upset—she was broken. The way she looked at herself, the way she couldn't see what I saw, it tore me apart.

I stepped closer, reaching out to touch her arm, to ground her, but she flinched, pulling away. "I'll tell you until you believe it," I said, my voice low, steady. "You're not what you think you are."

She shook her head, her tears falling freely now. "You don't know what I've done," she whispered, her voice thick with emotion. "You don't know what I am."

"I don't care," I said, stepping closer, refusing to let her push me away. "I don't care what you think you are. I know you, Sloane. I know the real you. And this—" I gestured to the room, to the paintings surrounding us. "This is you. Not what anyone else has to say. Not what the voice inside your head is telling you. Not what you've been forced to believe."

Her knees buckled, and she collapsed against me, her sobs racking her body as she buried her face in my chest.

"But that's just it . . . I haven't been forced into anything," she mumbled against my chest.

I froze. "What?"

She lifted her face and stared at me blankly, her walls fully up again.

"I *chose* this life. When I was eighteen, I was scared of having to leave my uncle's house. He offered me an opportunity to give up my virginity in exchange for money and stability . . . and I took it. I sold myself for designer clothes, a penthouse condo, and vacations to Malta. I chose that."

She sounded so certain of her culpability, but anyone could have listened to her and seen the holes in her story. She honestly thought that a decision at eighteen meant she was ruined forever? And that it was her fault?

"So that's it?" I asked, keeping my tone calm. "You woke up one day, decided you needed designer heels and thought, 'Hey, why not sell my virginity?'"

Her shoulders flinched, just barely. "It wasn't like that," she snapped, her nails digging into her arms. "I was scared . . . of going back to how I'd grown up. I was poor, Logan. Poor as in no food and living in shelters sometimes. There were so many times I wore the same outfit to school all week because I didn't have anything else." She lifted her chin, daring me to argue with her. "I saw a way out, and I took it."

I let the silence hang for a second, watching the tension in her shoulders tighten, before a dark realization hit me. "Wait, did you say your *uncle* gave you the opportunity?"

She nodded like it was nothing. "Everett made sure I didn't have to go back to that life. He organized an auction—he said I could finally take control of my life. He told me I was 'mastering my destiny.'"

The words hit me like a punch to the gut. Her uncle was her . . . pimp? He'd groomed her—there was no other way to see it. She flinched, and I realized I was holding her too tight. I released her, my head feeling like it was spinning. "Do you really believe that? That you had control?"

She whipped around to face me, her eyes flashing. "Yes," she snapped, but her voice cracked. "It was my choice."

"Was it?" I asked, my voice sharper now, cutting through her defenses. "Because the way you talk about him—it doesn't sound like you had much of a choice at all. Sounds to me like he groomed you for it."

Her jaw clenched and she looked away, her breath coming faster. "You don't know anything about it."

"Don't I?" I took a step closer, trying to keep my voice steady, calm, even though my anger was clawing at me. Not at her—at him. "Think about it, Sloane. Eighteen isn't exactly the age of sound decision-making. And you had someone whispering in your ear, dangling luxury and comfort in front of you like a carrot. Scaring you about what would happen if you didn't go along with what he was offering you. He made you think it was your idea, didn't he?"

She stared at the floor, and I could see her hands trembling. "You don't understand," she murmured. "It's too late, Logan. I've been this person for too long. It's who I am."

"No." I stepped closer, making sure she couldn't look away. "It's who you were made to *think* you are. That's not the same thing."

She shook her head, her voice shaky. "I can never be anything else."

"You're wrong," I said, my voice firm. She finally looked up at me, and the rawness in her eyes nearly broke me. "What would you tell another girl, Sloane? Someone you met randomly who was eighteen, and she was telling you she sold herself at an auction . . . because her guardian encouraged her. Would you tell her she was horrible? Would you tell her she was a whore, that she deserved everything she had coming to her?"

She blinked, her breath hitching, and I could see the cracks forming in the walls she'd built around herself. She shook her head. "What? I—no! Of course, not."

"Well, then why would you say that to yourself?" I said, stepping even closer. "Why are you different?"

Her lips parted like she wanted to argue, but no words came out. For the first time, she looked unsure. And that, to me, was a win. Small, but a win.

CHAPTER 33

LOGAN

Sloane had continued to pull away from me ever since our conversation about how she'd become an escort. I'd been doing everything I could to hold her close. But lately, it felt like I was clinging to sand—no matter how tightly I tried to grasp her, she was slipping right through my fingers.

She'd made me stay at her condo every night this week. I wouldn't have minded, not before that talk, but now her place carried the lingering feeling of him—her uncle. It was like his presence was burned into the walls, and every time I stayed there, it felt like I was stepping into the devil's lair.

More often than not, I'd wake up alone in her bed, the sheets cold and rumpled on her side. I'd find her in the studio down the hall, hunched over a canvas, dark circles carved under her eyes. She'd look at me like she hadn't slept in years, but when I'd try to convince her to come back to bed, she'd just shake her head and keep painting.

"It helps," she'd say, even though I could see the toll it was taking on her.

It was killing me to see her like this.

So, I decided it was time for us to move in together.

Even if she wasn't ready to have that conversation yet.

It was clear this place was haunting her. And since money was still being taken out of my account on a weekly basis, her uncle was still haunting her too.

What she really needed was to leave this place behind. And if she wasn't going to make that decision on her own, I'd just have to give her a little *push*.

I probably needed some help, though, I thought as I stared at her pretending to read on the couch next to me. Grabbing my phone, I sent the guys a text.

Me: Remember how vague Hero was about the dogs? How do we feel about rats?

Camden: What was vague? They were literally just dogs.

Ari: Were they, though? Because I remember a lot more happening that night. Like the loss of my big toe.

Lincoln: You didn't literally lose your big toe.

Ari: How do you know?

Lincoln: . . .

Lincoln: Because you're sitting in my living room right now with flip-flops on. Definitely seeing two big toes.

Ari: Knew you had a foot fetish, Golden Boy.

Lincoln: . . .

Me: Can we focus? We can talk about Lincoln's foot fetish at a later date. This is an emergency.

Walker: An emergency involving . . . rats?

Me: Well, yes.

Camden: Will it involve meat?

Me: What? Why would it involve meat? Are rats carnivores?

Ari: Hmm. Not sure about that, actually.

Walker: I'll look it up.

Ari: Of course you will.

Walker: I'm trying to be helpful!

Camden: Google says they eat both plants and meat. Not sure that helps.

Walker: Simp.

Ari: Flag on the play.

Lincoln: Why are we referencing football penalties now . . .

Ari: Parker influenced me.

Walker: What does my brother have to do with anything?

I huffed and Sloane side-eyed me. When I didn't say anything, she went back to her book.

Me: CAN WE FOCUS.

Ari: He's using shouty caps. I think he wants our attention.

Me: . . .

Me: Now that I have your attention.

Ari: It's a fleeting moment so take advantage of it.

Me: I'm going to use rats to get Sloane to move in with me.

> Ari: . . .

> Lincoln: . . .

> Camden: . . .

> Walker: . . .

> Walker: Not to be judgy—because really, to each their own. But why does Sloane have a thing for rats?

I stared at the phone incredulously, rereading because somehow I'd gotten offtrack in my messaging.

> Me: What? She doesn't have a thing for rats.

> Ari: I mean if you're into tail play, I don't think rat tails are usually what people go to, but again . . . good on you.

> Me: I'm not into rats! She's not into rats either. That's the whole point!

> Camden: I'm very confused right now. I think meat is involved.

> Me: I'M GOING TO USE RATS TO SCARE HER OUT OF HER APARTMENT SO SHE WILL MOVE IN WITH ME.

There was a beat of silence as I stared at the phone, waiting for them to answer.

> Lincoln: Well, why didn't you say that in the first place?

> Ari: Yeah, I mean your communication skills need major improvement. Who starts a text out asking how we feel about rats?

Camden: I know they were trying to be supportive, but no one likes rats.

Me: . . .

That was obviously exactly *why* my plan involved rats. Everyone was scared of them.

Walker: It's true.

Ari: Someone get Disney a muzzle. It's too much for me today.

Walker: I would say my feelings are hurt, but I'm still in possession of my two big toes and I have the cutest daughter in the world, so life feels pretty good.

Ari: . . .

Ari: Touché.

Me: Also, I need to borrow a Stanley Cupcake for this plan to distract Sloane.

Lincoln: I still can't believe that's the name we stuck with.

Ari: Walker's preening right now.

Walker: Ooh, Olivia can help! I mean I don't think we should mention the rats . . . or any other part of the plan. But she really wants to hang out with Sloane.

Ari: Hey, Blake wants to hang out with her too.

> Lincoln: Monroe wants to as well.

> Camden: Hey, I'm not as fast of a typer, but Anastasia loves Sloane and would definitely want to hang.

A warm feeling hit me hard. Fuck my dad. Fuck my mom for leaving me. But who gave a shit . . . look at the family I'd found.

Rubbing my chest at the sudden emotion, I finally typed out a reply.

> Me: Sorry, Grampalicious, type faster next time. Olivia's been chosen.

> Ari: Starting a group FaceTime to discuss this properly. If I can figure it out.

I got up from the couch and walked into the other room so Sloane wouldn't hear our discussion.

> Lincoln: Someone else do the call. He's never going to figure it out.

> Ari: I resent that, Golden Boy.

A second later Camden was starting the group call. The first thing Camden said . . .

"How's that for a Grampalicious?"

I stood in the lobby of Sloane's building, hands shoved into my hoodie pocket as Ari and Camden both lugged blanket-covered cages filled with rats through the side entrance. I didn't know how, but Lincoln had somehow procured hundreds of them, and I shivered listening to their tiny claws skitter across the plastic. Ari was muttering to himself, his shoulders hunched like he was bracing for battle.

"You know what? I prefer Fifi," Ari hissed. "At least she isn't a rodent. Did you know these things spread the Black Plague? We could be doing that right now!" His voice was a panicked whisper. He peered around the blanket as if a rat was going to jump out and get him right then and there.

Camden smirked. "You mean Fluffy, and *Fluffy* was a *he*. Lancaster, it's not hard to figure out what happened that night. You obviously offended the poor guy. Your big toe was his only option." He sighed as we stepped into the elevator, and I punched in Sloane's code. "But I agree, 'dogs' are definitely better than rats."

"You said 'dogs' weird again," Ari muttered as he stared at the cage he was holding. "These things are practically cats with tails. I saw them looking at me in the car. They've got murder in their eyes."

"Rats don't commit murder," I said, sighing exasperatedly. "They're more of a 'scurry and scatter' kind of creature. But also, quit talking about that night with Geraldine's dogs, it triggers my PTSD."

Camden smirked at me. "I don't know, Rookie, seems like a good time if it was immortalized in stone."

Ari growled at him and then shot us both glares. "Can we please not talk about Geraldine right now? We're on a break until she starts appreciating me." He winced as he adjusted his grip on his cage. "Also, you owe me for this. I'll accept steak-and-tacos dinners for a year."

"The only thing you want is steak and tacos?" Camden asked incredulously.

"Deal," I muttered, glancing at my phone and checking the camera in Sloane's necklace to make sure she was still out shopping with Olivia.

I grinned when the camera showed a rack of lingerie. Now, *that* was my kind of shopping.

"I want steak and tacos too," Camden said, and my smirk faded.

"Remember that whole thing about you owing me for the rest of my life after helping you get Anastasia?" I asked, raising an eyebrow as I tried not to think about . . . that night.

"Worth a try." Camden shrugged.

We slipped into the condo, Ari trailing behind us, struggling with the cage he was holding, looking like he was ready to bolt at the first sign of trouble.

The place was immaculate, as always. Light filtered through the tall windows, bouncing off the sleek furniture and polished floors. My gaze instinctively flicked toward her paint studio, the one part of the condo that truly felt like her. I'd promised myself I wouldn't let anything happen to it, and I intended to keep that promise. I strode down the hallway and closed the studio door.

Ari looked at the cage like it contained a ticking bomb. "How exactly are we releasing these things? Because I am not sticking my hand in there."

"You just open the door and let them do their thing," Camden said, lifting the blanket to reveal a cage full of beady-eyed creatures pressing against the bars. "They're just . . . rats."

"Says the guy who wasn't locked in a shed with one as a kid," Ari shot back, shivering. "You think they're just rats . . . until they turn on you."

"Why is that story just now coming out?" Camden asked. "It almost seems like you made it up, Lancaster."

Ari huffed. "I prefer not to talk about my trauma, Hero," he said primly. "Rookie, these are your rats and your plan. You come open this cage."

I snorted as I walked over.

Camden rolled his eyes and flipped the latch, tipping the cage on its side. "They're not going to bite you. Probably." The rats hesitated for a moment before scurrying out, their tiny claws clicking against the hardwood floors. Ari jumped back with a strangled noise, nearly tripping over the ottoman.

"Sweet mother of—get them away from me!"

Camden doubled over laughing, clutching his stomach until a rat ran over his shoe. "Ahh!" he screeched, jumping onto a barstool.

"You're not laughing now. Are you, Hero?" Ari snapped, darting to the other side of the room.

"Did you see the size of that thing?" Camden yelped, pointing toward the couch where the rat had disappeared. "It's a monster."

I shook my head, trying to ignore my queasiness as I opened the other cage, and the rats scurried out. They were already exploring, darting under the couch and disappearing behind the TV stand. One particularly bold rodent climbed onto the coffee table, sniffing the air.

"Where did Lincoln even get all these rats?" I asked as I backed toward the elevator. "There's like a hundred of them."

Ari and Camden carefully climbed off the furniture they'd mounted and were also backing their way toward the exit.

"A lot of things about Golden Boy are on a *need to know basis*," Ari muttered. "I don't think he's going to consider this a *need to know*."

Ari screamed as a rat darted past him, and he dove toward the elevator, crawling into it like a man escaping a burning building. "Close it! Close it! Close iiit! They're after me!"

The elevator doors slid shut as Camden and I both stared wide-eyed at Ari on the floor.

Camden took out his phone and took a picture.

"I'm showing Geraldine," he said. I snorted as Ari flipped him off and struggled to get up.

"What's wrong with you? Why are you acting like your legs don't work anymore?" I asked as I checked my phone. Sloane had just sent me a text saying they were wrapping up. Perfect timing.

Ari was muttering something about rats and tacos as the elevator doors opened into the lobby.

"Good idea, Lancaster. Let's get tacos," I told him, supremely happy with how things were working out. "But we need to make this quick. I'm sure Sloane will be calling me soon."

———————

When the call finally came, I answered on the second ring, putting on my most innocent voice. "Hey, baby. How was shopping?"

"Logan, there are rats everywhere!" she cried, her voice shaky.

"What?" I asked, trying to keep the amusement out of my tone.

"There are rats. In my condo. *Everywhere!*"

"Are you serious? How the hell did that happen?"

"I don't know!" she wailed. "But I can't stay in my place. I'm in the lobby . . . I need to get out of here."

"Okay, okay. Breathe, Sloane. I'll be right there. We'll get what stuff we can, and you can stay with me."

There was a pause, and I could almost hear the wheels turning in her head. Finally, she exhaled shakily. "Okay," she whispered, sounding unsure.

I bit back a triumphant grin. "I'll stay on the phone with you the whole time I'm driving."

"Thank you," she said softly, and I did a fist pump in the air as I started the truck.

I didn't feel an ounce of guilt on the drive over.

CHAPTER 34

LOGAN

The sun was relentless, glaring down on us as we walked onto the field, the announcer hyping up the fact that we were there to throw out the first pitch to celebrate winning the Stanley Cup before the Dallas Raptors MLB game.

It still felt surreal, hearing that. *Stanley Cup champions.*

The air smelled like sunscreen, overpriced hot dogs, and freshly cut grass—a weird combination that somehow worked.

We stopped just outside the pitcher's mound, decked out in freshly pressed baseball jerseys, customized with *Knights* stitched across the back in block letters. Lincoln, of course, had the honor of throwing the first pitch. Naturally. He was the captain. Our leader. The all-around Golden Boy.

"You nervous, Linc?" Camden teased, tossing the baseball between his hands like he was warming up. "Wouldn't want to ruin your image in front of all these fans."

Lincoln shot him a look, his mouth curving into a slow smirk. "You'd know all about that, wouldn't you, Hero? Didn't you get cut from JV baseball in high school?"

Camden feigned offense, clutching his chest. "I wasn't cut. I *quit* to concentrate on hockey."

Ari leaned in, grinning. "Translation: he couldn't hit the broad side of a barn."

I snorted, adjusting my cap as I scanned the field. It was surreal being out here. The stands were packed, fans decked out in jerseys and hats, waving their foam fingers and beers like maniacs.

"I can step in if you're nervous." Colt grinned.

Lincoln ignored him, rolling the baseball in his palm like he did this every day. He stepped toward the mound with the kind of confidence that only someone who wins at life as often as Lincoln does could muster. The rest of the team fanned out behind him, forming a loose line. Camden and Ari stood next to me, while Walker hung back, probably mentally calculating how much sunscreen he'd need to avoid burning.

"Hundred bucks says it hits the ground before home plate," Asher drawled, loud enough for Lincoln to hear as he came up beside me. His team happened to be the visiting team for the matchup, which was a win-win for me.

Lincoln threw a subtle middle finger over his shoulder without breaking his stride. He set, wound up, and let it rip.

The ball sailed through the air, a clean arc that ended with a satisfying *smack* into the catcher's mitt. The crowd erupted in applause.

"He's good at everything," Ari muttered.

"It's disgusting," Camden agreed.

Walker just whooped and clapped loudly.

The simp.

Lincoln turned back to us, smirking like he knew exactly what we were thinking. "You're welcome, boys."

"You're insufferable," Camden said, shaking his head. "We're leaving you here."

Lincoln turned to Asher, who was still standing out there with his hands on his hips, watching us with an amused smile. "What's the matter, Matthews? Jealous we're getting all the attention today?"

Asher raised his glove, shaking his head as he called back, "Keep talking, Daniels. You still couldn't hit a curveball if your life depended on it."

"Guess we'll never know," Lincoln shot back with a smirk. "I stick to sports where we *win* championships."

Asher scoffed and flipped him off, grinning as the announcer's voice boomed over the speakers, thanking the Knights for their appearance. We waved awkwardly as we made our way off the field and into the air-conditioned luxury of the box seats behind home plate.

———

"Asher's fucking good," Lincoln said as he watched Asher lay out for a ball and then somehow toss it to second base for the out.

"Really good," Sloane murmured.

I glanced down at her. "Hey, none of that," I growled, wrapping an arm around her waist and pulling her in for a kiss. I was going to have red lipstick all over my face, but it was worth it.

"What?" she asked, wrinkling her nose adorably.

"No complimenting other men."

Lincoln smirked, pulling Monroe closer to him like just the mention of "other men" made him nervous.

"You're ridiculous," Sloane murmured, and I grinned as Blake leaned over and whispered something in her ear. They both rolled their eyes and laughed, clearly making fun of me, and my grin widened.

She fit in so perfectly.

A ripple of noise in the crowd had me glancing back at the field. I turned just in time to see a woman, butt naked, bolting from the stands, sprinting across the field, her boobs flapping around as she ran. The entire stadium erupted into laughter and cheers as security rushed after her.

"Holy—" Ari started, leaning forward as he watched the chaos unfold. "Is she—"

"I think she's going for Asher!" Walker said, standing up from his seat.

And she was. The streaker was making a beeline straight for him, arms outstretched like she was going to tackle him to the dirt. The crowd was going wild—whistles, cheers, people on their feet, phones out.

"What the fuck are you doing? Run!" I laughed, slamming my hands against the suite glass.

Asher was completely frozen, a look of horror on his face as he watched her, and it was too late when he finally got his legs to move. His eyes went wide, and he took off, only making it a few steps before she dove and tackled him right at second base, sending them both crashing into the dirt.

The crowd lost it.

"Oh my gosh!" Sloane gasped, her hand flying to her mouth, her eyes wide in disbelief.

Lincoln was doubled over, laughing so hard he could barely breathe.

Security got there, but it took them a minute to drag her off him. The streaker was crying and screaming something at Asher as they took her away.

Asher . . . just lay there, staring up at the sky like he couldn't believe what had happened.

"And to think I almost didn't come today," Ari mused, wiping his eyes from how hard he'd been laughing. "Bring up any fond memories, Linc?"

Lincoln growled, and I smirked, remembering watching him on TV in a similar situation when I was in college.

Asher slowly got to his feet, brushing dirt off his uniform, his face redder than I'd ever seen it. He glanced toward our box, and even from down on the field, I could see the sheer humiliation in his eyes.

I waved at him, and he rolled his eyes dramatically before glaring at me.

The entire stadium was still buzzing, the replay of what had just happened flashing on the jumbotron for everyone to see—with her important parts blurred out, of course.

"I'm never going to let him live this down," I said dreamily.

"Unless he finds out about your . . . *sculpture*," Sloane pointed out. "I'm sure he'd have something to say about that."

"Let me have my moment, Red," I sputtered.

She grinned and nodded. "Fine. But only because I love you, and it will be fun to make fun of him for this."

My heart did that weird beating thing at the casual way she'd just told me she loved me.

Best day ever.

After the game I texted Asher.

Me: . . .

Asher: Don't you dare.

Me: I'm not doing anything.

Asher: You want to do something, though.

Me: I know someone that wants to do something . . .

Asher: That was terrible. Even for you. No wonder they're not letting you in the rhombus of despair.

Me: What?

Asher: You know, that thing you're so proud of. Triangle of trouble.

Me: No. Just no.

Asher: Oval of awesomeness.

Me: Circle of Trust! It's Circle of Trust. And by the way, I am on it.

Asher: On it or in it?

Me: Nope. This isn't happening.

Asher: What isn't happening?

Me: I texted you to make fun of the fact that you were tackled by a rabid streaker on national television.

Asher: . . .

Me: Excellent use of that by the way.

Asher: Thanks, Socks.

Me: But I still win this conversation.

CHAPTER 35

SLOANE

The knock on the door startled me. I wasn't expecting anyone. Logan was lifting weights with the guys, and I was anticipating a quiet evening until he got home. I had settled in on the couch, a blanket thrown over my lap, trying to relax.

Another knock.

I hesitated, still not used to the fact that this was kind of my place now too—at least until they decontaminated my condo. Something that seemed to be encountering delay after delay. At this point I wasn't sure when I'd be back there.

Or if I actually wanted to.

Everett had still been silent . . . something that didn't make me feel any better.

And then there was the fact that Logan was still paying him for my time . . .

Fuck. My life was a mess.

I got up and walked toward the door, the sound of my footsteps muffled by the big rug Logan and I had picked out the other day for the foyer.

Cracking the door open, I peeked through, only to find Blake, Monroe, Olivia, and Anastasia standing on the other side. Blake and Monroe held up bottles. "I've got wine." Blake grinned.

"And I've got the nonalcoholic stuff if you don't drink," said Monroe.

I stared at them, blinking, unsure of what to do.

"Are you going to let us in?" Olivia laughed, grinning from ear to ear. "The boys are all busy, so we figured it's the perfect time for a girls' night!"

My brain short-circuited. "A . . . girls' night?"

Before I could process it, Olivia pushed the door open wider and slipped past me. "Yep. It's time."

Anastasia followed, tossing her bag onto the couch. She flashed me a quick smile. "I brought cheese."

Monroe snorted. "She means she brought charcuterie. So lots of things."

"But cheese is the important part," Anastasia commented as she unwrapped the baking sheet she'd brought with her and unveiled a delicious charcuterie arrangement—with definitely more than just cheese.

"Ooh, give me that dark chocolate almond," Blake said, grabbing a few off the tray.

Anastasia smacked her hand, and Blake made a pouty face at her. "Sloane has to go first because we took over her place." She turned and held the tray out for me.

I stood there, rooted to the spot, staring at them and trying to resist the urge to cry. I'd once been fooled into thinking that I wanted to be like the women Everett had working for him, that they were who I should aspire to be in life.

But *these* women were who I wanted to be like. All of them funny, kind, beautiful, and already the sort of friends I only could have dreamed of.

"I . . ." I trailed off, searching for words, but nothing came.

"Come on, don't just stand there!" Blake grabbed my arm, dragging me toward the couch. "We've got snacks, we've got drinks, and we've got stories to share."

I didn't resist, letting her lead me to the couch. I'd hung out with them several times, I really should be less awkward at this point.

"Wine or apple cider?" Monroe asked as she dug around in the cabinets for drink glasses.

"Apple cider," I said softly, and she smiled at me sweetly before pouring me a glass.

The rest of the girls got drinks and began to settle in around me.

"Relax, Sloane. We don't bite," said Olivia, patting my knee.

I forced a smile, gripping the glass like a lifeline. "Right."

Blake plopped down next to me, so close I could feel the warmth radiating off her.

"To friends," Olivia sang as she held up her glass.

"To friends," the rest of us said.

And I'd never meant those words more.

The hum of laughter and clinking glasses filled the room. We were sprawled out across the oversized sectional now, wineglasses in hand, the coffee table littered with takeout containers and half-eaten charcuterie.

"We should make this a weekly thing," Blake said, leaning back against a plush cushion and sipping her drink.

"Sounds good to me," Monroe said with a lazy yawn. "If the guys can handle being away from us for that long."

Olivia snorted. "I could see them all waiting outside the door right now, waiting for the second we're done."

I giggled, and she raised an eyebrow. "You think I'm kidding. But I bet one of them is watching us right now."

"What?" I giggled. "What are you talking about?"

The girls exchanged smirks.

"Lincoln's got cameras all over our house . . . and they're not for security," Monroe said, rolling her eyes. "I'll tell him something happened, and he'll respond 'I know,' like a total creeper."

My mouth dropped open in shock, but her voice was dreamy-like . . . like she thought it was cute.

Blake nodded. "I'm pretty sure that Ari's always got his phone on, watching me either through my phone or with cameras. I'm not exactly sure," Blake muttered, tapping her chin as she thought about it.

"And you guys are okay with that?" I gasped.

Anastasia leaned forward. "She thinks we're crazy," she groaned. "She's never going to hang out with us again."

I shook my head. "I—I don't think you're crazy. It just sounds so—"

"Obsessive? Insane? Wonderful?" Olivia offered with a gleam in her eye.

I opened my mouth to respond and then closed it. Because honestly . . . it didn't sound that bad.

"All of us come from pretty fucked-up backgrounds. We've mentioned pieces of it to you, but . . . I think . . . I *know* it's what we needed. This all-consuming devotion. To know that we matter to someone more than anyone else." Blake shook her head. "Trust me . . . I never imagined I would be okay with what Ari did to my ex—which is a story for another day so you don't run away screaming," she said, winking at me.

"But it works for us," Olivia said softly, a faraway look in her eye like she was somewhere else. "I don't know that anything else *could* work for us."

I studied the ceiling as I thought about what she'd said. Logan was paying an obscene amount of money just so I couldn't work with anyone else. That was pretty crazy . . . right?

And I wasn't exactly screaming about the fact that he'd done that after I rejected him asking me out.

"So tell us, Sloane, how many times have you watched Logan's burger commercial?" Monroe asked in a lighter tone, wagging her eyebrows up and down.

I choked on my drink. "A few times," I said in a high-pitched voice.

Monroe snorted. "Well, it's been banned in my household. Lincoln said it was basically porn, and if I wanted that, he would film himself."

I shook my head, unable to hide my grin. "I think he secretly enjoyed it."

"Oh, for sure," Blake said, laughing. "It's also banned in my house, but Ari watches it every time he needs a pick-me-up."

"Camden swears it's Logan's best work," Anastasia added. "He calls it 'performance art.' But I'm also not allowed to watch it."

More laughter erupted, and another burst of warmth spread through me. I was pretty sure these women were my people.

"Alright, confession time," Blake said, sitting up straighter. "What's the most ridiculous thing Logan has done for you? Like, top-tier crazy."

I bit down on my lip, swirling the cider in my glass as a million memories flashed through my mind. How he'd hired me. The way he'd casually thrown himself into the deep end of my messy life without flinching.

"Well, he hired me after I said no to going out with him. Does that count?" I asked sheepishly.

There was a beat of silence. Then Monroe snorted, Blake spit out her drink, and Anastasia nearly fell off the couch laughing. Olivia already knew the story, but she was still grinning about it too.

"That's so sweet," Monroe said.

"Unhinged, but sweet," Blake laughed, before holding up her glass.

"And yet, somehow, it's still romantic," Anastasia said, shaking her head in disbelief.

"If you're watching this, I hope you're enjoying yourself," Blake suddenly yelled to the room.

I blinked at her and then glanced around, searching for cameras I would never have guessed were even a possibility.

Logan

Weights clanged around the gym, but I wasn't paying attention to any of it. My phone was propped up on the bench next to me, the screen showing Sloane's face as she laughed at something Blake said. Her smile was brighter than the overhead lights, and I couldn't look away.

"York." Lincoln's voice cut through my focus. "What are you doing?"

I didn't bother looking up, just flicked my fingers at the screen. "Watching some high-quality entertainment."

Lincoln snorted and held up his own phone. "They're funny, right?" He grinned as he turned his phone around and showed the video feed he was watching of Monroe.

Ari paused mid-rep, lowering the barbell onto the rack with a loud *clang*. He turned to face us, sweat dripping down his forehead. "Am I the only one actually working out here?"

"Says the guy wearing headphones so he can listen to everything Blake is saying," Camden muttered, setting his weights down and walking over. "Who knew a girls' night could be so educational?"

A minute later we all had our phones propped up in front of us, each showing a different live stream angle of girls' night, courtesy of the apps we all had installed on their . . . phones.

"This is better than Netflix," Walker admitted, his eyes glued to the screen.

"Does this make us creeps?" I asked.

"Is that a real question, Rookie?" asked Ari, his lips curled up in disgust.

"Of course it doesn't make us creeps," Camden said indignantly.

"Yeah, it makes us *devoted*," Walker mused.

"Devoted. I like that," I muttered.

The gym door opened, and a trainer walked in, pausing when he saw all of us clustered around the phones. "Uh, everything okay in here?"

"Fine," Ari said quickly, grabbing a random dumbbell and pretending to curl it. "Just taking a breather."

The trainer gave us a skeptical look but moved on.

Ari dropped the dumbbell as soon as the door closed behind him.

On the screen, Blake looked directly into the phone, mouthing something that looked suspiciously like *I see you, Ari*.

"That's my girl," Ari said dreamily.

We listened as the women started to discuss some of the "devoted" things we'd done.

"At least they aren't talking about everything," Lincoln said.

Ari side-eyed him. "I will get it all out of you at some point, Golden Boy."

Lincoln flashed his teeth. "I have no idea what you're talking about."

The girls got up to leave, and Walker groaned, putting his phone down. "Well, there goes the entertainment."

"Guess it's back to lifting," Camden said dramatically, grabbing a nearby barbell and pretending to struggle under the weight.

"Speak for yourself," Ari muttered, already heading for the water cooler. "I'm done."

"You know she's totally going to ask you about cameras when you get home," Lincoln said to me as we both downed some water.

I grinned.

"I know."

"And what are you going to say?"

"That there are no cameras installed in the actual apartment," I said carefully.

Lincoln snorted. "Atta boy."

CHAPTER 36

SLOANE

We were sitting on the couch the next night, the TV playing in the background, but his attention was entirely on me. Like usual.

Logan's hand brushed against mine, his thumb tracing circles on my skin.

"Have you ever thought about having kids?" His voice was casual, like it didn't matter to him either way, but the question felt like a dagger to my heart.

I blinked, trying to find the right words for how I felt about this particular subject. This wasn't something I wanted to talk about. Ever.

"No," I said quickly, the words bursting out of me. I stared at the TV as if the rerun of *The Office* was the most enthralling thing I'd ever seen. But I could still feel his gaze burning against my skin.

"After what I experienced with my mother," I softly added, "I wouldn't even know where to start."

He didn't say anything right away, just let the words hang in the air between us.

"You've mentioned a few things about your mom . . . but can you tell me more?" he finally pressed, and I sighed as he scooped me into his lap.

I frowned at him, and he huffed and pressed a soft kiss on the tip of my nose that for some reason had me feeling a lot better than I had before. An image of my mom's face right before she died popped into my brain, though, skeletal and almost gray-looking—and the good feelings went away.

"She was addicted to prescription painkillers for most of my life," I began softly, a myriad of memories filling my head. "And then when she finally got sober, and was acting like a mom for the first time in my life, she got sick—and got addicted again." I bit down on my lip, wishing there was a way to reach into your brain and pull out all the memories you didn't want.

Of course with my life experience, there wouldn't be much of my brain left.

I laid my head on his shoulder, allowing myself to soak up the good feelings I only seemed to get around him and his friends. "What was your mom like?" I hesitantly asked. I usually had a *don't ask personal questions* rule, but evidently I was blowing that off today.

"She died too."

"Oh, I'm sorry," I said, feeling callous that I'd been over here sulking and feeling sorry for myself, and he'd had loss too. "I know it was you and your dad growing up . . . but I'd thought she'd left—not that it's any different!"

Logan was the one staring at the screen now, his fingers absent-mindedly stroking across my skin. "She was beautiful and sad. I think my dad first brought another woman home when I was like three?"

"He brought her to your house?" I asked, my mouth falling open in shock.

He laughed, the sound harsh and disgusted and . . . wrong.

"Grant York doesn't care about a thing like decency or having respect for the mother of his child. Why should he? He's a football star. Everyone loves him," he said mockingly.

He shook his head. "I don't know if she ever loved him . . . but she did love his money. So she stayed for a while. She stayed when he fucked her sister in the closet while she was taking a nap in the same room. She stayed when he brought one of his mistresses to a Super Bowl party she was also at. She stayed . . . until I was six, and I'd started all-day school. And I guess that was what finally drove her to leave—all that alone time."

"She left without you?" I asked carefully.

"Who knows if she did it willingly or if he paid her off? Either way, she left. She died a few years ago in a car accident. My dad didn't even tell me until after the funeral."

I bit down on my lip, my heart aching for him. I wasn't sure what to say. I'd never been good at this sort of thing—being real with someone.

"So, what makes you believe that just because your mom sucked, you would suck too?" he finally asked calmly.

My mouth opened and closed.

"You're not scared that maybe you would end up like your dad?" I asked hesitantly.

He huffed and raised an eyebrow. "First of all, I could be blacked out, and my dick would still know the only thing it wanted was you."

I snorted, a rush of warmth floating through me . . . because I kind of believed him.

"But also, having a father like that—it makes you want to be the exact opposite. It makes you want to be better." He shook his head. "I'm not worried in the least bit," he said confidently. "And you shouldn't be either . . ."

I bit down on my lip at that comment, wishing we could have just stopped there. The silence stretched on, though, and something inside me finally snapped.

"It doesn't matter either way," I murmured, swallowing hard, a familiar lump forming in my throat. "I can't have them."

Logan's hands slid soothingly up my sides, like the news wasn't shocking at all . . . like it didn't make a difference to him either way. "What do you mean?" he asked gently, his voice soft, careful.

I took a deep breath, my chest tightening as the memories I'd tried to bury resurfaced. "There was a . . . surgery," I said, my voice barely a whisper. "It didn't go well. Too much scar tissue. I can't . . . I can't have kids."

There was a long pause, the weight of my words sinking in. I still couldn't bring myself to look at him. I didn't want to see the pity or the disappointment or whatever else he might be feeling. I didn't want to face it.

"It's fine," I added quickly, forcing a smile that didn't reach my eyes. "I've made peace with it."

Logan didn't say anything. Not at first.

Instead, he shifted closer, pulling me into his chest. His embrace was warm, solid, comforting . . . safe.

He finally grabbed my chin, tilting it up so I was forced to look into his soft green gaze. "I'm sorry that happened to you, Red," he said, his thumb stroking my cheek.

I leaned into his palm, my lip quivering as he continued to hold my eyes.

He leaned forward and brushed a heartbreakingly sweet kiss across my lips.

"Doesn't make a difference to me," he told me. The fierceness and sincerity in his voice caught me off guard.

I studied him, trying to find the lie.

But it didn't seem to exist.

"You actually mean that," I whispered, my voice and my chest and my *soul* full of wonder.

"I don't need kids to have a life with you, Sloane. I just need *you*."

He pressed another soft kiss on my face, this time on my forehead, and then let me bury my head once again on his chest.

"I love you."

The words burst out of me, soft and shaky.

But it wasn't those words that had me terrified. It was that I realized then I was finally ready . . . to tell Everett I was done.

Somehow, Logan had gotten what he was after.

My heart.

Logan stiffened slightly, and then his arms tightened around me like a vise, pulling me closer, like he never wanted to let me go. I could feel his heartbeat against my cheek, steady and strong, a contrast to the wild rhythm of my own pulse.

"Sloane, I love you so much," he said roughly, his body shaking as he held me. "You're everything to me, baby."

We stayed there in the quiet.

And unlike in the past when I would normally be thinking of the million reasons why I *shouldn't* be with him, for the first time . . . I couldn't think of any.

CHAPTER 37

SLOANE

I walked into the group home, pushing the thoughts of my upcoming conversation with Everett out of my mind so I could focus on Rome. Scanning the room, I spotted him in his usual corner with a stack of crayons and coloring books. His tiny body was hunched over, focused on whatever masterpiece he was working on.

"Hey, Rome," I said, smiling as I approached. He looked up, his big brown eyes lighting up when he saw me. That little flicker of joy was all I needed to make the rest of the world disappear.

"Hi, Sloane," he said softly, barely more than a whisper, but he smiled as he slid over to make room for me on the floor beside him. The fact that he'd immediately spoken to me was a huge step, and I was still a little in shock as I sank to the floor next to him. He'd been that way since he'd met Logan, seeming to be warmer with me every time I came.

"Whatcha drawing today?" I asked.

"Hockey stuff," Rome replied as I sat down, grabbing a crayon.

"Oh." My eyes widened when I saw he had a whole stack of hockey-themed coloring books. Those were new. The center must have gotten some new donations. Logan was going to get a big kick out of it next time he was able to come in with me.

We colored in silence for a while, and the tension in my shoulders slowly eased at the familiar routine.

After a few minutes, I noticed Rome glance up at me, then quickly back down, like he was thinking about something.

"What's on your mind, kiddo?" I asked, keeping my tone light.

He hesitated for a second, his tiny hands gripping the crayon a little tighter. "Do you not want to be friends with Logan anymore?"

I blinked at him and frowned. "Of course I do. Why?"

"He just comes to see me by himself now instead of with you."

His words caught me completely off guard. I blinked, trying to keep my voice steady. "Logan comes to see you?"

Logan had team events since that time he'd visited with me, and he'd been unable to come on my usual day. The fact that he'd been choosing to come himself . . .

He nodded, still coloring. "Yeah. He comes, and we color and play. But I'm glad that you guys are still friends."

I stared at him, the crayon in my hand hovering over the page but unmoving. I was struggling not to cry. Of course Logan had come to see him.

Because he was the most perfect guy in the entire world.

"What do you guys play?" I asked, my voice sounding a little too tight, a little too small.

Rome smiled. "We play hide-and-seek. He's not very good at it. I always win."

I couldn't help but laugh. "Yeah? He's a pretty big guy to be sneaking around."

Rome giggled, his eyes sparkling as he told me about how Logan always pretended to trip over things or made too much noise, on purpose, just to make him laugh. As he talked, I could picture it so clearly—Logan, towering over everyone in that ridiculous way of his, trying to make himself small for Rome. Not because he had to, but because he wanted to.

Something deep inside me cracked.

Suddenly I wasn't scared about severing ties with Everett.

I was excited about it.

"He's really fun," Rome continued, his voice soft again, like he was thinking about something serious. "And he talks to me like I'm big, like I'm important."

I swallowed hard, my chest tightening. Of course he did. Logan saw people. Really saw them, in a way that other people usually didn't.

"I'm glad he comes to visit you," I said quietly, running my fingers through Rome's hair gently. "You deserve that. And we'll come together again soon."

Rome glanced up at me again, a little frown creasing his forehead. "Do you like him?"

The question caught me off guard, and I felt the heat rush to my face. "What?"

He shrugged, his innocent gaze cutting through me in a way I didn't expect. "Do you want to marry him?"

I opened my mouth to answer, but nothing came out. I wasn't sure what to say. How could I explain to this sweet little boy that the answer was yes, but it was also so much more complicated than that?

"I . . . he's . . ." I stammered, but Rome just smiled, as if he already knew.

"I think he likes you too," he said simply, like it was the most obvious thing in the world.

I let out a shaky laugh, trying to hide the way my heart was pounding. "Yeah? You think so?"

He nodded, going back to his coloring like he hadn't just turned my world upside down with one innocent question.

And for the rest of the visit I tried to come to terms with the fact that . . . I wanted forever with Logan York.

CHAPTER 38

SLOANE

Y ou've been going to see Rome," I told him as soon as he walked through the door after a skating session.

He grinned and blushed. "Ahh, little rascal. I told him to keep that a secret."

"Logan, that's so amazing," I told him, a tear sliding down my cheek. "He's already improving so much."

"He's a fun kid," he responded as if it was no big deal. "And you're not allowed to cry about it."

"Why not?" I laughed, wiping at my face as he prowled toward me.

"Because I have plans for you. Something new we're going to try."

"What?" I asked, anticipation already building in my core.

There was a wicked glint in his gaze as he took my hand and led me down the hallway to the painting room he'd set up in his—our—place. "We're going to paint."

I raised an eyebrow, not saying anything as he led me inside and then walked me to the center of the room.

"I just need to move this," he mused, dropping my hand and going over to the settee on the far wall. He dragged it into the middle of the floor and fussed with the velvet cushions. I grinned as I watched him.

"Why exactly have you decided to pick up painting today?"

"Let's just say you've inspired me," he teased as he grabbed my hand and pulled me toward the couch.

"And what have I inspired you to paint?"

"You," he said, his voice turning low and smooth and sensual. Goose bumps ran across my skin as he slowly walked over to where I kept my paints.

"Take everything off," he ordered, and I immediately obeyed, my heart picking up speed in my chest. I could already feel my core softening, my panties getting wet. My nipples were budding and rubbing uncomfortably against my bra.

As I bit down on my lip, a rush of heat flooded my cheeks at the way he was looking at me. I wasn't sure how it could be like this every time. Like he was in awe of what he saw.

I kept waiting for it to fade. But it never did.

I pulled the shirt over my head. Then took my pants off, doing an awkward shuffle as I slipped out of them. I was learning that it was difficult for me to be practiced and cool around Logan.

Probably because for the first time, sex meant something. It wasn't just a performance where I was going through the motions.

"Now your bra," he said roughly, a splash of color in his cheeks as he continued to take me in.

"Do you think you'll ever stop looking at me like that?" I whispered, an edge of vulnerability to my words.

His features softened. "Never," he swore fiercely.

"How do you know?" I asked, unable to keep the desperation out of my voice.

He cocked his head, taking his time as he undid the cap of a blue tube of paint and squeezed some out on a palette.

"I know I'll never stop looking at you like I'm in love, because every time I see you, it feels like the whole world is holding its breath, waiting for you to steal it over and over again.

"I know I'll never stop looking at you like I'm in love, because of the way you walk into a room like you own it but still can't help being a little shy. Somehow, you don't know you're the most beautiful thing anyone's ever seen.

"I know I'll never stop looking at you like I'm in love, because of the way you light up a room without even realizing it, like you're carrying a little bit of the sun with you wherever you go.

"It's the way your laugh sounds like it belongs in a song. And the way you look at me sometimes, like I'm worth everything. It's how you always surprise me—whether it's with something you say or just the way you see the world—it keeps me on my toes in the best way.

"It's the way you let me in, even when you're scared, like trusting me is a risk you're willing to take.

"And it's the way you make me feel. Like for the first time in my life, I'm enough.

"I know I'll never stop looking at you like I'm in love, Sloane, because I *am* in love with you. Now and forever. You are my everything.

"So the question is, how could I *not* look at you like this?"

My breath came out in a gasp as his words stitched themselves to my skin. I undid my front clasp, and my bra sprung open, the air cool on my nipples and making them pebble even more. His gaze grew hungry, and his tongue peeked out and slowly slid across his bottom lip.

"You're so fucking beautiful," he rasped, his eyes squeezing shut for a moment like it was hard for him to look at me. I slowly slid my underwear down my legs until I was completely bare.

He cleared his throat and gestured to the couch. "Now, lie down so I can paint you."

"I can think of better things we can do," I told him as I reluctantly sat down. What I really wanted to do was jump on him and throw him on this couch so I could get what I wanted.

But I guessed I could play along. For a little while.

Logan studied me intensely, his gaze raking across my skin, and then he studied the myriad of paints he had laid out to use, picking a few of them and squeezing them onto the palette to join the blue.

"There's blank canvases in the cabinet," I told him, pressing my legs together because somehow all of this was turning me on.

He hummed in response, squeezing out some gold and a lighter blue before he picked up a brush. "I have another canvas in mind," he finally murmured before he slowly stalked toward the couch.

He circled me, and I watched, my heart pounding as he dipped the brush into the blue paint. "Turn over," he said, his voice growing hoarse.

As I rolled over, the velvet brushed against my chest. I was so wet that a trail of liquid fell down my thigh as the cool bristles gently touched the back of my neck. I shivered and a sigh fell from my lips.

"I'm obsessed with your body. The first thing I noticed when I saw you up in the stands was how poised you were, the way you were holding your head. I'd never seen anyone who looked so . . . I don't even know how to describe it. It's like you were a queen sitting among your courtiers."

I swallowed hard, feeling the paint cool against my skin as he continued, moving the brush down my back in long, deliberate strokes.

I turned my head to look at him, watching as he switched colors, dipping into a fiery orange that he spread across my ass. "This reminds me of the fire inside you. You can't see it like everyone else can. But you're a survivor, and the fire inside you that's kept you going is the strongest I've ever seen—the strongest I've ever felt."

A tear slid down my cheek as he dipped the brush through my crease, briefly brushing against my slit before circling the other ass cheek.

He abruptly turned me over, and I shivered as I flopped onto my back. I sucked in a breath as he dragged the brush down my neck, over the curve of my breast, and around my waist. I was shaking—whether from the cold paint or from the way he was looking at me, I couldn't tell.

Logan stepped back, eyeing his work for a second before dipping the brush into a deep, rich purple. "I think about your curves constantly. I'll be skating across the ice and realize that I've been lost in my head the entire time thinking about the next time I can have you. I can't ever come back from this. I won't be able to. I'll do whatever it takes to keep you." He dipped the brush into my belly button, his voice casual, like his words weren't rewriting my DNA.

I felt like I was going to melt. My body tingled where the paint touched, but it wasn't just the physical sensation. It was the way he spoke, the way he looked at me, like he was seeing more than just skin. Like he was pulling me apart piece by piece.

He dipped the brush in red next and, starting from my knees, began to paint my inner thighs. Each stroke of the brush got closer and closer to my core, and I couldn't help the moan that slipped from my lips.

"You're soaking wet, Red. Your thighs were wet before I even started painting you." He dipped the brush through my slit, circling my clit until I was mewling, my head thrown back in agony because I wanted him so much.

He laughed darkly for a moment before bringing the brush up to my left breast and painting the skin over where my heart was beating wildly.

"You're a masterpiece," he said softly, still holding the brush, his eyes dark and full of something I couldn't quite place.

I swallowed, my throat tight. The paint was drying on my skin, and I was feeling exposed and raw, but also . . . *seen*.

"This is the best prize I've ever won," Logan purred, the paintbrush continuing to move over my heart. "Tell me, pretty girl. Give me what I want to hear."

I stared into his eyes, the words on my lips.

Yes, he'd won my heart. A thousand times over he'd won it. Even if the words were still hard to speak.

"I love you," I whispered.

He grinned, like my words really were a prize. He leaned over and brushed his lips against mine. "I know."

I huffed. "So sure of yourself."

My words didn't have the intended effect that they should have because of the breathiness in my voice that I was sure told him all he needed to know. He was still hovering above me, and I couldn't get myself to look away and break the spell.

The paintbrush was still pressing into my skin, and I suddenly yanked it away, reaching up and painting a streak of red across his face.

Logan didn't bother trying to get the brush back; he wiped his hand through the paints on the palette and then streaked it across my chest, groping my breasts while he did it. Of course.

"That's not playing fair," I said, my voice half moaning as I streaked red across his lips this time.

As soon as I moved the brush, his lips were on me, smearing the red between us. I could taste some of the paint on my tongue—probably not great for my health.

But everything else about Logan was.

His tongue slipped into my mouth, long, aggressive licks that had my core clenching.

He pulled away, breathing hard as he stared at my face, and then my chest, his dark gaze raking over my breasts. My skin felt flushed and tight.

With his paint-streaked hand, he once again dragged his palm over my breasts before he suddenly shoved a hand under my back, pulling me up and onto his lap. I clung to him, the paintbrush clattering to the wood floor as I straddled him.

"Logan," I whimpered, my bare ass on his denim-covered thighs. I watched as he dipped his fingers into the paint once again, stroking the paint across my face as he stared at me intensely.

"Fuck me," I begged, and his grin was like a flame flickering to life in the darkness. I wanted to live in it. His hands tangled in my hair, and he groaned as his lips claimed mine once again, our mouths and tongues tangling together.

He reached between us with one hand, undoing his jeans and pulling out his cock, fisting it slowly as he continued to devour my mouth.

"You want my big dick so bad, don't you?" he growled, biting down on my lip, his eyes gleaming dangerously.

"Yes," I moaned, replacing his hand with my own as I lifted up and rubbed his tip against my clit. Sparks of pleasure heated my core.

It wasn't enough, though. Nothing would be enough but him inside me.

"Beg me for it."

Mmm. This was new. I was definitely going to add this to the list of things that I liked.

I pulled back, shifting my hips as his hands curved to my back and then down to my ass, squeezing it and pushing me against his cock.

"I'm waiting," he said roughly.

My hands moved back to his shoulders, gripping them as I rubbed myself up and down his length.

"Please, baby. I need you inside me," I begged.

I was dripping wet, soaking his cock as it moved through my folds.

It felt so fucking perfect.

"Yes, that's it. Use me. Get what you need," he murmured, pressing another bruising kiss against my lips. The light was fading in the room, catching on the perfect planes of his face.

"How badly do you need me?" he said silkily, maintaining much more control than I was capable of at the moment. His dick was rubbing perfectly against my clit, and my head dropped to his chest.

"I want you more than anything. Please, Logan, please," I moaned, my fingers digging into his skin as I tried to sit up higher so that I could have him.

The bastard laughed. "My poor impatient girl. Do you need me to take care of you?"

"Yes," I whimpered.

His mouth moved against my ear, his tongue tracing the edge and sending shivers racing down my skin. "Please," I whispered again.

"As you wish," he breathed, his voice finally thick with the arousal I was feeling.

He kneaded my ass cheeks one more time before lifting me up and positioning the mushroomed head of his perfect dick at my opening.

I was about to beg again when he slammed me down, impaling me on his huge length.

My head fell back, and I moaned, trying to adjust to the fullness and learn how to breathe again. It was still a miracle every time he fit inside me.

His shirt was still on, and I pulled at it, frantic to feel his skin against me. He growled and ripped it open with one hand, buttons clattering to the floor around us. I clutched him desperately, my eyes finally fluttering open as I adjusted to his size.

"You're choking my dick, baby," he groaned, the sound so erotic that I gushed around him, my essence soaking our thighs.

"I love your dick," I told him as my body started to move.

"And me. You love me, too," he reminded me.

I moaned in response, his cock hitting that perfect spot in my core that only he could reach.

He captured my kiss, his tongue thrusting in, aggressive deep licks that I could feel everywhere.

I rocked against him, working my clit each time I shifted my hips.

"Yes, you're perfect," he murmured against my lips, his hands guiding my body in the perfect rhythm.

Sometimes it felt like he had been made just for me. From the fit of his dick, to the taste of his mouth . . . to how he knew just the pressure and movement to get me off.

Everything about him was perfect.

I cried out, an orgasm shooting through me, surprising me with its suddenness. He continued to move, working me up and down his dick as the pleasure coursed through me. "That's my good girl," he said, his voice smug as he leaned forward. "Now do it again."

My pussy clenched at his words, and it was easy for the pleasure to build as his mouth closed around my nipple, sucking and pulling at the tender flesh while he slammed me onto his cock.

"You feel so fucking good. Your tight pussy is taking me so well," he growled as he released my nipple and thrust up inside me, his gaze glued to where his dick was stretching my entrance.

"Logan," I whimpered.

"That's it, baby. Come one more time."

My hands slid from around his neck, brushing against his cheeks as I stared into his green eyes, trying to center myself, to stay in the moment by focusing on the stubble on his cheek, the way he smelled, the feel of his huge length as it rutted in and out of me.

Hoarse cries were slipping from my lips as our bodies worked together, the pleasure building until my vision grew hazy. I was shaking and jerking against him as I came, the sensations stronger and brighter than anything I'd ever experienced before.

His groans joined mine, and a second later he was filling me with hot bursts of cum, so much that the liquid seeped out between us.

Between our . . . fluids and the paint, we'd destroyed this couch.

Worth it.

Logan shifted us and laid me gently back, somehow staying inside me as we moved. The look in his eyes had me thinking of that word again . . . *forever*. He rolled us so that we were both on our sides, and I was cradled in his arms.

I was sticky, and there was dried paint coating my skin. But as he brushed a kiss against my forehead, I was also sure that I'd never felt better.

CHAPTER 39

SLOANE

I stood outside his office, the familiar chill of dread creeping up my spine. My palms were sweaty, and my heart had pounded harder with each step to the door. I'd done a lot of things I hated in my life, but walking into Everett's office and telling him I was done—that I wasn't going to work for him anymore—was probably one of the scariest.

I hated this mansion. I hated the memories and the reminders that this was where I'd chosen to ruin myself. I never came here if I could help it.

But I'd had to today. I'd had to do this in person, so he knew I was serious. I was done. I'd made up my mind.

Everett would respect my choice. He might be stern and scary, but he'd never hurt me. Everything was going to be fine.

And Logan was going to be so happy when I gave him the news.

I pushed the door open and stepped inside, the cold, sterile atmosphere hitting me immediately. Everett sat behind his oversized mahogany desk, studying some papers. He had the same cold, calculating look on his face that he always did when he was in business mode.

"Everett," I said, my voice stronger than I felt inside. "I need to talk to you."

He didn't respond right away, continuing to flip the pages of whatever file he was looking at. It was annoying that he always did that, making sure I knew who was in charge.

The silence stretched, my nerves buzzing, but I forced myself to keep going.

"I'm done," I said, the words coming out in a rush. "I'm not doing it anymore."

That got his attention. His eyes flicked up, cold and unreadable, the corner of his mouth twitching like he was fighting off a smirk. "Doing what?"

"Working for you," I said, my voice faltering.

"You're done?" he repeated slowly, his tone mocking. "And what exactly do you think that means, Sloane?"

I swallowed hard, trying to hold my ground. "It means no more clients. No more selling my body. It's over. I don't know what I'm going to do . . . but it's not going to be this. Not anymore."

There. I'd said it. The truth was out, and my heart felt like it was about to burst from my chest, it felt like a weight had been lifted off my shoulders. Logan had changed everything for me. I wasn't going to be trapped in this nightmare anymore.

But my uncle—he just laughed. A short, sharp bark of laughter that made my skin crawl.

"You think you've fallen in love. That's what this is about, isn't it?" he said mockingly, shaking his head like he couldn't believe the audacity. "With who? That hockey player? *Logan York?*"

I clenched my fists, trying to ignore the sick feeling in my stomach. "Yes. I—I love him, and I'm leaving this behind. It was my *choice* to start, and it's my *choice* to quit."

The word *choice* felt different as I said it, though. The last few weeks with Logan—away from Everett—had made me actually start to think.

Maybe . . . Logan was right.

What if that first night hadn't been my choice? What if Everett *had* manipulated me?

He leaned back in his chair, folding his hands over his stomach, and that mocking grin stretched wider across his face. "You're a fool, Sloane. A naive, *stupid* fool."

My heart stuttered in my chest, but I didn't move. "I'm not a fool. I've just figured out what I want out of life."

"And you think that's him?" His voice turned crueler. "You really believe someone like him can love you? That this is some fairy-tale ending for you?"

My insides twisted at the sneer in his voice, but I didn't back down. "I know it is."

Everett leaned forward, his eyes narrowing as the smirk dropped from his face. "He'll get tired of you. And then what will you do? You have no skills, no education, no money. You'll be out on the streets or struggling in a miserable apartment again. It's going to hit even harder after you've been living like a plush pig for the last few years."

The words hit me like a kick to the ribs, and I took a deep breath. Because his words were familiar.

That was what he'd said before.

That was what he would say *anytime* he could feel me faltering. Scaring me about the past had been his favorite and most effective tool to convince me to go along with whatever he wanted.

And even though I *was* still terrified about ending up back in the miserable ruins where I'd started life . . . something about Logan lessened Everett's effectiveness.

It wasn't Logan's money either. It was his steadiness, and that I could feel his love for me in every word he said, everything he did.

There was also the fact that I should have some money left over after all these years of work—even after my expenses.

"You can pay me what I've earned over the years or let me sell the condo. I'm sure that's enough to get me by if something were to happen," I told him, proud of how my voice had leveled out . . . and I sounded more confident.

Everett smiled then, dark and triumphant, leaning back in his chair like he was enjoying every second of this. "No."

"What?" I asked, the blood draining from my face. All these years he'd promised he was keeping my money safe, that he was investing it for me for when it was time for retirement. He'd told me that was how he handled finances for all the women who worked in the business.

He'd taken care of all my bills, my clothes . . . everything. But he'd also always told me when he was depositing money in my account. Even though I'd never seen it, never been able to use it freely, it had felt like mine.

But maybe it was just another way I'd been stupid and completely missed him manipulating me.

I was such a fucking idiot.

"That's *my* money."

"I own you, Sloane. Everything you have is because of me." He shook his head, like I'd disappointed him. "This is your last chance. If you choose to do this, I'll have no choice."

"No choice?" I whispered, my voice barely audible.

"But to treat you like the property you are," he said, his voice dripping with venom.

He picked up his papers and began reviewing them again.

The threat sank into my chest, and a stark fear filled my insides. I'd had all sorts of emotions about my uncle over the years, but the terror I was experiencing right now . . . that was new.

"What about everything you've said over the years . . . about how this job was me choosing power. Huh? What about that?" I threw out desperately, hoping I could get him to see reason.

Everett glanced up, a cruel smirk dancing across his lips. "Haven't you felt powerful? You sold your body at eighteen because you were so scared of actually having to work hard. You were a miserable, weak, useless girl, and I made you into someone that made men drop to their knees. You were nothing. And I made you into this."

He pushed up from his chair and leaned forward.

"Everything comes with a price, and transforming someone as worthless as you . . . well, the price was far more than you'll *ever* be able to pay."

My hands trembled, my body shaking from the weight of his words. Tears burned at the back of my eyes, but I refused to let them fall.

"I hate you," I managed to choke out, my voice cracking.

He shrugged and walked around his desk, his smirk never fading. "It's better that you get this through your stupid brain before it's too late. *You* have no choice. You made sure of that at that auction. And now you'll *never* have a choice. You belong to me, and you'll *never* escape."

I stumbled back, my legs shaking as I tried to process what he was saying. My chest was tight, my throat burning with the threat of tears.

His hand shot out before I could react, his fingers clamping down hard on my chin, forcing me to look up at him. The grip was painfully tight, his eyes dark and full of rage. I tried to pull away, but he held me there, his face mere inches from mine.

"You really think you can walk away from this?" he hissed, his voice low, dangerous. "You think you can just waltz into my office, spout some nonsense about love, and that'll be the end of it?"

I couldn't answer, couldn't move. His grip was like a vise, and my fear of him only grew.

"Answer me!" he shouted, shaking me hard enough that my teeth rattled.

"I—" The words caught in my throat, but I didn't get a chance to finish. His grip shifted to my shoulder, and before I could do anything, he threw me to the ground.

I hit the floor hard, the impact sending a jolt of pain through my body. But before I could even try to get up, I heard the unmistakable sound of leather sliding through a belt loop.

I froze.

"I think I'll give you a taste of what you can expect if you choose wrong, Sloane. Remind you what I do with useless things," he said coldly, stepping toward me, the belt hanging loosely in his hand. "It seems like the right thing to do, don't you think?"

I rolled over and tried to scramble away, my heart pounding in my chest, but I wasn't fast enough. He raised the belt, and the first strike came down hard across my back, the sting of the leather biting into my skin. I cried out, curling in on myself, but it didn't stop him.

The belt came down again. And again.

I lost count after the third hit, my mind slipping into a fog of pain and fear. Each strike sent a sharp, searing pain through my body, and the sound of the leather cutting through the air was the only thing I could focus on. My arms wrapped around my head, instinctively trying to shield myself, but it was useless.

I don't know how long it went on—minutes, hours, it all blurred together in a haze of pain. But finally, after what felt like forever, he stopped. The belt hit the floor with a dull thud, and I heard his heavy breathing as he stepped back.

"You'll return to your condo and wait for my instructions. You will not see Logan York again. And most of all . . . you'll remember your place," he growled. "You'll never be free of this. Of me. I *own* you."

Without another word, he turned and walked out.

I lay there for a long time, the silence in the room pressing down on me. My body throbbed with pain, and the tears I'd tried so hard to hold in, they blurred my vision as I sobbed. Everything hurt—my skin, my heart, my hope.

I had thought I could escape. I had thought love would save me.

But as it turned out . . . love wasn't enough.

CHAPTER 40

LOGAN

Something was wrong. When I looked at my phone after practice, my app showed that Sloane wasn't at our place—she was at her old condo. The one I kept paying contractors to mess up so she wouldn't be able to ever move back in.

Why was she there?

Grabbing my bag, I hustled out of the locker room, ignoring the guys calling after me.

Something had happened.

I tried to call her all the way to my truck . . . and then the entire drive over to her condo.

But she didn't pick up.

Checking the camera in her necklace, all I could see was dark brown—meaning she'd set it somewhere.

I kept pulling up the app, making sure it said she was still at her building. And every time it confirmed it, my stomach tightened. After everything that had happened—everything she'd told me and the things I'd pieced together—I couldn't stand the thought of her being there.

By the time I pulled into the lot outside her high-rise, my jaw was clenched so tight it ached. I killed the engine and stalked inside, ignoring the polished lobby and the false sense of security it tried to exude. The elevator loomed in front of me like a challenge. I punched in the code to get up to her penthouse, tapping my foot anxiously as I waited, but the screen blinked red.

Fuck. She'd changed the code.

I stood there for a second, glaring at the keypad, before spinning on my heel and heading for the empty front desk. No one ever manned it. You had to press a buzzer and then someone came from the back. A useful setup for when I'd gone up to her place that first night . . . and the rat situation, but annoying now.

I pressed the buzzer five times, sighing in relief when an employee— a wiry guy with thick glasses and a wary expression—opened a door and peeked out.

"Hey," I called, trying to summon up my charm, even though the last thing I felt was charming. "I need to get up to my girlfriend's place. I forgot the code and she's not answering her texts." I sighed and rolled my eyes. "She's probably wrapped up in a *Real Housewives* episode or something. She did this to me the other day too."

He squinted at me. "You forgot the code?"

"Yep," I said, trying to keep my tone steady. "I'm usually with her, so I haven't needed it that much. Guess I learned my lesson."

He stepped all the way out and stared at me, his eyes widening as he really took me in. Yeah, I guess all my tats and the fact that I was built like a god were probably a little intimidating.

After what felt like the longest wait of my life . . . he gulped and shook his head. "Can't let anyone up without clearance. Building policy. Can you try just calling her some more?"

Fuck, he even had a quiver in his voice and everything. Just another reason that Sloane couldn't stay here anymore. The security was ridiculously bad.

"Right." I dug into my wallet, pulling out a couple of crisp bills. "How about now?"

His eyes flicked to the cash.

"Sorry, the answer's still no. I'll lose my job if anyone finds out."

I pulled out some more cash. "How about now?" I growled, waving the bills in the air. I pulled out my phone as well, showing him some pictures of Sloane. "These are texts from her. I'm clearly her boyfriend."

For a second, I thought he was still going to refuse, like any good employee should have. But then he lunged forward and grabbed the bills from my hand. "Fine. But if anyone asks, I didn't help you," he told me, unable to even look me in the eyes.

"Deal." I followed him to the elevator, where he fished a keycard out of his pocket, swiping it against the elevator panel. The doors slid open, and I stepped inside, already bracing myself for what I might find upstairs as it started to ascend.

The elevator doors slid open with a metallic hum, and the silence of her place was the first thing that hit me. My gut tightened as I walked into her foyer, the air sharp with the faint scent of cleaning products. The place looked immaculate—pristine even. Not a speck of dust, not a single out-of-place object. My teeth ground together. The contractors must have stopped dragging their feet on repairs. They'd be hearing from me later.

I walked around, glancing into rooms to see if she was there.

I hated every square inch of this place. Every time I was here, I wanted to claw at the walls . . . burn the whole fucking building down.

My jaw tightened when I saw the closed door to her bedroom. I tried the handle and the worry inside me only grew.

It was locked.

"Red?" I called through the door, my voice echoing in the sterile quiet. No answer.

I knocked again, harder this time. "Sloane, open the door. Whatever it is, I'll fix it."

Still nothing.

My knuckles hit the door once more, even harder, and my patience snapped. "Sloane, if you don't open this motherfucking door, I'm busting it down."

"Please," she finally said, her voice trembling. "Just go away, Logan."

Fuck. She had obviously been crying. Her voice didn't sound right—it was small, shaky, like it had been stripped raw.

"Sloane." I pressed my forehead against the door, my hand flat against the cool wood. "Let me in. Talk to me."

My chest was heaving now, the red-hot edge of panic clawing its way up my throat. I didn't bother knocking again. I stepped back, scanning the frame, and took a breath. One good hit should do it. I wouldn't need to replace the door. Because she was never going to be in this place again.

The lock gave way with a loud crack as I slammed my shoulder into the wood. It flew open, slamming against the wall, and I froze in the doorway.

Sloane was on the bed, lying on her stomach, completely still. The room was dim, the only light coming from the faint glow of a lamp on the nightstand. Her head was turned away from me, and she hadn't even flinched at the noise I'd made breaking in.

A sick, twisting feeling settled in my gut as I stepped inside. "Sloane?" My voice sounded rough and hoarse, even to me. She didn't respond.

I crossed the room in two strides, crouching down beside the bed. My heart was hammering as I reached out, my fingers barely brushing her back. The instant I made contact, she screamed—a sound so raw, so filled with pain, that it stopped me cold.

She tried to move, to pull away, but the sheets slid down as she twisted. That was when I saw them.

Welts. Bruises. Dark, angry marks covered Sloane's back like a twisted map of every second of pain she'd endured.

"Fuck." The word slipped out before I could stop it. My hand hovered uselessly above her, not daring to touch her again, not knowing how to help. Rage and helplessness warred inside me, leaving me shaking.

Her breathing was shallow, uneven, and she clutched the pillow beneath her like it was the only thing keeping her anchored.

"Sloane," I said again, my voice breaking. I couldn't keep the anger out of it, even though it wasn't directed at her. "What—?"

She didn't answer, just turned her face into the pillow, muffling a quiet, broken sob. It sliced through me like a blade.

I moved around the bed, crouching again so I could see her face. Her eyes were squeezed shut, tears streaking down her cheeks. She looked utterly defeated, like a shell of the woman I knew.

"I'm going to kill him," I said, my voice low and full of fury. I didn't even need her to say it. I knew who was responsible. I'd known the moment I walked in and saw her like this.

"Logan," she rasped, her voice barely audible.

I leaned closer, trying to catch what she was saying. "I'm here, Sloane. I've got you. Just tell me what you need."

Her eyes opened just a crack, glassy and filled with pain. "I told you . . . I don't need saving. Because . . . I can't be saved."

My chest tightened, and I shook my head, taking a deep breath and trying to gentle my voice. "Come on, baby. Let's get you home," I said soothingly.

Her eyes widened, panic flashing across her face. "Logan, I can't—"

"You can," I interrupted. "And you will. Because I'm not leaving this condo without you."

Her lips parted, but no words came. For a long moment, she just stared at me, as if she was trying to decide whether to fight me or let me in.

Finally, she exhaled shakily, her shoulders slumping. "Okay," she murmured.

Relief coursed through me, but it was tempered by the simmering rage in my veins, rage that was only growing the longer I looked at what he'd done to her. I wiped a trembling hand down my face as I thought about all the ways I was going to make him pay.

One way or another, her uncle was going to pay.

But for now, all that mattered was getting her out of this place and somewhere I could keep her safe.

I carefully lifted her into my arms, not bothering to grab anything else as I stalked back to the elevator. Her tears were soaking my shirt, and every tear made me want to die.

"Logan, I went to him to tell him I was done," she whispered as I stepped onto the elevator.

My whole body shuddered as the elevator descended.

"That's my good girl," I finally got out in a choked voice, even though every cell in my body was busy planning his demise. "That's my *good* girl."

I paced the length of my living room, my phone clutched tightly in my hand as I waited for Lincoln to pick up. My apartment was too quiet, save for the faint murmurs coming from the bedroom where the team doctor was helping Sloane. Every now and then, I caught the sound of her voice, soft and trembling. The image of her lying on that bed, beaten and broken, was burned into my mind, fueling a rage I couldn't contain. The only thing keeping me from leaving and finding her uncle right now was because murder was a crime that would end up with me separated from her forever, something that was obviously unacceptable.

I was hoping Lincoln would have a plan.

The call finally connected. "Logan," Lincoln answered, his voice calm and steady, the kind of voice that never wavered, no matter what.

"I need your help," I said immediately, not bothering with pleasantries. My words came out sharp, clipped. "Sloane tried to be done tonight. Her uncle—" It was hard to finish. There was so much rage and hate inside me right now. "He beat the fucking shit out of her."

There was silence on the other end of the line, heavy and deliberate. Then Lincoln's voice dropped, colder than I'd ever heard it. "He won't be a problem for much longer."

"He's not going to let her go," I said quietly, pacing faster, my free hand raking through my hair. The anger boiling in my chest was spilling over, making it hard to think straight. "I need to figure something—"

"We'll make sure he doesn't have a choice," Lincoln interrupted, his tone leaving no room for argument. "I'll get to work on it."

Before I could respond, the line went dead. I pulled the phone away from my ear, staring at the screen. I hadn't even given him the details—no names, no specifics, nothing. Which could only mean one thing.

Lincoln already knew.

A sharp, humorless smile tugged at my lips, something I didn't think I was capable of at the moment. "Fucking stalker," I muttered, shaking my head as I let the phone drop to my side.

The bedroom door creaked open, and I turned to see the team doctor stepping out. His face was grim, but there was a professionalism to his expression that kept my panic at bay.

"She's resting now," he said, his voice low. "But she's in a lot of pain. I don't think we need to worry about internal bleeding, and I don't think anything's broken. It mainly looks to be severe bruising and welts. She'll need time to heal—and someone to watch over her."

I nodded, my throat tightening as his words sank in. "I'll be here," I said, my voice firm and unyielding. "Whatever she needs."

The doctor studied me for a moment, then gave a short nod. "Good. She needs a safe place. I gave her some pain meds and something to help her sleep. The bottles are on the table next to her, along with instructions for when she needs them next." He gathered his bag and left without another word, leaving me standing alone in the quiet apartment.

I turned toward the bedroom door, staring at it like it could give me all the answers to every question that had been clawing at me since I'd found her like that.

The only thing I did know—I wasn't going to let it happen ever again.

My fists clenched at my sides as I exhaled sharply, forcing myself to relax before I opened the door and joined her on the bed.

Lincoln was working on the problem. I didn't know what he'd do, but honestly, I didn't care.

Just as long as it ended with Everett bleeding and suffering and completely . . . destroyed.

Sloane

And you know what I do with useless things . . .

I was back at Everett's estate. The memories are disjointed, surreal, but so vivid I could feel the cold stone beneath my feet, the silence that hung in the air. The housekeeper had brought home a dog. A scrappy, brown mutt with wiry fur and eyes that I immediately loved. Its job was simple: hunt the rats and small animals sneaking into the estate. Nothing more.

At first, he did exactly that. Focused, determined, his nose always to the ground, darting after anything that scurried. But then he found me.

I wasn't supposed to pay attention to the dog. I knew that. Everything had changed after the auction. Everything about my life had a purpose, a role. And yet, when those big, hopeful eyes met mine, something inside me cracked. I started sneaking him food under the table, small scraps I could hide in my hand. I'd crouch down when no one was looking, running my fingers through his coarse fur, whispering words I couldn't say to anyone else.

It didn't take long before the dog stopped hunting altogether. He followed me instead, his tail wagging whenever I came near. He didn't want to do his job anymore—he wanted my attention, my love.

I should've known it would end badly. I should've seen it coming.

The scene shifted, and suddenly I was sitting on the porch steps. The dog lay beside me, his head resting on my knee as I scratched behind his ears. His long tail thumped lazily against the wooden planks, a soft sound that somehow felt louder than anything else in the quiet estate. For that brief moment, I let myself believe he was mine—something warm, something real in a place that had turned so cold.

The next morning, I looked everywhere. Around the estate, the gardens, the stables where it used to chase the rats. My calls echoed in the stillness, unanswered. Panic clawed at my chest, growing with every passing hour.

Later in the afternoon, I heard Everett's sharp tone with a disappointed edge that made my stomach churn. "Looking for something, Sloane?"

I turned to see him standing there, his hands in his pockets, a faint smirk playing on his lips. My heart sank. "Rory," I said quickly, the name slipping out before I could stop it. "The dog—I mean. Have you seen him?"

Everett's smile grew, but it wasn't kind. He gestured for me to follow, and I did, my legs heavy, dread pooling in my stomach with every step. He led me to the edge of the estate, past the tool shed. And that was when I saw him.

The dog's lifeless body lay crumpled on the ground, its fur matted and its eyes dull. My breath caught in my throat, the world tilting beneath me.

"Why?" The word escaped in a broken whisper, barely audible over the roaring in my ears.

Everett's voice was calm, matter-of-fact, like he was commenting on the weather. "He was useless. A dog that doesn't do its job has no place here."

I stared at the body, disbelief and grief crashing over me like a wave. Rory had trusted me. He'd stopped chasing the rats because he wanted to be with me. And now he was dead—because of me.

"You softened him," Everett said, his voice cutting through my spiraling thoughts. "Made him weak. This is on you, Sloane. His death is your fault."

His words hit like a blow, stealing the air from my lungs. Tears burned the back of my eyes, but I couldn't move, couldn't speak. I just stood there,

*staring at the small, broken body, guilt settling deep into my chest like an
iron weight.*

*Everett leaned down, his voice a harsh whisper that sliced through the
silence. "I don't keep things that don't serve a purpose. Remember that."*

I sat up with a gasp in the dark, tears streaming down my face, the dream
lingering on my skin like the smell of rotten milk.

How had I ever thought Everett was a good man, that he had my best interests at heart? What kind of person kills a dog like that . . . and for that reason?

How had I been so stupid that those first two years of spoiling and kindness had somehow blinded me to how he really was? Why hadn't I recognized the fact that he was a monster?

"Sloane?" Logan's anxious voice called out, and then he was carefully
folding me into his lap, making sure not to touch my back.

"It was just a bad dream," I whispered, hating how weak I sounded.

"Of him?" he asked.

I didn't answer, because we both knew. All my bad dreams the last few
nights had been of Everett.

"I know you've already told me I'm wrong—but sometimes I can't help
but think . . . what if I had just walked away that night? What if I'd walked
out of the house, just tried to make it on my own?"

Logan was silent for a moment.

"I don't think he would have let you have the choice," he began som-
berly. "He was giving you the illusion of a choice so he could manipulate
you later on . . . but that night, it never would have ended up different."

He was right. I knew he was right. I didn't know why I'd been so insistent all these years that I was the one solely responsible for ruining my
life . . . when the truth had been right in front of me all along.

The last few days I'd been going over everything that had happened over
the years and what he'd said and done leading up to my eighteenth birthday.

My "choice" had been an illusion all along, and I'd spent these years
playing into his hands by hating myself every single day for something I
couldn't have avoided if I'd tried.

As terrible as it was . . . that realization that I'd never had a choice at all,
it was eye-opening. I hadn't let myself even think of that possibility before
I'd met Logan. But now that I'd come face-to-face with it, I felt my self-
loathing and guilt drift away.

For the first time, I felt . . . lighter. Innocent. Like the pieces of myself I'd
given away had just come back to me.

I was free.

CHAPTER 41

SLOANE

The phone vibrated on the nightstand, Everett's name flashing across the screen like a beacon of dread. I froze, my chest tightening. Logan was beside me, his jaw clenching as he looked from the phone to me, his expression a mix of frustration and concern.

"Don't answer it," he said, his voice low, commanding.

I hesitated. I wanted to listen to him, but something deep in my gut told me I couldn't ignore this.

"I have to," I murmured. "I'm not going to cower. Not anymore." I grabbed the phone before he could argue further. Tapping on the screen, I put it on speakerphone. My voice was shaky as I said, "Hello?"

"Good morning." Everett's smooth, venom-laced tone filled the room, curling around me like a noose. "Judging by the fact that you aren't in your condo, it appears you've made the wrong choice."

I swallowed hard, my fingers tightening around the phone. Logan's hand brushed mine, steady and grounding, even as his eyes burned with barely restrained rage.

"I told you I was done," I finally said, proud of the strength in my voice.

Everett's silence stretched unbearably before he clicked his tongue, a sound that always made me feel like a disobedient child. "You *are* done, Sloane. I've decided you'll be sold. Permanently. The bidding will start in a virtual auction at five."

Logan went rigid beside me, his entire body coiling tight like a spring about to snap. His jaw clenched so hard that the muscles in his neck stood out in sharp relief, and his fists curled against his thighs, the knuckles white with pressure. My breath hitched, my body freezing like ice had shot through my veins.

Sold.

The word echoed in my head, hollow and damning. My knees threatened to buckle, but I locked them, forcing myself to stay upright.

"You can't do that," I managed, though my voice cracked on the words. Logan's hand was now a steady pressure on my back, his touch both comforting and desperate, like he was trying to hold me together.

Everett ignored me entirely. "And Logan," he continued, his tone shifting to something darker. "Don't try to intervene. You can't win. If you want Sloane to live—or if you value your own life—you should take my advice."

He'd been watching us.

Logan's hand jerked, his body taut beside me like a bowstring about to snap. His rage was tangible, radiating off him in waves. He grabbed the phone from me. "Listen, you little sick fuck. I will—"

"Enjoy your last day," Everett interrupted with cold indifference. Then the line went dead.

For a moment, the room was silent except for the sound of my uneven breathing. My hands trembled as I set the phone down on the nightstand. I couldn't meet Logan's gaze. My head was spinning, and bile was coating my throat.

"Five," I choked out.

"What the hell does that mean? That he's *selling* you?" he asked, his voice sharp but laced with worry.

I closed my eyes, the weight of the truth crushing me. "The wife auctions," I said finally, the words falling from my lips like stones. "They're . . . it's where the highest bidders . . . they buy us permanently. I'd heard about them, but I never thought . . ."

Logan swore under his breath, pacing the room like a caged animal. "I'm going to kill him. I'm going to cut his dick off and ram it down his throat—and then I'm going to kill him," he growled.

"You can't do anything." My voice broke, my hands gripping the edge of the nightstand to steady myself. "These men that participate in these things . . . they're powerful. They don't care about rules or the law. They *are* the law. They take these types of exchanges very seriously. They'll kill you too if you try to interfere."

"We'll see about that," he bit out, his eyes blazing as he turned to me.

The conviction in his voice was unshakable, but it didn't stop the fear clawing at my chest. Everett's words echoed in my mind, a promise of destruction that felt inescapable.

Logan moved closer, his hands gripping my shoulders firmly. "Listen to me, Sloane. He's not going to win. I don't care what it takes or who I have to go through. You're going to get your happily-ever-after."

Happily-ever-after.

I'd never thought about those words until him.

I wanted to believe him. I wanted to fall into the safety of his words and let him shoulder the weight of this nightmare. But all I could think about was the cold, calculating tone in Everett's voice. The certainty in it.

I nodded slowly, even though I wasn't sure if I believed it. "Okay," I whispered, though my chest felt like it was about to cave in. "Okay."

But deep down, the terror refused to let go.

Logan

I leaned against the kitchen counter, phone pressed to my ear, my other hand gripping the edge hard enough to make my knuckles ache.

Lincoln answered on the second ring. "York."

"Sloane's uncle is trying to sell her in some kind of sick fucking auction, and I need to know what to expect."

There was a beat of silence before Lincoln sighed. "Logan, why would I know something like that?"

I snorted, pacing now, the tension in my chest too much to keep still. "Because you're like *Batman*, that's why. You know everything, even the dark, messed-up shit. Don't act like you're not three steps ahead of all of us."

I wasn't sure of all the details, but after Lincoln had met Monroe, he'd organized some kind of hostile takeover and basically pushed his father out of the business. The man had been involved in all sorts of shady shit, which was why it seemed obvious that Lincoln would know things.

There was a low laugh on the other end of the line. "You better never tell Ari you think I'm Batman. He'd never shut up about it."

"Do you know how much these things usually go for or not?"

Another pause. "Millions," he said finally, his voice grim. "It's usually millions of dollars."

"Fuck," I groaned. "I figured you would say that."

I paced the room, rubbing my face. "I'm going to need a hell of a lot more burger commercials for this."

Lincoln's humorless chuckle wasn't reassuring.

I may have been a top draft pick, but NHL players didn't make as much as football or basketball players. I'd had a lot of endorsements this year, but a lot of that money had also gone to paying Everett for Sloane in the first place.

"So . . ." I muttered, my mind racing. "Is there any way to stop these things?"

"No," Lincoln said flatly. "Not unless you're planning to take down an entire network of powerful men by five o'clock. They don't play by any rules you can use against them."

I cursed again, my hand tightening into a fist. The thought of those men sitting in some room, throwing around money like they were buying a new yacht while deciding Sloane's future, made me want to destroy something. "Then I'll have to buy her."

The words came out harder than I intended, but as soon as they did, an icy surety rushed over my skin. If the only way to keep her safe was to play their game, then fine. I'd play it. I would just have to figure out how. I'd do whatever it took. I'd drain my accounts. I'd call my dad if it came down to it. Beg him to loan me money. Although . . . I didn't know if he had that much cash available, even if I somehow convinced him to help me in the first place.

Fuck.

"Logan—" Lincoln started, but I cut him off.

"I'm serious," I said, my voice steel. "If that's the only way, then I'll figure it out. I don't care what it takes."

There was a long silence, and then Lincoln's voice softened, losing some of its usual edge. "You don't have to do this alone."

"What?" I asked, thrown off by his tone.

"I've got you," he said simply. "I know you don't have the money. I do. We'll figure it out."

I exhaled slowly, some of the pressure in my chest easing just slightly. Lincoln didn't offer things like that lightly. When he said he had you, he meant it.

"I'll pay you back," I murmured in a choked voice, my throat tight.

"It's what family is for, Rookie," he added, his voice teasing now. "You can repay me by not telling Lancaster I'm Batman. I don't need him showing up at my door with a cape."

Despite the weight of the situation, a small, broken laugh escaped me. "Deal."

"I'll get my PI to get the details of the auction, and I'll wire money into your account. I need to move some money around to get what you'll need, though. It's going to take me some time."

"Thanks," I said, rubbing at the tightness in my chest again.

We hung up, and I stared at the counter for a second, pulling myself together so I could have a strong face in front of Sloane. Then I walked into the room where she was . . . packing.

"What are you doing?" I growled, stalking forward and grabbing the clothes out of her hand that she was about to throw in the suitcase.

"Protecting you," she spit out. "These types of auctions . . . there's no way to win. I'm going to leave and wait for the results on my own. I'm not going to let you get involved and get hurt when you try and stop what's coming. What's *inevitable*."

"You're not going anywhere," I said firmly, moving closer.

Her eyes darted toward the door, and I knew exactly what was coming. "This isn't your decision to make. Maybe I love you enough to do whatever it takes to protect you too."

I took a deep breath and then pulled the handcuffs from my pocket and held them up, the metal glinting under the light.

Her eyes widened in disbelief, and then she snorted. "Okay . . . and what do you think you are going to do with those?"

"Making sure you don't do something stupid," I said calmly, stepping forward.

"Logan, you can't seriously think—"

Before she could finish, I grabbed her wrist, snapping one cuff around it. She gasped, her eyes flashing with fury, but I didn't stop. I secured the other cuff to my own wrist, the cold metal biting into my skin.

"What the fuck, Logan?" she snapped, tugging at the cuff. "Take this off. Right. Now."

"Not until I'm sure you won't leave," I said, my voice steady. "We don't need self-sacrifice right now, Sloane."

She yanked on the cuff, trying to pull away, but all it did was drag me closer. "This is insane! Let me go!"

I met her gaze, unflinching. "I'm going to save you. And you're going to trust me to do it."

Her chest heaved, her breaths coming fast and shallow. "You don't get it, Logan. He'll never stop. You can't protect me from him."

"Watch me," I said, my voice low, my grip tightening just slightly. "I'll do whatever it takes to keep you safe. Even if it means pissing you off."

She glared at me, her eyes blazing. "You don't get to make this choice for me. It's my life, my—"

"And I'm not letting you throw it away." I cut her off, my voice sharp. "You think I'm going to just stand by and watch you walk back into that nightmare? Think again."

The fire in her eyes dimmed slightly, replaced by something softer, more fragile. Fear. Pain. She looked down at the cuff on her wrist, her fingers brushing over the metal. "I'm scared," she whispered.

"I know, baby," I said, my tone softening. "But you'll see . . ."

She didn't respond, her gaze fixed on the floor. I reached out, gently lifting her chin so she had to look at me. "I'm not your enemy, Sloane. I'm on your side. Even if you hate me for it right now."

Her lips pressed into a thin line, but she didn't pull away. For the first time since Everett's call, I saw a flicker of something other than fear in her eyes. It wasn't trust, not yet, but it was a start.

"Fine," she said, her voice barely above a whisper. "But I'm just saying . . . handcuffs are not hero behavior."

A small smile tugged at my lips. "Not trying to be a hero, Red. Just trying to keep my future wife safe."

"There you go again . . . talking crazy," she said sadly. "Whores don't become wives."

For the first time, the way she'd said *whores* didn't have quite the same self-loathing as it had in the past.

I pressed a kiss to her lips and proceeded to lead her to the kitchen so I could make her breakfast. The handcuffs were staying on. "Good thing you never were one of those," I finally told her over my shoulder.

Her eyes narrowed slightly, but she didn't argue.

That was also a start.

CHAPTER 42

LOGAN

The link to the auction room came through while Sloane and I were sitting anxiously in my office, my laptop open to some protected web browser that supposedly would keep me hidden from the feds. The PI had sent the auction link with a short message: *This is your in.*

Sloane sat beside me, perched on the edge of the leather chair like it might swallow her whole. Her hand that wasn't still handcuffed to mine was clasped tightly in her lap, and she kept rubbing her thumb over her palm—a nervous tic I'd noticed she did when she was trying to hold herself together. Her breathing was shallow, her chest rising and falling rapidly, and she was staring at the laptop screen like it was a ticking bomb.

I was staring at it the same way. The auction was about to start, and I still hadn't heard from Lincoln or received a wire transfer yet. Which meant I was about to start bidding with money I didn't have.

I clicked on the link, and the screen loaded with a dimly lit room, where a video of Sloane appeared. Sloane gasped and averted her eyes from the tape as it began to play, and my stomach dropped. It was her, but not the Sloane I knew now. This was from before—before me, before anything resembling hope or love in her life. She was wearing some barely-there black lingerie, her walk deliberate and sexual, her expression vacant yet practiced. She was moving toward someone off-screen, and then she slowly sank to her knees.

The bile rose in my throat, and I looked away, unwilling to watch even a *past* her with another man.

"I'm sorry," she murmured beside me, and I grabbed her hand.

"Nothing to be sorry for, Red," I said sternly.

A chime rang out, and I stared at the screen again. The bidding was beginning.

I tightened my grip on the mouse, watching as the numbers began to climb. A million.

Okay, I could pay that myself.

Two million.

Five million.

Fuck.

The numbers began to make my head spin as I struggled to comprehend that this was an actual thing, buying people like this. There wasn't a number that equaled what Sloane was worth—what any human being was worth.

But it was still money I didn't have.

I glanced frantically at my phone, desperate to see something from Lincoln. But there was still nothing there.

Fuck. Where was he?

Sloane gripped my arm, her nails digging into my skin. "Logan. You have to pay immediately if you win. You can't make a bid if you can't pay it. Please. Don't even try."

"He's going to come through," I told her, even though my own panic was building with every second that passed.

The screen showed the bids accelerating, the numbers leaping higher, faster. My chest tightened with every increase, fury . . . and fear bubbling under the surface.

Nine million. Ten million.

I leaned back, my jaw clenched.

Thirteen million.

Fourteen.

The countdown clock to the end of the auction was ticking in the corner of the screen, every second dragging out like an eternity. Finally, the bids slowed, hovering just under fifteen million. I sat there, staring at the screen, my hand trembling over the mouse as the final seconds ticked away.

And then it stopped.

Fifteen million.

"Logan. Please. I might as well be dead if something were to happen to you because of me. Don't click that button," Sloane begged.

I swallowed, an icy resolve sliding through me.

And then I clicked the button signaling I was making a bid.

Sloane was sobbing next to me when the screen shifted, showing a message that the auction had ended. My chest heaved as I exhaled, not realizing until that moment that I'd been holding my breath.

I'd won.

I glanced at my phone screen desperately. But it was still blank.

A second later, wire instructions popped up on the laptop screen and a five-minute timer began.

"I have to call Everett, Logan. I have to tell him to start the auction over. Please, you don't understand."

She tried to grab her phone, but I pushed it out of her reach.

Lincoln was going to come through. He had to.

Fifty seconds left . . .

"Come on, come on," I muttered under my breath, my fingers hovering over the keyboard. I had everything ready, but without the funds, it was pointless.

My phone buzzed.

Lincoln.

The message was short and to the point: *Done. Wire it.*

"Holy shit," I breathed, my hands moving on autopilot as I entered the transfer details. My fingers flew over the keyboard, sweat slicking my palms. Five seconds. Four. My heart was pounding so hard it felt like it might burst. Three. Two.

The confirmation screen popped up.

Transaction complete.

I sat back in the chair, my chest heaving as I stared at the screen. The auction was over. The final bid was mine. She was mine.

She was *safe*.

Fifteen fucking million.

I'd figure out how to pay Lincoln back later. But we'd done it, Sloane was free.

Sloane was gaping in disbelief at the screen, her face pale, her cheeks still streaked with tears.

Before either of us could say anything, her phone rang. The same fucking phone that had started all of this.

Sloane stared at Everett's name on the screen but didn't make any move to reach for it.

"You did it," she choked out, her voice trembling. "You won the auction."

I grabbed the key out of my pocket and unhooked the handcuff from her wrist with a quiet *click*. She didn't move, her gaze searching mine, tears still streaming silently down her face.

"And now you're free," I said, my voice low and rough. "It's over, Sloane. You're done. No one gets to decide what happens to you ever again."

Her breath hitched, and for a moment, we just sat there, the weight of everything that had happened pressing down on both of us. Then she collapsed against me, her body shaking as she sobbed into my chest. I wrapped my arms around her, holding her as tightly as I could, as if that alone could erase every awful thing that had brought us to this moment.

"You're free," I whispered again, my voice breaking. "You're mine, but only because you want to be."

She blinked, and one last tear slipped down her cheek.

"I'm yours."

CHAPTER 43

SLOANE

'd never felt like this, so alive, so changed . . .

So free.

And suddenly, I was starving. Not for food.

But for him.

"Logan," I murmured, getting up from my seat.

"What do you need, baby?" he asked.

"You."

It was taking him too long to understand, so I grabbed his hand and pulled him toward the bedroom. Once inside, I let him go and slid my leggings and thong down my hips and legs before kicking them away.

He stared at me, hunger growing in his gorgeous green eyes.

"We don't have to do this. And your back . . ." he protested feebly.

"I know we don't *have* to do this. I want to. And my back is why I'm going to be *riding* that big cock."

"I mean, when you put it like that . . ." he growled, finally stalking toward me and grabbing me by my waist. He pressed a bruising kiss to my lips, and I could feel it. All the fucking relief that it was over now. Everett was still out there . . . no doubt a lot richer—

"I can't believe that just happened. Fifteen million," I said in between breathless kisses.

"It wasn't enough," he insisted as he undid his jeans with one hand and pulled out his enormous dick . . . the red outline of my lips stark against the pale skin. "There's no amount of money that would ever be enough."

He sat back on the bed, pulling at my legs as I moved into position over his jutting cock. I teased him for a second, sliding my wet folds across his tip.

"Fuck," he groaned.

"Tell me you want me," I purred. I felt like a different person. Like I was more.

Like I could do anything.

"Yes, fuck. I want you," he begged.

His hips thrust up, and I shook my head. "Now, that's not being a good boy. I'm in charge right now."

He smirked and stopped moving. "Yes, ma'am."

I grabbed his length and lowered myself back into position, rubbing up and down his shaft, pressing against my clit with every stroke.

"Please, baby," he breathed desperately, his gaze trained on the sight of me moving against him.

My clit was throbbing from the perfect friction, and I was so turned on, I forgot that I was supposed to be playing with him. I gasped and then . . .

He surged inside me—only halfway, but enough to make me cry out from the fullness.

"That's my good girl," he said wickedly, grabbing my hips and thrusting in all the way.

We both groaned at the sensation, and I fell against his chest, trying to get a hold of myself.

"Fuck me, Red. Use my cock," he hissed, his fingers digging into my hips.

"Yes, sir," I whispered to him, and he groaned as I began to ease up and down, trying not to die of pleasure with how good it felt as his thick cock stretched me just right.

I was soaking wet, and even with the tight fit, I glided up and down easily. His thighs were coated with my wetness, his desperate moan had me rocking up and down faster, wanting to give us both what we wanted.

Grabbing his shoulders, I leaned forward, trying to ride him harder. My clit rubbed against the coarse hair at the base of his cock, and I moaned with how good it felt.

"Yes, yes, yes," I chanted as I clenched around him. Logan tore at my shirt, pulling it up so my breasts were bare to him.

I winced for a second as my shirt brushed against my damaged back, but we were both too far gone for that to stop us.

His hips and thighs flexed, pumping into me as I moved. He bent over and latched onto my nipple, sucking it hard before he bit down gently.

"Fuck," I panted as my orgasm crashed over me. He sucked my nipple again, and my entire body convulsed, squeezing his dick as I tried to survive the pleasure.

"Yes," he growled as his mouth released my breast, his head falling back as his cock jerked inside me, his hot cum filling me up. I shuddered as I came down from the orgasm, my forehead falling to the crook of his neck as I tried to get my breath back.

We stayed like that for several long moments until I finally got my wits back enough to lift my head.

"Don't ever handcuff me again . . . unless I ask you to," I whispered, my lips brushing against his mouth.

His dick jerked again.

Logan grinned, his green eyes gleaming, a piece of his hair falling across his forehead. "Absolutely no promises, Red."

Logan

The notification lit up my phone just as I was finishing my second cup of chai tea—props to Lancaster for introducing me to it. This stuff was the shit.

I unlocked my phone and saw the email from the PI. The subject line read simply: *Everett.*

There was a link below his name, and I clicked on it, my pulse picking up speed as the screen filled with a series of documents, photos, and emails. There were client lists—high-profile names—and payment records tied to the escort service Everett ran under the guise of a "consulting firm." But it didn't stop there. Hidden deeper in the files were records of a trafficking ring, complete with photos of women and girls who had been coerced, manipulated, or outright taken from their lives to serve his "business interests."

My stomach churned as I clicked through image after image. Financial statements showed large payments funneled through shell companies, and email chains painted a picture of Everett as the cold, calculating architect behind the operation. He didn't just run it—he thrived on it. The names of some of his clients popped up in my head like a taunt. Politicians. Executives.

One particular email stopped me cold. It was from Everett himself, instructing someone to "prepare" a new recruit. My blood boiled when I saw the language he used—clinical, detached, as if these were products, not people. *Make sure she's docile. No mistakes this time.*

I gripped the edge of the table, fighting the urge to throw my phone across the room. He wasn't just a monster. He was the devil in a tailored suit.

Before I could fully process it, my phone buzzed again.

> **Lincoln:** Everything you need to bury him. Use the server I gave you to send it as an anonymous tip so you don't get caught up in it. The PI removed your and Sloane's names from the docs. Don't screw this up.

> **Me:** How the fuck do you always have this stuff ready to go so fast?

His response came almost immediately.

> **Lincoln:** It's a Circle of Trust thing.

I snorted.

> **Me:** So it does exist.

> **Lincoln:** . . .

Sliding over to my laptop, I pulled up the secure server Lincoln had set up for me. Uploading the files felt both satisfying and sickening. Every document, every photo painted an unmistakable picture of Everett's guilt, but the faces of those women, their hollow eyes staring back at me in the photographs, made my chest tighten.

With one final click, the files were sent.

I leaned back in my chair, staring at the confirmation message on the screen. The weight in my chest eased just slightly. The tip had gone through, hopefully anonymous and untraceable, and it was only a matter of time before the fallout began.

Everett was going to lose everything.

CHAPTER 44

SLOANE

The apartment was quiet, except for the clinking of my fork against the plate as I finished the last bite of Mrs. Bentley's stuffed French toast. I'd been painting all morning while Logan was at practice and had almost forgotten to eat.

I moaned around my last bite like some kind of crazy person. The guys liked her burritos, but her French toast may have been better than anything I'd ever tasted.

Even if I wasn't head over heels for Logan, it might be worth sticking around just for access to them.

Snorting at that thought, I reached for the remote, flicking on the television more for noise than anything else. I barely glanced at the screen as the bright logo of a news channel filled the space, the familiar anchor's voice droning on about the usual chaos of the world.

And then I heard it.

"Breaking news this afternoon: Prominent business tycoon Everett Wells has been arrested on charges related to human trafficking and running an extensive prostitution ring."

The fork dropped from my hand, clattering onto the plate as my head snapped toward the screen. My breath caught as they showed footage of him being escorted in handcuffs, his suit rumpled for the first time in memory.

My heart thundered as the anchor continued, her voice polished and detached, like she wasn't dismantling the man who had controlled every aspect of my life for years.

"An anonymous tip provided authorities with detailed evidence of Wells's operations, including high-profile clients connected to the ring. One name already making headlines is Congressman Jared Stroople, who has been linked to the case. More details are expected as this story develops."

I sank to the floor, the cold hardwood pressing against my legs as my body shook. My mind raced through a frenzied storm of emotions—relief, disbelief, anger, grief, and something else I couldn't quite name. It wasn't just that Everett was gone. It was that the entire foundation of his power was being obliterated.

The weight of it all crushed me in waves, and for a long moment, I just sat there, trembling as the images on the screen blurred together.

———

An hour later, the sound of the front door opening jolted me out of my haze. I scrambled to my feet, my heart pounding all over again. Logan was barely through the doorway when I ran to him, throwing my arms around his neck with a force that startled even me.

"Thank you," I breathed, my voice breaking as I clung to him. "Thank you."

He pulled back just enough to meet my gaze, his lips curving into that cocky, infuriating grin that never failed to make my chest flutter. "Don't thank me," he said smoothly. "Thank Batman."

I blinked, the absurdity of his words cutting through the heaviness in my chest. "Is that some name you're going by instead of Rookie? I'm *not* calling you that in bed."

The grin turned into a full-blown smirk as he winked. "I'd never ask you to."

I let out a shaky laugh, burying my face against his chest as the tears started to come. He held me tightly, his arms a fortress around me as I let it all out—the fear, the relief, the gratitude. For the first time in what felt like forever, I wasn't crying out of despair.

I was crying because I was truly free.

———

Two months later

"Are you sure you want to do this?" Logan asked for what must have been the millionth time as we sat in the truck outside the federal penitentiary that was housing Everett.

I shook my head. "I have to do this. I *need* to do this."

He sighed like this was going against his better judgment, but he still got out of the truck and walked around to let me out.

"Remember he can't touch you anymore. He's nothing," he told me as he led me inside. We went through security, and then I stopped him in the visiting room before he could go any farther with me.

"I want to do this myself," I whispered, hating how he flinched at my words.

There was a long silence as he searched my face for something, and then he finally nodded. "You've got this, Red."

The guard led me through the sterile hallways, the echo of my heels against the concrete feeling oddly satisfying. I wasn't here to find closure— I'd already claimed that for myself. I was here to face Everett Wells and leave him with nothing, just like he'd left me so many times before.

When I stepped into the room, I saw him sitting at the metal table, his orange jumpsuit a sharp contrast to the cold steel of the chair he occupied. His once-perfect hair was streaked with gray at the roots, and the air of control he once used as a shield was gone. Now, he just looked like . . . a nothing. Just like Logan had said.

"Well, well, well," he said, leaning back in his chair, his handcuffs clinking against the table. "Look who decided to visit. To what do I owe this honor, Sloane? Have you come to grovel? Or maybe thank me for the life I gave you?"

I didn't sit. Instead, I stood just inside the door, my arms crossed, my back straight. "I came to see what powerlessness looks like," I said evenly.

His smirk faltered for a moment, but he quickly recovered, narrowing his eyes at me. "You've grown bold since I've been in here."

I took a step forward, my heels punctuating the silence. "You don't scare me anymore, Everett."

He chuckled, low and bitter. "Don't I? You're more naive than I thought if you believe that. Do you think because I'm in here, you're done? That you're free?" He shook his head, his expression full of disdain. "You've just stepped into another cage, Sloane. And you don't even know it."

"What are you talking about?" I scoffed, rolling my eyes at the flicker of smugness in his gaze.

He gestured toward my chest. "That necklace you're wearing—the one you think York gave to you out of love . . . there's a camera in it."

I scoffed. "You're full of shit."

His mouth twitched. His employees were never allowed to curse. He leaned forward, his eyes narrowing. "He's watching you. Every second. *Every* move."

I fell back a step, his words catching me completely off guard. I reached up, my fingers brushing the cool metal of the necklace against my skin. It was such a delicate, beautiful thing. Could it really have been a tool for control?

Everett's smirk grew, sensing my uneasiness. "See, Sloane? You've traded one master for another. The only difference is that this one is watching you in real time."

I met his eyes, steadying myself as my mind reeled. I thought of Logan, of the way he looked at and treated me like I was the center of his world. Of the insane, over-the-top things he did to keep me close.

"*It works for us,*" Olivia had said that night. "*I don't know that anything else* could *work for us.*"

A smile curved my lips, slow and deliberate. My mind was made up. "Maybe that's exactly what I need," I said softly.

Everett blinked, the smirk slipping from his face. "What?"

"Maybe I need someone who's a little crazy about me," I said, my voice growing stronger with every word. "Because someone who loves me like that? Who's willing to cross every line for me? That's a fuck ton more than you ever gave me."

His face twisted, the cracks in his carefully constructed mask showing. "You don't know what you're saying," he hissed. "He'll ruin you, Sloane. Just like I did."

I stepped closer, leaning down until I was face-to-face with him. "The difference is, Everett, I get to choose this time. And I choose . . . Logan."

"Said like a true nobody."

My grin widened. "I'm pretty sure, *Uncle*, that you're the one who's a *nobody* now. And when people hear your name, they won't think of wealth or power. They'll think of handcuffs, orange jumpsuits, and a *sad* little man who got exactly what he deserved."

Everett's face turned red. "You think you've won? You think this is over?"

"For me, it is," I said, straightening up and smoothing my blazer. "But for you? This is just the beginning. Enjoy your cage, Everett. It suits you."

I turned on my heel and walked out, the sound of my heels echoing in the quiet hallway like a victory march. The necklace lay cool against my collarbone, and I realized . . . it felt like armor. A reminder that I wasn't alone anymore—and that someone out there would do whatever it took to make me happy.

Even if his methods were a little . . . crazy.

After this, Everett Wells was going to be nothing more than a bad memory.

Logan

The news had a different story the next week. A report that Everett Wells had been strangled by an inmate and been killed.

Sloane hadn't even cried at the news. Instead . . . she'd simply smiled.

I didn't know how. But I knew he'd done it.

Batman had struck again.

An hour later my phone buzzed.

> Lincoln: I've taken the liberty of getting my money back from his accounts. So no need to pay me back, Rookie.

I grinned . . . extremely relieved about that.

> Me: You surprise me, Golden Boy. I thought you enjoyed my burger commercial. You're going to miss out if I don't need to do them anymore.

> Lincoln: . . .

Shaking my head, I set my phone down and went to join Sloane . . . in the shower.

CHAPTER 45

LOGAN

> Ari: I'd like to file a complaint.

> Lincoln: . . .

> Ari: This is serious, Golden Boy. And it's against you.

> Walker: The drama queen is in this morning, boys.

Ari Lancaster removed Walker Davis from the chat.

I grinned when a second later:

Lincoln Daniels added Walker Davis to the chat.

> Me: What's the problem, Lancaster? I'll be judging complaints today.

> Ari: Ha. I just Lol'd. Blake gave me a look. As if that would ever be your job, Rookie.

I scoffed.

> Me: It could be my job.

Camden: No, it could never be your job.

Camden: But it could be mine.

Ari: Well it can't be Lincoln's, and we know Disney is just his simpy pawn, so I guess you'll do.

Walker: Did you really just call me a simpy pawn?

Ari: If the shoe fits.

Me: . . .

Lincoln: Look at Rookie, thinking he's all grown up and able to . . . people.

Me: What does that mean? "Able to."

Me: I have a tattoo on my penis. And a butterfly on my back, might I add! That completely counts.

Lincoln: Nobody wants to hear about your dick, Rookie.

Me: I would actually venture to guess by the ten million views I have on my burger ad that there's a lot of people out there who want to hear about my dick.

Lincoln: . . .

Walker: . . .

Ari: Back to me, please.

Ari: I'd like to file a complaint against Lincoln "Golden Boy" Daniels for the misappropriation of my alter ego.

Camden: Maybe I shouldn't be the judge. Because I'm really confused right now.

Walker: No worries, Hero. I'll step in. But also, I have no idea what you're talking about either, Lancaster.

Ari: Batman is what I'm talking about. BATMAN.

I snorted. Because out of all the things he could have said . . . that was not what I would have expected.

Wait a minute. I gasped in outrage.

Me: We said we weren't going to discuss this with him, Daniels! We said this was a secret.

Lincoln: Well, evidently it's not a secret when he gets stuck inside Blake, and I have to help him again. That's very Batman type behavior, isn't it?

Ari: THIS IS AN OUTRAGE!

Lincoln: Just because you dressed up as Batman once at a Halloween party . . . does not a Batman you make.

Ari: That made absolutely no sense.

Walker: It made perfect sense to me.

Ari: Of course it did, Disney. Because you're a simpy pawn. It's definitely what a simpy pawn would say.

Camden: I mean, I'm definitely not a "simpy pawn" unless that means certified badass. But . . . Lincoln does kind of act like Batman.

Me: It's true. He always knows things. And he knows people. Very Batman-like.

Ari: Let me let you all in on a secret. He learned everything he does from me.

Lincoln: . . .

Lincoln: That's an outrage for you to even say that about Batman.

Ari Lancaster removed Lincoln Daniels from the chat.

I grinned as I added Lincoln back in.

———

Sloane

This was the first time I'd ever been excited about going to a hair appointment—the first time I'd felt buzzed with energy and possibility. The scent of hair spray and shampoo lingered in the air, mixed with the faint aroma of coffee brewing somewhere in the back. The hum of hair dryers and the low murmur of conversation created a kind of white noise that wrapped around me, settling my nerves and, at the same time, lighting them up.

This was it. I was finally doing it.

The hairdresser, a woman in her late thirties with vibrant pink curls that looked like they belonged in a music video, met me with a friendly smile. "Hi, I'm Melanie," she said, leading me toward a station near the back of the salon. She had this effortless cool vibe that made me feel like maybe, just maybe, I could pull this off.

I sat down in the chair, staring at my reflection in the large mirror. It was just me, as I'd always been. My safe, brunette hair, no crazy colors, nothing wild or bold. It was safe. Pleasing.

Exactly what Everett had wanted.

Melanie looked at me in the mirror, comb in hand, ready to start. "So, what are we doing today?"

I didn't even pause. The words flew out of my mouth before I could second-guess myself. "I want to dye it lavender."

For a second, her hands stilled, the comb hovering in midair. She blinked at me, her surprise barely hidden behind her professional smile. "Lavender? That's a bold choice."

I grinned. "Yeah. But I think I'm ready for something bold."

She raised an eyebrow, studying me for a moment, then smiled. "You've got the features to pull that off. I think it'll look amazing on you."

I appreciated her validation, but it really didn't matter. I didn't care if I looked amazing or if lavender hair was the "right" choice. This was about so much more than just hair color. It was about the freedom to choose, to do something just because I *wanted* to. No one was making this decision for me. I wasn't doing it for anyone else. This was for me—and that was thrilling.

"Let's do it," I said, my heart beating a little faster as the words left my mouth.

Melanie nodded, her smile widening as she walked away to grab the bleach and dye necessary to change my dark hair. "You got it."

———

Melanie began applying the color, and I closed my eyes, letting myself sink into the sensation of the brush running through my hair. Each stroke felt like shedding a layer of the past, like I was finally breaking free of the invisible chains that had held me down for so long.

"So, what made you decide to go lavender?" Melanie asked casually as she worked.

I shrugged, though the real answer was complicated. "I guess I just wanted a change. Something different."

She smiled, nodding as though she understood more than I was letting on. "Lavender is definitely different. But in a good way. You'll turn heads for sure."

I smiled and let the process happen, letting the minutes tick by as she carefully worked the dye into my hair. I was nervous, sure, but more than that, I felt excited. I'd never been this excited about something so simple.

When the timer went off, signaling the end of the process, Melanie led me over to the sink to wash out the dye. The warm water ran over my scalp, and I closed my eyes again, feeling the last remnants of my old self wash away.

"Alright," Melanie said after she'd finished rinsing and drying my hair. "You ready to see it?"

I nodded, my heart pounding as she turned the chair around to face the mirror again. And there it was—lavender hair. Soft, subtle, but undeniably bold. The color framed my face, transforming me in a way I hadn't expected. I stared at myself for a moment, barely recognizing the person looking back.

"Wow," I whispered, running my fingers through the soft strands. It was different. So different. And I loved it.

"You like it?" Melanie asked, watching me with a grin.

"I love it," I said, a genuine smile spreading across my face. For the first time in a long time, I felt like I was seeing myself—really seeing myself. And it was someone I liked.

After leaving the salon, I headed straight home.

I couldn't wait to show Logan.

He was waiting at the door when I got there, leaning casually against the frame, but the second he saw me, his eyes lit up. That familiar grin spread across his face as he took in the change.

"Holy shit," he said, his voice filled with awe. "You look hot."

I laughed, feeling a blush creep up my neck. "Yeah?"

"Yeah," he said, stepping closer and reaching out to run his fingers through my hair. His touch was soft, lingering. "This is . . . wow."

I smirked, raising an eyebrow. "Don't get too attached. I might change it tomorrow."

He laughed, his grin widening. "What? You're gonna go from lavender to something else that fast?"

"Maybe pink," I teased, shrugging like it was no big deal. "Or blue. Or maybe I'll shave it all off."

Logan shook his head, still smirking as he leaned in closer. "You know, I always thought Smurfette was hot when I was a kid, so blue works for me. But I'm not so sure about the shaving part. If you do that, I won't be able to hold on to it as I fuck you from behind."

My breath stuttered. "Oh . . . maybe I won't shave it off."

His grin was beautiful. "Good girl." He tucked a lavender strand behind my ear. "You look amazing, though."

I bit my lip, the compliment sinking in. "Thanks. It *feels* amazing."

"Good," he said, brushing his lips softly against mine.

Later, as we sat on the couch, my head resting on Logan's shoulder, I found myself running my fingers through my hair again. It still felt strange, like I was getting to know this new version of myself. But it also felt like another step toward freedom.

Free to choose. Free to change. Free to be with the person I love.

And finally free to love myself.

"Handcuffs are definitely underrated in my opinion," Logan groaned as he thrust into me.

I was on my stomach, my hands handcuffed behind my back, my hips propped up on a stack of pillows as he fucked me from behind.

"Yes, let's add them to the list," I moaned.

The newest *list* we were making had been Logan's idea. Since I'd only ever done what other people wanted me to do, I didn't know what I liked—besides sex with Logan, of course. Logan had suggested we try everything to figure out what *my* favorites were.

Try everything once, and twice if we like it, so to speak.

So far I was a big fan of blindfolds, ropes, hot wax, and . . . handcuffs. But the list was definitely growing.

"Can't get enough of you," Logan groaned, his tongue licking down my spine.

"It feels so good." I bit down on my lip as I rocked back against him.

One hand slipped under me and massaged my clit. "Yes!"

Thwack. I cried out as his other hand came down on my ass cheek, sparks of pleasure shooting through me.

"Fuck. I need to see your face," he growled, abruptly pulling the pillows out from under me and flipping me over in one smooth move.

Thankfully, my back had long since healed, and we could do this.

"There's my girl," he murmured, staring into my eyes as he slid all the way in, until it felt like I was in danger of being split in half. His lips sealed over my mouth, his tongue tangling lazily with mine.

"I fucking love you, Red," he breathed, his hand cupping my breast as he teased the nipple with his thumb.

I was overwhelmed with all the sensations—the prick of the handcuffs against my ass as I lay on them being top of mind, actually. I wanted to touch him, but that was probably part of the lure of the things, feeling a little bit helpless because I couldn't.

His mouth slid down to my breasts, and he sucked hard on the tips, groaning as he took long, hard pulls.

"Please move, baby," I begged, desperate for more friction.

He was intent on taking his time, though, moving to the other breast and giving that nipple the same treatment. Logan released my tip with a pop before dragging his tongue softly across my skin . . . and then suddenly biting down. The combination of hard and soft had me thrashing underneath him, a chorus of my cries echoing around the room.

"Please, please, please," I panted.

"We're going to try something new," he rasped, suddenly working his cock at a different angle that rubbed along my front wall.

"What—are you doing?" I gasped as he pressed down on my pubic bone.

"Just feel it, sweetheart, I'm going to make you feel so good."

He rubbed harder, with his dick and fingers, and suddenly I was exploding. White-hot pleasure surged through me as I squeezed his cock. I was faintly aware of the fact that I was *gushing* all over him, but it felt too good to care that much.

"Fuck. You're making me come," he growled as his head fell back, showcasing all that glorious, straining, tattooed muscle. I felt his long, hot streams of cum filling me up before he collapsed on top of me.

"Oof." I was still feeling tiny bursts of pleasure in my core . . . and wetness, so much wetness. "What the fuck just happened?"

Logan groaned and rolled off me, propping himself up with one muscled arm. A huge smile stretched across his pretty face. "You squirted, and it was the fucking hottest thing ever. Can we add it to the list?"

I shifted, feeling how much . . . liquid there was . . . everywhere.

"Possibly," I finally said, before wiggling. With the handcuffs behind me like this, my chest was arched out—not the most comfortable thing. Although Logan seemed to like it based on the way his eyes were suddenly glued to my breasts. "Can we take the handcuffs off before I decide?"

"If I must," he said, like I'd asked the world of him. He gently shifted me and then popped open the handcuffs. I sighed in relief as he began to massage my wrists.

"I love you, Sloane," he murmured, nuzzling against my cheek as I felt his dick somehow hardening . . . again.

Suddenly he was slipping something onto my ring finger.

My eyes widened as I glanced down and saw a ring with a huge ruby surrounded by an insane amount of diamonds.

"You're going to be my wife, Red," he said, holding my hand up in the air so we could both lie there and stare at it.

"You're talking crazy, York," I whispered, the happiest tear I'd ever experienced sliding down my face. "But of fucking course."

I guess it turned out that I was going to get my happily-ever-after . . . after all.

CHAPTER 46

SLOANE

They're going to see it," Logan muttered, his face a bright red color as if I hadn't seen him naked a million times.

And he wasn't even naked right now, he had his briefs on—which happened to be the same ones that he'd worn for Geraldine's sculpture.

"They're not going to see it," I huffed, cocking my head as I tried to get the shadow of his abs just right.

"Where are you going to put it so they won't see it? You know Ari has a habit of nosing around places. He'll sense it when he gets into our place, and then I'll be done for."

"We can hang it in here. I never let *anyone* in here," I soothed, biting down on my lip as I tried to concentrate around his panic.

I'd gotten the idea to paint him after another dinner party at Geraldine's. If she got a life-size replica of him in stone, it only seemed fitting that I get a replica of him in paint—even if I got the real-life version every day.

"Make sure to get the proportions right," he said, gesturing to his erect dick that was poking out from the top of his briefs. "They can at least be shocked and awed when they see it."

"They're not going to see it," I repeated for the twentieth time.

He muttered something under his breath that sounded a lot like "you'll see."

"Is there anything you can do about—" I gestured to his cock. As much as I loved the thing, it was very distracting when I was trying to concentrate.

"Nope," he said with a grin. "How else is it supposed to be when you're painting me dressed like that?"

The fact that he'd only agreed to let me paint him if I did it in lingerie had been his main negotiating point when I'd first suggested the painting.

I'd regretted it every session—although it did help with me getting proportions right.

It's just that it also made it difficult to make it through a session. I was only human. How could I be expected to keep away from him when he looked like this?

I tried to paint for a few more minutes, but when the head of his dick popped out from the briefs all the way, I was done for.

It was a perk of the job, I decided as I set my brush down and walked toward him, my insides throbbing with need.

"Let's add after-painting sex to the list," he growled as he pulled me on top of him.

"Sounds good to me."

———

Sometimes it was still difficult to keep the demons at bay—to keep away the memories of those nights and those days, and the years I'd spent hating myself for a choice I actually hadn't made.

Sometimes it got overwhelming thinking of all that had been taken from me.

But every time that happened, Logan would just hold me close, make me laugh, make me come, and make me forget because the present was so good it outweighed the past.

With Logan, I found a freedom I couldn't have imagined. Not just a freedom to move from the past and be happy, but a freedom to feel all the things that I'd tried so hard to keep at bay. He didn't care if there were times I cried or raged, or when I couldn't sleep because the monsters in my head had escaped.

He told me it was a privilege to be there for me, that every piece I showed him only made him love me more.

And I believed him.

I believed him now when he told me everything would be alright.

I believed him when he told me he loved me and promised me a lifetime of smiles and laughs.

I believed him when he told me someday we'd be the best parents to our kids we would adopt, and we'd give them what our parents never did.

And with that belief came a rebirth. I'd thought that I would never be able to get my pieces back, but what I'd really needed was to make new ones with him.

I was scattered, and I didn't know that what would put me back together again . . .

Was a pucking wrong, *crazy*, *perfect* . . . rookie.

EPILOGUE

SLOANE

One year later.

The gallery was buzzing with people, voices mixing with the soft hum of background music, but all I could focus on were the walls lined with my paintings. My work. My soul poured out onto canvas for the world to see. It still didn't feel real, standing there in this beautiful gallery in New York, surrounded by my art, watching as people whispered in admiration and reached for their wallets to buy pieces that once felt too personal and tragic to share.

I'd never imagined this moment. Never thought it could happen. But Logan, Olivia, and the rest of our friends—my family—posted my artwork on their social media, flooding their followers with images of my darkest moments and my brightest ones. It felt like exposure, like standing in front of the world completely bare. And then, a call from a curator in New York. A huge art show. Me, in this space, with everything laid out in front of strangers who suddenly saw value in the pieces of myself I'd kept hidden for so long.

I walked through the gallery, brushing my fingers lightly against the frames. Some of the paintings were dark, heavy with pain and shadows, but others . . . the more recent ones . . . were filled with light, hope, and the kind of brightness I never thought I'd find. The contrast between them mirrored my own journey—darkness to light, broken to whole.

"Sloane, this is incredible," Olivia said, coming up beside me, her eyes wide as she took in the paintings. "Every piece is just . . . wow."

"I want them all," Monroe added, her eyes glued to the painting in front of us.

I smiled, my heart swelling. "I still can't believe people are buying them."

"Believe it," Logan said, wrapping his arm around my waist and pulling me close. "You're a fucking genius, and now the whole world knows it."

I leaned into him, grateful for his unwavering belief in me, but my eyes were drawn back to one painting in particular—the one I wouldn't be selling. The girl sitting on the pier under the cloudy night sky. The one that marked the day everything changed. It was dark, yes, but it was also the beginning of something new. Something better. That painting wasn't for anyone else. It was mine, and it always would be.

"I love that one," he told me, his eyes softening because he knew the story behind it.

"That one I told them I'm keeping," I murmured, more to myself than anyone else. "It's . . . special."

Logan followed my gaze and nodded. "Yes it is."

As I stood there, surrounded by strangers and friends, admiring the work I'd poured my heart into, the door to the gallery opened, and in came Ari, Blake, Camden, and Anastasia—this time with Rome in tow. I couldn't help the way my heart skipped when I saw him, the little boy who had changed everything for me. We'd adopted him six months after we'd gotten married, when I'd felt mentally healthy enough to be a great mom to him, and every day with him had been better than the last.

His eyes scanned the room until they found me, and then his face lit up like the sun breaking through the clouds.

"Mommy!" he cried, his little voice cutting through the noise, and before I could blink, he was running across the gallery, his tiny arms wrapping around my waist.

I froze for a moment, the word *Mommy* echoing in my mind, filling every empty space with warmth, just like it always did. I knelt down, pulling him into a tight hug, my chest aching in the best way possible. "Hey, baby." I smiled, my voice thick with emotion.

Rome looked up at me with those big, trusting eyes. "I missed you."

"I missed you too," I said, brushing a stray piece of hair behind his ear. "Did you have fun with Ari and Blake?"

He nodded enthusiastically, his face glowing with happiness. "But I wanted to see your pictures. They're so pretty, Mommy."

My throat tightened, tears prickling at the edges of my eyes as I glanced around the room. My paintings, once a symbol of everything broken inside me, now felt like they belonged here. I belonged here. I looked down at

Rome, our son, and I still couldn't believe just how perfect things had become.

"There's my buddy," Logan growled, scooping Rome up and setting him on his shoulders. Rome squealed in delight, and I immediately took out my phone to take a picture of them—to join the five million others I'd taken just like it.

Logan rested the hand that wasn't holding Rome on my shoulder, his voice soft and full of pride. "I'm so fucking proud of you, Red."

"Uncle Logan, that's a dollar in the swear jar," Walker and Olivia's tiny daughter, Isabella, told him, yanking on his pants.

"He said one this morning when he spilled his coffee," Rome tattled.

"Hey, we said we were going to keep that one a secret," Logan griped, smirking down at me.

I smiled at them all, unable to find the words to describe how much this moment meant. Everything had changed, and somehow, despite all the pain, all the struggles, I was okay. More than okay—I was happy.

As I looked around the room one more time, from the dark paintings to the light, I saw the reflection of my journey in every brushstroke. The highs, the lows, the moments I thought I wouldn't survive, and the moments that saved me.

And then, through the large windows of the gallery, I noticed something. It was raining. Hard. But the weather didn't feel like a threat anymore. It wasn't a storm to fear, a sun when it shouldn't be shining, or a sign of something bad. It was just weather.

I smiled, pulling Rome closer to me. The rain fell steadily outside, but inside, everything felt . . . perfect. I didn't need the sun to shine every day. I didn't need everything to be easy. I had what mattered most—family, love, and a life I never thought I'd have.

And in that moment, I knew I was whole.

DALLAS #9 KNIGHTS

SECOND EPILOGUE
LOGAN

One year later

We were sitting around, taking a break after practice, when Walker glanced over at me, holding his youngest daughter, Jovie, in his lap. She was adorable, all pink cheeks and wide eyes, but Walker had this serious look on his face, which immediately made me suspicious.

"I'm filing a complaint."

"What?" I asked.

"Your son," he started, his voice low and mock-serious. "He has been giving my daughter the look."

I blinked, pausing mid-drink, before raising an eyebrow. "Rome?"

"No. Sanders," he growled.

I blinked at him, my lip curling up in amusement. "Disney, he's a month old. How is he giving her the look?"

We'd been able to adopt Sanders as a newborn, and Sloane, Rome, and I were in heaven having a new baby in the house.

Walker nodded, completely deadpan. "I don't know, man, but I saw it. He's been eyeballing her every time we hang out. I don't like it."

I set my drink down, trying not to laugh. "Eyeballing her? He barely opens his eyes."

"Except when he shits," Ari added. "His eyes were definitely open when he shit all over my shirt yesterday."

Lincoln snorted and shook his head.

"Yes, that's true," I mused.

"I'm going to set the rules right now." Walker lifted his chin, glancing down at his daughter with exaggerated protectiveness. "There will be no commingling with these two. It's not happening."

I leaned back in my chair, raising both eyebrows this time. "And what about Isabella and Rome?"

Walker sighed. "It's too late for them. Isabella's already in love. But if I start young enough, before Sanders is too cute to cloud my judgment . . . Jovie might have a chance."

"Hey, Sanders is cute right now," I complained.

"He looks like a wrinkled grandpa," Lincoln said, his eyes glued to the video of Monroe he was watching on his phone.

"It's true. Like a cute little prune almost. A grandpa prune," said Ari.

Camden, who was sitting nearby, snorted into his water bottle, clearly trying to hold it together.

"Well," I said slowly, rubbing my chin like I was considering this deeply. "I will take what you've said under consideration. Because you're right, gotta nip that in the bud. Wouldn't want my month-old son scheming on your daughter."

Walker narrowed his eyes. "It sounds like you aren't taking me seriously. It's bad enough that Isabella asks to see Rome twenty times a day . . ."

"No, I am," I said, a smirk spreading across my face. "I'm going to have a serious talk with Sanders tonight. A real heart-to-heart."

"He's probably just mad because he's plotting for one of his kids to marry into Lincoln's family, but Lincoln has no kids to offer yet," Camden said, standing up and grabbing his bag.

Ari pointed an accusing finger at Walker. "That's exactly it. But I have news for you, Disney. If Lincoln Daniels ever has children, my future children will be the ones to have claim on them."

"This is a really weird conversation that I don't want to be a part of," Lincoln said as he stood up and walked toward the locker room door.

"Just think about it," Walker desperately called after him.

"I'm not thinking about it," said Lincoln before he left the room.

"He's definitely thinking about it," said Ari, sitting back in his chair and folding his arms in front of him. "But Golden Boy and I already made a pact about this. So you're out of luck."

"There's no way he made a pact with you about this," said Camden, rolling his eyes.

"Okay, Grampalicious. So it was a silent pact. But it means the same thing. I could tell he meant it," snarled Ari.

I snorted and got up from my chair, clapping Walker on the back and wiggling my finger at Jovie as she stared up at me with a pacifier in her mouth.

"We can't help who we love, Disney. You should know that by now," I told him as I walked away.

I certainly hadn't had a choice.

And I'd never regretted it a single day.

THIRD EPILOGUE

LOGAN

The ball cracked off the bat, a slicing foul toward the stands, and before I could blink, Asher was off like a rocket from his spot at shortstop.

"Holy fuck, he's going to run into the wall," I muttered under my breath as I watched.

He leaped, literally *launching* himself into the stands like he thought he was Spider-Man or something.

And completely overshot the ball.

Instead of catching anything, Asher ended up diving straight into the lap of a fan. And not just any fan, either—a young, pretty, *female* fan.

I watched it happen in real time, but it still felt like slow motion. Asher, sprawled across this girl's lap, both of them wide-eyed in shock.

And then Asher completely lost his mind. While the whole stadium watched, Asher leaned in . . . and *kissed* her.

The crowd went nuts, laughter and gasps rippling through the stadium.

"Wow," Sloane said from next to me. "That's one way to make *SportsCenter*."

I snorted, because my girl had an excellent sense of humor.

The girl's face turned from shocked to pissed in about two seconds flat. She shoved him hard, and Asher tumbled backward out of the stands and landed on the field with a thud.

"That probably hurt," I mused, shaking my head. "I can't believe that just happened."

The crowd erupted in more cheers and laughter, no doubt enjoying this more than the actual game since baseball was one of the most boring sports on Earth.

Asher stayed there for a few seconds on his back, a huge idiotic, lovestruck grin on his face.

But, of course, he wasn't done.

He got up, dusted himself off, and turned back toward the girl. And then he raised two fingers to his eyes and pointed them at her, mouthing "I'll be seeing you" like a fucking serial killer.

The crowd lost it again, roaring with laughter and applause, while the girl just rolled her eyes, crossing her arms like she didn't believe him.

But I believed him. Because I'd had Asher's same look before.

And I knew exactly what it meant.

Asher was a goner.

BONUS SCENE

Want more Logan & Sloane? Come hang out in my Fated Realm for an exclusive bonus scene. Get it here: https://www.facebook.com/groups C.R.FatedRealm

MRS. BENTLEY'S
STUFFED FRENCH TOAST

rvings: 6 people

gredients

UNCES CREAM CHEESE , SOFTENED

CUP SOUR CREAM

ABLESPOON LEMON JUICE

CUP POWDERED SUGAR, OR MORE TO TASTE

ABLESPOON PLUS 1 TEASPOON
NILLA EXTRACT

SLICES BRIOCHE

RTON OF SLICED STRAWBERRIES

GGS

UP HALF-AND-HALF

EASPOON GROUND CINNAMON

ABLESPOON BUTTER

ABLESPOONS GRANULATED SUGAR

TIONAL TOPPINGS: SLICED STRAWBERRIES,
PLE SYRUP, NUTELLA, WHIPPED CREAM

structions

A MEDIUM BOWL, BEAT TOGETHER THE CREAM CHEESE, SOUR CREAM, LEMON JUICE, POWDERED SUGAR, AND
ABLESPOON VANILLA EXTRACT UNTIL YOU HAVE A SPREADABLE CONSISTENCY.

OUT 6 BRIOCHE SLICES ON A PLATE. SPREAD A THICK LAYER OF CREAM CHEESE FILLING ON ONE SIDE OF
CH SLICE. ARRANGE STRAWBERRIES IN A THIN LAYER ON THE FILLING AND THEN SPREAD ANOTHER THIN
ER OF FILLING ON TOP. TOP EACH SLICE WITH A SECOND SLICE OF BRIOCHE, FORMING A SANDWICH WITH
EAM CHEESE AND STRAWBERRY FILLING IN THE MIDDLE.

A SMALL BOWL, WHISK TOGETHER THE EGGS, HALF-AND-HALF, CINNAMON, GRANULATED SUGAR, AND 1
ASPOON VANILLA EXTRACT. DIP THE SANDWICHES IN THE EGG MIXTURE TO COAT COMPLETELY.

LT BUTTER ON A GRIDDLE OR SKILLET OVER MEDIUM HEAT. COOK SANDWICHES UNTIL GOLDEN BROWN ON
TH SIDES.

WITH STRAWBERRIES, SYRUP OR NUTELLA, AND WHIPPED CREAM.

ACKNOWLEDGMENTS

To my incredible Renegades,

This journey would be nothing without you. Your unwavering support, enthusiasm, and passion for these stories keep me inspired every single day. Whether it's your thoughtful messages, book posts, or just the simple act of picking up one of my books, it means the world to me.

You've made the Circle of Trust come alive, not just in my mind but in yours, and there's no greater gift for a writer than to share that connection with readers like you. Thank you for embracing the chaos, the love, the red flags, and every twist and turn along the way.

Here's to more late nights lost in these worlds, more drama llamas (#IYKYK), and more unforgettable moments. Thanks for letting me live my dream.

This is just the beginning.

. . .

XOXOXO,
C.R.

A few thank-yous . . .

To Raven aka My Moon: I couldn't do this career without you. Your constant support, brilliant ideas, hilarious memes, endless brain-storming, and our late-night sprints made this journey not only possible but unforgettable. You're not just an incredible writer (seriously, you amaze me), but you're also the kind of best friend who shows up, cheers the loudest, and loves without limits. I'm so lucky to have you in my corner. ILYSM.

To my incredible beta readers and dear friends, Crystal, Blair, and Lisa: You three are my rock, my cheerleaders, and my steady support system. Your thoughtful comments, unwavering encouragement, and constant presence mean more to me than words can say. Thank you for giving so selflessly, for always showing up, and for being the wonderful friends every writer dreams of having. I'm so lucky to have you in my corner.

To Stephanie, my amazing editor: Your commitment to this story and to me has been beyond amazing. The effort and heart you poured into every word didn't go unnoticed, and I'm so thankful for the way you treated this book with such care. You helped shape Logan and Sloane into something truly special, and I couldn't have done it without you. Thank you for your brilliance, your patience, and your complete dedication.

To Jessa: Your friendship is a gift I treasure every day. Thank you for always being there with laughter, wisdom, and unwavering support. You inspire me, ground me, and make life infinitely brighter. I'm so grateful for you, always.

To Alexis: Your talent, enthusiasm, and constant support mean the world to me. I can't imagine this journey without you—you're a tier 1 friend, no question.

To my PAs and BFFs, Caitlin and Sarah: I love you both forever and always—thank you for being in my corner, no matter what.

To my husband: You are my anchor, my safe place, and the love of my life. Thank you for being my biggest support and for reminding me every day that love is not just real, but extraordinary. This journey wouldn't mean as much without you by my side. I love you, always and forever.

ABOUT C.R. JANE

A Texas girl living in Utah now, C.R. Jane is a mother, lawyer, and now author. Her stories have been floating around in her head for years, and it has been a relief to finally get them down on paper. Jane is a huge Dallas Cowboys fan and primarily listens to Taylor Swift and hip hop (. . . don't lie and say you don't, too.)

Her love of reading started when she was three, and it only made sense that she would start to create her own worlds, since she was always getting lost in others'.

Jane likes heroines who have to grow in order to become badasses, happy endings, and swoon-worthy, devoted (and hot) male characters. If this sounds like you, I'm pretty sure we'll be friends.

Visit her C.R.'s Fated Realm Facebook page to get updates, and sign up for her newsletter at **www.crjanebooks.com** to stay updated on new releases, find out random facts about her, and get access to different points of view from her characters.

Podium

FOR A GOOD TIME

follow us on our socials